RISE

of the

BEAST

BOOKS BY
KENNETH ZEIGLER

Heaven and Hell

The War in Heaven

AVAILABLE FROM DESTINY IMAGE PUBLISHERS

RISE

of the

BEAST

HELL ON EARTH

KENNETH ZEIGLER

DESTINY IMAGE® PUBLISHERS, INC.

P.O. Box 310, Shippensburg, PA 17257-0310

"Speaking to the Purposes of God for this Generation and for the Generations to Come."

This book and all other Destiny Image, Revival Press, Mercy Place, Fresh Bread, Destiny Image Fiction, and Treasure House books are available at Christian bookstores and distributors worldwide.

For a U.S. bookstore nearest you, call 1-800-722-6774.

For more information on foreign distributors, call 717-532-3040.

Reach us on the Internet: www.destinyimage.com.

Trade Paper ISBN 978-0-7684-3283-1

Hardcover ISBN 978-0-7684-3499-6

Large Print ISBN 978-0-7684-3500-9

Ebook ISBN 978-0-7684-9086-2

For Worldwide Distribution, Printed in the U.S.A.

1 2 3 4 5 6 7 / 13 12 11 10

DEDICATION

Dedicated to Cecilia Celeste Farnsworth,

the woman whose life inspired

The Tears of Heaven series.

A CKNOWLEDGMENT

I would like to thank my wife,

Mary Zeigler,

who offered continuing editorial guidance.

Ｈow art thou fallen from heaven, O Lucifer, son of the morning! How art thou cut down to the ground, which didst weaken the nations!

(Isaiah 14:12)

CHAPTER 1

It was well past 11 P.M. as Leland James and his number one made their way through New York's Central Park. Leland was a handsome and well-established African American man in his late thirties. He had grown up in New York City, though not in this part of town. No, he had grown up in Harlem, in a rundown apartment with his single mother and his sister. Those were far different days.

Tonight, he and his comely companion were on their way to his current home, an upscale condo on Central Park West. He'd partaken of the spirits rather heavily tonight at the party. Why else would a savvy, street-smart New Yorker be cutting through Central Park at this hour? Certainly not because it was the quickest route home—that was screwy logic, the logic of a man some distance short of sobriety. The nighttime dangers of the park were rather overstated in the stories told to frighten the tourists away. Still, he was not typically a person who cared to tempt fate.

In his younger days, he had conducted his share of drug deals in the park, some of them after dark. They had been small-change deals, really—an ounce of weed here, a couple pills there. He'd never been a hard-core dealer. He didn't have the temperament for it. He didn't do drugs himself either—not then, not now; that wasn't good business. The bottom line in business was making money, not getting high. Those who learned that rule lived longer and got richer, and he had. But he wasn't involved in that sort of thing anymore. It was just too risky. Most of the dealers he knew from his younger days were either doing hard time or had taken up permanent residence six feet under. No, today he dealt in a different commodity—love.

He gazed over at his fine young lady, a blond–haired, blue-eyed girl just over half his age. She was his number one, his best hooker. When he'd first set eyes on her three years ago, she was an underage runaway from Richmond. He'd seen her potential even then, as she stood in line at the women's shelter. He'd taken her away from all of that. And she hadn't become some strung-out street vendor either, dealing in the pleasures of the flesh. No, in his hands, she had been molded into the finest lady of the night, a beautiful princess with both feet squarely on the ground, available for the right price. He took good care of her, pairing her up with only his finest clients.

Yet now it went deeper than that. Of all of his women, and there were many, she was the one he spent the most time with. In fact, during the past two months, Krissie was the only one of his ladies he had spent time with. She was special to him, and he knew that he was special to her.

Leland wasn't a difficult person to become enamored with, really. He was a handsome man, and despite his lowly beginnings, he was highly intelligent and quite clever in so many ways. He certainly had a way with the ladies. He was a true gentleman in every sense of the word. He took care of his women, made sure that they wanted for nothing. His rules for them were simple: no drugs, and alcohol only in moderation. If they were uneasy about particular clients, they were to walk away. He dealt in quality, not quantity, and quality didn't come cheap. In reality, he himself set up most of their encounters, assuring the quality of their clients. Those clients were businessmen, bankers, stockbrokers, and politicians, New York's finest. When the finest didn't treat his women right—well, he had contacts who dealt with those problems too.

He and Krissie were nearly to the underpass. He was more than halfway home.

"Hey, big man, ya got a light?"

Leland turned to see four young Hispanic men step out of the shadows of a tall oak tree. They looked to be in their late teens, maybe 20. He could see their gang affiliation from their colors, the Latin Kings. This was not good. "Sorry, guys, I don't smoke," said Leland, not knowing what to say.

"Well, that's okay," said the one in the center, a muscular, heavily tattooed man. "But you still gotta pay to go through our territory."

Leland evaluated the situation. This youth was right; he was a big man. He could make short order of one of these punks, but the other three—that was the problem. It was his move. Still, there might be a way out of this short of fighting or surrender. "Don't you think that you should find out who you're dealing with before you start making threats?"

"OK, homie, I'll bite. Who are ya?" said the youth, who didn't sound impressed.

"Someone who works for Louie Pagoni," replied Leland. "I'm sure you've heard of him. You mess with me, you're messing with him. If you're short on change, well, out of respect for the Kings, I'd be willing to drop a 50 for each of you. You can consider it the toll."

The youth looked at his compatriots and smiled. "Hey, this homie knows our gang colors, what do ya think about that?"

There was an uneasy round of low laughter among the youth's comrades. Leland figured that he had taken the wrong approach.

"I'll make you a counteroffer, homie," said the youth. We'll accept your offer, out of respect for Louie Pagoni. But you gotta sweeten it a bit. Leave us that little lovely as well, and you can go on your way. We'll take good care of her, return her to you when we're finished with her. When you get her back, she'll know a few more tricks."

"Leland?" whispered Krissie, fear in her voice.

"Hush," said Leland, who turned once more to the youths. "Not gonna happen."

"Then I think we are at an impasse," said the youth, drawing a glistening knife. "You should have taken my offer when you had the chance."

Leland had some experience in street fighting, and should have been focused on that blade, yet something else had caught his attention. About 30 or 40 feet behind the four teens, near the entrance to the tunnel, what looked like dozens of glistening stars and a blue mist had suddenly appeared. From the mist stepped two men in long, dark-hooded cloaks of a sort that might have been worn by a proper gentleman a century or more ago. They removed their hoods in unison to reveal two handsome, and middle-aged men, both of whom had short, dark hair with just a touch of gray. They advanced in the direction of the growing altercation.

Apparently, the youth had noticed Leland's expression and turned to see the approaching men. "Well, what do we have here? Why I think we got more travelers needing to pay the toll."

The men eyed the four youths carefully as they approached. It was the one on the left who spoke. "You young men wouldn't happen to be bothering these good people, would you?"

The youth looked at the man angrily. "I'd say that was none of your damned business, homie."

"Oh, I'm not your homie, I assure you," said the man, setting down his briefcase and drawing closer. "I do, however, have business to discuss with that gentleman behind you. So if you will be so kind as to move along, I will leave you in peace, at least, for the moment."

"You gotta be kidding," said the youth, brandishing the blade in the businessman's direction. "Maybe I ought to cut you up a bit, just to teach you some manners."

"Bad decision," replied the man, reaching over his left shoulder and drawing a three-foot sword that must have been hidden somehow behind his back. He went to business on the gang members at lightning speed. Within seconds, the leader's head had been parted from his neck by a single, swift slash of the shimmering blade. The arms of the headless body reached for the neck, which was spouting blood like a fountain. Then the body collapsed.

Another tried to grab for the other man in black, but barely laid a hand on him before being pushed back. He was run through by the man's sword before he had time to react. Another of the youths tried to flee, yet it was already too late. Two swift slashes to the abdomen sent his entrails tumbling out of him, even as he tried to contain them with his hands. He tried to run, yet was unable to hold his own guts in. He tripped over his own intestines, screaming in a shrill, terrified voice.

The fourth youth, who had hardly moved a muscle, just fell to his knees begging for mercy, as the sword-wielding businessman stood over him. "Oh please, don't hurt me," he pleaded.

"And what am I to do with you, young man?" asked the businessman. "You would have shown no mercy to these nice people. Had they pleaded with you for mercy, your black heart would have been closed. Let me tell you something, boy; I have listened to more than a few people like yourself pleading before me, many more than a few. I have dispatched them in ways that you cannot even begin to grasp." He looked to Leland and Krissie. "But, I will allow this gentleman and his lady friend to decide your fate. Those whom you would have done harm to shall decide your destiny, not me. What shall it be, kind people?"

The youth gazed up into the stranger's eyes. They were so dark, so cold. There was something terrible there, something indescribable. They were like a dark, infinitely deep pools of nothingness. He clearly wanted to flee, but he couldn't seem to will his body to move. Then he looked to Leland and Krissie, as if to plead for leniency.

For a moment there was total silence. It was Krissie who spoke up first. "Please, let him go."

The businessman's eyebrows rose slightly. "Indeed. And what say you, sir? Do you agree?"

"Yes," said Leland, hesitantly. "Let him go. I think he's suffered enough."

"Very well, then," said the man, sheathing his sword. Again he looked to the youth. "It would seem that your life has been spared, for the moment. Run, if you can. Yet, I tell you this; you will be mine in the end, no matter how far you run. You can't escape from me, boy; you can't run from Lusan."

The young man didn't have to be told twice. He fled in total panic, even as the other businessman put the disemboweled youth out of his misery with a quick thrust to the heart.

"Are the two of you unharmed?" asked the businessman.

"Yes," replied Leland, "thanks to you and your friend." He gazed about at the incredible carnage around him. One thing was certain; these people weren't a couple representatives of the guardian angels. He prayed that Krissie and he had not just passed from the frying pan into the fire.

"But forgive me," said the businessman. "We have not been properly introduced. I am called Lusan, and my associate is Duras."

"Happy to meet you," said Leland, who didn't know what else to say.

"I think that we should depart this place," suggested Lusan. "Bodies tend to attract attention and unwanted questions, especially bodies in the state in which these are in. I don't think we desire either on this night. Anyway, we have important business to discuss."

Leland nodded. "Maybe we could go to my place." He almost regretted the suggestion the moment he posed it.

"An excellent idea," said Lusan, a slight but devious smile coming to his face. "You must have been reading my mind. I was about to suggest it myself."

"Please, sir, this way," said Leland, pointing the way to his home.

Leland and Krissie walked side by side while the two dark-clad strangers followed some steps behind. Krissie looked back at their newfound benefactors, then at Leland. "Do you think this is a good idea? I mean, taking them to our home?" she whispered. "We don't know what sort of people these guys are. They just killed those men."

"I really don't have a lot of choice," whispered Leland. "But, after all, they did save our lives. Anyway, I've got to find out what these guys are all about; I've got to know who they are."

"I'm not sure I want to know," replied Krissie. "I have this terrible fear about them."

"You're nearly in shock," replied Leland, placing his hand around her. "That's all it is."

"Is there a problem?" asked Lusan.

"No, not at all," assured Leland. "My companion is just a bit shook up."

"I'm not surprised," was the reply. "She has had a dreadful fright on this night. I fear that my compatriot and I did little to calm her nerves." He turned his gaze to Krissie. "I assure you, young woman, you have nothing to fear from me or my associate. I assure you, we are friends."

"I'm not afraid," replied Krissie, though her quivering voice betrayed her.

A few minutes later, they were crossing Central Park West. It was quite nearly deserted at this hour. They walked through the great glass doors on the ground floor of Leland's condominium complex. The rather large concierge looked at the two dark strangers suspiciously.

"It's OK, Henry," assured Leland. "They're friends of mine."

"Yes, of course, sir," confirmed the concierge, giving the strangers a wide berth.

"My place is on the eleventh floor," said Leland, leading the way to a wide hallway, with three elevators on either side.

They only had to wait a few seconds for the elevator, and they were on their way up. Within the confines of the elevator, Krissie was shivering. Leland noticed it right away. He drew her close; it didn't seem to help.

What was it about these men that so disturbed her? He couldn't say. If someone should have been afraid, it was him. He had seen them materialize out of nowhere. Krissie hadn't.

"I feel like I'm suffocating," she whispered.

What a strange comment. Leland just didn't get it.

On the 11th floor, it was but a dozen yards or so from the elevator to the door of Leland's place. He opened the electronically activated door lock with his hand control and disarmed the security system within. The group beheld a plush domicile, just about the best New York had to offer. It was 1,500 square feet of pure heaven.

"I picked it up during the worst year of the meltdown a few years back," announced Leland, "when property values had really tanked. It's worth twice what I paid for it now."

"Leland, you shouldn't go on like that," said Krissie.

"No, it is quite all right," assured Lusan. "There is nothing wrong in having a measure of pride regarding the victories of one's life. Treasure them, my friend. Your King Solomon spoke wisely when he said that the pleasures of this Earth are fleeting. Enjoy them while you yet live."

"Can I get you something to drink?" suggested Leland. "Maybe a glass of wine?"

Lusan smiled. "Yes, I believe that I would like a glass of wine, thank you. We have had a busy day, and refreshments would be welcome."

"Please, have a seat," said Leland, motioning to a sofa and several fine chairs by a large window that offered a lofty view of the park.

The strangers made their way to the sofa and sat down, gazing out at the park. The site of their previous activities was just visible from here, though, judging by the quiet darkness, it appeared that no one had come upon their handiwork just yet.

Krissie was still shaking a bit, yet she didn't sit down. She shadowed Leland, as he made his way to the bar.

"I wanted to thank you again, both of you," said Leland, as he offered to pour an additional glass of wine for Krissie, who declined. "I don't know what we would have done if you hadn't happened by."

"It was my pleasure to be of assistance this night," said Lusan.

Duras nodded in agreement, but said nothing. It seemed to Leland that Lusan was the leader. Duras seemed to be little more than a servant, who likely spoke only when spoken to.

Leland walked over to the sofa, Krissie at his side, and handed a glass of wine to his two benefactors, then sat in the chair next to them. He paused; who was he kidding? This wasn't just a casual meeting on the street, and these weren't ordinary people. "But I saw what you did. I saw the two of you step out of thin air, in the middle of blue, sparkling lights. People don't just come and go like that."

Krissie became suddenly pale. "What?"

Lusan chuckled. "No, people don't, but angels do."

"Oh, sweet Jesus," gasped Krissie, looking toward the strange visitors and back toward Leland.

"We don't usually put on such a spectacle, but it was unavoidable," continued Lusan. "We are here on a mission. Rescuing the two of you was only part of it."

"Rescuing us?" asked Krissie. "Why would angels rescue people like us?"

"You shouldn't talk like that," said Lusan, his tone suddenly stern. "Think you that your choices in life, your lifestyle, your chosen profession, are reasons for the Father of us all to love you any less? I tell you that this is not true. His love for you is undiminished. Surely, our presence here should assure you of that."

There was a pause. Neither Leland nor Krissie said a word; they were just too overwhelmed.

"But, allow me to come to the point," continued Lusan. "In order to accomplish our mission, we will need your help."

"Our help?" echoed Krissie. "What could we possibly do for you, an angel?"

"Offer us shelter, a place to stay first of all," came the reply. "Lot did just that when angels came to his door so as to deliver him from the sins of Sodom and Gomorrah. Still others have entertained angels unaware."

"You can stay here," said Leland, not the slightest hesitation in his offer. "I have two guest bedrooms, very nice ones."

"Thank you," replied Lusan. "We shall accept your kind hospitality."

"You spoke of a mission," continued Leland. "Can you tell me what it is?"

Lusan shook his head, then took a sip of wine. "This is really quite good. It has been some time since I have partaken of the fruit of the vine. I am not at liberty to discuss all of the details of our mission. I will tell you that I and my friend are in need of your assistance. We are strangers here. You have contacts in high and low places. You have business associates who could make clear the way for our venture."

"I have a business," replied Leland. "I guess you know that. It gives me important contacts in business and government. I even have an associate's degree in accounting. But there are so many others with more experience. It's not that I'm not grateful; I am. I just don't know how much help I can be."

"You can be of immeasurable help to us," assured Lusan. "You have run a very risky business for many years. You have been discrete, even gentle. You have provided a port of refuge to those women. You have taken good care of them in all ways. I happen to know that you have even provided well for their future, though many of them are unaware. Yes, I know even that. Your employees trust you, even love you. You are a good man, Leland James, despite what you might think. But allow me to come to the point."

Lusan took a moment to open his briefcase. Within it, Leland and Krissie beheld many bars of shimmering metal. It looked like gold.

"It is gold, if that is what you are wondering," confirmed Lusan. "Specifically, it is gold from Heaven itself. Gold is of no value to me, but it can buy influence and commodities, which we shall require to complete our mission. I need someone familiar with people and business who can convert some of this gold to American dollars. I will also need a human identity that will allow me to establish a bank account and a foundation to do the master's work here on Earth. I need someone to manage my affairs. I need you, Leland James."

"Manage your affairs?" gasped Leland. "Why me?"

"Have you so little faith in yourself?" asked Lusan. "That is the second time you have told me why you are not worthy. Please, don't continue. When the Nazarene walked this Earth, he didn't choose kings and princes, priests and scribes, to further His Kingdom. No, He chose people that society looked down upon, common people. He chose people of the streets, even prostitutes."

Lusan turned his gaze toward Krissie. She seemed to shiver.

Then Lusan turned back to Leland. "Your William Shakespeare put it this way: 'Be not afraid of greatness. Some are born great, others achieve greatness, while still others have greatness thrust upon them.' Need I continue, my friend?"

"No," replied Leland. "I get the picture. I'm sure I can find a way to convert your gold to cash or establish a bank account with it, if that's what you want. I don't know exactly how to do it, but I know people who do. You get to know plenty of people in my line of work. I'll help you; I'll be honored to."

A broad smile came to Lusan's face. "Yes, I knew that you would say these very words." Lusan turned to Duras. "Did I not say that he would be as this?"

Duras smiled. "Yes, indeed you did."

"Then it is settled," said Lusan. "You will begin tomorrow."

Leland nodded.

"Then there is a Heaven," interjected Krissie, who seemed to have overcome her fear of this strange being.

Lusan only nodded.

"Please tell me about it; what is it like? I mean, is it a spirit realm, or is it solid like here? Please, tell me what it's like."

Lusan laughed. "Tell you about Heaven? That might take some time. It is so big, much bigger than your Earth. It is a world of both humans and angels. It is seven different worlds in seven different realities, joined by bridges of a sort, bridges that you yourself form as you need them, bridges that allow you to travel from one to another freely. Each of these seven worlds has its own unique beauty. In one, there is a city of grandeur beyond description, a city that covers over a thousand square miles, a city with buildings of marble and glass and streets paved with gold. On other planes, there are forests beyond compare, mountains that reach to the sky, and warm oceans of pure sweet water. And, I assure you, it is very real, Krissie, more real, more vivid than this world; of that you may be sure. I have been away from it for but a few days, and I already miss it terribly."

"And I suppose Hell is real too, isn't it?" asked Krissie, a trace of fear in her voice.

Again the angel nodded. "Yes, Hell is real, too. It is like the most terrible prison you can imagine, a place from which there is no escape. There you become a forgotten soul, cut off from the rest of the universe, cut off from everyone and everything you ever loved. It is a realm of wailing and gnashing of teeth, a realm of pain and suffering. And that suffering takes on so many dreadful forms. Satan and his minions have had millennia to explore the techniques by which pain and horror are most effectively delivered. You cannot even begin to imagine it. And like Heaven, it is an eternal realm; nothing grows old, and no one dies. No wound is fatal, and all recover to face the reality of it all again. It is a realm where God the Father is not." Lusan paused. "But why would you want to know about such a place as that?"

"Because I'm afraid I'm going to end up there someday," said Krissie, a tear appearing in her eye.

"Krissie!" scolded Leland. "Why would you ever think such a thought?"

"Because, maybe it's true," she replied. "My mother used to say that when I did things I shouldn't. She would tell me that it was a place where bad little girls went."

"Your mother was a nut case," retorted Leland. "You and I both know it."

"Enough," said Lusan. "Let us have no more of that foolishness. God has seen fit to send an angel to you, Krissie. Yes, child, to you. Is this the act of one who intends to condemn you to Hell? I tell you, no. God loves you very much. Believe me; I know. Don't let your heart be troubled by such thoughts. Put your faith in me and all will be well. I will guide you back to His grace, I assure you. It is a significant part of my mission."

By now Krissie was smiling through her tears. "Really?"

Lusan returned her smile. "Yes, Krissie, really. Those were the words of the Father."

"But can't you tell me a little more about your mission?" asked Leland. "I'd really like to know."

Lusan paused; he seemed deep in thought for a moment. "Yes, I shall tell you more. It had not been my intention to do so tonight, but I shall nonetheless. It is important that you know if you are to serve me in this venture. I do not wish for you to serve me blindly. I am here to help ease the suffering of mankind, to alleviate some of the struggling and hardship. We have come to show the sad, heartbroken people of this world a new way to reach their Creator."

"A pretty lofty goal," noted Leland.

"Indeed," replied Lusan, "but attainable. Understand this; one of the most divisive things in human society is religion. How many wars have been fought over it, fought in the name of God? Well, God has decided to say, no more. He will set the record straight. He will instruct humanity as to how to worship Him. We shall bring His words, His love, and His grace to humanity."

"Why doesn't God just tell us Himself?" asked Krissie. "Couldn't He appear in the form of a thousand burning bushes, speak from the clouds, or something like that?"

Lusan laughed out loud. "Oh, Krissie, if you only knew God like I do. As your people might say, it is simply not His style. He does not operate that way. He is not nearly so heavy handed, at least not usually. In Heaven there is a place called the Holy Place. It is a vast open-air mall where tens or even hundreds of millions of people come to talk to and worship Him at one time. At the very center of it all, you can see God and His court of elders and angels. Yet, even there, His voice is not a thundering voice from the sky, but a soft, quiet voice as He speaks to everyone in the crowd individually. His is a kind voice. He is everyone's loving Heavenly Father. He does not demand their worship; they all give it willingly, out of love for Him. So you see, a thundering voice from the clouds, even a burning bush, just isn't His way. Rarely does He resort to such theatrics."

"So, what are we going to do?" asked Leland.

"My friend, we are going to educate people," replied Lusan. "You have a name for it, a nonprofit corporation. The Divine Light Foundation, yes that is what we shall call it. But creating such an entity is not such a simple thing as it once was. There are tax codes, corporate laws, requirements of the Department of Homeland Security, and so on. I do not have the time or the inclination to see to such things. You shall be my chairman of the board, my chief advisor on all things human, the new, born-again Leland James." There was a pause. "Understand, you will have to leave your old life behind. It will only get in the way. That life must become a thing of the past. Peter did that; Paul did that; can you do that, Leland James?"

Leland smiled. "I have to; yes, I can do that."

"I will ask you many questions in the days and weeks to come. I must know that your answers are true to the best of your knowledge and ability," continued Lusan.

"I won't have all of your answers," said Leland, "but what I don't know, I will find out."

Lusan nodded approvingly, "I can ask for nothing more than that, my friend. Your new life will be an exciting one, and I will not ask you to give up your beautiful home, your cars, or your wealth to follow me. It is not necessary. Our base of operations will be right here on Manhattan, in the new city. You will not need to move. I will be staying with you for a time, but only for a time. Eventually, Duras and I will find our own private accommodations, accommodations more suited for our own unique needs."

Leland stepped to the window. Two police cars, their blue and red lights flashing brightly, were converging on the region of the park where they'd had their encounter just an hour ago. He couldn't quite see the scene of the incident from here. It was hidden by trees and the underpass itself. "I think the police have discovered your handiwork," he said.

Lusan rose to his feet and gazed out into the night. "It would seem so."

"Mr. Lusan, I want to make sure I understand something," said Leland.

"Please, just Lusan," was the reply. "Angels don't have titles, as such."

Leland smiled. "OK, Lusan, you came looking for me tonight, me specifically, right?"

"And Miss Cartright, yes, that is correct," confirmed Lusan.

"God, the creator of the universe told you to seek me out?"

"Yes," replied Lusan. "We have been over all of this before."

"Well, I guess I'm just thinking that there is more to it than you're saying," said Leland. "Excuse me, I don't mean to offend, but I'm thinking that we were chosen for some specific reason, a reason you haven't told us yet."

This time Lusan laughed openly. It dispelled some of the stress that seemed to be building up in the room. He turned to Duras. "Did I not say he was intuitive, that he would come to this conclusion?"

Duras smiled. "Yes, you most assuredly did."

"First and foremost, it was the Father's will," said Lusan. "We angels are not exactly like you humans. We are creatures of duty; we do as the Father instructs. But there is a second reason. It may be the reason that I was selected for this mission. Tell me, Leland, who were you named after, do you know?"

"Yes," confirmed Leland. "Supposedly, I was named after my great grandfather. He was a preacher who got his start as a young man in the Azusa Street Revival a century ago. He got into that Pentecost stuff; spiritual healing, prophecy, speaking in tongues, that sort of thing."

"He did indeed," confirmed Lusan. "What would you say if I told you that I know your great grandfather personally?"

Leland was caught off guard by that one. "You know my great grandfather?"

"I know him well," continued Lusan. "He leads a large congregation beyond the veil of this life. Thousands follow him. He has accomplished feats that would truly astonish you. I would like to think that I had a hand in putting him where he is today, opening up the opportunity for him. I don't expect it to occur overnight, but I would like to think that it is within you to follow in his footsteps. He would be so proud of you."

Leland wasn't easily moved, but there was a tear in his eye now. "Look, I've been a sinner. I admit it. I've never killed anyone, but I'm sure I've broken all of the other commandments somehow, somewhere."

"All have sinned and fallen short of the Father's glory," assured Lusan. "It doesn't matter. God has made provisions for humanity."

"Jesus," deduced Krissie.

Lusan nodded. "Yes, He loves you that much. That is why I say to you not to worry."

Quite abruptly, Lusan and Duras underwent an incredible transformation. No longer were they two humans dressed in somewhat archaic apparel, they were beautiful winged angels dressed in white. Their faces still looked the same, yet everything else about them was different. They were practically radiant.

Krissie dropped to her knees. Lusan quickly pulled her back to her feet. "No, do not kneel to me. I am but a servant of Him who is truly worthy of your supplication." He looked to Leland. "I did not wish to alarm you, but wanted you to see us as we actually are. I wanted there to be no doubts in your heart. We shall do this for none other. Only you shall share our secret."

"But why can't others see you like this? It would make you more credible," said Leland.

"We don't want people to follow us because of what we are, but for the message we bring," said Duras.

"Exactly," confirmed Lusan. "But we are weary. We have been a long time without sleep."

"Angels sleep?" asked Krissie.

"Of course," confirmed Lusan, who once more took on human form. "We sleep several times per month, not often, more if we are on Earth, farther from the center of God's power. Like you, it gives us time to absorb the events of our lives, to put them in perspective."

"Please, follow me," said Leland, escorting the two angels to the guest bedrooms. "I have one for each of you."

"No need," assured Lusan. "We will require but one. We will not even use your bed. Our needs are simple. You see, we angels sleep resting on our wings."

"That doesn't sound very comfortable," noted Krissie.

"I assure you, it is," replied Lusan.

The large bedroom was indeed lavish, with a beautiful view of Central Park from its large window. Leland was happy that he kept it constantly ready for guests, though he didn't have them often.

"Oh yes, this is nice," said Lusan. "I thank you for taking in two weary travelers."

"Of course," confirmed Leland, "I am looking forward to getting to know you better."

"And you shall," assured Lusan. "You will find that we angels are an open book. There is not much that we will not discuss with you. Prepare to come face to face with a world of wonders." Lusan sat his case on the bed and removed two of the gold bars. "Here, take these with you tomorrow. We shall need them converted into cash. Be certain that you put some aside for yourself to see to your own affairs in changing your line of work."

"I understand," confirmed Leland.

"I'll have additional instructions for you tomorrow morning before you leave," continued Lusan. "I look forward to our relationship."

"I do too," said Leland, backing out of the room. "Goodnight."

"And, thank you," added Krissie.

Lusan and Duras smiled, but said nothing as Leland closed the door and walked back into the living room. His mind was awash in emotions.

"Leland, tell me I'm not tripping out," said Krissie, taking his arm. "Those were angels, real angels."

"I saw it too," said Leland. "If it's an illusion, then we're both tripping, babe."

"So, what do we do?" asked Krissie.

"Right now, we go to bed," said Leland. "We're both tired. Maybe we'll think better in the morning." He held up the two blocks of gold that must have weighed ten pounds each. "If these are still here in the morning, I'd say we have some adventure ahead of us. I think our old lives are behind us."

"I'll never turn another trick again," said Krissie, who seemed to be speaking as much to God as to Leland. "Oh Lord, please forgive me for all the bad stuff I've done."

"I think He already has," said Leland. "Still, I need you to contact the other girls as soon as you can. Tell them that I'm going out of business. I'll see to it that they all get one hell of a retirement package: $5,000 a piece for a start, more to come later once we get our share of this gold. I'd rather have them find some other line of work, go to college, beauty school, or something. If they want to stay in the business, I'll find good men who will take them, treat them nice. But I'm done with it. I'll never go back."

"How are you going to explain that to Mr. Pagoni?" asked Krissie.

"I'm really not sure yet," said Leland. "I could tell him I've found religion. I don't think I'll tell him that two angels saved my life in Central Park. I've known him most all of my life; he's been very good to me. He is not a bad person; really, he isn't. If I want to make a clean break, he will wish me well and let me go."

"I hope so," replied Krissie. "I don't know what I'd do if something happened to you. I love you so much."

"And I love you," confirmed Leland. "I can let the others go, but I don't think I could let you go. If I am to be a man of honor, of virtue, I can see only one role for you. Would you consider being the wife of a former sugar daddy pimp like me?"

Krissie was taken aback by that one. "You're serious?"

"Yes," confirmed Leland, "I've wanted to say that for a long time, but I couldn't. What do you think; could you?"

Krissie didn't have to think long about that. She put her arms around him. "Oh yes, nothing would make me happier."

"Then, let's start planning it, babe," said Leland. "Let's you and me start changing the world, starting with us."

From the guest bedroom, Lusan was staring out the window, overlooking the city. In another time, it seemed an eternity ago, he had offered all this to the Son of God, only to be spurned. Venomous hatred welled up in his heart again, threatening to boil over. It would not happen again. He would take back this world that was rightfully his. As for the Son of God, the thief who stole his place of honor, he would see to it that He was soon forgotten. If he had to put every last one of his followers to the sword, so be it

Duras turned to Lusan, interrupting his thoughts of vengeance. "That went very well, my lord."

"Indeed," confirmed Lusan, quickly composing himself. "This Leland James is someone we can use, a human we can depend on. Still, there is one more thing I must take care of before I rest this night."

"The other youth," deduced Duras.

"Yes," confirmed Lusan.

"Has he spoken to others of the incident?"

"No," replied Lusan. "He walks the streets, seeking what he shall do. He has not sought out the authorities, his family, or his fellow gang members. It is just as well; then it is only he that must be dealt with." Lusan pulled a yellow crystal from his cloak. He inspected it closely. "This teleportation device is nearly exhausted. If only the Archangel Michael would have had more of these little gems in his quarters. It would have made our lives here far simpler. Nevertheless, it still has enough energy left to open a few more ethereal doorways."

With no further delay, Lusan opened a doorway that had the appearance of twinkling stars in a blue, glowing mist. He stepped into it and vanished.

CHAPTER 2

Seventeen-year-old Julio Mendoza stumbled on through the night. His mind was swimming in a pool of dark madness from which it couldn't escape. He tried to tell himself that it hadn't happened at all. Juan, David, and Miguel were still a part of his life; but they weren't. He'd seen them cut down in Central Park by two dark strangers. Never had he seen men move as fast as they had. What sort of people carried swords like that around with them anyway? This was nuts.

In reality, he and his friends hadn't expected to encounter anyone in Central Park tonight, not at that hour. It was just somewhere to hang, something to do. It had been Miguel's idea. Now Miguel's head and his body lay separate amidst the blood-stained grass. That image would haunt him for the rest of his days. But how many days would that be?

Should he go to the cops? He'd thought of that. Thing was, that black guy and his white chick might come forth to testify what he and the boys had been about that night. When it all came down, he might end up in juvie until he was 18 or, worse, be charged as an adult and spend serious time on the inside.

But if he didn't go to the police, the police might come looking for him. There were people that had seen him in the company of the others tonight. It might be difficult to explain why he hadn't gone to the police right away.

Then there were his brothers in the Latin Kings. How could he explain to them what had happened tonight, how the others had been cut down while he had been spared? How could he explain what had happened to Juan to his mom?

Then, on top of it all, there was that guy who stood over him, prepared to become his executioner if need be. Never had he been in the presence of someone like that. His eyes—he couldn't get them out of his head. Even now, he could see them staring back at him, cold and lifeless. It was like he wasn't even human. He was like the Devil.

Julio stumbled into an alleyway on the lower east side. He sat down in the darkness and began to cry. His life would never be the same. If only he'd stayed home tonight with his mom. She would have liked that.

He thought about his mom. Many of the guys in the gang had parents who were gang members themselves. The Latin Kings was a family tradition in their homes. They really didn't have a choice in the matter when it came to joining. They were in it sometimes to the third generation. When they turned 13, they underwent the rites of passage into the Kings; they were beat up to within an inch of their life.

But he was different. He'd entered it of his own free will; he'd accepted the rights of passage with his eyes wide open. And now where had it gotten him?

He felt it before he saw it: darkness darker than the alleyway, a cold darkness that he could feel in the air and within the depths of his soul. He wasn't alone.

"Did you really think you could hide from me, boy?" said the voice.

Julio looked up to see that same stranger who had stood prepared to execute him just a couple of hours ago. Had he been following him all of this time?

"Every act of man has its consequences," said the stranger in a deep, commanding voice. "But you're just beginning to realize that now, aren't you, Julio?"

Julio gasped, but said nothing. Perhaps he had been expecting this all along. Hadn't the stranger said something about catching up with him eventually? He hadn't expected it to come so soon. He cried like a child.

"Would you stop that?" said the stranger, his tone firm, but not necessarily threatening. "You humans grovel and cry so much. I am quite tired of it."

"I promise, I won't tell anyone about tonight," pleaded Julio, between his sobs. "I won't go to the cops; just let me live."

"You really are quite pathetic," said the stranger. "I assure you, I do not intend to harm you."

Had Julio heard him right? Could he believe him? "You don't?"

"Really, for a young man you don't listen very well," complained the stranger. "I am not accustomed to repeating myself, but I will tell you this one more time. "I do not intend to harm you; you have nothing to fear from me."

"Oh, thank you," wept Julio. "I promise I won't tell anyone what I saw; I won't."

"I believe you," said the stranger. "Now, pull yourself together, Julio."

That shocked Julio. The stranger had called him by name twice. "You know who I am? Have we met somewhere before?"

"No," said the stranger, "we have not met, at least not formally. My name is Lusan. Not Mr. Lusan, just Lusan. And if you can manage to pull yourself together, I have a business proposition for you, one that will be mutually profitable for us both." Lusan extended his hand to Julio. "Here, allow me to help you to your feet."

Julio hesitatingly extended his hand to the stranger, who helped him up. Somehow, he'd almost expected the hand to be electric or icy cold, but it was just another human hand, soft and warm.

"You keep bad company," noted Lusan. "That is your main problem. Still, when the others drew their blades, you kept yours in your pocket. That was the one act that saved your life this night, the one act of intelligence. Now, they are dead and you still live."

"I didn't know what they were going to do tonight," replied Julio in a meek voice. "We were just out to have some fun."

"Of course," replied Lusan. "But you shouldn't have been out here at this hour at all, with or without them. After all, it's a school night."

"I haven't gone to school since I was 15," replied Julio. "My mom practically begged me to stay in school, but it just wasn't my thing, you know? I was good at it and all; I got OK grades. They just didn't have anything to teach me anymore, that's all."

"Is that a fact?" queried Lusan, more in the form of an observation than a question. "And the Latin Kings did?"

"Well, I…I don't know," admitted Julio.

"I assure you, I can teach you far more than school or the Latin Kings ever could."

"Teach me?" asked Julio, still quaking.

Lusan placed his arm about the youth. "Of course. Come, Julio, we have places to go and things to discuss. If you are going to work for me, you must come to understand how I do business."

"Work for you?" asked Julio, who seemed more confused than ever.

"Why not?" asked Lusan, guiding the youth out of the alley. "I could see it the minute I laid eyes on you; you were perfect for the job. You pick and choose your fights wisely; that is why you still draw breath. If you were not useful to me, I assure you, we would not be having this conversation right now. Understand, I am not looking for a heavy-handed person like your friend Miguel, no, not a heavy-handed person. I am looking for someone who can be subtle, even clever, when the situation demands it. And I will tell you this; working for me can be lucrative in ways that you cannot even dream of. I can grant you the deepest desires of your heart: money, power, even women. All you need to do is serve me faithfully. I think you owe me that much. Wouldn't you agree?"

Julio didn't know what to say. This dreaded meeting wasn't turning out the way he figured at all. They strolled up the almost empty sidewalk. "Yes, I guess I do," he finally replied.

"I would think so," continued Lusan. "If you really insist on being a member of the Kings, I think you should be the leader. Wouldn't you agree?"

"The leader," gasped Julio. "I'm only seventeen. There are people in the Kings who are in their fifties."

"There you go," said Lusan. "The first thing I need to teach you is to stop with the negativity. If I am behind you, I assure you, you will become the leader of the Kings. Things in this city are about to change. We've tried it their way for long enough; now we'll do things my way."

Julio wasn't so sure about the sanity of this guy, but he wasn't about to say anything about it. He wasn't even sure if thinking it was safe. Still, what he said was appealing. Suppose he could deliver on his promises? Julio wasn't so certain that he couldn't. But who was this guy, some sort on ninja? That would explain his skill with the sword. No, he couldn't be a ninja; they were all Japanese. At least, that was what he thought.

They walked on for a few more minutes until they arrived at a high-rise autoparking garage. All the while Lusan spoke of the benefits of serving him. Yet, he spoke in generalities. Julio still didn't know what organization he represented. However, it became apparent that he was high on the ladder of authority, perhaps even the leader. Lusan directed him toward the elevator.

"Where are we going?" asked Julio.

"To a meeting," said Lusan. "I'm going to introduce you to some of the others. I especially want you to meet the individual, the operative you will be working with. It is not a good idea for you and me to be in contact directly. He will give you instructions, teach you our ways. He will help you to achieve all that I have spoken of."

They stepped into the elevator and traveled to the top floor, 11 levels up. They emerged from the elevator and onto the almost empty parking lot, over 150 feet above the city streets. It was open to the sky, whose low clouds reflected back the predominantly amber glow of the great city. It was misty and threatening to rain. Some distance away, the top of the Empire State Building penetrated the low overcast.

Julio scanned his surroundings carefully as they walked away from the elevators and out into the lot itself. There wasn't anyone here, at least no one he could see. "I guess we're the first ones here," he deduced.

"Oh no," said Lusan. "They're here. I assure you, we are far from alone. I'm anxious for you to meet them."

Julio was starting to feel ill at ease once more. Something was wrong. Things weren't as they seemed. They walked to the edge of the lot, where a thick four-foot-high wall guarded the precipice.

Lusan gazed down at the almost empty street below. For but a moment he seemed lost in thought. "I enjoy high places," he noted. "I always have. But let us move on to the business at hand. I wish you to meet my associate, Krugloe."

Lusan motioned toward seemingly empty air across the lot. Julio followed his hands. At first he saw nothing. Then he noticed a mist. No, not a mist, a distortion. Those things beyond it seemed to twist and contort, like a distant landscape viewed across waves of rising heat on a summer's day. But this distortion took the rough shape of a cloaked human form, and moved, or more accurately, drifted toward them. As it drew still closer, Julio felt a chill. It came to a halt about five feet before them. It was a ghost, a spirit, and it was all too real.

"Allow me to introduce you to Krugloe," said Lusan. "Please excuse his appearance. He is but an ethereal vapor, a spirit in this world. The two of you will be working as a team. He will provide the mind, the will, while you will provide the physical form."

"I don't get it," replied Julio, who was rapidly becoming more agitated.

"Oh, I think you do," replied Lusan. "You humans have a name for it. You call such a union demon possession."

"Mary, mother of God," gasped Julio. "Demons aren't real; possession isn't real."

"I assure you, God has no mother," said Lusan. "As for demons; I ask you to look before you, young man. Is not seeing believing? Go ahead, Julio, invite him into you; that is all that is required of you. He will do the rest. No doubt, you will sleep much of the time. He will do all of the thinking for you."

"No, I can't," said Julio. "I don't want that thing in me."

"He can't enter you uninvited," replied Lusan. "Allow me to present your options to you; they are really quite simple. You can accept Krugloe into you willingly, or you can fall to your death over that wall. It's a long way down, young man. It is totally up to you."

"You promised that you wouldn't hurt me," said Julio. "You promised."

"And I'll keep my promise," said Lusan, his voice betraying the impatience he was trying to hide. "You can allow Krugloe to take possession of you, or you can climb onto that wall and from there jump to your death. I won't touch you, I assure you. You yourself will do it for me."

"I won't commit suicide," insisted Julio. Yet he was already walking slowly to the wall at the edge of the lot. The next thing he knew, he was scaling it. No, he didn't want to do this, but he couldn't seem to stop himself.

"It's not too late," assured Lusan. "You can still choose life. Nonetheless, it is your choice. What shall it be, boy? None shall suspect that what happened here tonight was anything short of suicide. You were distraught, not thinking clearly after witnessing the death of your friends. It was just too much for you, so you took your own life."

Julio found himself standing upon the two-foot-wide wall, looking down into the street. How had he gotten here? He didn't want to do this. Yet he was inching toward the edge.

"It is not just death you're facing," noted Lusan. "No, you are not so fortunate as that. It is your eternity in Hell that lies before you. Do you have any idea how long eternity is, boy? No, of course you don't. And it shall be I who decides exactly how you shall spend that eternity. In my mind, the punishment always fits the crime. Do you know who Salome was? Probably not, I doubt that you've read the Bible. She was the stepdaughter of King Herod Antipas. Dressed in the finest, most colorful silks, she danced sensuously before the king to secure from him a favor—vengeance for her adulterous mother. She asked for the head of John the Baptist, and she got it. Now, in Hell, she dances for me, alone, continuously, for all eternity. She dances in tattered, gray rags, with her hands shackled above her head, barefoot within a hot chamber whose floor is but a mass of burning coals. On occasion I go to watch her dance, to take my mind off of my many responsibilities. But mostly she dances alone, for no one, to the tune of her own screams."

Julio was horrified beyond imagining. He was terrified of heights. He struggled for control, but in vain.

"Are you up for a long, hot swim within the Great Sea of Fire? I can arrange it for you, in much the way I arranged it for the great Adolph Hitler. He caused unimaginable suffering during his reign of terror. Six million people, boy, that is how many human beings he killed in the concentration camps." Lusan laughed. "Now, he himself is both fried and cremated throughout all eternity. There, afloat in the boiling black oil, surrounded by the towering flames, he has come to know the real meaning of suffering. His suffering has already exceeded the sum total of that he dealt out during his reign, and eternity is just beginning."

"But I didn't do anything like that," cried Julio. "I've never killed anyone."

"But sin is sin," retorted Lusan. "It doesn't matter how minor it is; it still brings God's judgment down on you. But you aren't some little sinner, are you? You dishonor your mother. You lie and steal. You think God is love? Ha! God has given up on you, turned you over to me to do with as I please. What I shall do to you in Hell is beyond your imagining—no less terrible than what I have done to Salome or Hitler, just different."

There was a pause in Lusan's ranting. Perhaps he desired to allow the horror of the current situation to sink into Julio's soul. It was working only too well.

"However, I am in a charitable mood tonight," continued Lusan, in a more reasonable tone. "I'll allow you to delay your fate for a while if you make the right decision. But your time is running out. What shall it be, boy?"

Julio felt like he was losing his balance; he was on the threshold of plummeting to the street below. Why couldn't he seem to pull back? "All right, I'll do it," he said, tears in his eyes.

"Good," said Lusan. "Now you're being sensible. Now step off that wall; you could fall from there."

A few seconds later, Julio found himself at Lusan's side, facing the frightening apparition. It was drawing ever closer.

"Now, just stretch out your arms and invite Krugloe into you," said Lusan. "It won't be all that bad. You might even grow to like it. Many people do. This isn't like some grade B movie, you know. Most possessed individuals don't foam at the mouth, curse God, and generally behave like raving lunatics. Only on rare occasions do I require such melodrama from my minions. No, far more possessed humans go about dressed in a suit and a tie, beguiling others with their demons' clever tongues. These far better serve my purpose. They are businessmen, politicians, even preachers. You will be like one of them. However, you shall be my witness on the streets, among the gangs of New York. You shall bring a new unity into their midst."

"Who are you?" asked Julio.

"Oh come on, boy. I thought the answer to that question was obvious," laughed Lusan. In an instant, Lusan had changed. His eyes had taken on an almost orange hue while his face, which now bore a small goatee, had grown pale and sinister in appearance. From his forehead a pair of small white horns had materialized. "Do you recognize me now, boy?"

How could he not? "Oh God in Heaven," cried Julio.

"Why don't you take another guess?" laughed Lusan. "Are you afraid to say my name out loud? Then I will say it: Satan. Now you know. Stretch out your arms and invite Krugloe in or return to the parapet and complete your act of suicide. It matters little to me which road you choose."

In that moment, Julio gave up all hope. He stretched out his arms toward the apparition before him. "Come into me demon, just get it over with," he said.

Julio felt a shock of electric cold as the ethereal vapors seemed to sweep into his warm flesh. He fell to his knees, whimpered in fear, as terrible thoughts of all manner of evil swept through his mind. For but an instant, he knew the mind of a minion of Satan, knew the true heart of darkness, of depravity. Then he was shut out, locked away from that aspect of his new being. He would not be privileged to the demon's thoughts as his thoughts were to him. Julio was trapped, locked away within the flesh of his own body.

Then the youth arose to his feet once more, but he was no longer Julio. He smiled a devious smile. "This one is weak-willed indeed. He will be easy to control." There was a pause. "The horns, eyes, and flesh were a nice touch, my lord."

Satan smiled back at his minion. His appearance had nearly returned to its former state. Only the goatee remained. "I simply gave him what he expected to see, what he feared to see. Return this young man to his home; you know the plan.

"Yes, my lord," said Krugloe through the lips of the youth. "I shall indeed enjoy this assignment."

"I'm sure you will," said Satan. "Treat him gently. I suspect that he will be very useful to us."

The youth bowed before his master and then turned toward home. He had much to accomplish in the coming days.

Satan stood there until the former Julio had stepped into the elevator and vanished from sight. "Promising beginnings," he said. It was not clear if he had spoken to himself or to other invisible entities hiding in the night. He gazed out across the sleeping city. "Oh humanity, if only you knew what was in store for you. You might stand in line to leap from this parapet, anything to spare your-self from the days that are to come. But for now, sleep; sleep children of Adam; sleep children of Eve. The day will dawn when you shall worship me as god."

Satan made his way toward the elevator and stepped in. A minute later, the elevator door opened to the street to reveal an empty car with a lingering trace of faint mist.

The walk home was a nightmare for Julio. He lapsed in and out of consciousness, yet he could feel his legs moving and his heart pumping, sense the chill of the night air. But he was but a spectator to it all. Any further intervention in his own life was beyond his control.

"What are you going to do?" asked Julio. His voice was not heard in the real world. He could not stir his vocal cords to vibrate nor move his lips. It was a voice of the mind. "Can't anyone hear me?"

"Yes, Julio, I can hear you."

It was another voice within his own head that answered him. It was the voice of the being who had possessed him, the voice of a demon. "You cannot possibly imagine how good it feels to be physical once more, even in a weak mortal body such as your own. To answer your question, we are going to your home. We, or shall I say I, have much to do in the coming days and months. If I could kick you totally out of this body, claim it as my own, I would in an instant. However, that is not how the game is played, at least not yet. What I can do is lock you up in a small corner, a cell, within your own brain. Don't harbor any hope of escape, of retaking your body. I assure you that it is quite impossible. I've had many thousands of years to learn how to dominate your kind, and a 17-year-old delinquent like yourself isn't going to stop me."

"Please, don't hurt my mom," said Julio. "Do what you want to me, but don't hurt her."

"My, what a change in attitude," noted Krugloe. "You've broken that good woman's heart for years. Don't deny it. I know all that you've done. Now, suddenly, you're concerned about me hurting her. There is a place in Hell for your kind. The master did not speak of it openly, but I think I know what he intended. It is a place of heartbreak. Only there the heart of the offender is broken by an arrow piercing the chest and not merely by words or deeds. And it is an ordeal repeated over and over again, just like those who break the hearts of those they love do it not once, but time and time again. Perhaps we can make a place for you there when this is all through, shackled to that heavy wooden trestle for all times facing a loaded crossbow with a hair trigger trained upon your heart."

Julio did not respond. He was way beyond the point of being terrified.

"But fear not on that account; I do not plan to hurt her. In fact, I plan to start treating her the way she deserves to be treated—that is, so long as she serves a purpose to me, to the master."

It took close to an hour to get home. Julio practically ran up the steps of the old apartment building to the third floor. He inserted the key and quietly crept in.

"It's late," said his mother, looking up from her book. "Where have you been?"

"Mom," he said in surprise. "I didn't think you'd still be up."

"Where else would I be?" she asked, setting down her book and walking toward her son. "Where have you been, Julio? Out with your friends?"

Julio walked toward his mother, a thin woman with long, dark hair and sad, dark eyes. "I left my friends hours ago," he began. "They wanted to go to Central Park, have some fun, but I didn't go with them." He lowered his head a bit. "I don't know, Mom. I just didn't want to be a part of what they might do. I had this bad feeling, you know? I can't explain it. I've been walking around the city for hours, just thinking."

"Thinking about what?" asked Consuela, placing her hand upon her son's shoulder.

"I don't know, Mom, just thinking about my life, about the Kings. Things are happening. They didn't bother me at first, but now they are."

"Like what?" asked Consuela.

"Well, people are getting hurt, in and out of the gang," continued Julio, "and it's the guys who are doing it. I guess, I'm just fed up, that's all. It just isn't me. I'm not like that." There was a moment of hesitation. "Mom, I think I want to go back to school, get my GED at least. There is a GED class starting up in another two weeks, isn't there? I think that's what you told me."

"Yes," replied Consuela, "there is. It's being held only a few blocks away, at the old high school. I'd love so much for you to enroll."

"It's a night class, right?"

Consuela nodded.

"I think I want to enroll in it," said Julio. "I've even thought about community college afterward."

Consuela's smile was literally beaming. "Julio, you really mean it?"

"Yeah, I think so," confirmed her son. "I can't keep living like this. A couple of my friends are already dead. I don't want to end up like them."

Consuela wrapped her arms around her son. "I'll go with you. We can get you enrolled tomorrow morning if you're really serious."

"Yeah," confirmed Julio. "Thanks Mom, I'd like for you to go with me. I mean, I don't know the first thing about getting enrolled to go back to school."

"I'll be glad to help you," said Consuela, wiping away her tears of joy. "But if you're going to be getting enrolled in school, you'd better get some sleep."

"Sure, Mom," said Julio, kissing Consuela on the cheek and heading toward his bedroom. "Get me up early, OK? I want to be sure and get a place in that class."

"Sure," said Consuela, whose smile hadn't dimmed. "I love you."

"I love you too, Mom," said Julio. "Thanks for not giving up on me."

Consuela only nodded as her son closed the door. She prayed as she turned off the lights and headed to bed. "Oh Mother Mary, please, don't let my son change his mind," she whispered. "Oh, Jesus, guide him."

"See how easy it is to be nice to your mother?" said Krugloe. "Don't you feel better now?"

"What are you going to do now?" asked Julio, in a voice that was heard only in his mind.

"Exactly as I said we shall do," was the silent reply. You are getting your GED, and you are going to be a good student and a good son. Then you are going to go to community college. You are going to major in criminal justice. We need you, Julio."

Julio faded away to sleep. He didn't seem to have much choice. In sleep was his only release.

Flashes of the cameras illuminated the Central Park crime scene as 29-year-old detective Bill Strom looked over the grim landscape. He'd earned quite a reputation over the last four years as an astute investigator, but for the moment, this one had him mystified. He turned to his boss, Lieutenant Phil Stoddard, a 44-year-old NYPD veteran. "The wounds have an almost surgical precision about them. One clean slice in each case."

"You think it was done with a machete, maybe, or something like that?" asked Stoddard.

"More like a broad sword," replied Strom, jotting down an additional note in his book.

"Okay, what are we looking at here?" posed the lieutenant. "Three Latin Kings, sliced down like this, no apparent witnesses beyond the perpetrator or perpetrators—you think maybe the Bloods?"

"They're in the midst of a war with the Kings right now," confirmed Strom. "Still, I've never seen the Bloods do something like this. It's just not their MO. And they usually leave a calling card of some kind, but not this time."

"I'm thinking it could be a hit by the Mob," posed Stoddard, looking about at the carnage. "The Kings were horning in on one of their pet operations so they used this act as a something-less-than subtle statement to the Kings to stay out.

"Could be," said Strom. "Still, in your 22 years with the force, have you ever seen the Mob do a hit like this?"

"No," replied Stoddard, "can't say I have."

"I'd not be surprised if we have a new player in town, someone with a grudge against the Kings," said Strom.

"Who, the Samurai?" said Stoddard, almost jokingly.

Strom smiled, though only slightly. "I don't get it, Phil. These were just kids. Who'd want to go to this kind of length to kill them?"

"Someone they tried to mess with?" posed Stoddard. "Some guy walking around the city with what, a three-foot broadsword hidden in his trench coat? You'd be surprised at the stuff we've found hidden in trench coats over the years."

Strom nodded. "You're thinking maybe this is the work of some sort of vigilante?"

"I don't know," said Stoddard. "Your garden-variety vigilante might shoot them, maybe even knife them, but this—this is practically a ritual killing." He shook his head. "Maybe we'll know more once the forensics guys have a better look at this."

"Yeah, I'll follow up on that," said Strom.

Stoddard scanned the scene one more time. "This work isn't getting any easier with the years. This isn't quite the same city I knew as a patrolman in the early '90s. It changed some after 9/11, but that was only the beginning. America itself has changed, and not for the better."

"The meltdown was rough on everyone," noted Strom.

"That isn't even all of it," continued Stoddard. "The city is just getting weird. It feels like there is this evil, oppressive spirit hanging over the city, you know? And what happened tonight is just a part of it." There was a pause. "I feel like it's going to get a lot worse before it gets any better." Again Stoddard paused. He seemed a mile away.

"You OK, Lieutenant?" asked Strom.

"Yeah, OK," confirmed Stoddard. "Let's get this place cleaned up. It will be light in another hour. I don't want these bodies here when the joggers hit the trails. Still, cordon the area off. Maybe we'll be able to pick up some more clues in daylight that we're not seeing now."

"Sure, Lieutenant," confirmed Detective Strom, who made his way over to the place where a set of bodybags lay prepared to accept their cargo.

Strom and the forensics guys were still there as the first joggers hit the trail. In three hours, the investigation had turned up very little evidence and no leads. Strom really hadn't counted on that. He would pursue other avenues, start building a picture as to who was here late last night.

CHAPTER 3

It was just after nine in the morning as Leland James walked into the offices of Manhattan Gold on Sixth Avenue dressed in a dark and very conservative business suit. To say the least, its proprietor, Dale Silversmith, was surprised to see him, and just a bit nervous.

"Leland," he said, offering a warm handshake. "What brings you over here to my establishment? I mean, there isn't anything wrong, is there?"

Leland chuckled slightly. "I'm here on business." Dale's expression told him that he really needed to reword that opening statement. "Oh for heaven's sake, Dale, not that kind of business—precious metals business. I need your advice on an important matter. Can we talk somewhere privately?"

"My office," said Dale, pointing the way. Leland followed.

No doubt about it, for a while, Leland's new life was going to be a bit awkward. He knew Dale through his other business; Dale was a regular customer. He had a particular fondness for Denise, one of his girls. Thing was, Dale was married, had been for 20 years. He'd been a player for at least ten. Keeping things on the QT was of vital importance to him. He'd developed this business using his wife's inheritance money, and it had paid great dividends. The gold market had been very good to him. The uncertain economic and political times had brought him lots of business, and with that business had come the need to relieve some of the stress that went along with it. Still, if his wife found out, he could easily lose it all.

"Leland, you understand the danger in you coming here during the business day, right?" queried Dale, closing the door behind them. "I mean, I can't have people talking."

"Oh come on, Dale," said Leland, a smile on his face. "You're completely safe. No one here knows anything about me. I'm just another customer. For heaven's sake, man, you're my friend. As a matter of fact, I'm out of the love business for good. Don't worry, I'll see to it that you can still make your contacts with Denise, discretely, of course, if you still want to."

"If I still want to?" asked Dale, sitting in his chair.

"That's right," said Leland. "Only now, the two of you will have to make the arrangements on your own."

"So awkward," mumbled Dale.

"Would you just listen to me, man?" asked Leland, sitting in the chair across the desk, and pulling something from his briefcase. It made a rather loud thud as it landed on the oak table.

Dale's eyes grew as round as saucers as he picked up the large and somewhat irregular block of gold. After dealing with it for so many years, he knew that this was the genuine article. "You've gotta be kidding. This thing must weigh ten pounds. My electronic balance won't weigh anything this massive. Where in the hell did you come by this monster?"

"It's sort of a long story," replied Leland, "a story for another time. A good and reliable friend has asked me if I could get this converted to cash money. Now, before you start asking—no, it's not from drug dealers or any other illegal activity. It's all on the up and up, I swear. You were the only person I could come to, the only person I knew that could tell me what to do with a thing like this. Come on, Dale, I need your help."

Dale pulled out his reading glasses and examined the bar carefully. "You realize that a thing like this could easily be worth $200,000? You realize that, right?"

"I sort of figured it," was the reply.

"Who gave this to you?" asked Dale.

"An angel, OK?" replied Leland. "It doesn't matter. I've got dozens of these things, and I've got to unload them over the next three months. How do I do it?"

"Dozens of them, dozens you say?" asked Dale. "You have dozens of gold blocks this large?"

"At least," confirmed Leland. "I haven't actually counted them."

"I've never held so much gold in my hand at one time," said Dale, "and I've been in the business all of my adult life."

"So how do we sell them?" asked Leland.

"Well, first of all, we don't want to flood the market," said Dale, who seemed to drift deep into thought for a moment. "To start off, we have to determine how pure this gold is and what impurities, if any, it has. The impurities themselves might be valuable. Darn it, Leland, if it were a bunch of gold kruger-rands it would be easier, but this is raw gold. It has to be sent off to be analyzed, assayed. I can't do it here. There is a guy who does it right here in New York; that will take at least a few days. He will certify its purity. Then we can search for a buyer, offer it on the precious metals market a little bit at a time. You can't dump it all at once, and you'll need to break it down into smaller units. That big of an ingot might bring up questions you're not prepared to answer." There was a pause.

"Then you'll help me with this sale?" asked Leland.

"Sure," said Dale. "But answer me this; what is this guy going to do with the money?"

"He is going to do God's work, start a ministry like the modern world has never seen," said Leland. "He is going to bring the word of salvation to the nations. That's why this is so important. It was important enough to convince me to give up the love business that has brought me my fortune. Does that tell you something about him?"

Dale shook his head. "Not really. So what will you do now, become a minister, a missionary?"

"I don't think so. I don't know my way around the Bible well enough for that. My grandmother does, but she didn't pass it on to me. I was never that interested. For the moment, I'm the owner's representative, his financial advisor," replied Leland.

Dale seemed taken aback. "You, a financial advisor?"

"Sure," said Leland. "Remember, I do have an associate's degree in accounting. I wasn't about to trust anyone else to keep my books for my most recent business."

"You keep books in your business?" asked Dale.

"Of course," said Leland. "I make what I do look as legal as what you do."

"I'll try not to take that personally," said Dale.

"Would you like me to leave this block of gold with you?" asked Leland. "If so, I think I'll need a receipt."

"Leave a thing like that with me?" asked Dale, in an incredulous tone. "I can't believe you brought that thing over here in a brief case. Most normal people would insist on an armored car."

"I don't have an armored car," said Leland. "Anyway, I've never been robbed in New York. It's a safer city than most people think. Then again, nobody had any idea what I had in the briefcase."

"I'll cut off a few slivers, just a fraction of an ounce of it; gold is relatively soft. Then I'll take it over to the assay office myself," said Dale. "I'll draw up a standard contract with you for the assay work. I'll probably need my lawyer to draw up a contract for me to act as your broker for the sale of the metal. You are getting a percentage of the proceeds, aren't you?"

"Sure," confirmed Leland.

"I can see why you're giving up your old business," observed Dale. "Even a one percent commission on the sale of that much gold would make you wealthier than Midas."

Leland shook his head. "No, Dale, you aren't getting it at all. I'm not doing it for the money. I'm doing it because it's the right thing to do. I've lived on the far side of God's will for a long time, all of my life, really. Don't you see? This is my chance to settle up the account with God, do something for Him to be on the right side for a change. That's what it's all about."

Dale looked at Leland incredulously but didn't respond.

It didn't seem to Leland that Dale was really getting what he was telling him. What he and Krissie had experienced last night was an indeed personal matter. They were prepared to give up everything if need be and follow Lusan. Surely he would lead them back into God's good graces, to salvation. That was worth all of the wealth, all of the possessions he had acquired. What would it profit a man if he gained the whole world but lost his soul? That was in the Bible; Leland remembered his grandmother reading it to him.

"This guy you met must be some salesman to change you so profoundly," noted Dale, as he and Leland made their way to the door. "You really seem different."

"I feel different," proclaimed Leland. "Call it being born again, call it what you wish. For once in my life, I'm a part of something special. I'm going to have a part in changing the world."

Leland stepped from Manhattan Gold and headed toward Seventh Avenue. He had a long walk ahead of him, better than two miles, but he would walk it. He needed time to think about what he was going to say to Mr. Pagoni. He'd spoken to his executive assistant this morning, arranged the meeting. It wasn't difficult; everyone down there knew and liked Leland James. He was sure, however, they weren't going to like what he had to say.

It was about an hour later that Leland walked into the 50-story, high-rise office building. Louie Pagoni had a suite of offices on the top two floors. On paper, Pagoni owned an international shipping business, a very large and profitable one. In fact, most of his dealings were totally legit. He employed over 3,000 people worldwide, yet if there was a grand godfather of the Italian Mafia, he was it.

Leland had first met him when he was only 19 years old, running games of chance for some hustlers on the street over in Brooklyn. Pagoni had taken a liking to him right away and offered him a series of much better jobs. Leland had done a number of odd jobs for Mr. Pagoni, most of them legal. It was Pagoni himself who got him set up in his current gig 13 years ago. Now he was setting it aside. That would take some explaining, and he still didn't know exactly what he was going to say. He wasn't scared as such, but he was nervous.

Leland checked in at the main desk, then walked through the metal detector. It reminded him of a TSA checkpoint, as he set his gold-laden briefcase on the X-ray machine. The security agent looked at it in disbelief as he opened the case at the far end of the machine and removed its contents.

"Yes, its gold," confirmed Leland, "I don't know how pure."

The second security person gazed upon it, picked it up, even shook it.

"It's solid," confirmed Leland.

"Where did you get this thing?" asked the security guard.

"I'm sorry, I really can't say," said Leland. "That information is for Mr. Pagoni alone."

The security officer stepped aside and keyed his radio. Leland couldn't hear the contents of the conversation, but it went on for over a minute. Then that officer turned to the other. "He can go on up. It's OK."

Leland was escorted to the elevator by one of Pagoni's muscular security people, who inserted his special key that whisked them to the penthouse.

"Mr. Pagoni will be seeing you in his private quarters," noted the security officer. "He has invited you to have brunch with him. You should feel honored; he rarely accepts guests in such a manner."

"I do," said Leland, watching the floors click off at lightning speed.

The elevator door opened and Leland came face to face with Mr. Pagoni's two massive bodyguards. Now Leland was feeling a bit nervous.

"Mr. James, welcome," said a pretty, well-dressed young women, stepping between the two muscles. "I'm Sylvia, Mr. Pagoni's personal assistant. Please follow me. You're right on time. Mr. Pagoni will appreciate that."

They walked down the wide brightly lit hallway, a hallway lined with beautiful paintings of sylvan landscapes. Leland had never been up here. It made his own condo pale by comparison.

"Mr. Pagoni has told me a lot about you," said Sylvia. "I can tell that he really likes you."

They stepped into the main dining area with its long glass table. It offered a panoramic view of the New York skyline through large windows that spanned two of the walls. At the head of the table stood Mr. Pagoni, dressed in a blue business suit.

Pagoni was a relatively tall and thin man in his early sixties. He was quite handsome and had graying hair and a broad, open smile. He walked toward Leland, his arms wide open. They embraced. "Leland, my boy, it is so good to see you again. The man who keeps New York's finest businessmen and statesmen happy and content is always welcome here."

"It's good to see you too, Mr. Pagoni," said Leland. "You have such a gorgeous home."

"Thank you so much," said Pagoni. "We should have done this long ago. Please, have a seat."

Leland sat by his boss, even as their omelets were set out before them by the chef, who also happened to be a young and beautiful woman. For a time, Pagoni engaged Leland in chitchat. He asked about his grandmother, about his feelings on New York politics, and especially about his young women. It was then that Leland dropped the bombshell.

"Getting out of the business?" asked Pagoni, incredulously. "Why Leland, you are at the height of your game; you're the best."

"It is hard to describe, sir," said Leland, deciding how best to filter the information without outright lying to his boss. It wasn't out of fear so much as out of respect for this man that he so very much admired.

"Does it have something to do with a large block of gold?" asked Pagoni.

"Yes, in part," said Leland gingerly pulling the ten pound ingot from his briefcase and placing it on the table.

Pagoni picked it up and examined it. "I'm no expert on gold," he admitted, "but it looks genuine enough." He handed it back to Leland. "Tell me, Leland, where did you get this?"

And so the story began. Leland spoke of the rescue in the park, of the two strangers, of his calling to bring the message of God to the world. He spoke of Lusan, without referring to his otherworldly nature. He spoke of his need to get out of the business and why.

Through it all, Mr. Pagoni sat there quietly and thoughtfully. When the tale was told, he leaned back in his chair. "An incredible story," he noted. "Still, the gold seems to bear it out. I believe you Leland. I'm glad that you came to me with this, and I understand why you want to leave the business of love. Still, it's a pity. You were so good at it." There was a pause as Pagoni contemplated the situation. "I'm still willing to help you in your new business, Leland. I could have helped you to market that gold as well; still, let us allow Mr. Silversmith his day of jubilee. What is it that you need from me? How can the company help you?"

Leland was overwhelmed. He had not expected Mr. Pagoni to be this under-standing. He could sure use his help. During the next hour they evaluated the situation, solving many of the problems that Leland had not been able to crack. Coming up with forged identity documents for Lusan and Duras that were ab-solutely watertight was one of them. Getting initial funding, office space, office staff, and business licenses to operate in the city of New York was another.

By the time Leland left Mr. Pagoni, virtually all of the sticking points had been overcome. Before they parted company, Leland and Mr. Pagoni even took a minute to pray for the success of this venture. Having the Italian Mafia clearing the way for the ministry of God's Word seemed an incredible concept, but there it was. God truly did move in mysterious ways.

"Hey, Phil, we've got the forensics and autopsy reports back on those kids who were killed in the park three days ago," said Detective Bill Strom, as he walked into the lieutenant's office. "I sure hope you're in a good mood."

"Because you're about to tell me something that will sour my mood regard-less," deduced Phil Stoddard, turning from his computer. "Out with it."

"OK," said Bill, "it looks like one of those kids grappled with his assailant or assailants before he went down. Forensics found two dark hairs and some skin beneath his fingernails. The guys in forensics took it in for genetic typing. Thing is, the hair turned out not to be human, neither was the skin."

"Maybe it was from his dog," suggested the lieutenant. "Two of the kids had dogs, didn't they?"

"Yes they did, but here's the creepy part," continued Bill. "It wasn't canine, or even feline. The skin and hair don't match any of the 50 or so animal ge-nomes in the database. It's close to human, really close, but not quite."

"Maybe it's from an ape of some kind, or maybe the lab just fouled up the test. I don't know. I've never really understood all that genetic stuff. If you're trying to tell me that little green men or Big Foot killed those kids, well, I don't have the time. Our assailant was human, a damn weird one to be certain, but he was human." There was clear frustration in the lieutenant's voice.

"Look Phil, I worked with forensics for three years," continued Bill. "I know a little bit about the science; they're not making this stuff up, and there's no mistake. I don't know what I'm trying to tell you beyond the fact that it's weird, that's all. They will be expanding their search. Maybe it will be something simple that we're just overlooking. We all know that it was a man who wielded the blade that killed those gang members." Bill paused. He really hated to bring up the next issue. "There's something else. Some blades leave a trace of their identity behind, and this one left a doosey, an almost microscopic fragment. There were faint traces of titanium and iridium in two of the wounds."

"Iridium?" asked Phil. "I've heard of titanium, but iridium? That's some kind of crazy, rare metal, isn't it?"

"It is," confirmed Bill, "four times rarer than gold and real;y expensive."

"So, the sword, or axe, or whatever it was, was made of what, an alloy of titanium and iridium? What kind of crazy blade is that?"

"One that never existed before," said Bill. "I don't know a whole lot about metallurgy, but this is a new one on me. It combines one of the least dense metals with one of the most dense. Who knows what the properties of a metal alloy like that would be. The lab guys are looking into it. They are even sharing their findings with one of the professors over at New York University. Maybe he can shed some light on this."

"We have a few clues, but they just don't add up," lamented Phil. "No eye witnesses have stepped forward, and we don't have any suspects. There are no security cameras with a good view of that region of the park, either. The papers are suggesting that this was the work of a vigilante. I can't eliminate that possibility, but I have my doubts. Unless someone comes forth with new information, we might have to put this one on the back burner for now."

"Maybe not," said Bill. "There are no security cameras in the park, that's true, but there are cameras on the far side of Central Park East and Central Park West, several of them that give us a good image of the perimeter of the park. I may have found something."

Bill placed three rather dark and somewhat blurry photographs on the lieutenant's desk, showing two people, a man and a woman, entering the park from the east. The lieutenant examined them closely.

"These two individuals are the only people who crossed into that area of the park anywhere near the time of the murder. They are way too far away to ID them, but it looks like a fairly large African American man accompanying a small, thin Caucasian woman." Bill pointed to a building on the photograph.

"They seem to have left this building here. It's an upscale apartment complex. Then they cross the street and enter the park on the same path on which the murders took place."

"Did you see where and when the gang members entered?" asked the lieutenant.

"Not yet. I haven't seen where and when these two left, either, but I'll keep searching. Maybe someone in that apartment complex knew them, maybe the doorman. I'm going to check that out this afternoon. And here is something else, according to the mother of one of the murdered youths—there might have been a fourth gang member who accompanied the others to the park that night. Then I turned around to find that the kid in question actually came down to the precinct with his mother and filed a report yesterday after they heard what happened. He claimed that he left the group earlier in the evening and didn't see anything. Now that may well be true, but I'm following it up nevertheless. I'm going over to see him this afternoon."

"Good work, Bill, mighty good work," confirmed the lieutenant. "Maybe we'll get a break in this case yet."

"My son has been very upset by the death of his three friends," confirmed Consuela, looking over at Detective Bill Strom, who was setting in the comfy chair in their living room with a notepad in his hand. "It frightens me to think that he was with them earlier that night, that I could have lost him."

"I was with them earlier that evening," confirmed Julio, sitting on the love seat by his mother's side. "They were going to hang out in the park. We did that sometimes."

"We went over to the precinct and filed a report on Wednesday," said Consuela.

"Yes, I noticed that here," noted the detective. "Thank you for coming forth, Julio. What time did you leave your friends?"

"About 9:30," was the answer.

"About an hour and a half before they were killed," noted Bill. "What were they planning on doing in the park?"

"They'd planned on playing toll taker in the park that night."

"Toll taker?" asked Bill.

"Yeah, we'd hang around until someone came along. Then we'd tell them that this was our territory and that they would have to pay a toll to get by. Some people would just run; others would fork out some cash. Not too many would think about fighting us. I mean, there'd be four of us, you know? I mean, we'd never hurt anyone, it was just a game."

"Sounds like a game that could get you in trouble," noted Bill. "It might have been what got them killed."

Julio seemed to tremble for a moment, as though there were strong emotions just beneath his cool exterior. "I'd played the game a few times; I admit it. But I didn't that night. I've been in trouble. I guess you know that. I'm on probation now, will be for another month. I don't want to end up in juvenile hall. I've been clean for nearly six months now, no drugs, no felonies. I wasn't going to play. I left them at the edge of the park, across from that new Brookmoore Hotel. I walked around for a while, thinking it out, and then went home. You see, I had a bad feeling that night, I don't know why." For a moment, he hesitated. "It was like something was telling me to get out of there. Maybe it was the Spirit of God or something. I know that sounds crazy."

The detective smiled. "No, Julio, I don't think that sounds crazy at all. I think it sounds sensible."

"Julio is going to be starting GED classes here in another week," said Consuela. "He is really trying to turn his life around. I'm proud of him for that. It's not easy to walk away from the gang."

"No, it's not," said the detective, turning to Julio. "But it's the best decision you've ever made."

"I hope so. I just couldn't stay," said Julio. "I'm hoping to major in criminal justice in college, after I get my GED. I'd like to be a detective someday. I'm just worried about my juvenile record getting in the way."

"Don't worry about that," assured Bill. "I've had a look at that record. It's just a juvenile record, and you haven't been involved in any really serious trouble. Down the road, if you want to join the NYPD, give me a call. I'll help you."

The detective rose to his feet and handed Julio his card. "If anything else comes to your mind that you think might be important, would you give me a call?"

Julio stood up and smiled, though slightly. "I sure will, and thank you Detective Strom."

The detective shook Julio's hand. "Thanks for coming to us, Julio; I know that took some courage."

"I just wish I could have been more help, detective," said Julio. "I want you to get whoever did this to Miguel and the others."

Bill smiled. "We'll get them Julio. You just keep looking up. And keep up the good work. One of these days I hope to see you in our department. We need good men on the force, ones who really appreciate what we're dealing with. Stay in touch, Julio, even if you just need someone to talk to, OK?"

"I will," confirmed Julio.

"That was a little help," muttered Bill, as he walked down the hallway. At least he knew now what the youths had been doing in the park and why they might have gotten into trouble. Meeting Julio was a pleasant experience, too. That in itself had been worth the trip. To see the lights go on in a young person's head, to see kids change course before it was too late, always gave Bill a good feeling. It didn't happen often enough. He'd try to keep an eye on Julio, help him if he could.

It had been the better part of a week since Leland had encountered the angels in the park. Since that time, his life had become more hectic than ever. He had 16 girls in his employment. They were flabbergasted when Krissie gave them the news that Leland was going out of the love business. They were even more surprised when they were each presented with a check for $5,000 out of Leland's private account.

"This is just the first of it," explained Krissie. "Leland has promised to provide you additional money for schooling or refer you to someone else if you really want to continue in the business, but he is out of it for good."

When asked why such a successful pimp was closing his doors, he answered that he had found religion. There were no specifics, just religion. Still more astonishing was the revelation that Krissie and Leland were planning on getting married. Imagine that. It seemed that Leland was full of surprises this week.

But Leland didn't hold the monopoly on surprises. His friend Dale, from Manhattan Gold, had some good ones, too. "Meet me in my office; the assay is in." That was the sum total of the message on Leland's answering machine. When he arrived at Manhattan Gold, Dale practically spirited him into his office.

"The assay is in on your gold," he announced. "They ran it three times. The news is good, really good. That sample is 86 percent pure gold, but all of the rest of it is iridium, a dense and very expensive metal, with a market value equal to the gold. It has a number of scientific and manufacturing uses. I already have a buyer, if you're interested."

"Already?" asked Leland, who seemed genuinely surprised.

"Yes, already," confirmed Dale. "He is willing to purchase five of those ingots initially and still more later. His offer is very generous, $980 an ounce. I think that he is mainly interested in the iridium, myself. He is a buyer for a large semiconductor manufacturer. Minus my commission and expenses, that will net you about $942 an ounce."

"Sounds good to me," replied Leland.

Dale reached into his file cabinet and produced a stack of paperwork. He placed it on the table before Leland. "I took the liberty of having my lawyer draw up the contract. Once you have your lawyer look it over, we can move forward."

"That's OK," assured Leland. "I'll just want to take a quick look over the papers and sign them before I leave. I trust you. I want to get this deal moving as quickly as possible."

Dale looked at Leland incredulously. "You're talking about a deal worth over a million dollars. It is one of the largest individual deals I've ever brokered. I really think you should discuss it with your lawyer first. Yes, I'm your friend, and no, I wouldn't screw you over on this. We're in this together. I want to keep you as a client. Still, you need to take some time on this, make sure this is the route you want to pursue."

"I'll take the papers home, show them to Lusan and get his approval, but I want to keep my lawyer out of this for the moment," said Leland.

"Lusan?" queried Dale. "That sounds French. This is the guy who gave you the gold?"

Leland realized that he had just slipped up. He didn't do things like that usually, but the past few days had been so fast paced. He had to think quickly. Pagoni's people had been working on creating an identity for Lusan, one that would hold up to careful government scrutiny if it came to that. This deal would go far in covering those costs, which were considerable. "Yes, that is the guy, Andre Lusan. He actually hails from Casablanca, but, yes, he is French."

"So, he's in mining, is he?" asked Dale.

"Well, indirectly," was the reply. "He purchased the gold from an independent third party that hit a rich vein of gold deep in the Moroccan desert. They were the actual miners. I'm sorry. I really can't tell you more than that."

Dale nodded. "I fully understand. Thank you for the information. It makes more sense to me now. I still want you to take the papers home and think it over. If your client likes the deal, then bring them back tomorrow. Oh, did you want me to arrange for an armored car to come and pick up the gold bullion?"

"No, I'll just bring it in with me tomorrow," said Leland, placing the papers in his briefcase.

Dale nodded, but said no more. He was getting accustomed to dealing with Leland and his cavalier attitude toward security.

It was later that evening when Leland presented the papers to Lusan at dinner. It was true that Lusan and Duras really didn't need to eat, but Krissie's cooking was exceptional. At any rate, they needed to fit into human society, learn the customs and habits of humanity, including dinner table discussion and etiquette.

"Yes, Leland, this is totally acceptable," said Lusan, setting down the last page following dinner. "You have done better than I had dared to hope during the first week."

Leland smiled. "Yes, it was one week ago tonight, wasn't it?"

"Indeed it was," confirmed Lusan, who then turned to Krissie. "You have been such a kind and gracious hostess this past week. You have made Duras and me feel truly welcome in your home. We are most grateful."

"Indeed, we are," confirmed the usually silent Duras. "I particularly enjoyed our visit to the Metropolitan Museum of Art. Seeing firsthand the artistic nature of humanity was most spiritually enlightening. Thank you, Krissie."

Krissie smiled a broad smile. "And I enjoyed taking you, both of you. You are beginning to fit in with people really well."

"Getting a more appropriate wardrobe was helpful," noted Duras.

"Yes," said Krissie. "Your old wardrobe sort of made you stand out in a crowd. No offense meant."

"Oh, none taken," assured Duras, smiling broadly. "If we are to minister to humanity, we must learn to be more human. You are an excellent teacher, Miss Krissie."

Krissie nodded. She was becoming more at ease with the two angels, particularly with Duras. Duras seemed more open, more willing to help. Despite his quiet nature, he was actually the more considerate of the two. In fact, he had helped her prepare dinner this evening. She smiled a lot and laughed often when he was around. He could be quite amusing at times. Lusan was gracious, incredibly charming, but difficult to read. There were times that he made her feel very uneasy, though she wasn't quite sure why.

"Mr. Pagoni's people are almost finished with your new identities," said Leland. "Both of you will have very authentic looking French passports tomorrow. Even if someone were to check the French government's electronic records, they would only find a confirmation of the validity of your passports. I don't even pretend to understand how that was accomplished, but the people doing this for us are good."

"Excellent," said Lusan, "I was a bit dubious about involving the Italian Mafia in this ministry, but I am pleasantly surprised so far. What of the bank accounts?"

"We will be able to establish those once your passports and other necessary French documents are ready," said Leland. "I don't want to jump the gun on that one. I want things to go right the first time. Give it another three or four days, a week at most."

"Excellent," repeated Lusan. "My faith in the two of you has not been misplaced. I can see that now. If you don't mind, I think I will accompany you to Manhattan Gold tomorrow morning, put its proprietor more at ease."

"Good idea," replied Leland. "I think it would help."

The following morning found Leland and Lusan in Dale Silversmith's office at Manhattan Gold. Lusan had the five gold bars tucked away in his brief case. Though it weighed over 50 pounds, Lusan carried it as though it was filled with feathers.

"I understand that you are French," noted Dale, extending his hand to Lusan.

"Heureux pour vous rencontrer, mon nom est Andre Lusan," said Lusan, introducing himself without hesitation. *"Je suis reconnaissant pour votre aide dans cette matière."*

"You're very welcome," assured Dale. "Pleased to be of service."

Lusan removed the five gold ingots from the case and placed them on Dale's desk, an act that brought a look of pure astonishment to his countenance.

"Remarkable," said Dale. "I'll see to it that these end up in the safe right away. You will have a signed receipt before you leave. I am grateful for your business."

Lusan bowed slightly, but said nothing.

"The papers are all signed," said Leland, handing them to Dale. "How long before we can expect payment?"

"Within the week," assured Dale. "I will have the proceeds deposited directly into your account if you wish."

"We will be placing the proceeds in Mr. Lusan's account, which should be established by then," replied Leland. "Dale, I suspect that we will be giving you a lot of business over the next year or so."

Their meeting was amazingly short for a transaction so large. Fifteen minutes found Leland and Lusan back out on the city street. It was windy and distinctly chilly. A cold front had ushered in the first cold weather of the season. It was clear that the Indian summer of the past two weeks was over.

"I'd like to show you the office space Mr. Pagoni has provided for you," said Leland, turning to Lusan. "It is in the new Davidson high-rise downtown. You will have two complete floors, the 31st and 32nd floor. Those are the two top floors. It's a bit pricy, but it offers plenty of room for expansion. Mr. Pagoni will pick up the first month of rent until we establish our own bank account. It will also offer you and Duras living quarters that meet the special requirements you described to me. You will have total privacy and total security, the entire 32nd floor. The elevators will not even go to that floor without a special electronic key that only you will have. It has a tremendous view of the city. As I recall, you like that. It won't take long to get a business license for your organization. Mr. Pagoni has seen to that. But to establish it as a 501(c)3 charity that will be tax exempt may take six months or more. We should be ready to sign the lease within two weeks once you have an established bank account. Still, you might want to hold off getting the entire two floors of office space until all of the non-profit paperwork is complete."

Lusan shook his head. "The salvation of the world can't wait, my friend. We must get started now. If this office is acceptable to me, and I suspect that it will be, we must proceed with all due haste."

Leland nodded. Lusan had been running his legs off this past week. Still, he could see the need for swift action. The world was in a mess. Leland saw that more clearly than ever. Right now, what the people needed was what Lusan had to offer.

It had been fully three weeks since Julio's experience in the park. The demon's control over the youth's body was now absolute. The old Julio was locked away securely, able to do little more than watch and feel what the demon felt. Still, to the outside world, this was an improvement. The new Julio was the perfect student in his GED class, very different from the old Julio. He had also become the perfect son for Consuela, and she couldn't be happier. Still, there were some loose ends to tie up. His old brothers from the Latin Kings were bothering him, urging him back into the fold. It was on a Friday night that he stepped into their basement meeting place and announced his intention to quit the Kings.

"I'm not mad at any of you," he said, standing before the group. "It is just that I need to live my own life. The deaths of Miguel, Juan, and David made me realize that life is just too short, especially if I continue on here."

"You don't walk out on the Kings," said Angel, a six-foot-two, 240-pound original gangsta.

"Unless we beat you out," said Carlos, their leader and most senior member. "Look, Julio, you're a smart guy. I like you, always have. I know how bad you feel about Miguel and the others. He was my youngest nephew; how do you think I feel? But being beat out of the gang; well, that might make your life even shorter, *comprendo?*"

"I'm willing to take that risk," replied Julio, "are you?"

That comment elicited both laughter and shock from the members present. This kid couldn't be serious.

"You sure this is what you want?" asked Carlos. "If it is, I can't protect you."

"Yes, it is," said Julio, no hesitation in his voice. "Just let me walk. I don't want to hurt any of you."

Carlos looked at Julio incredulously. "Yo—you, afraid to hurt us? It's you that needs to be afraid."

"You don't even know what kind of powers have my back," replied Julio. "Those powers are all around me, protecting me—protecting me from you if it comes down to it. Just let me go, Carlos. I promise that I won't ever do or say anything to diss the Kings."

"Then step up, Julio, and accept what's coming to you," said Carlos. "Let's see if those powers protect you."

Julio shook his head sadly. "All right."

A way was made through the crowded room as Julio moved toward the center. He found himself standing before Angel.

"There will be no blades," warned Carlos, gazing about at the crowd and then focusing on Angel.

Angel returned his leader's gaze, but said nothing. He knew the rules; he didn't need a lecture, and he sure as hell didn't need a blade.

"Stand back," warned Angel, turning to the crowd, which numbered over 50 men and women. "I get to be the first to mess this little traitor up. I'll put so many bruises on him, break him up into so many pieces, that his own mama won't recognize him."

Through all of Angel's ranting, Julio stood there calmly. He didn't seem a bit afraid of this muscular man that towered over him.

Angel's first blow was a right fist directed at Julio's chest. He seemed astonished when that blow was stopped in mid-air by Julio's open hand.

"Don't do this, Angel," warned Julio, applying ever more pressure to the big man's fist.

Angel threw his other fist, only to find it intercepted like the first.

Julio applied an opposing twist to each arm; that was accompanied by a sickening crack. An instant later, Angel had been cast into the crowd, with both wrists broken.

The silence that followed was stark, even frightening, but it didn't last long. Another gang member charged Julio from the rear, yet Julio swung around to sweep him right off of his feet with his left leg. Julio's moves seemed superhuman.

Julio's swift rotation continued so as to bring his fist squarely into the chest of yet another attacking member of the gang. To his right, a gang member managed to plant his fist into Julio's cheek, only to find himself thrown over Julio's head, his right arm wrenched from its socket.

Although Julio was at the center of the struggle, other totally inexplicable things were happening around the room. Pictures flew off walls and the concrete floor shook, for no apparent reason. Around the room, some of the gang members were fighting with each other. Still more inexplicable were flashes of light and shadowy ethereal forms that appeared randomly about the room.

After a minute and a half, the fury was spent. Julio had put eight big men and a woman on the floor, while suffering only three punches. He had no other challengers; none were so foolish.

Julio turned to Carlos, who had taken no part in the violence of the past minute and a half. "Is it over now?"

Carlos was visibly shaken. What he had just seen was supernatural, and he knew it. "Whose hand is protecting you, Julio? Tell me."

"I think you know," replied Julio. He turned to the others. "I didn't want to hurt you, not any of you. I love you all. But I have a calling on my life, a calling from God. It's his angels that have protected me. They've been here all along; they're still here. I want you to know, they're calling you, too. They'll bless you if you let them." Julio turned to Carlos. "Am I free to go now?"

"You can go," replied Carlos, who turned to the others. "No one stops him; no one hurts him, not now, not ever. Give him room."

The others made way as Julio walked from the room. Who was there to stop him, anyway?

Julio was halfway down the long alleyway before he heard someone calling his name. He turned to see Salvador and Karina, two of the gang members about his age. He stopped.

"We're not going to hurt you," said Salvador, approaching him slowly.

"I know that," said Julio, wiping a trace of blood from his lower lip.

"I don't think we could," noted Karina.

Julio chuckled. "Probably not; then again, I don't think the two of you would want to anyway. You're my friends. I know that."

"We are," assured Salvador. "We saw what you did. Whatever it is that you've gotten into, we want to be a part of it. We're with you Julio."

"Even if it means leaving the Kings?" asked Julio.

"Even if it means leaving the Kings," confirmed Karina.

Julio placed his arms around his two friends. "I'm really glad the two of you are here," he said. "My life would be a lot lonelier without you. I want you to be a part of what I've found. Maybe I should say that it is what has found me."

The blank expressions that he got from his friends told him that they didn't understand. "Yo, it's off da hook!" he continued. "You just got to experience it for yourselves."

"We want to," said Karina.

"Then I'll tell you all about it," said Julio. "I'll tell you the whole thing. Then, if you still want it, it's yours for the taking. We're going to be a part of a great awakening, my friends. It's gonna be poppin'! We are going to change the world!"

Within the prison of his own mind, the real Julio was screaming. "No, not Karina, not Salvador, no you can't."

But it was no longer his decision. He had given up his rights to this body on that rooftop three weeks ago. Now Krugloe called the shots. As the three walked down that alleyway, Julio realized that the nightmare was just beginning. Already, he felt the demonic spirits gathering around them. Now he would have company in his strange, fleshly imprisonment; now Salvador and Karina would know his pain.

CHAPTER 4

A chilly wind was gusting out of the southwest, bringing with it the musty odor of dust. Forty-two-year-old Will Reinhart was only too familiar with the odor, though at this point he wished he wasn't. Another one of those damnable dust storms was brewing. He gazed out into the darkness, beyond the glare of the floodlights. He didn't have to see it to know that a billowing cloud of dust was sweeping in. The visibility would be plummeting within the half hour. They would probably have to suspend operations even sooner.

"Great. All we need is another delay," he mumbled under his breath, even as another section of pipe joined the growing stack building up at well number 14. There were just a few more sections to go. Maybe they would get the old bit out before the weather closed in on them.

They had reached a depth of just over 10,600 feet before the bit had crapped out on them. Five hours; that was how long this bit had lasted, five hours. The last one had only lasted four. They should have lasted twice that long.

Will was a veteran of 24 years at this profession. Bringing in oil wells was his life, and he loved it. He'd started as a roughneck in the oil fields of Oklahoma when he was only 18. He'd brought a lot of oil wells in over the years—in Oklahoma, in the deep waters of the Gulf of Mexico, in the arctic wilderness of northern Alaska, and now here, in what used to be northern Iraq, now the Autonomous Kurdish Republic of Kurdistan. The job had taken him all over the world. Oil was becoming more difficult to find; he realized it only too well. They were drilling deeper and coming up with more dry wells than they used to.

His mind wandered back to his suburban home just east of Vancouver, British Columbia. He was tired of traveling, of being away from home for six months at a time, of being a long-distance husband to Mary, and a long-distance father for his two boys. Nonetheless, he wouldn't have dreamed of bringing them to this place, even with the company's supposedly safe gated compound.

Kurdistan was, by far, the most politically stable of the two nations that had arisen from the ashes of war torn Iraq. Its government hadn't been engulfed by the fundamentalist Islamic fever that had swept like a wildfire through most of the Middle East. There were still a few moderate nations, like Egypt, Jordan, and Saudi Arabia, but the rest of the region was a real powder keg.

In truth, the Kurdish Republic had tried to distance itself from the chaos to the south, even going as far as petitioning for membership in the European Union. It would never happen, of course. Turkey had tried for 30 years without success. The European Union was a pretty exclusive club, and they planned to keep it that way.

Still, the locals sort of liked having the Canadians here. They brought in shiploads of money to the economy of the Kurdish Republic, decent jobs, and the best that Western culture had to offer. Nevertheless, the oil field was only 20 miles from the border of Iraq, and that border was far from secure. To Islamic terrorists, the hundreds of miles of remote border territory, with its poorly guarded fences, were no obstacle. They resented the oil wealth of the north, and they made their displeasure felt quite frequently. Yes, the pay here was out-standing, but it was hazard pay to be sure.

Last September, a suicide bomber with a truckload of explosives had driven his way onto the site of well number 11, something that shouldn't have been possible. It was, by all accounts, the work of a husband and wife team. They'd gotten past security and driven to within a couple hundred yards of the well before the guards nailed them. Fortunately, the only fatalities were the bombers themselves. If they hadn't left a suicide video, there would have been no way to have identified them.

The attitudes of these radicals were positively creepy, and recent incidents around this well hadn't helped matters, either. There was the five-year drought, the freak windstorms, and now, by some accounts, a haunted oil well. That's right, a haunted oil well. In all of his years in the business, Will had never heard of such a thing, but here it was.

This project had started ordinarily enough. They were even ahead of schedule for a time. The trouble began when they hit 8,500 feet. It was there that they first encountered the strange rock strata. It defied classification. It was an incredibly resilient metamorphic rock, one altered by heat and pressure. But its crystal structure and elemental makeup were like nothing their chemist had ever seen. It was incredibly rich in sulfur and in no less than four rare earth elements. These elements were so rare that, at first, he hadn't even recognized them. It took researchers back at the University of Washington to finally identify them: promethium, lanthanum, osmium, and iridium. They'd drilled all over this valley and brought in seven good wells brimming with light crude, but they'd never encountered anything like this. This strata ate up their expensive drill bits for lunch, and it just went on and on.

Then at 9,100 feet they hit the first of many pockets of that damnable liquid. Bill and his crew thought they'd finally broken through the cap rock and into the oil.

At first, just traces of it came up with the mud, then, the better part of a 1.000 gallons of the black viscous liquid erupted from the well casing and unto the platform before they were able to cap it. A cheer arose from the roughnecks; the work had all been worth it. Troublesome number 14 had finally paid off in a big way. But their jubilation had been short lived for this was like no oil they'd ever seen. It was black, but it lacked the smell of normal crude, and it was incredibly high in sulfur. You could actually smell the stuff. Within two minutes of reaching the surface, the still hot substance had burst into flames, sending everyone scattering. The flames danced across the liquid, sometimes swirling and then suddenly erupting dozens of feet into the sky. After a couple minutes, the fires went out by themselves, only to erupt again several minutes later. The liquid burned with the odor of sulfur, but with virtually no smoke. What the hell was this stuff? After half an hour, the liquid had cooled and become inert, but it had left a lasting impression. Bill had never seen the likes of it before, though it reminded him of something that he'd read about a few years back. No, that was absurd, he'd quickly dismissed it.

Analysis in the lab revealed the presence of heavy organic compounds within that mysterious liquid that looked like bits and pieces of amino acids, even proteins. Nevertheless, its combustive properties mystified their chemist. A sample of the liquid had been sent back to Vancouver for more detailed analysis.

More recently, they'd pulled the bit out to find that not only had it been dulled by the hard rock, but twisted and distorted by forces unknown. It was like it had been partially melted. But how could that be? The temperature at the bottom of the well was scarcely 250 degrees: hot, but not that hot. They'd called in the company's best metallurgist to examine the bits, but he couldn't explain what was happening either.

If Will had his way, they'd have capped this well for good two weeks ago, but the company said to keep drilling. Whether it was a matter of economics or just scientific curiosity on their part, he couldn't say.

Then two mornings ago, one of the roughnecks came into his office as white as a sheet. He was scared, really scared. They'd just pulled in the line and were preparing to replace the bit. It was quiet, on the normally loud and busy platform. He'd taken a break right beside the casing. It was then that he heard it; cries coming from the depths of the well: the cries of people in pain. Had it not been for the multitude of bizarre incidents over the last month, Will might have dismissed the story. He had gone out to hear for himself, but he heard only silence. Since then there had been two more reports of the same thing from experienced, no-nonsense roughnecks. People were getting scared, people who usually didn't spook easily.

The last of the drill collars had hit the stack, and the crew was working on changing out the bit, when the storm hit with 40-mile-an-hour winds. They finished securing the well and ran for cover.

Will couldn't explain why, but he didn't join them. He put on his goggles and made his way over to the well for an inspection. He looked about; his crew had done a good job of securing the site. The crew had stacked the drill string perfectly according to company standards; they always did. He was turning to leave when he heard the sound coming from the well, a sound that could be heard even over the howling wind. He knelt by the 20-inch-diameter casing and listened.

The winds were beginning to die down. This was incredible; he could actually hear it. It was like the distant moaning of a person from somewhere below. Not a multitude, just one person. No, there had to be another explanation—venting of gas, something. A deep melancholia swept over him, though he knew not its source.

"Help me," cried the distinctly human voice from far below.

Will lurched back. No, this couldn't be. There was someone down there.

But how could that be possible so far below ground in all of that heat? Will approached the well once more. "Hello, can you hear me?" he yelled, into the casing.

Only silence answered his cry. It was then that the lighting on the rigging went black. It sent a chill of fear up his spine. He quickly recovered. The wind had knocked down a power cable; that was all. But what about the voice he'd heard? He had heard it. There was no doubt in his mind. Again, he gazed into the casing.

Somewhere, far below, he could see light, a faint blue light. He removed his goggles and put on his glasses to get a better look. It was getting brighter, no, not brighter, closer. Something was coming up the casing toward the surface. He stifled the urge to run. He pulled the flashlight from his belt and directed its beam down the casing. It didn't help. Then a terrible realization dawned upon him. He reeled back, barely in time, as a tower of glowing blue gas erupted from the casing amidst a terrible roar.

Will was on his back gazing up as it dispersed into the air. Yet, it wasn't a single cloud, but a multitude of smaller ones. They took a common form— ethereal beings with glowing wings, yet they were as inconsequential as vapor. Will gazed at them, hundreds of them, in wide-eyed terror.

Then one erupted from the well, only to swing back toward him. It hovered before him, towering above him, a cloud of vapor in the shape of a winged demon, and that shape was becoming ever more distinct. He could sense the darkness, a darkness beyond the blackness around him, as it reached for him. It drew ever closer.

In his terror, only one heartfelt response erupted from his lips. "In the name of Jesus Christ, my Savior, leave, you have to leave!"

The being seemed to dissolve back into a nearly formless cloud and raced away from him. Half a minute later, the terrible phenomena ended.

Will quivered in fear from head to toe. Then he just broke down and cried. That was how his crew found him a minute later. They'd seen the pyrotechnical display, but not in the detail Will had.

They helped him through the darkness back to his office. They stood about him, flashlights in hand. It was over a minute before he came to himself. "Oh my heavens," he gasped.

"What did you see, Will?" asked a concerned roughneck.

"I don't know," said Will, further composing himself. "I'm sorry guys; I guess I wasn't prepared for that."

"For what?" asked the roughneck. "I didn't think anything could faze you."

It was then that the lights came on once more. It gave everyone a start.

"Yeah," said Will, rising to his feet on trembling legs. "Saint Elmo's fire, that must have been what it was, had to have been." Then he was fully composed once more. "Sorry guys, sorry to turn weird on you. Well, let's check for any damage and get the new bit on and back down the casing. We have a well to bring in."

After a few seconds, the crowd dispersed, noticeably shaken, all save that one roughneck. He closed the office door.

"Saint Elmo's fire?" he repeated. "Come on Will, it would take more than Saint Elmo's fire to put that kind of fear into the likes of you. What did you see out there?"

"I don't know, Sam," admitted Will. "I think I just saw the gates of Hell swing open and release a legion of demons."

There was a long silence. Sam looked into Will's eyes; he was serious. "Yeah, OK, Will. Look, you've had a busy night. Why don't you take it easy for a while, OK? The well is in good hands."

Sam headed out of the trailer and closed the door behind him, leaving Will alone with his thoughts.

"Sweet Jesus, what did I just see?" asked Will, sitting down once more. He turned to his computer and went onto the Internet. He had someone he had to contact, and they weren't at the central office. Right now, he didn't know who else to turn to.

"We had a packed house tonight," noticed Pastor Martin, walking out of the chilly fog and into the old rectory with his visiting evangelists from America. "There is revival in Cornwall this autumn. Sometimes it takes a crisis to bring God's people close to Him."

"Like the possibility of Earth being hit by a comet?" said Serena Davis, almost jokingly.

"Or turning 40 next March," joked her husband, Chris.

"You're only two months behind me," retorted Serena, laughing. "Get used to it, Chris. We're not as young as we used to be."

"You ought to try 62," noted Pastor Martin. "On the issue of age, I can remember when the average age of my parishioners was probably about 60. Not anymore. There are young couples, teenagers, and children in the Church again. There is surely a spiritual awakening sweeping England, even as we speak. I'm thankful that I've lived to see it. It was a long time in coming. Eleven people gave their heart to the Lord at this evening's meeting. Last night there were four. There was a time when I'd have been thankful if there had been a single individual come to the altar during the course of a year."

"The latter-day harvest," said Serena. "It has been wonderful to come to England and see it for ourselves."

"When you can see it through the fog," noted Chris.

"England in November," said the pastor. "It wouldn't be England without our pea soup fogs, I assure you. I'm sorry to see you go."

"We've had a great three weeks here," assured Chris. "We have to be on our way back to misty, rainy Oregon. We have a revival scheduled there in another two weeks. It's back to London for us, and then we're on our way to Portland by the end of the week. That will give us five days to tour jolly old London."

The pastor smiled. "Well, I'd best let you Yanks get some sleep if you want to get an early start. Remember, you drive on the left side of the road here."

"Yeah," confirmed Chris, "I gotta remember that."

"I do believe that you're starting to get a few gray hairs," noted Chris to Serena as they were getting ready for bed.

Serena just shook her head, brushing her long hair all the more vigorously. "A few months in Hell's Great Sea of Fire will do it to you," noted Serena. "Sometimes I feel like it added years to me. When I think of all of the people still there, oh, it sends shivers up my spine. If people only realized that they are only one heartbeat from eternity."

"I can hardly imagine," noted Chris, switching on his laptop and logging onto the Internet before bed.

They got a lot of email, mostly about their book, *Tears of Heaven*, the full account of their otherworldly adventures seven years ago. He had been so fortunate to have experienced it—nearly half a year in the realm beyond this life— in Heaven. He still cherished the friendships he had made on the other side of eternity in that glorious realm. His route there had been through a fatal auto accident that had never really happened—or had it? That aspect of the adventure still made his mind reel. His friend David Bonner could explain it. Then again, he was a genius, with the resources of all of Heaven at his disposal.

He sure missed David and the others. Surely, no human on Earth had ever been as blessed as he had been. He had interacted with the great men of science, Johann Kepler and Nikola Tesla, during his stay in Heaven. He had spoken directly to Jesus, even God the Father. He had walked the streets of gold in Zion and strolled through the meadows of Heaven. Now he had the responsibility of conveying the wonders he had experienced to the world. During the past six years, he had done his best to accomplish that.

Then there was his wife. Her task was not nearly so pleasant as his. He did his best to be sensitive to that fact. Even as he had spent half a year in Heaven, she had spent the same amount of time in Hell. As he spoke of the wonders of Heaven to the congregations, she spoke of the terrors and agony of Hell. She had witnessed and felt so much horror and pain for one so young. She had experienced the darkest place in all creation, and it had a profound effect upon her. She had witnessed the suffering of others and then experienced that same suffering herself. He couldn't even begin to imagine what it must have been like to struggle amidst a vast, turbulent sea of scalding, black oil. Had it not been for her own courage and the assistance of the dark angel Abaddon, she might well have spent all eternity in that realm beyond God's love.

Chris scanned their emails. As always, there was so much. His eyes caught the odd title on one email message: "Urgent apocalyptic event, need your help." "Hey, Serena, do you know someone by the name of Will Reinhart from Canada West Petroleum?"

Serena had to think about that one. "I'm not sure," she admitted.

Chris opened the email. "It is dated today, only about half an hour ago. He says that he met us at the crusade in Vancouver back in 2011. He said that he and his wife spoke to you for some time after the meeting. He was one of the organizers of the crusade."

"Oh yes, I think I do remember him," said Serena.

As Chris continued to read the lengthy email over the next few minutes, he seemed to grow quite pale. "Serena, I think you'd better read this for yourself. I don't know what to think. This is your area of expertise."

Serena had a seat by her husband and started to read its contents. It was the story of oil well 14. It read like something out of the tabloids. She tried to remember back to their meeting with Will Reinhart. She didn't remember much beyond his name and that he was a foreman for a petroleum exploration company. What sort of man was it who would write such a thing? It seemed so incredible, yet she couldn't dismiss it.

"He has his cell phone number down here at the end of the email," said Serena. "He said to call him anytime, that it is important."

Chris glanced at the number. "We've gotten our share of weird emails over the years. There are a lot of nut cases out there. Do you think this guy is one of them? I honestly don't remember him."

"I do," replied Serena, reaching for her cell phone. "I'm going to call him."

Serena caught Will still at work, still in his office, though it was past midnight there. They spoke for over half an hour. During that time, he made a believer out of her. He was right; only she would be able to confirm his suspicions. It was crazy, but she needed to go to Kurdish Republic. Will would cut through all of the paperwork and red tape for her. She would be acting as a consultant for them. He would explain it all to his boss later. She and Chris would fly to Hamburg tomorrow and from there they would fly on the company's biweekly supply plane to Kirkuk. Will Reinhart would meet them there.

"This is pretty crazy," said Chris, as Serena put away her cell phone. "You know that we're flying into a virtual war zone; you know that, right?"

"Yeah," said Serena. "But we shouldn't be there long, just a day. We'll be back in London in time to catch some of the sights and the flight back to Portland."

"So we trade the fogs of London for the deserts of the Middle East," noted Chris.

"I have to do this, Chris. I've got to know. When Aaron came to visit me, he said that the time was short, that Satan was right here on Earth. And you know how well Satan and I get along—not so well. I figure that eventually he will come looking for me. I've got to figure out what the score is, rain on his parade if I can."

To anyone else, that would have sounded crazy, but not to Chris. He knew him too, and the last time they had crossed paths, the meeting hadn't been exactly friendly. In fact, he had definitely rubbed him the wrong way. He was very certain that few humans had spoken as boldly to the Prince of Darkness as he had that day. He'd been downright caustic. "I think you've been raining on his parade for quite a few years now."

"We both have," noted Serena.

By the time they had turned in for the night, they had two plane reservations to Hamburg, Germany for the following morning. Chris thought back to the good old days, living with his mother in Heaven. How he missed her. He thought of the adventures he'd had there. In contrast, life on Earth seemed boring. That is, until now. He suspected that things were about to get interesting.

The following morning found Chris and Serena on the road to London, traveling through a dense English fog. They'd allowed plenty of time to get to Heathrow Airport; they needed every minute of it.

They touched base with Will Reinhart over the phone. Nothing unusual had happened at the well since the following night. The drill bit was in the hole once more and they were making depth. Still, Will was concerned. Had it been their drilling that had released the demons? Might they have just popped the cork on a Hell that was a mere two miles below the surface of the Earth?

Chris had tried to use the little hyper-dimensional physics he understood to explain to Will that Hell itself was not actually located within the Earth. The gravity well formed by the Earth simply made the depths of our world the most convenient exit point for demons traveling from Outer Darkness. In reality, Hell lay somewhat deeper down than the center of the Earth. Judging from Will's puzzled response, he figured that his explanation had lost something in translation. Johann Kepler did a much better job at explaining this sort of thing.

Upon arriving in Hamburg, Chris and Serena were faced with more than the usual problems in changing planes. They had to go all the way from the passenger terminal to the cargo terminal. They made it with less than an hour to spare.

As Will had promised, they were expected and got first-class treatment, such as it was. Their plane to the Kurdish Republic was not quite what they had envisioned. It was a 50-year-old, prop-driven, C-119, flying boxcar that looked like it was on its last engines. It did, fortunately, have three rows of wide, comfortable seats just behind the cockpit, first-class accommodations on a third-class flight. At least they wouldn't have to sit on one of the crates.

The company wasn't bad, either. The pilot, copilot, and engineer were true veterans of this run. They had been flying this route twice a week for the past eight years, and they had their share of stories to tell. Their tales ranged from dodging insurgent rockets to discovering a young woman who tried to get out of the country on their plane by hiding in a wooden crate.

When asked what they would be doing up at the oil field, Chris had simply said that they were guests of Will Reinhart and that they would be taking a tour of the operation. That explanation had sufficed until they were flying over the Black Sea. It was then that the flight engineer put it all together.

"Hey, wait a minute; I know who you folks are. Yeah, you're the ones who wrote that book a few years back. It was a best seller, if I remember right."

"That's us," confirmed Chris.

"Yeah, yeah, it was a book about a journey through Heaven and Hell, *The Tears of Heaven*, right?"

Chris nodded.

"My son read that book from cover to cover when he was in high school. He really loved it," said the engineer. "It got him going to church again. I'm not that much into that stuff, religion and all. Still, I guess I read about a third of it." There was a pause. "All of that stuff really happened to you?"

"It all happened," confirmed Chris.

At this point, they had the attention of the whole flight crew, who suddenly realized that they had real celebrities on board.

"*The Tears of Heaven*," said the pilot. "I think I've heard of that book, too, a few years back."

"Oh yeah," replied the engineer, turning to Chris. "It sold a million copies or something like that, didn't it?"

"One and a half million," said Chris.

"That's pretty cool," said the pilot. "You're about the most famous people we ever had on this plane."

"Except for that House of Representative guy from Oklahoma," said the copilot, glancing back. "What was his name?"

The pilot just shrugged.

The engineer's attention turned to Serena. "The part I read was mostly about you, about Hell. It was like a vision, right?"

"Nothing like that," assured Serena. "It was as real as being in this plane. Every sight, every sensation was real. I was actually there."

"But it was a vivid dream, wasn't it?" asked the engineer. "I mean, I read this book once, about a woman who traveled to Hell in her dreams night after night. She went though some pretty scary stuff too."

"No, it wasn't anything like that at all," replied Serena. "I think I know the book you're talking about. What she saw and felt wasn't the same as what I experienced. You see, she experienced a vision, or a series of visions. I was actually there. For six months, I experienced the real thing, what it was like to be a damned soul in Hell. It seemed so much longer than that. Pain tends to make time drag out, and I could never have imagined that someone could feel so much pain for so long. Words can't describe my time in that hot oily sea. I wanted to die, I wanted it to all be over, but it just went on and on. There was no death, and there was no escape."

"Oily sea?" asked the copilot?

"Yeah," said the engineer. "In the book, the Devil let her take a sort of tour of Hell. Only it wasn't underground like you usually think of it. It was on this whole other planet. There were birds feeding on people chained to altars, people flailing around in boiling filth, burning skeletons in fiery pits, all sorts of stuff. At the end of it, she was forced to throw herself from this high cliff into a sea of fiery boiling oil, where she was supposed to spend the rest of eternity."

"A sea of boiling oil?" said the pilot. "That sounds pretty ghastly. What would a thing like that be like?"

"What can I compare it to?" posed Serena. "Imagine placing your hand into the deep fryer at your local fast-food restaurant all the way up to your wrist. Now imagine keeping your hand in there for a minute, an hour, a day, a year. On Earth, you couldn't do that, of course. But you could in Hell, because there your flesh is never really destroyed, at least not permanently. It just keeps coming back, regenerating. There is nothing that can be done to your body that can't be undone given an hour or so, for you are eternal, immortal. Oh, it hurts, hurts like you can't believe, just like it would on Earth. Thing is, you're already dead; you can't die again."

A strange silence fell over the group.

"Let's take it a step further. Imagine a deep fryer large enough to swim in. You can't get out of it, no matter how you try. Your blood, what little remains of it after a while, boils within your veins, but you still can't die. The flames roar over top of you again and again, charring what was once skin. Your flesh seethes in the heat, becoming a mass of boils. All the while the demons are not far away, working to ensure that you don't cheat your fate. Once you can imagine that, then you might be able to imagine what it's like."

"And this really happened?" asked the pilot.

"It really happened," confirmed Serena. "It's only by the mercy of God that I was allowed to return to warn humanity of what could lie ahead. Only the sacrifice of Christ separates us from an eternity like that. Without Him, we're all doomed."

It had become an uncomfortable subject. The pilot changed it by drawing the attention of all to a Russian warship in the sea below heading for the Bosporus. From there, the topic changed to the instability of the region. Serena's adventure did not again emerge as a topic of conversation.

After a rough five-hour ride, they found themselves descending into the small municipal airport of the City of Kirkuk. Chris recalled that this had been the center of some pretty fierce fighting during the Iraq War. It was a lot calmer now, assured the pilot. He'd been flying this run for years without incident. The Kurds were really nice people, not the sort that made religious violence a spectator sport.

As they pulled up to the tarmac, Will Reinhart was there to meet them in one of the company jeeps. After just a few minutes of customs red tape, they were on their way to well number 14. They had chewed up another bit and were in the process of pulling it out. It would be out soon after they arrived. Then it would be quiet for a while.

It was a long ride to the well site, across cool, rolling desert landscape on a pitted blacktop and then on a gravel road. It reminded Serena a bit of northern Arizona, a sort of magnificent desolation. This was her first trip to the Middle East, and as a precaution against offending the locals, she wore a headscarf, as Will had suggested.

"It's a mighty strange place out here," noted Will. "The locals are darned friendly, really. And they like Westerners. Many of them even speak English. But things can change just like that. This is not a Christian nation. They are a bit more tolerant here than in most Islamic countries, but you don't try to tell them that you've found a better way through Christ. Be a Christian by example, but don't preach it too loudly. The man you reach with the Gospel today might be killed by his own family tonight because of it."

Serena nodded. It seemed strange to her that so many people found it necessary to suppress the truth. Islam was spreading into Europe at an ever-increasing rate. Much of the opposition to the Christian revival that was now spreading across the continent from west to east had come from the Islamic community. Certain factions had gone as far as to burn churches and kill ministers of the Gospel over it.

It was a nearly two-hour drive to the drill site. They passed the two fences and the checkpoint and headed onto company property. By the time they reached the well, the sun had reached the horizon. They pulled up to the well, its tower rising 100 feet over their heads. It was very quiet. Only noise from the number 15 well a mile across the valley broke the silence.

"We've stopped drilling for a few hours," explained Will. "I gave the first shift the rest of the day off. Second shift won't be here for another hour or so."

The three made their way to the platform. Will took some time to explain how roughnecks drilled for oil. It was a tour that was of more interest to Chris than Serena. She was more interested in the spiritual manifestations that had invaded this place. She gazed down into the seemingly bottomless well casing; she listened, but heard nothing. But there was something else, something neither heard nor seen, but felt within her spirit. It was an uneasiness, the feeling that something very bad, yet very familiar, was near at hand, and it was down there.

"I'd like to show you the black liquid," said Will. "I need to know if, well, you're familiar with it."

Serena's face held an indeed odd countenance. Was it fear? Chris placed his arm around her.

"Are you OK?" he asked.

"Yes," she replied. "Let's see it. It's what I'm here for. I'm the only one who will know for sure."

"There was so much of it," explained Will. "We didn't know what to do with it. Some was sent off for analysis, but most of it ended up stored in 55-gallon drums over in the warehouse. I'll drive you over there."

The warehouse was only half a mile away. It was a large structure, actually, an old aircraft hangar. Daylight was fading as Will switched on the bright over-head lights. This place was filled with great stands of pipe, large wooden crates, heavy machinery, and near the back, at least 100 sealed 55-gallon drums. Will had already pried the lid of one of them loose. He walked ahead and opened that drum for inspection.

Serena cautiously approached, gazing down into the black liquid. The odor hit her; then her finger touched its surface. She almost immediately stumbled back. Chris had to grab her to prevent her from collapsing to the floor.

"Serena," exclaimed Chris.

At first, she said nothing. Then she wrapped her arms around her husband and started to cry.

Immediately, Will placed the lid on the drum. "Maybe this wasn't such a good idea. I'm sorry, Serena."

"No," replied Serena, "I had to know. That's it; oil from the Great Sea of Fire."

Chris looked into his wife's eyes. "Are you sure?"

"Yes," she replied, trying to get hold of her emotions. "Yes, I'm sure. The smell, the way it feels. Only, the last time I felt it, it was much hotter. Still, I know that's it."

"Sweet Lord Jesus," murmured Will. "I can't explain why what you wrote in your book came to mind the first time I saw it. I'd read it years ago."

"I'll never forget that awful stuff," said Serena, still clinging to Chris.

"I noticed that it doesn't stick to your skin like oil," said Will. "It was one of the first things I noticed about it. In that respect it's almost like mercury."

"More cohesive than adhesive," noted Chris.

"Yeah, that's what our chemist said about it," said Will. "It has something to do with a specific chemical in it. I don't remember what it was, our chemist knows. He'll be here in the morning."

"I want to go back to the well," said Serena. "There is something we have to do."

"Sure, we'll go there right now," said Will, leading the way back to the jeep.

Five minutes found Serena standing over the well casing, gazing into the abyss. Daylight was fading fast.

"Second shift will be here in about 20 or 30 minutes," said Will. "It will give you an idea as to how we lower the bit and collar back into the well to continue drilling. It will take about…"

"Quiet, please," said Serena. "There is noise coming from the well."

Will and Chris knelt down by Serena around the well. Yes, there it was; the distant sound of crying.

"Strange," whispered Chris.

"It's starting again," confirmed Will.

It was getting louder and louder, a sound of crying and moaning like people in great pain. Then Serena saw it, a faint blue glow at the bottom of the well, and it was growing brighter.

"We've got to get clear! They're coming again!" cried Will, stepping away from the casing.

Serena stood there like a statue, motionless. "This is what you saw last night?"

"Yes," confirmed Will. "You really don't want to stand there when they come through."

"I'm not standing anywhere else," said Serena. "This world is in enough trouble. We don't need any more of those things coming in."

"You haven't seen how it happens," argued Will. "You can't stop them."

"You're right," confirmed Serena, "I can't, but the Holy Spirit can. You realized that last night. You stopped one with the name of our Lord. If you can stop one, you can stop them all. I'm not letting them get past."

"Neither am I," said Chris, standing at his wife's side.

Will looked on in amazement and then joined them in a circle about the well. They all joined hands and began to pray. He prayed for faith as much as for anything else.

The glow below grew ever brighter, and with it came a strange cold that touched not the flesh but the soul. Serena especially could feel it. Her mind was carried back to her time as a damned soul in Hell, to the agony of the Great Black Sea of Fire. Her months in that horrible cauldron without end had threatened to rip both her sanity and her humanity from her. It was agony on the grandest of scales. She focused on her prayers, and as she did, her fear was being replaced by something else—anger. But it was not a malicious anger, the likes of which can poison the soul; this was a righteous anger. She prayed for the right words. She found them.

Serena gazed down into the well, its casing now glowing a bright blue. The entity or entities were hovering but 20 feet below her. "Hear me demons," she said in a loud voice. "You have no right to come to this world. Go back to where you belong, to Outer Darkness, to Hell. I command you as a child of the living God, saved by the blood of Jesus Christ His Son."

"How dare you stand in our way," said a deep and unearthly voice that all three in the circle heard. "I know you, Serena Farnsworth, and I know what you were and will be again—a damned soul doomed to the Great Sea of Fire. The sea will soon welcome your flesh once more."

"You're wrong," retorted Serena, confidence in her voice. "I am a daughter of the living God. And let me tell you something; you and your fellows have no dominion over me, none whatsoever. And, for the record, I am Serena Davis, not Serena Farnsworth. Now, leave; go back to your place of exile. Tell your friends that this portal into our world is closed indefinitely. Now go, or face the consequences."

There was a moment of silence before Chris spoke. "You heard her, now go."

"Go, in the name of Jesus," said Will, who had gained a new boldness.

"Very well," said the demonic voice. "Enjoy your victory, for it is small and short lived. But mine shall be the final victory. I shall see you grovel in agony before me begging for mercy."

"Are you deaf as well as stupid?" asked Chris. "Go away!"

The glow faded, as the demonic forces retreated back down the well, vanishing half a minute later. Peace had returned to well number 14.

"Thank you, Jesus," said Will, who then turned to Serena. "It's all true, just like you said in the book."

"Yes," confirmed Serena. "You didn't think I made it all up, did you?"

"No," said Will. "It's just that I never imagined in my wildest dreams experiencing anything like this."

"Neither did I," replied Serena. "I wish I had. It would have saved me six months of pain and uncertainty in Hell."

"Now you know," said Chris. "Welcome to the war."

"Well, what next?" asked Will.

"First of all, you need to become a sort of spiritual sentry here at the well," said Serena. "I don't think they'll come back, not anytime soon at least. But you need to be here, guarding, praying, and having the faith it takes to hold Satan's forces at bay. You've done it twice now; you can do it again."

"I reckon I can do that," said Will.

"There is something else," said Serena. "You and your people have to find out what is going on. Why is this all happening here and not somewhere else? If we knew that, we might have another tool in fighting Satan's plans. And there is more you need to know as well, things that only Chris and I know, but I think it's time to bring you in on it as well."

They headed into Will's office, where Chris and Serena spoke of the recent

War in Heaven, of their angelic messenger, Aaron, and of the presence of the Prince of Darkness right here on Earth. It left little doubt but that the end times were upon them.

"I'm with you all the way," vowed Will.

Their meeting was interrupted as two trucks pulled up in front of the trailer and six men in hard hats stepped out.

"It's the second shift," said Will. "They will be lowering the new drill back into the casing and continuing where we left off this afternoon."

"I'd like to watch that," said Chris. "I have a bit of the jitters after what has just happened."

"Sure," replied Will. "I'll get you a hard hat and overalls if you like. Welcome to oil well drilling 101. I'll give you the full experience. It will take our minds off of what has just happened, too. You want to join us, Serena?"

"I think I'll pass on that one," she replied. "But you guys have fun for right now. I need to go somewhere quiet and rest for a while. It's been a rough day for me."

"There's a comfortable cot in the other room," noted Will. "We will only be gone for an hour or so. Then I'll take the two of you to our guest quarters to get some well-deserved sleep. We'll have you on your way back to Hamburg first thing in the morning."

Will wasted no time in getting Chris outfitted for his roughneck experience. Then they headed for the brightly illuminated well. Serena watched them for a time. Chris seemed to be having so much fun. He always did. She was the serious one. Her experience in Hell had opened her eyes and fortified her spirit, but it had wounded her too in ways that no one else could see. How could it not? She had endured more concentrated pain and horror than any woman alive. Earth could surely not render up its equal, for death held such experiences in check. In Hell there were no such safeguards. The memories of that place kept her focused and drove her from revival to revival, but they also tormented her. On occasion, Serena's nightmares took her back there, back to that terrible world beyond the stars.

As she and Chris prepared for bed that night, he spoke of his experience with the crew at the oil well. He had a really good time, yet Serena was already focused on something else.

"I wonder what Satan is up to," she pondered. "I wonder where he is right now."

"At the very heart of the storm," replied Chris.

"If we only knew where that was," lamented Serena, "maybe we could do something."

"I think we already have," said Chris.

"He'll know where we are," continued Serena. "We have a Web site, a revival, and book signings scheduled; he'll know right where to find us, and he'll come."

"Then we'll know where he is," observed Chris. "Stop the turning wheels in your head for the night. Let go and let God."

As the lights went out, it was tough for Serena to fall asleep. Yes, God was in control. He would protect them, but still, she was troubled. She felt certain that she would soon have to face the Prince of Darkness again. Only this time, it would be on her turf, not his.

CHAPTER 5

Serena found herself standing barefoot atop the precipice of a high and very sheer cliff. Before her, all the way to the amber horizon, a stormy sea heaved and swirled, with the violence of a great tempest. Its waves crashed upon the base of the cliff 50 feet below her. She could feel the force of every wave as it echoed through the bedrock. The hot, arid sea wind hit her squarely in the face, carrying with it the aroma of vitriol and raw sulfur.

But this was no sea like those along the coast of Oregon. No birds soared upon the thermals, and no greenery graced the land around her. This was a slick, turbulent sea of black oil, reflecting the roaring flames that danced across its surface. This was Hell's Great Sea of Fire.

She looked down to find herself dressed in a ragged gray top and skirt, the terrible garb of one of the damned. She had worn such an outfit once, during her time in Hell.

"Not real," she whispered. "Wake up, Serena, it's not real."

"Are you so sure?" said a voice from behind.

Serena spun around to see a middle-aged man draped in a long, black robe. Oh, she recognized him all right. He was the author of the worst time of her life. He was the master of Hell, Satan. For a moment, her heart was full of terror.

"Remember this place?" he asked with a twinkle in his eye. "You should." He pointed off to a crumbling peninsula of land, a section of the cliff that jutted out into the sea. "It was just over there that you took the plunge into the Great Sea of Fire so as to begin your eternal service of pain to me. This place was and shall again be your destiny. It is in your blood, what little of it that shall remain once the heat boils away the rest. You can't fight me, Serena, so don't even think of trying. Cooperate, and I might feel disposed to go easy on you."

Was this a dream, a manifestation of her subconscious, or an ethereal visit from Satan himself? Serena wasn't quite sure.

"I might feel compelled to bring you here every night," continued Satan. "You're dressed for it. You could experience anew the sights and sensations of being deep fried within this sea, my greatest creation here in Hell, my greatest work of art."

Up to this point Satan had been playing on her fears. Serena had tried to wake up, though in vain. If this was but a dream, she was, nonetheless stuck here. It was time to play hardball. She prayed that she had the strength.

"I really wish that you'd shut up!" said Serena, her tone both confident and firm.

"No one talks to me that way!" roared Satan. "I've put you in that sea once, and I'll do it again if it so pleases me. Therefore, I command you to jump from this precipice and into the fiery cauldron below. It is my will, and you dare not disobey."

Serena could feel the power of Satan's will, but even now she focused her mind and soul elsewhere, and as she did, the force of the Holy Spirit welled up within her. In but a second her clothing had changed from gray rags to the nice blue dress that she often wore to her revival meetings. The change seemed to anger Satan, even as it gave Serena renewed confidence.

"Jump in! I command you!"

"Oh, you'd like that!" retorted Serena. "I've stood here and listened to you rant on like the megalomaniac you are long enough. Now, listen to me. I'm not jumping in there. In fact, I'm putting you on notice. I know what you've been up to, that you're here on Earth, and I'm going to find you. You were defeated in Heaven, and you will be defeated here. Your reign is over, you pathetic excuse for an angel."

Satan screamed out in rage. He lunged at her, yet his hands met with nothing but empty air. He was as inconsequential as vapor. "This isn't over, Serena!" he yelled.

"No, it isn't," confirmed Serena, "at least not yet. But the day is coming when you'll be cast into a pit to be chained up for a thousand years. And I hope that pit is hot and unpleasant for you. Your days are numbered."

Before her, Satan dissolved away into vapors as did the dream. She awoke in bed, Chris at her side. It was nearly five in the morning. No, she wouldn't wake him up. There was no need. She'd tell him about her adventure later. They had another hour to sleep. The plane didn't depart until after 11 A.M.

On the far side of the world, Lusan arose from his contemplative state, his eyes full of rage. He gazed out from his 32nd floor window. "You will pay for your insolence, Serena," he cursed. "Make no mistake about it. You will pay."

Serena had cast a shadow across what would otherwise have been a productive day. He had been here now for nearly a month. In the offices below, their ministry had already begun. His 58 employees had flooded the Internet and filled the papers of the world with their message of peace, of a new age of faith that borrowed from so many different religions. It was as appealing as it was generic, a new faith for a new century. Tonight, in a rented Harlem auditorium, he would make his début. He himself would preach it to a downtrodden humanity. The event would begin with a rich, but completely free, meal for the hungry masses and climax with his message. He would have some surprises for them too, oh such wonderful surprises.

And across the world, his minions were making progress as well. They too had found humans who opened the door for them into the cultural, financial, and political world of humanity. They had slit the arteries wide open to allow Satan's own brand of poison to flow into humanity's veins. Sure, they had faced opposition, but tonight, they would deal it a decisive blow.

The scattered forces that had retreated from the battle in Heaven in defeat less than three months ago had networked through the World Wide Web. They held financial stakes in dozens of international businesses and had taken possession of so many humans that had been ripe for the harvest.

Lusan's thoughts returned to Serena. He was tired of her meddling. She was the fly in the ointment; she had been for years. Perhaps, after today, that would change.

"Thank you for all of your help," said Will as Chris and Serena prepared to board the plane for the trip to Hamburg.

"I think we sort of added to your problems," noted Chris, almost jokingly.

"No, I think you just gave my Christian walk meaning," said Will. "If I ever had doubts, lapses in faith, they are all gone after what I saw last night. I'll guard that well with my life, I promise. Nothing gets into our world while I'm on duty."

Serena gave Will a hug. "I think we're in good hands."

A few minutes saw them back on that venerable, twin-engine, flying boxcar, and on the way down the taxiway. They had the same flight crew they had on the trip out. Serena wondered if her experience in Hell would become a topic of conversation on the long flight to Hamburg.

Serena couldn't help but notice that, amidst a stack of core samples and packages for the folks back home were three metal drums containing a mysterious liquid marked with a hazard label. It made Serena a bit nervous, though not overly so. The captain's warning about some rough weather along the route didn't help much, either.

Nonetheless, half an hour saw them at their cruising altitude of 15,000 feet above the mountains of southern Turkey. Amidst the occasional chitchat with the crew, Chris and Serena were examining their options. Serena's tale of the previous night's dream both interested and concerned Chris.

"You know, Chris, something else has me confused," continued Serena. "The things that tried to enter our world through the well, where did they come from? Aaron said that Sheol was destroyed, that demonic spirits could no longer make the trip back and forth between Hell and Earth. The spirits that are already here on Earth are stuck here as disembodied spirits. So where did these things come from?"

Chris shrugged. "Maybe they're spirits of demons that were destroyed during the war in Heaven."

Serena leaned back in her chair. "But still, that doesn't seem quite right," she replied. "How would they make the trip from Heaven to Earth and emerge from underground? If I'm understanding it right, they would be coming in from a higher plane, wouldn't they?"

"Oh yeah," said Chris. "Maybe they were caught in transit, neither here nor there when sheol was destroyed. Maybe they were spirits sucked into that vortex in Hell that your mother wrote about, remember? That would also explain the human voices that Will and the others heard. It would explain the sea oil, or whatever you want to call it, sucked up from the Sea of Fire and into the vortex. Somehow, it ended up here, two miles down."

"That makes more sense," noted Serena. "But why here?"

Chris shook his head. "There are a lot of unanswered questions, aren't there?"

"How did it go over at well 14?" asked the engineer, sitting down across the aisle from Serena.

"How did you know we were at well 14?" asked Serena.

"It wasn't hard to figure out," said the engineer. "That is the haunted well, the place where all the weird stuff is happening. There's a lot of disturbing stories coming out of there." He motioned to the drums near the back of the plane, "And some really strange material, too."

Serena only nodded.

"And lastly, that is the well where Will is the foreman. If you were visiting him, you were at well 14."

Chris couldn't help but chuckle just a bit.

"A real Sherlock Holmes, that one," said the pilot.

Quite suddenly, the engineer's expression became quite serious. "That stuff, that oil no one seems to be able to identify, it's from the Great Sea of Fire, isn't it?"

Serena looked incredulously into the man's eyes. She could discern that he was dead serious. "Yes, it is."

"What are we doing out there at well 14, drilling into the heart of Hell?"

"We're not sure," admitted Serena. "We only know that it is a doorway into our world that Satan's minions are taking advantage of."

"Oh boy," said the engineer, who seemed genuinely concerned. "I was listening to what you two were talking about. Sorry to be eavesdropping. Look, I'm not religious, never have been, but your explanation, well, it all makes sense. It's about the only one that does. There is the stuff in the drums for one thing. How else can you explain that crazy stuff? It still has our chemists scratching their heads."

"We talked to one of them this morning," said Chris. "All that he could tell us is that it's not like any oil he has ever analyzed before, and that its properties change radically when it's heated. When it's cool, it's safe to handle, but heat it just a bit and it becomes suddenly very dangerous. He said the only place they've found it is at the bottom of well 14."

"Yeah, well 14," said the engineer. "There are a bunch of strange stories coming out of there."

"Tell them about the guy who rode home with us last week," interjected the pilot.

"Yeah," said the engineer. "Get a load of this one. We had this roughneck who caught a ride back to Hamburg with us a week ago. I'm here to tell you, he was in a state. He went on and on about well 14 for most of the trip. To hear him tell it, you'd think that the well was more than just haunted, it was possessed. I guess he was there on the platform by himself one night, picking up some tools. The well was shut down for maintenance, I suppose. The rig lights were off. Only a couple of the deck lights were lit. Anyway, he heard a sound and went to investigate. He talked about glowing lights from a mile down, and then he heard the voices, voices coming up from well 14. One of the voices was talking to him. He said something about hearing the voice of his dead mother, crying out to him from Hell. She claimed to be on fire, burning with a blue flame."

"His story gave me the willies," interjected the pilot. "It was the way he told it. I tell ya, he broke down and even cried at one point."

"Then he talked about glowing things flying out of the well," continued the engineer. "Demons, he called them. Well, I guess he didn't wait around for introductions. He just ran. He swore he'd never go back there." There was a pause. "I know something happened out there last night, from what you've said.

Please tell me about it. I'd really like to know."

Serena hesitated. She looked over at Chris; he nodded. Then she opened up. She told of the events at the well last night. She even told the flight crew about letters from Heaven and Hell, letters from her mother, Chris's mother and others that they had encountered in that realm beyond death. They had been letters hand delivered to her by an angel. She had never told that story to anyone beyond Chris and, more recently, Will.

The telling left the flight crew in stunned amazement. It was a disturbing revelation. It was then that the copilot came up with some disturbing revelations of his own. He turned to the pilot. "Frank, I'm showing dropping oil pressure in the starboard engine."

The pilot looked over, even as the tachometer reading started to fall. "Damn, wasn't that engine just serviced before last trip?"

"Sure was," confirmed the engineer, rising from his seat and stepping between the pilot and copilot. He scanned the panel. "I'm very much afraid we're going to lose it."

By now, even Serena could discern the change in the sound of the engine. It sounded like it was running rough. Its pitch was dropping.

"What are our options?" asked the pilot.

The engineer walked over to his station and looked at his panel. "If I were you, I'd divert to Istanbul. I'd declare an emergency. Still, we shouldn't have any trouble making it, even on one engine."

The pilot nodded. "OK, let's get all the miles out of the starboard we can before we feather it. Give me a heading and an ETA for Istanbul's Ataturk airport while I fly the plane." He turned to the copilot. "Hal, inform Ataturk of our situation." Then he turned to Chris and Serena. "Folks, sorry about this, but I think you'd better buckle up, just in case. We'll be fine, this sort of thing happens only once in a blue moon, but we have plenty of altitude and Istanbul can't be more than 200 miles. We'll make it on one engine; we'll be fine. We'll be on the ground within an hour, safe and sound. You'll just have to wait till we get this engine fixed or catch another flight home, that's all. Ataturk is a major international airport; you won't have any problems."

Chris and Serena did as requested. Their pilot sure made this problem sound routine. If they were in serious trouble, he sure didn't show it.

"Frank, I can't raise Ataturk," announced the copilot. "I've tried them on VHF twice. I even tried Unicom; no luck."

"We can't be out of range," said Frank. "Try the satellite phone to Hamburg. Have them relay the message to Ataturk."

"GPS is out," announced the engineer. I can't get a heading or distance for you."

"OK, then go on our last known position," replied Frank, frustration now evident in his voice. "Give me a heading."

There was a long pause. "OK," said the engineer, "turn to heading 175; that should get us close. We should be able to pick up the coast in about 20 minutes and then we can VFR our way from there."

The C-119 banked to the south, even as their starboard engine gave up the ghost. Before them, an impressive line of menacing-looking clouds stretched across the horizon.

"Feathering starboard," announced the copilot.

"There's that stationary front," observed the pilot. "I'd taken a more northerly course to try to stay out of that stuff."

"Now here we go straight into it on one engine," observed the engineer.

"I can't raise Hamburg on the satellite phone," said the copilot.

The pilot looked at him incredulously. "I can see a failure in flight, even a double failure, but this gives us a quadruple failure. What's wrong with this picture?"

What was wrong with this picture? Serena had a pretty good idea, though she hesitated to bring it to the crew's attention. This was the work of Satan's minions. In all of her years of service to the Lord, she had never seen the equal of this. She began to pray, both for the souls on board this flight and for personal guidance.

They had been on the new course less than five minutes when the port engine began to falter. They were beginning to lose altitude, even as the air became ever rougher. And all the while she prayed.

"We're dropping below 10,000 feet," said the pilot. "It's looking more and more like we're going to have to ditch."

"In those seas?" objected the copilot.

In the midst of the growing crisis, an odor caught Serena's senses. It made her suddenly ill. She turned around to see vapors rising from the three deadly drums near the rear of the plane. A second later, the engineer noticed it, too.

He raced back to the place where the barrels were secured by several steel straps. Already a small puddle of black, shiny ooze had dripped from the steel canisters. He touched the nearest one. "This stuff is hot!" he exclaimed. "But how can that possibly be?"

If there had been any doubts in Serena's mind as to who was behind all of this, they had just evaporated.

The engineer literally staggered to where Serena sat praying. The cool exterior of this seasoned veteran of the air had vanished. "You know why this is happening, don't you?"

Serena gazed into the engineer's eyes. "I think so."

"Eight thousand feet," said the copilot, who was still trying to raise anyone on the radio, though in vain.

"Folks, get out your life jackets," announced the captain. "They're in the cabinet on the wall in front of you."

"What can we do?" asked the engineer.

"Come on, Cal, we need you up here," said the captain.

"We can pray," said Serena.

"Come on, Cal," repeated the captain.

"Serena," said Cal. "I know you can do something."

In that moment, Serena knew that Cal was right. More than that, she knew what it was. She immediately unbuckled her seatbelt. "You and the others have done everything that you can do, are you willing to let me try now?"

"Yes," said Cal, not the slightest hesitation. "Come on."

Cal helped Serena to her feet and forward into the cockpit. The pilot turned about in amazement.

"Get her back to her seat," he demanded.

"No, she can help," objected Cal. "Don't you see what's behind all of this? Even the barrels back there, barrels filled with oil from Hell's Great Sea of Fire, are about to explode. We're fighting the Devil here, Frank."

"You're talking crazy," objected Frank. "We're not fighting the Devil. This is just a weird series of events, triggered by a freak power surge or something. There is no Devil, and you know it."

"Are you so sure?" asked the copilot. "Right now, I'm not. How would a power surge affect the satellite radio? It's a self contained unit."

"Ron, don't you start on this, too," objected Frank. "I need you to stay with me."

"I am," objected Ron. "I know what's going to happen if we try to ditch in seven or eight foot seas. If there's even a chance that she can do something, I'm willing to let her try."

Frank glanced over at Serena, who now stood between him and Ron. "OK, what do you want to do? What can you do?"

Serena opened her heart before the Lord, and in a second she knew what to do. "We're going to restart the feathered engine," she said in a calm voice.

"But that engine is dead," objected Frank.

"Restart it," repeated Serena, placing her left hand on the back of the captain's right. Her voice was calm, almost angelic.

"All right," relented Frank, "I don't know what good it's going to do."

He unfeathered the engine, threw the ignition switch, pushed the primer, and attempted to restart it. All the while, Serena's hand was upon his. All the while she prayed in some indecipherable tongue.

By now, Chris stood behind Serena, one hand on her shoulder, the other raised before God.

The engine windmilled in the gale force winds that roared across the wing. At first, it added additional drag to the plane. The pilot applied more rudder pressure to compensate for it. Then, a growing rumble emanated from the apparently dead engine. Suddenly, in a flash of fire, the engine exploded into life. Like Lazarus, it had risen from the dead in a mighty roar. Their air speed increased, even as the nose slowly pitched up. They were flying straight and level at just over 5,000 feet.

Then the pilot's hand reached for the throttle of the other engine. With little more than a touch of his hand, the engine was running smoothly once more. And, of course, Serena's hand was on his through it all.

"This is Ataturk approach control," said a voice over the radio. "November niner three Echo, what is the nature of your emergency?"

Through a break in the clouds, the Turkish coast came into view. As quickly as the crisis had arisen, it had passed.

It took but a few minutes for the copilot to appraise flight controllers of their situation. They had experienced electrical problems, lost an engine, but they had managed to restart it. Things were under control.

In the end, they returned to their previous heading. They would continue on to Hamburg.

The rest of the flight was uneventful. It gave Chris and Serena the opportunity to share their testimony and the good news of salvation with the grateful crew. The roles of the saints grew by three souls that day. None would deny that what they had just experienced was nothing short of a miracle. Nonetheless, they vowed to keep most of what had happened to themselves. After all, who would believe their story?

As Chris and Serena parted company with their newfound friends and brothers in Christ and prepared to board the plane for London, they realized that a new chapter in their ministry had begun.

In New York, Lusan was none too pleased with the news that his spiritual assault on the plane carrying Chris and Serena Davis had gone badly. He had considered the possibility that Serena might appeal to the Father in such a crisis, had considered the likelihood of divine intervention, but he had decided to take the chance nonetheless. Nothing ventured, nothing gained.

Many people turned to the Father every day; they had from the very beginning. It seemed to Satan that the Father had His favorites, those whom He was more disposed to come to the aid of in a crisis. Serena certainly met that criteria.

But why her? What made her different? Why had He seen fit to deliver her from the pains of Hell and not some other lost soul?

Well, he wouldn't dwell on that minor setback, not when the grand event at the convention center in Harlem had gone so splendidly. The new convention center had been the center point of the city reconstruction effort some years ago during the depths of the global meltdown. Now it had become a new center point, the first strategic initiative of his global crusade.

It had been Pagoni who had pulled the strings to make the center available to him on such short notice, and it had been time and money well spent. The merchandizing aspects of this new venture would pay Pagoni and his organization great dividends and improve his image as a concerned community leader.

Lusan had preached to over 8,000 fascinated attendees. Never had he been so moving, so passionate. His words alone had captured the hearts of the masses, words of a global community, of reconciliation, even of love. And he had spoken of the healing powers of the spirit. Not of the Holy Spirit, but of a sort of nebulous force that pervaded the entire universe.

Indeed, he had done more than just speak of it. People had come forward, people who had been persecuted by his minions for years, not knowing the real source of their afflictions. Some were blind, others had a form of demon-induced mental illness and nervous disorders. Lusan's hand had alleviated their sufferings by removing the offending spirits, and he had done it before thousands of witnesses. It was a bold gambit—Satan casting out Satan, but it had worked. Come the morning, the papers and Internet would be filled with the stories of the new spiritual healer on the scene.

His lines of communications with his global partners, his minions cast out of the great war in Heaven, had also been reestablished via the World Wide Web. They worked tirelessly to invest the gold they had brought from Heaven. They invested in stocks, bonds, commodities, and, of course, Lusan's ministry. Soon, he would turn the world of humans upside down.

His mind returned to Serena. He would have his way with her in time, only in time. He would enjoy sweet vengeance. He could not send her back to his kingdom to resume her service of agony, but perhaps he could make her suffer here on Earth. For the moment, he would put the issue of Serena Farnsworth aside and concentrate on more pressing matters, but her day was coming.

CHAPTER 6

Sam Florence felt a sense of motion, of acceleration. He opened his eyes to find himself hurtling through cool, damp mists. Then he burst forth from a bank of billowing clouds to behold a starry sky. Yet, the sky was also filled with dancing, auroral light that took on many different forms and colors. He must have been 20,000 feet up, at least, but he didn't feel cold. Nor did he seem to be having any trouble breathing. Was he actually breathing at all? He thought so, but he just wasn't sure. He stretched out his hand only to discover that he could see the thin crescent moon right through his palm. He was practically transparent. Now he was freaked out. If this was a dream, it was like none other. It was so incredibly real.

A minute later, he passed through the shifting curtain of aurora at the very top of the atmosphere. He looked behind him to see the receding Earth, the aurora and the light of its many cities were a thing of beauty. He was like a spirit, free of the limitations of his natural body, hurtling into the universe.

It was then that a terrible thought crossed his mind. Was he even still alive? Had he somehow died in his sleep, only to begin life's final journey? In his mind, he reviewed his life and the choices he had made. One of those was to place his faith in Jesus Christ when he was only 15. It was a faith that he'd never abandoned. He felt a confidence in his salvation, in his Savior. If this was the end, he was at peace about it.

In a flash of light, the scene changed. He was traveling amidst tenuous streams of colorful mists. Where was he? How had he gotten here? To his left and below, he saw a sort of intense beam of light surrounded by swirling clouds and raging bolts of lightning. It seemed to stretch out into infinity before him. He was both mesmerized and frightened by this otherworldly display of raw power. Even from here he could feel its powerful, electric presence. Thankfully, he wasn't moving toward it, but rather parallel to it. For several minutes his path followed it. Then it seemed to end abruptly before him. Again the scene changed.

Sam found himself with his feet planted firmly on the ground once more. He was relieved to find that he had taken on a physical form again. He now stood upon a very real, barren, rocky hill overlooking a black sea with tongues of fire leaping from its turbulent surface. It was like a scene from Dante's Inferno. Yet it wasn't hot here; indeed, it was rather cool. In the distance, over the terrible sea, a towering thunderhead, alive with blue bolts of electricity, cast a rain of glowing blue light and gray mist to the sea below.

He turned his attention to the sky overhead; it was dark and cloudless, yet not a single star graced that blackness. However, the air itself held a pungent odor of sulfur compounds, sulfur dioxide, he thought. It was not present in lethal concentrations, but it definitely made its presence felt.

It was then that Sam turned his attention to the storm once more. He noticed the color of the storm clouds. They weren't white, but faintly yellow. Again he looked at the sheets of glowing rain and he understood. He'd been a chemistry major for three years before turning to astronomy. "Oh my God, it's a storm of sulfuric acid droplets, not water. It's raining burning pellets of sulfur and sulfuric acid. Where am I?"

"I think you know the answer," said a voice to Sam's left.

Sam turned to see a winged being, dressed all in black, who stood well over six feet tall. His mighty wings were like those of a great raven, his face smooth and without blemish. He had a short beard and his deep brown eyes seemed to look right into Sam's soul. He was an angel of some kind, not a demon, of that much Sam was certain, though he had never quite pictured one looking this way. Sam might have been truly terrified had it not been for the kind face and the aura of this being. He had an aspect of peace and kindness about him.

"Don't be afraid, son of God," said the dark being, "for it has been appointed unto you to understand what has happened and what is to come." The angel pointed to Sam's right.

Sam turned to see the great vortex of swirling vapors. It looked like multicolored liquid swirling down into a dark drain. A strong wind blew into the great abyss, spiraling into its depths, carrying dust and sand with it. The great storm over the sea also seemed to be drawn inexorably toward this otherworldly corridor.

"Tell me, son of God; what do you see?" said the angel.

For a moment, only silence answered his query. Then Sam spoke. "What do I see? I don't know. Crazy as it all sounds, I see a rip in space, a wormhole."

"Yes, continue," bid the angel. "Where does that corridor lead?"

"Well, that thing isn't a black hole; it doesn't lead to the crushed remnants of a dead star. It leads to Earth. Wait, this all makes sense. This must be the thing that caused a burst of powerful radiation that lit up the night skies for days last year. No one had ever seen the likes of it. But eventually it ended. This wormhole was closed somehow."

"Yes it was," confirmed the angel.

There was a brilliant flash of light from the heart of the swirling vortex, and in a moment, it dissipated, leaving fading eddies of dust.

Sam shook his head. "How does a thing like that get started? Physicists have theorized about their existence. They don't violate the laws of physics, but no one has ever figured how to create one."

The angel nodded approvingly. "Know this, beloved son of God. This rip in space, this wormhole, as you call it, was a consequence of a great war between Hell and Heaven. In war, desperate and not-so-well-thought-out actions can often lead to unforeseen calamities. So it was in this war. In an attempt to defeat Satan's forces, certain well-meaning saints of Heaven accidentally created this thing that you saw. It was through a cooperation between both sides that disaster was averted—a disaster that would have consumed both Hell and Earth in total destruction."

"You mean to say that saints, people redeemed by the blood of Christ, worked with Satan to close this rent in space time?"

"No, not with Satan," corrected the dark angel. "One could not work with him. He is simply too vile. But they did work with certain of his minions without his knowledge, minions who realized what was to be lost if they did not cooperate."

"Then this place, the place where I'm standing, is Hell?" gasped Sam, who finally gave voice to what he'd already suspected.

"Yes, a small part of it," confirmed the dark angel. "But don't be afraid, you are in no danger, I assure you."

Again Sam looked about into this dark realm of desolation illuminated only by the fiery sea. "Somehow I hadn't quite pictured Hell as looking like this."

"Most people don't," replied the angel. "They think of hot claustrophobic caverns filled with the screams of the damned. There are places like that here, but there are places like this as well." The angel pointed to a range of mountains further to their right. "It might be pleasantly cool here, but a hundred miles beyond those mountains, the climate is like your continent of Antarctica, a climate that lends itself to a multitude of cruel ordeals for those souls so unfortunate as to call this place their eternal home. Hell is a realm as vast and diverse as your own Earth, just not as pleasant."

"You said something about a war," said Sam. "You mean there are wars beyond life, in Heaven and Hell?"

"Yes," confirmed the angel. "It was Satan himself that precipitated this war, a war that stretched from the barren plains of Hell, to the beautiful meadows of Heaven.

"It was his desire for accolades, his desire to dwell at the center of God's universe, second only to God, that led him to plunge us into war. The War in Heaven was fought on a scale that you can hardly conceive of, with weapons that would stretch your imagination. It involved angels and saints, demons, and damned souls, but the forces of Heaven prevailed, barely. Satan was driven out of Heaven, but he was not vanquished, not completely. Now the conflict has spilled over to Earth. Earth shall be the final battlefield."

"Do you mean that there will be demons and angels fighting here on Earth, clashing swords, or whatever they do in war?" asked Sam.

The angel shook his head. "Not at first. Satan hopes to win the hearts and minds of humanity with his slick tongue. He hopes to confuse them, lead them away from the path of salvation that God's only Son provided."

"But hasn't he been doing that all along?" asked Sam.

"Yes," confirmed the angel, "but not like this. This shall be the final falling away, and Satan shall see to it personally. Those he cannot lure away, he will destroy. Those who openly oppose him will be eliminated with great prejudice. He will bring a season of darkness upon your world the likes of which humanity has never seen. Even now, his work has begun."

Then Sam understood. At least, he thought he did. "The comet—it's his doing, isn't it? We're not going to be able to stop it."

"No, son of God, the comet is not his doing. On the contrary, it might be his undoing. He tried to prevent you from discovering it, but the angels were watching over you, protecting you. He even tried to kill you, but his plan was defeated. You may be certain that he holds you in great contempt, and now he walks among humanity, right there on your green Earth."

Sam had done his best to remain calm up to this point. Nonetheless, he was pretty shook up. "OK, so what am I supposed to do? Answer me that one?"

The angel placed his hand on Sam's shoulder. "You do what you have done all along, place your faith in the Father and His Son. But there is something else. There is a person, a woman, who can help you. There are many who claim to have had divine visions of Heaven and Hell, but only a few of those visions are true. There is one on Earth who spent nearly a year in Satan's realm, one who understands the master of lies like none other. It is to her that I am sending you. She shall help you stand in this trying day."

Sam considered who that might be. He'd read a book or two about people who had experienced the dark realm beyond life. Somehow, most of their stories never quite rang true to him. There were just too many flaws in the web of logic they tried to spin. They certainly sounded sincere, but might they have been nothing more than vivid dreams? No doubt, people would say the same thing about him if he told them where he had just been.

"In reality, your paths shall cross naturally," continued the angel. "Her name is Serena Davis."

Serena Davis—that name rang a bell with Sam. He'd heard of her all right. Like so many others, she'd written a book about her experience, though he had never personally read it.

"Tell her what you have seen this night," continued the angel. "She will believe you. Remind her of the purple roses sent to us from Heaven, the ones that had no thorns. Tell her that I still have them in my garden to remind me of her and our time together."

"I don't understand," said Sam.

"You will," assured the angel, turning to leave.

"But wait," said Sam, "who shall I say sent me? What is your name?"

The angel turned toward Sam once more. He smiled, though slightly. "Tell her that Abaddon sent you."

The angel vanished into what looked like a starry mist, leaving Sam standing alone upon the hilltop. A sound of thunder caught his attention. He gazed out at the pale yellow clouds of the thunderstorm coursing with lightning. The storm was growing closer even as winds laden with the smell of sulfur compounds kicked up the dust around him.

"Oh great," said Sam, focusing on the gray acid rain that descended from the base of the clouds of the storm in great sheets. "This isn't good."

Again the thunder rolled, mixed with a sound that might best be described as electrical static. The sound of the static was growing louder, even as the stench of sulfur increased. Then he heard the distant sound of singing: *Don't you know I've always loved you, even before there was time. Though you turn away, I tell you still, don't you know I've always loved you, and I always will.*

"Third Day?" said Sam. "I know that song."

The scene around him dissolved. He opened his eyes to find himself safe and sound in his Tempe, Arizona, apartment. He reached over and turned off the radio alarm clock. It was 8:00 A.M. He glanced over at the duffle bag setting by the closet. His mind came into sharp focus. Tonight was the first night of his two-night observing run at the Discovery Channel Telescope. He had a 150-mile drive ahead of him, followed by a long night at the telescope.

In the shower he went over the contents of his dream again and again. Usually he'd have forgotten most of a dream by now, but this one was coming into ever-sharper focus. Serena Davis probably had a Web site. Her book was still pretty popular. He knew a little bit about the story. Supposedly, she and her husband had some sort of vision on their way home from a Christmas party about ten years ago. In a fraction of a second, they had lived the better part of a year in Heaven and Hell. Serena had gotten the short end of the stick and spent that time in Hell.

He'd seen Serena and her husband Chris on TBN a few years back. It was a pretty wild story. It was an interesting story, all right. Actually it was one of the best life-after-death stories he had heard. Still, he had dismissed it as some sort of phantasm, an illusion. That sort of thing didn't really happen to people, did it?

Then again, one didn't pray over complex electronic instruments only to find them miraculously restored, either. That very thing had happened to him last year at the telescope. That act had allowed him to be the one to nail down an orbit for Comet Florence, had made him the discoverer of what some people were now calling the Doomsday Comet. It had given him something more than his share of fame. This rather dubious discovery had at least netted him a full-time teaching and research job in his field of study right here at Arizona State University. At least something good had come out of it. That was, unless Comet Florence really did hit Earth. That would sure put the kibosh on his new career.

As Sam prepared to head out to the car for the trip to Flagstaff, he stopped at his computer to see what he could find out about Serena's book signing schedule, if she had one. Yep, there was her Web site, thetearsofheaven.com. Yeah, that was the name of her book, *The Tears of Heaven*. A chill shot up his spine when he discovered that she and her husband would be in Flagstaff tomorrow, speaking at a local bookstore and autographing their book.

"Too weird," gasped Sam. "What's going on here?"

Before leaving, Sam shot off an email to them, speaking of his desire to talk to them regarding unusual goings on that might be of interest. He knew of no other way to describe it. He hoped that they wouldn't think he was some kind of nut. He was certain that they got loads of that sort of email. He did have some name recognition, his 15 minutes of fame. Perhaps that would contribute to his credibility.

On his way out of town, he picked up a copy of their book at a local bookstore. He wanted to have it read before going to their book-signing tomorrow afternoon. He'd check into the lodge at Happy Jack and sit down with the book. He'd try to finish it during the observing run.

The mostly cloudy night at the telescope gave Sam a lot of time with the book. As it turned out, Ken, the telescope operator, had read the book several years back. He was astonished as Sam related to him the contents of the previous night's dream. He urged Sam to read on, though he declined to give an explanation for why he did. Sam soon came to understand the reason. The acid storm and the Great Sea of Fire he had seen in his dream were described in perfect detail in Serena's book. Even the name of the angel, Abaddon, was there.

Ken largely took over the observing program to give Sam more reading time. There really wasn't that much to do. The weather made this night pretty much a wash out. Still, he seemed to realize just how important this all was.

Sam was about halfway through the book when he finally put the book down to rest his eyes. "Serena was really there," he announced. "I can hardly imagine just how much she suffered in that awful black sea."

"Your vision was a gift from God," observed Ken. "You know that, of course."

"Yeah," replied Sam, "I sort of figured that. He didn't quite know how to describe what he was feeling right now. Was it elation or fear? He felt like he'd actually been to Hell in his dream."

"I cannot say what sort of ministry the Lord has for you," continued Ken, "but I'm sure you'll know soon enough."

It was just past midnight when a light rain began to fall, forcing the closing of the dome and the ending of their observing night. It was just before dawn, back at the lodge in Happy Jack, that Sam finally finished the book. Now he knew the score. The next move would be his.

In the months that followed, Serena's life settled back into the more familiar routine of evangelism, seminars, and book signings. Fall turned to winter, and winter to spring, yet no more attempts on her life were made. As always, she and Chris were on the road a lot, doing their best to bring the good news to the world. They resisted the temptation to bring the world the bad news, the news that Satan walked among them. They kept their eyes and ears open in search of telltale signs of his hand in human affairs. Those signs were everywhere, but at the present, they could see no clear pattern emerging.

Will Reinhart stayed in contact with them, mainly through emails. Yes, well 14 still had more than its share of weird phenomena, voices, power failures, and the like, but not of the magnitude they had experienced that night. To his knowledge, nothing had escaped from the depths since. He did, however, relate to them one curious incident. The many barrels of that mysterious oil that had been stored on site had been moved. When they hit new pockets of it, the oil was quickly contained and shipped to some buyer in France. Apparently, someone was exploring the chemical and industrial potentials of this terrible substance. The very thought of it made Serena shudder. Hell's number-one export to Earth—what was it being used for?

Will had sought that answer, but had been unable to find out too much beyond the name, Roan Chemical. Both he and Serena had looked it up on the Web. It was a French company, operating out of Marseilles, involved mainly in the development of new space-age polymers, plastics. They'd had several contracts with ESA, the European Space Agency, over the past 20 years, as well as with other private and government entities. They'd fallen on hard times during the global meltdown, but had managed to ride out the storm. Word on some of the blogs indicated that they had recently been purchased by some third party, though who that third party was wasn't exactly clear. Will was determined to pursue it further.

To Serena, it seemed a curious turn of events, though she wasn't prepared to say that she saw Satan's hand in it. Looking for the hand of Satan in a world of nearly seven billion people made the old adage of looking for a needle in a haystack seem simple by comparison. There were lots of possibilities, lots of candidates, but no one of them stood out at this point.

She had reached out to others to help her in her search, people whom she felt were true children of God with a warrior's heart. One of them, an investments analyst, spoke of strange goings on in New York City, of people trading in large quantities of raw gold with odd properties. Again, it was curious, but it didn't hit her outright as evidence of the hand of Satan.

It was early evening in April in Flagstaff, Arizona. Chris had just pulled their motor home into the RV park and hooked up the utilities. They'd have another book signing tomorrow, another opportunity to warn people of what was to come. Chris was relaxing after the six-hour trip from Vegas, surfing the net, when he noted a new email message.

"Hey, Serena, you gotta see this one," he announced. "We got an email from Doctor Sam Florence, you know, the guy who discovered the Doomsday Comet."

"Yeah, I know who you mean," replied Serena, sitting on the bed next to

Chris. "I wonder why he'd be emailing us."

"He doesn't say exactly," replied Chris, "only that it's important, something of interest. He'll be there at the bookstore tomorrow and wants to talk to us afterward. Actually, it sounds like he mainly wants to talk to you."

"Really?" asked Serena, looking over the brief message on the computer. "I wonder what it's all about."

"I guess we'll find out tomorrow," replied Chris. "You're the family astronomer; maybe he needs advise. After all, you've boldly gone where no person on Earth has gone before."

"Very funny," said Serena, who didn't seem to much appreciate the comment. Her mind wandered back to that terrible realm, the planet of Hell. For a time she'd imagined herself as an explorer on a different world, but only for a time. She'd lost the desire to explore it pretty quickly as she witnessed the terrible suffering going on all around her. Knowing that her eternity of suffering was but hours away didn't help. After her experience in the Great Sea of Fire, all she could think of was to hide in that cave, the sanctuary where she had spent so many months. She had never wanted to set foot outside of it again. Her whole world became that subterranean garden. Strangely, her interest in the sciences had faded quite a bit after that, and it had never really returned.

Apparently, Chris hadn't noticed that he'd touched on a sensitive area. He went on about the new comet and how bright it was predicted to be, then about tomorrow's book signing. Yet he had lost Serena's attention some ways back.

The turnout for the book signing was pretty light. But that was OK; Serena really wasn't in much of a signing mood this Saturday.

It was two in the afternoon and the book signing was almost over when the young, lanky man in the sport coat approached them. Serena recognized him almost immediately. She'd seen him on a late-night show a few months ago. Since his discovery of the comet, he'd done the talk-show circuit. He was sometimes heralded as the discoverer of the Doomsday Comet, at other times as the man who might well have saved the Earth. He didn't seem to care for either title. Actually, he looked a little bit like a young Carl Sagan. He even spoke like him.

At least Serena thought so. Seeing him in person only reinforced that opinion. He held a copy of her book in his hand.

He'd made no mystery of his faith on the talk shows. He'd gotten a little bit of flack over it, too. Imagine it, a Christian astronomer. In this day and age, it seemed strange indeed.

After the signing at the bookstore café, Sam spoke of the events surrounding the discovery of the comet, of an unusual equipment failure, and how a prayer had seemed to correct it. Had it not been for that prayer and its answer, it might have taken another year or more before the danger posed by the new comet was realized. By then, it might well have been too late.

"I can't get the Revelation story of the flying mountain Wormwood out of my mind," he admitted. "I mean, it all fits. The Bible speaks of the flying mountain hitting the sea, and right now, the Mid Pacific is the most likely impact point for the comet, if it hits us at all. Still, I don't know. More recent orbital calculations are looking encouraging. The odds of impact are dropping. We might just dodge the bullet on this one. Best estimates call for the comet to miss us by about 27,000 miles. Still, world governments are going ahead with the plan to deflect it, just in case we're wrong. If we don't need to this time, well, we will have the infrastructure in place for the next time. Building it is not a waste of money."

"I'm sure it's not," confirmed Chris, munching down on some fries. "Having insurance is a good thing. This must all be really exciting for you."

"I don't know if that is the word I'd use or not," admitted Sam, chuckling slightly. "I have become sort of the voice of this whole project, though I'm not all that involved in the nuts and bolts of it any more. Right now, it's more of an engineering problem than a scientific one. I'm here in Flagstaff to obtain additional images of the comet to refine its orbit. It's still real faint, only within the reach of a handful of telescopes, and one of them is here. It's supposed to be clear tonight."

"Still, lots of people are saying that you may well have saved the Earth from a cosmic catastrophe," said Chris. "That has to be worth something."

Sam nodded. "We're not out of the woods yet. Still, I think my dissertation went a little smoother with this discovery under my belt. I'm getting my 15 minutes of fame, that's for sure. Still, even with the odds of impact decreasing, I have a bad feeling about it all. I just can't shake it. I feel like all is not right in the world tonight. It's not just the comet; there is something else going on."

That comment caught Serena a bit by surprise. "I can understand that," she confirmed. "I've had that feeling a lot myself lately. What do you think it is that makes you feel that way?"

"I thought you might be able to answer that question," said Sam

"Me?" replied Serena. "Why me?"

"I've seen and experienced things during the past year that I'd never imagined seeing or experiencing," replied Sam, "like the intense aurora display last year. To my knowledge, nothing like that has ever happened before—such intense aurora, I mean. And its source wasn't the sun, like a normal aurora. The sun has been unusually quiet for years. The high-energy particles causing it were coming in from somewhere else in deep space. It was like we had a beam of radiation focused right at us from somewhere out there. It knocked out a dozen or so satellites and fried their electronics. Had it continued, there might have been serious ecological implications. We would have been in a world of hurt, real Revelation, angels blowing their trumpets sort of stuff. I don't think people realized how serious a situation we were in."

"Good thing that it only lasted for a few days," said Chris. "I didn't hear until later about all of the things that might have happened if it had gone on much longer."

"Then there's the comet." Sam hesitated. "But there was something else. I'm afraid it's not very scientific. It is really the reason I'm here. I hadn't read your book until yesterday. What I'm about to tell you sounds incredible, but I swear it's all true."

"Incredible stories are our specialty," said Chris. "Go ahead."

And so began the story of the dream. Serena said very little during the telling. She wasn't sure what to think about it all. Chris was more interactive, pushing for every detail of what Sam had seen. To Serena, it almost looked as if Chris were trying to trip him up.

"It was near the end of the dream or vision or whatever you want to call it," said Sam. "By that time I was thoroughly shook up. I mean, nothing like that had ever happened to me. It was like something out of Daniel or Revelation. It was then that I decided to ask the dark angel his name. Now, keep in mind that I'd never read your book before. He told me that his name was Abaddon. He told me that I should seek you out. It turned out to be easier than I'd ever imagined. I mean, I had no idea you were going to be here today."

The silence that followed wasn't encouraging. Serena looked at Sam incredulously. Right now she didn't know what to think. He'd described Abaddon perfectly. Chris had pushed Sam for a detailed description of the dark angel, a more detailed one than they had offered in their book. Sam had provided it. He had passed the test.

"There was one other thing," said Sam. "Abaddon told me to tell you that he still had the purple roses from Heaven in his garden, the roses without thorns. I got the feeling that you'd be pleased to know that."

Now there were tears in her eyes. Yes, Serena remembered the roses. She had never told anyone about that. The cuttings had been a gift from her husband's mother in Heaven. How she had nurtured them in the meager subterranean soil. They had been so beautiful. Never had she seen such roses. They had become a little piece of Heaven in the depths of Hell. She believed Sam's story.

"I'm sorry," said Sam, his voice faltering. "I didn't want to hurt you."

"You haven't hurt me," replied Serena, smiling through her tears. "I'm just so happy."

"You were really there," said Sam, his tone telling of his astonishment. "There have been so many stories, so many tales of near-death experiences. There have been books written about them, but I never really believed them. But your story was true. I know that now. God's promises are not a matter of faith to you, either of you. You know it as a fact because you've actually been there and come back. You know there is life after death. You have knowledge, priceless knowledge, that virtually no one else on Earth possesses."

"And I paid dearly for that knowledge," said Serena. "For many months, months that seemed like years, I suffered the agonies of Hell. Within the Great Sea of Fire, I came to realize what it was like, what it felt like, to have my blood boiling within my own veins. I understand the meaning of pain like no other woman on Earth. It was a hard lesson. It has made me a sadder but wiser person. I rejoice only in God's gift of salvation to the world because I know exactly what He saved us from. I am grateful that He gave me another chance."

Sam nodded. "I'm sorry. You're right. I have no idea what that must have been like."

"You've had a real, God-given vision," noted Chris. "There's no other explanation."

"I guess so," said Sam. "But there are things that you haven't told me, things that I need to know. What's going on? We're in trouble, deep trouble, I know that."

"We are," said Serena. "We've told only a few people about it so far. I think it's time you found out. If the Father allowed Abaddon to speak to you about it, then it seems only right that you know what we know."

And so began another story, one more than the equal of the one Sam had told Chris and Serena. It was a story that ranged from letters delivered to them from Heaven and Hell, to wars in Heaven, to Satan's arrival on Earth.

"It's worse than I thought," admitted Sam. "For much of human history, many generations have figured that they were living in the last days. The thing is, this is it; we're in the last days now."

"I'm afraid so," confirmed Serena.

"What is going to happen next?" asked Sam.

"I don't really know," admitted Serena. "I guess its Satan's move."

"Heck of a thing," said Sam, shaking his head. "I feel so helpless. Please tell me that you've got some sort of plan."

"We do," assured Chris. "Right now we're following a trail of bread crumbs. We're trying to figure out what form Satan has taken, what his plans are. We have some leads, some suspects, if you will. Thing is, there are so many crazy things going on right now. Maybe he's behind some of them; maybe he's behind almost all of them. But he'll tip his hand. He can't hide forever."

"He's not hiding," said Serena. "It isn't in his nature. We'll find him."

"And do what?" asked Sam.

"Follow God's Holy Spirit wherever He may lead," replied Chris. "When the time comes, we'll know what to do."

"I don't know what to say," admitted Sam as they prepared to depart. "The world is the same as it was yesterday, but it sure doesn't feel that way."

"Knowledge has a tendency to do that to you," assured Chris. "It sure did it to me."

"But it does bring freedom," observed Serena. "Now you know what we know. Do you wish you didn't?"

"No, I guess not," admitted Sam. "Maybe I can help. I'll sure try. I feel humbled, really humbled, that God saw fit to bring me into the light. Now that I know the score, I can't hide my head in the sand. I'm with you for the duration."

CHAPTER 7

"Leland!" said Claire, placing her arms around her favorite grandson, "Oh, don't just stand there on the porch, come on in."

Leland stepped into his grandmother's old Brooklyn townhouse. It was over a hundred years old, but it was truly in beautiful condition, with a fresh coat of white paint and flowers blooming in the window boxes and along the sidewalk. It was the sort of place that might have been featured in *Better Homes and Gardens*, and it boasted both.

Leland had seen to it that her home got painted by professionals last year. Had he not, his grandmother would surely have been out there on a ladder herself painting the second-story eaves. Even as it was, she was on the front line helping them with her roller and paintbrush, seeing to it that the job got done right.

Like the house, his grandmother was something to behold. She was the picture of health; appearing and acting much younger than her 83 years, she was constantly on the move. She was a slight woman with brown eyes and gray hair. Right now she was involved in a baking project, and her house was full of the wonderful aroma of a freshly baked cake.

"Yes, I baked a cake for you," she confirmed. "It's angel food, your favorite."

Leland chuckled, pointing to his belly. "Do I look like I need cake, Grandma?"

Claire took but a glance at her grandson's 42-inch waistline. "It wouldn't hurt."

Leland laughed openly. How he loved his Grandma Claire. Through the bad times, the dark times, she had never abandoned him. She had said that he would return to the Lord one day. She'd said it for years, and she had been right.

"Oh, why didn't you bring Krissie with you?" asked Claire. "How I love seeing the two of you together."

"She's busy getting ready for the wedding next Saturday," replied Leland. "You're still coming, right?"

Claire smiled. "Oh Leland, I wouldn't miss it for the world."

"Now, I don't want you to drive the Ford into Manhattan, driving in the traffic and looking for parking," cautioned Leland. "I'll send a limo over for you. The chauffer will see to everything, so let him do all the work, OK Grandma."

"So, you're sending the chauffer to gather up madam," said Claire, trying to sound as aristocratic as possible. "Thank you, kind sir."

"You deserve to be treated like a queen," said Leland. "Your crown in Heaven must be full of jewels by now. You've put up with me."

"You're easy to put up with," said Claire. She hesitated for a moment. "I suppose that Lusan guy will be performing the service."

"That's right," confirmed Leland. "The service will be held in our New World Faith Center in Manhattan. It's amazing what we've managed to do to that old church; you'll be surprised."

"I'm sure I will," replied Claire. "Look, dear, don't get me wrong. I'm glad you've found your faith. It's just that, well, I don't know about this Lusan fellow."

"What do you mean, Grandma?" asked Leland. "He's done some pretty incredible things. Last weekend at the service he healed at least seven or eight people. And when he heals them, they stay healed. This is no hocus pocus, Grandma, no smoke and mirrors; it's the real thing. Believe me, I know."

Claire shook her head. "Oh, Leland, dear, I'm not saying that he doesn't have a gift; he does. I'm just a bit leery about his message, that's all. He doesn't give the glory to God the way he should. He doesn't hardly say a word about our Savior, Jesus Christ. He goes on and on about unity and bringing all of the faiths of the world together. Well, I'm just not buying it. There is only one name in Heaven or Earth by which a man can be saved. But you'd never realize it listening to this Lusan. Look, if you mix a little truth in with a pack of lies, they're still lies. Leland, I have a bad feeling about him. Something isn't right."

Claire sat in her favorite chair in the living room, and Leland sat beside her. Yes, they'd covered this territory before. Why was Grandma being so stubborn? Was it her age, or was she just being difficult? "Grandma, Lusan leads us in prayer every morning at the center. He insists that we live a moral, upstanding life. And we talk about Jesus. He is a son of God."

"He is the first and only true Son of God," corrected Claire. "His followers have the honor of being adopted as God's children."

"But you're still coming to the wedding, right?"

"Yes," confirmed Claire, "that snake oil salesman notwithstanding."

Leland hesitated. Getting his grandmother's approval was so important to him. Was it important enough for him to divulge a secret he'd revealed to no one else? "I never told you about how I met Lusan," he began.

"You told me you met him in the park," said Claire. "That's true, isn't it?"

"It is," replied Leland. "I just haven't told you all of the details. Maybe once you've heard them, you'll understand."

"Go ahead, dear," bid Claire.

During the next 20 minutes, Leland gave her the incredible details. He felt like a repentant sinner giving his confession. As he did, a great weight seemed to be lifting from him, though he couldn't understand why. Through it all, Claire seemed transfixed, asking few questions. Yet, by the end, she was practically in a panic.

"Oh Leland, I understand now," she replied. "Why didn't I see this before? Don't you see? No angel of God would have done all of the things you've told me about. I don't know for sure who you're serving, but he's no angel of God. He's a Deceiver, and I'm afraid to even think who he might be."

Leland realized that he'd just made the situation all the worse.

"There have been people at my church and in others saying that he's a false prophet, maybe the false prophet of Revelation, but from what you've just told me, he could be the Devil himself," Claire paused for a minute. "You said something about him knowing your Great Grandfather Leland, knowing him in Heaven."

"Yes," replied Leland. "He said that he led a great congregation there. I'd think that knowing that would please you."

Claire took a deep breath. "It would, if it were true. Leland, I never told you a whole lot about him. Your mother, God rest her soul, seemed to have put him on some sort of pedestal. I don't know why. She never knew him at all. He died way before she was born. All she knew was that he'd been the founder of a great church."

Leland was confused. "But he was part of the Azusa Street Revival, wasn't he? I mean, he was a holy roller Pentecostal when it wasn't fashionable to be one."

"Sure," replied Claire, "but that didn't make him a saint. He had a true experience with God when he wasn't much more than a child; I don't doubt that. He spoke of it often. He built up his own church, Faith Fellowship, when he was barely 30. I mean, he ran against the grain—a black preacher in a church that was truly interracial. Martin Luther King would have been proud of him. He was way ahead of his time. He preached the fire and brimstone Gospel from the pulpit. He brought sinners to tearful repentance, but that didn't make him a good man."

"I'm not following you, Grandma," admitted Leland. "If he did all of that, how could he not be in Heaven today?"

Claire shook her head sadly. "I don't like telling you this, believe me, dear. You see, I really loved him when I was a little girl. I remember him running around the house, with me on his shoulders. He used to call me his princess. Oh, we had so much fun. I looked up to him so much. Most daughters are that way with their fathers, I guess. I think his whole life centered around me. He was always kind and loving to me. I haven't brought this up in years, haven't spoken to anyone about it."

Claire almost teared up. Her lips were trembling. Leland reached for her hand.

"You OK, Grandma?"

"I'm OK," confirmed Claire. "I really haven't thought about those days in so long. There was a tenseness in our home. It's hard to describe. My father was awfully demanding when it came to my mother. The house had to be just so; she had to dress just so, and he'd lecture her about responsibility when things weren't the way he liked them. You didn't question my father's decisions. His word was law. My brother had sort of a rough time understanding that. I guess he was sort of strong willed. Still, it was what my father did outside our home that was the bigger problem."

"I don't understand," admitted Leland.

His grandmother hesitated. "Well, word on the street was that he had an interest in other men, if you get my meaning."

"What?" gasped Leland. "He was homosexual?"

"And more," assured Claire. "I'm pretty convinced that he molested my older brother at least once. Tommy never told anyone about it, except me, and then only years later, after Papa had been in the grave ten years or more. I believed him."

"I really don't know what to say," said Leland. "Mom had me believing he was some sort of saint."

"As I said, she never knew," replied Claire. "In death, I guess, he became larger than he was in life. At Faith Fellowship he has achieved a status approaching sainthood—their glorious founder. But it was all show—a sham. The real Leland Brown cheated on my mother, did it with grown men, and very well might have molested his own son. He went to terrible places with his lovers and stole money from his own church to pay for it. I was about 16 when he was murdered, right there in back of his own church. They never found the killer. Some said it was the clan; others said it was a spurned male lover. I don't rightly know. I'd be amazed if he were in Heaven today. Still, God's mercy is a wonderful thing. I truly hope, no, I pray, that Lusan is telling you the truth."

Now Leland was confused. He didn't know what to say. Could Lusan have lied to him?

Claire squeezed Leland's hand. "I'm sorry, dear. I don't mean to be hurtful, really I don't. I know how you feel about Lusan. He might have saved your life. I owe him that much, saving the life of my grandson." For a moment, Claire seemed deep in thought. "I want you to do something for me. I want you to tell me that Jesus is your personal Savior, not some angelic being, but Jesus. I want you to tell me that you've invited Him into your heart, and that you love Him with all your heart and all your soul and all your mind. I want you to mean it."

"Oh, I do, Grandma," said Leland, looking straight into her eyes. "I love Jesus with all of my heart and soul." Leland chuckled. "I've finally read the Bible from cover to cover. Lusan told me that I should. Grandma, he's just a vessel of God's will. He doesn't want anyone's worship; he said it that very first night I met him."

"And he's still that way?" countered Claire. "Is he still that selfless, noble person you met that first night, or has all of the fame gone to his head?"

That comment made Leland think. Was Lusan the same? In some ways he was, but when he thought no one was looking? "I'm not sure."

"Then I'll ask another favor of you," said Claire. "Introduce him to me at the wedding. Go out of your way if you have to. I believe I'll recognize the Deceiver when I see him. At least, I hope so."

Leland nodded. "And if you decide he is, what would you do?"

Claire shook her head. "I haven't thought that far ahead yet. I won't make a scene, if that's what you're worried about."

"I'll do it for you," replied Leland. "Still, I think you'll be disappointed."

"Disappointed?" replied Claire. "I'll be relieved. Now let's, the two of us, dig into that cake—an angel food cake for my angel."

There was something Leland and his grandmother could agree on. He'd begin the diet tomorrow.

The demon Klothock bowed low before his master within the darkened room on the 32nd floor. Nearly all of the ministry's business operations were confined to the floor below. Very few indeed were those who were permitted access to this level.

Klothock was but a spirit, trapped between Hell and Earth in the ethereal abyss by the destruction of the great city of Sheol. He'd come to this place by a most unlikely route, through an oil well in the Middle East. He appeared as little more than a faintly glowing vapor. He was a visual distortion within the room, not unlike that seen across a hot road in the middle of the summer.

"And he told his grandmother everything?" asked Lusan, making sure that there were no misunderstandings.

"Yes, my lord," confirmed Klothock. "In all of the time I have followed him, he has told none other."

"I do not know if she would recognize me, were she to confront me in person," noted Lusan. "How could she? Still, these followers of the Nazarene continue to be an affront to me. The day shall come when I turn the world itself against them, but I am not ready yet." Lusan considered his options. "She is an old woman; her death would serve me well."

"And by what means should she die?" asked Klothock. "Shall it be made to appear as a result of natural causes, perhaps a heart attack? I'm sure that I could terrify an old woman to death. Or shall it be an act of random violence? One of the many humans we have possessed could do the job and make it slow and painful. It is your choice, my lord."

"Choices, choices," chuckled Lusan. "I would prefer her death be a violent one, both painful and terrifying. See to it."

"An excellent choice indeed," replied Klothock.

"I want it done just before the wedding," continued Lusan. "But I don't want Leland or his lovely bride to suspect anything has happened until after. I want it to be a happy day for them, at least the first part of it."

"It will be as you command, my master," confirmed the demon.

"Then go, my friend; see to the preparations."

The demon bowed, then vanished into the ether.

"Into every human life, a little sorrow must come," said Lusan, who now stood alone within his chambers. "Now, Leland, perhaps I shall preside not only at your wedding, but at the funeral of your grandmother as well."

Julio Mendoza, the real Julio, had little influence on the day-to-day life he now lived. The demon Krugloe now ruled over his physical form. Julio just went along for the ride, a prisoner within his own body. He'd seen so many horrors during the past months. He'd seen his friends die at the hand of Lusan. Still others had been possessed as he had and now lived a waking nightmare as they awaited their entry into Hell. He had repented a thousand times for what he had done with his life, yet it seemed to do no good. He had tried to retake control of his own body, yet without effect.

On the outside, Krugloe had made so many improvements to Julio's life. Julio now held a GED, graduating at the top of the class. He was taking night classes at a local community college, majoring in criminal justice. He had established a sort of student mentor relationship with Detective Strom, who had taken an interest in him. Even his relationship with his mother had improved, though he suspected that she was beginning to sense that something was wrong. And if he suspected it, then so did Krugloe. What would Krugloe do if she got in his way? He didn't like thinking about that.

But now things were worse. He found himself in the passenger seat of a car, driven by Karina, a former girlfriend and member of the Latin Kings, now just another possessed soul trapped within her own body.

"She is just an old woman," said Karina, smiling slightly. "She has been a follower of that Nazarene for many years. Now she is making trouble for the master. She knows things that she should not know. You need to rough her up before you kill her. Do with her as you please. You will have one hour before I return. Remember, it must look like a case of random violence. Don't make any mistakes."

"Don't lecture me on procedure," replied Krugloe, a bit of anger in his voice. "Lest you forget, Molon, it was I who obtained that fine body for you. I know how you prefer the females of this detestable species. I brought to you a fine specimen."

"That might be so," replied Molon, in Karina's voice. "But she is a fighter, this one. She constantly opposes me, struggles against my every action. She is a drain on me. She makes me uncomfortable. She is not like yours, all self-pity and resignation."

"I didn't promise that she would be easy," said Krugloe, "I just said that you'd like her."

That brought a slight smile to Karina's face. "She is interesting."

Karina pulled off to the side of the road, near the corner of Carroll Street and Brooklyn Avenue. "Remember, one hour," she repeated.

"Yes, ma'am," replied Krugloe, his tone expressing a sense of hostility.

He was on his way. "Ingrate," he cursed, under his breath.

It was a Saturday, but the streets weren't particularly busy. He had it all figured out. Six minutes to walk to her house, four to accomplish entry by the back door, three to locate the old woman, then a half hour or more to bring her to the point where she would be pleading for death. It would take a few minutes to verify that he had left no evidence of any account behind, and he would be on his way. He'd be in time for Leland and Krissie's wedding, no problem. It was all so perfect.

He worked his way down the back alley, then through an unlocked wooden gate at the back of her narrow yard. The back yard itself was a virtual jungle of fruit trees and lush gardens. It provided perfect cover. Then he was at her back screen door. He was surprised to discover that it wasn't even locked. He slipped in.

He was way ahead of schedule. He checked his black bag, which contained rope and a gag to keep her quiet while he worked on her. He had it all figured out. This was going to be so easy.

He waited just inside the door for several minutes, listening, attempting to evaluate the situation. He heard her upstairs, walking from room to room, and she was singing. It made him smile to think of how her life was about to change, then end.

He heard a lawnmower start up in the yard a door or two down the street. It was a particularly loud one. It would likely mask any noise she might make before he gagged her. This thing just kept getting better and better.

He moved toward the stairway and then crept up the stairs. All the while, Julio watched helplessly within his prison of the mind. No, he couldn't allow this to happen. But what could he do?

Krugloe reached the top of the stairs and looked down the short hallway. He identified where this woman was; her voice was coming from the room before him. It was time. He stepped into the room, only to come face to face with his victim. She was dressed for the wedding. She was quite becoming for one so old, this Claire James.

The woman seemed stunned, not expecting to come face to face with an intruder. Then the fear vanished from her face. "I'm almost ready," she finally said. "I hadn't expected you so soon. You really should have knocked."

Krugloe was confused, a state that he rarely found himself in. Adding to it, Julio had started to fight him again. Indeed, never had Julio struggled with him so desperately. He stood there like a statue.

"The present is setting on the end table in the living room," she continued. "If you want to go ahead and load it up, I'll be down in about ten minutes. Oh, and there is an apple pie on the drain board in the kitchen. Go ahead and help yourself to a piece while you're waiting."

Still the intruder stood motionless. It had been a long time since Krugloe had encountered such resistance from one he had possessed. It caught him completely by surprise.

Claire approached Julio, concern on her face. "Are you OK, young man?" Then she saw the blade in his one hand the cloth and strand of rope in the other. "Oh my," she gasped.

In that brief moment, Julio took control. He fell to one knee. "Run, get out of here, please," he gasped, as if fighting for every word.

Julio expected this woman to flee screaming, but she didn't. A moment later he felt a hand on his shoulder and with that hand a sense of power. Then he heard her speaking. Yet, her words were not in English or Spanish, but in some tongue the likes of which he had never heard.

"You have not the right!" raged Krugloe, using Julio's own voice. "How dare you?"

"By the blood of Christ," replied Claire, her tone suddenly forceful. "That is who gives me the right. Get out of this boy! Persecute him no longer. Go back to that wilderness you came from, demon." There was a pause. "Get out of him, Krugloe."

Julio was astonished. This woman had called the demon by name.

Then Julio fell to the floor, convulsing violently as the demon threw him in what seemed to be all directions at once. Then there was silence and peace. He opened his eyes to see the kind eyes of the woman looking into his. Her hand was on his forehead and she was still praying in some unknown language. It was only then that Julio realized that Krugloe was gone. He was free. Julio started to cry like he hadn't cried since he was a child. He was free. "Thank you Jesus," he wept. "Oh thank you."

"You're thanking the right person," said Claire. "For I tell you it was Him and not me that freed you." There was a pause. "It was that Lusan that did this to you, wasn't it?"

Julio nodded. "I'm so sorry I did this. But I'm so happy now."

Claire smiled. "What is your name, young man?"

"Julio, Julio Mendoza."

"You know my grandson, don't you," she continued.

Julio just nodded. Right now, he wondered how much this woman did know. Yet a second later her expression changed. She seemed to be having trouble breathing. She fell to her knees, even as Julio rose to his. "Ma'am, what's wrong?"

"My heart," she gasped. "Oh God, what's happening?"

Julio looked on in horror as she collapsed before him. What was he going to do now, run? No, not now. He picked her up and carried her to her bed. His eyes scanned the room. Then he saw what he was looking for, her phone. Without the slightest hesitation he dialed 911. Right now he didn't care what people might think. He couldn't let Claire die.

For Claire the terrible crushing pain lasted for less than a minute. Then all of her pain, even the stiffness she had felt for years vanished. She sat up on her bed. "I'm OK, Julio," she said.

He didn't respond. He had the 911 operator on the line, was describing Claire's symptoms, telling him where to send the paramedics. He walked back toward the bed, phone in hand. Claire was noticeably confused as he walked straight through her and knelt by the woman on the bed—her.

Claire looked on in wonder. It was her. She looked at her hand. No longer was it wrinkled; it was soft and smooth as it was in her youth. She touched her face to discover that it was in the same condition. She looked in the mirror. She was there. She almost expected to see nothing. Yet she looked different from the other objects reflected in the glass. She somehow looked more real, more vivid. Stranger still, she was young again. She looked as she had when she was 30. No, she was even more radiant than that.

It was then that she saw what looked like a star shining in mid-air near the door. Swirling clouds appeared around it until it had taken on the form of a sort of corridor of clouds. At its center, in the far distance, was an object that looked as bright as the sun, yet it didn't hurt her eyes.

She looked back at the bed where Julio was trying to do CPR on her, apparently following the instructions of the 911 operator. The brilliance of the light didn't seem to have any effect on the room, only on her. She was literally gleaming in its luminance. She felt love all around her; it was wonderful, and its source was the light at the end of the tunnel. She needed to get going.

Claire took a step toward that wonderful tunnel only to stop. Oh she felt drawn to it all right, and she wasn't afraid in the least. She knew who awaited her at the end of the tunnel. She so wanted to go and see Him, yet she hesitated. No, she couldn't go. She was needed here. Leland needed her. He had to know what she knew. But if she stayed, what could she do? Again she called out to Julio, but he didn't respond. What could she do?

"Oh Lord," she cried. "I want to be with You, but I'm needed here. People have to know."

"Claire," said a voice from behind her.

She turned to behold a man dressed all in white. He had a short beard, long hair, such a kind face, and deep blue eyes. She knew at once who it was. She smiled through her tears as she fell into His arms. "Jesus," she wept.

"It's OK, Claire," He said reassuringly. "I decided to come to you. Let's go home, together."

"No, I can't go," said Claire. "Lord, can't you see what's happening here?"

Jesus nodded. "Yes, I can. The last days are almost here."

"But I can't leave my grandson in the hands of that, that Monster," wept Claire. "Oh Lord, I can't leave Julio like this."

"But you can't stay," replied Jesus, his words kind and gentle. "You have run the good race all of the way to the end." He pointed to Julio, who was doing everything he could to save her. "Look what you've done for him. I tell you, my child, he is going to make it. He is going to find the Kingdom of Heaven, I promise you. It will happen because of you, because of your love."

"But I have more to do," objected Claire, her tone insistent. "Please Lord, give me just a little bit more time."

Already she could hear the sirens. The paramedics were on their way.

"Please, Lord, they need me." Claire looked into her Lord's face to see a broad smile.

"OK, Claire, you shall have a little more time," said Jesus. "Make the best use of it you can for I shall call upon you again soon. You see, I have need of you as well. We have important work to do, and it cannot wait. There are terrible days ahead, and I intend to spare you from them. You are so faithful, so loving. I can tell you that our Father loves you very much. You have done well. But for now, you can stay in this troubled world." Jesus gave Claire a kiss on the cheek. "I'll see you again soon."

Jesus turned to the swirling vapors, vanishing into them but a few seconds later. Then everything went dark.

A moment later, Claire opened her eyes to see Julio. She smiled slightly. "Thank you, Julio."

"She's awake," he said to the operator. "Yes, she seems to be breathing fine, she's talking to me." Julio turned from the phone. "Oh thank God you're OK. I'm so very sorry."

Claire looked into Julio's eyes and she knew him, knew all about him. It was amazing. "It's OK, Julio, really it is. It wasn't your fault."

There was a knock at the door. Apparently, the paramedics had arrived.

Julio was off like a flash, the portable phone still in hand. He brought the paramedics back with him only half a minute later. By that time, Claire was sitting up in bed.

They immediately went to work, checking her heart, blood pressure, and her eyes.

"All this fuss," said Claire, smiling slightly. "I just fainted, that's all."

"Blood pressure looks fine," said one of the three paramedics.

"Heart seems normal, too," said the other.

"Really, I'm fine," said Claire. "I guess I just lost my balance for a minute, that's all. I'm sure glad that Julio was here for me."

"Ma'am, you still should come with us to Good Samaritan so you can be checked out," said the first paramedic. "From what Julio said, it sounds like you had a heart attack. It's just a precaution."

"A heart attack? No, I just got a bit dizzy, took a fall, that's all. I must have gotten up too fast. I mean, I'm not as young as I used to be. Anyway, I have my grandson's wedding to go to. The chauffer is going to be here in an hour. Look, I promise to go and get checked out later if I'm feeling badly. I'm sorry to be any trouble to you gentlemen."

The paramedic smiled slightly, "Mrs. James, you aren't being any trouble at all. We're just concerned, that's all."

The paramedics remained with Claire and Julio for another 20 minutes, monitoring her vital signs, and asking plenty of questions. It became clear that they would not be able to convince her to go to the hospital. They didn't have the authority to insist that she go with them. Then again, there was no sign that she'd actually had a heart attack. Maybe it had been something simple, indigestion perhaps. In the end, it took a promise from Julio that he would stay with her and bring her to the ER if any further problems arose before they would leave. Claire even saw them to the door, offering each of them a piece of one of her famous apple pies in the process.

As she closed the door, she turned to the young man at her side. "Now, Julio, I want you to tell me about everything that's happened. I want to know how you got into this mess and what you know about Lusan."

And so the story began. It was worse than Claire had anticipated. This young man had been through a nightmare during these past months. It was almost unimaginable. But now he openly offered his heart and mind to Christ. He knew only too well what was at stake. He was just thankful for another chance. They prayed for guidance right there in Claire's living room. Claire took a little bit of olive oil and anointed the young man. She proclaimed that he would put on the whole armor of God, that he would be a great spiritual warrior. When it was all though, Julio was in tears.

"Now I really know what people mean when they say born again," said Julio. "I just don't know what I'm going to do next."

Amazingly, Claire knew exactly what to do. Never had she felt such a strong leading by the Lord. "We're going to get you into a good church. I think I know just the one. But first, we're going to confront Lusan. No, I won't dignify him by that name. We call it, we call him, what he is: Satan."

"I don't know if I can face him now," admitted Julio. "He'll kill me to keep me from talking."

"No he won't," said Claire. "I'll be with you every step of the way."

"But you can't be with me 24/7," objected Julio. "His demons are going to come after me. Even now, there is one waiting for me."

Julio seemed amazed when Claire began to smile. "Is there, now?" she said. "I suppose we'll just have to see about that. And about being with you 24/7, Julio, I don't know how much time I have. But when I'm gone, you're going to do even greater things than I've done. God has His mighty hand upon you, Julio. Demons will flee from your presence. Even Satan himself will not be able to stand before you."

Julio shook his head. "He practically made me commit suicide, jump off a roof. If I hadn't done exactly what he said, let that demon in me, I'd be dead and in Hell right now."

"That was then," corrected Claire. She looked over at the clock. "Oh my, the chauffer is going to be here in half an hour. Let's deal with this demon, this possessed young woman, and get on our way to the church. You have a change of clothes, don't you?"

"In the bag," said Julio.

"Well, you can change here after we deal with this. Let's go."

Julio seemed reluctant. Indeed, he was truly scared. Nonetheless, he followed her.

They proceeded up the street. It took only a few minutes before they turned a corner to see Karina, sitting at the wheel of the car. She seemed impatient.

"These are just kids," murmured Claire, shaking her head. "Oh Devil, you are going to pay."

Karina didn't seem to notice the two approaching until Claire and Julio stood at the driver's side door of the car. She seemed shocked to be staring at a woman who was supposed to be dead. "You!" She gasped. Then she looked at Julio, rage in her eyes.

Amazingly, it was Julio and not Claire who made the next move. "Fight him, Karina," he said. "You've got to fight him. I'm free, and you can be too."

"Your time is up, demon," said Claire. "I command you to leave this girl, in the name of Jesus. Now, go."

Karina hissed like some horrible, wild animal. "This wench is mine." Karina cursed, scrambling for something under the driver's seat. She came up with a menacing-looking nine-millimeter pistol. In a second, the safety was off. "Looks like I'll have to do this old bat myself."

Julio jumped between Claire and Karina. "No, you're not doing that; I won't let you. I love you, Karina. Fight him! I know you can!"

The evil-looking gleam in Karina's eyes was not encouraging, yet her hand was shaking. She was trying to speak, or at least it looked like she was, yet no words came from her lips.

"I'm sorry I got you into this," continued Julio. "I never wanted to hurt you, not ever. Call on God. He'll hear you."

Karina was a living contradiction, as two minds fought for control. Her shaking grew. At any second the demon might find the way to pull that trigger. Surely, Julio must have realized it. Yet he didn't budge."

"Leave her, Molon," repeated Claire. "You have no right to her."

Abruptly Karina turned the gun to her own head. Her finger trembled. Pressure on the trigger increased. Then her hand went limp and the gun fell to the floorboard. Karina let out an unearthly screech and then slumped back into the seat.

Julio opened the door and reached for her. At first he was afraid that she was dead, yet she was breathing regularly. It was but half a minute before her eyes opened and the tears started to flow.

"She's going to be fine," said Claire. "This is the way it usually is when a demon is cast out."

"How many times have you done this?" asked Julio.

"Twice," said Claire, "counting this time."

Julio looked over at Claire incredulously, but said nothing.

It was about ten minutes later that Claire and Julio helped Karina into the house. Karina was just thankful to be herself once more.

"I don't want that thing to ever come back," said Karina, still crying.

"Then you need to replace it with someone else," said Claire. "When a demon is cast out of someone, he finds himself in a terrible wilderness. He wanders for a time before returning. If he finds that heart and soul swept clean, he will go and seek seven other demons, each more foul than himself to join him. No, you must invite Christ into your heart. Let Him dwell there and you will be safe. Never will demons enter you again."

It didn't take much convincing. Within minutes, Karina too had invited Jesus into her heart. Never would she turn her back on Him again.

"The two of you will have each other," announced Claire, turning to the two youths who now sat arm in arm. "You'll each support the other because you know what's at stake." The sound of a car pulling up in front of the house caused Claire to look out the window. "It's the limo," she announced. "It will take us to my grandson's wedding. I think you were both invited."

"No, I can't go back there," wept Karina. "There will be all kinds of demons there, visible and invisible."

"But you can't run away from this either," said Claire. "There is surely no place to hide. You've got to face them; we all do. We'll do it together."

CHAPTER 8

"Oh, you just look so gorgeous," said Denise, Krissie's maid of honor, giving the bride a big hug.

Krissie's stomach was full of butterflies as she adjusted the veil on her long white wedding gown. In another half hour she would be heading down the aisle at the New World Faith Center in mid-Manhattan.

It had been over seven months since Leland had popped the question, seven months since Lusan had entered their lives. Oh, how she had been looking forward to this day. They had thought to make it a simple ceremony, perhaps go to Vegas, but Lusan wouldn't hear of it. No, they had waited until this grand old church could be renovated to become the very heart of his worldwide mission, his vision of a grand new faith. To be married by an angel—how many people could make such a claim?

Of course, no one beyond her and Leland knew Lusan's true identity. They had gone to great lengths to keep it a secret. During the past half year, she had grown more at ease with Lusan. One only had to see the great work he was doing to become enamored with him. There were even young people within the gangs of New York whose lives had been turned around by his tireless efforts.

As ironic as it all seemed, one of the leaders of this new peace movement was Julio Mendoza, the one gang youth who had survived the altercation with Lusan and Duras that fateful autumn night. Apparently, God could deal with the heart of even the most wayward youth. Now he worked closely with Lusan toward the goal of global unity.

All in all, it had been a hectic half year for Krissie, but she was happy, more so than she had ever been before. Like Leland, she worked for Lusan. She became the voice of his organization here in New York City. Lusan never gave interviews, so it was Krissie who spoke to the media on his behalf. Despite her youth and background, she was an exceptionally gifted spokeswoman.

She made no mystery of her background. She had been a hooker, rescued from that oldest of professions by the hand of the Creator. Now she worked tirelessly to tell others that none were beyond redemption, none need perish. There were many routes to God, not just one. It wasn't necessarily who you put your faith in that mattered; it was the fruit that your faith bore that counted. It was, love, compassion, and striving to create a better world that mattered.

Her pleas for unity were both impassioned and compelling. She claimed that Lusan would lead humanity into a new age of enlightenment, out of the darkness of the past. There were some who claimed that she followed a false gospel, but still more related to her. She had become an overnight celebrity. The people knew what she had been, but they loved her anyway. Now her marriage to Leland would be the social event of the season.

Over the course of a very short time, Lusan had made many powerful allies, not the least of which was the mayor of New York himself. At one of Lusan's many crusades, the young son of the mayor had been brought forward, a boy suffering with a multitude of neurological problems, including epilepsy. A touch from Lusan had sent the boy to the floor and, a minute later, back from the depths of his own private hell. He was free and in his right mind once more.

The church was absolutely packed with well-wishers, reporters, politicians, and even family. Though her mother still refused to have anything to do with her, her younger brother and sister held places of honor among the well-wishers in the church, which included the mayor.

Sure, the movement had its detractors. Evangelical Christians refused to accept the simple fact that theirs was not the only path to Heaven. They spoke out against Lusan, calling him all sorts of horrible things. Sometimes their rhetoric frustrated Krissie, but she would hold no grudges against them. She still had faith that their narrow-minded view of God would change. Surely they could see that the blessings of God were upon Lusan.

Krissie returned to the here and now, turning to Denise. "I only wish my father could have lived to see this moment." There was the trace of a tear in her eye.

Denise smiled. "Don't you start to crying, sis; you'll ruin your makeup. You want to look your best for Leland. Oh, you are so lucky. And to have Mr. Pagoni walking you down the aisle, giving you away—that is way cool."

Krissie smiled. She had worked closely with Pagoni on so many projects during the past six months. They had become close. She had never imagined just how approachable and friendly he really was. Now she realized why Leland liked him so much. They had often had breakfast together in his penthouse, discussing business. Somewhere along the way, she had captured his heart too.

Denise glanced at her watch. "It's time, sis. Let's go."

Krissie thought back. Denise had been one of Leland's girls too. Now she was out of the business for good. Like her, Denise had become a part of Lusan's organization. She was glad to have her here today.

They headed out the door to find Mr. Pagoni wearing a black tux. He smiled broadly when he saw Krissie.

"Oh, my dear, you look so lovely. Such a beautiful bride." He gave Krissie a kiss on the cheek. "I consider it a privilege, no, an honor, to be walking you down the aisle."

"I'm the one who should feel honored, Mr. Pagoni," said Krissie, smiling broadly.

"Oh enough of the Mr. Pagoni. We're way past that. We're like family, you and me, and Leland too. Call me Luis."

"Thank you, Luis," said Krissie. "I just appreciate all you've done for us. I am looking forward to our trip to Naples, to your villa. It's such a wonderful wedding present."

"My, pleasure, Krissie, my pleasure," assured Pagoni. "I just hope that Mr. Lusan can get along without you for two weeks."

"He was delighted we're going," she said. "He said he'd manage somehow without us."

"He is an interesting character," said Pagoni, though he didn't elaborate.

In the sanctuary, Lusan looked out at the vast crowd before him. Even with the extra chairs they'd put in the back, it was standing room only. He looked on, apparently with some degree of satisfaction, at the empty chair reserved for Leland's grandmother.

It was a fact that had Leland glancing at his watch about every three minutes for the past 15. The service was set to begin in five minutes. "Come on, Grandma," he whispered, "I really need you here."

As if on cue, the back door of the sanctuary opened and in strolled Claire. Leland was surprised to discover that she was being helped along by a young man and woman. They were members of Lusan's youth ministry team. Leland was particularly surprised to discover that the young man on her left was Julio Mendoza. How was it that he was with his grandmother? They were talking and smiling like they were old friends. It was curious. Leland didn't remember the name of the young woman on his grandmother's right. However, he did recall that she too was a former gang member. She seemed more reserved, almost frightened. He'd have to ask his grandmother about this later. They all came up to the front row, and after some discussion with the usher, all sat down together.

Claire looked over at her grandson and waved, smiling from ear to ear. Yes, Leland was sure that she had some story to tell.

Leland glanced over at Lusan. For a moment, he was certain that he discerned a look of surprise—and maybe even anger?—upon his countenance, though it quickly passed. He had little time to contemplate these curiosities. A moment later, the wedding march began to play and the procession of the bridesmaids commenced. It was several minutes before the bride appeared at the rear of the church, accompanied by Mr. Pagoni.

Leland turned to his grandmother, who was smiling broadly. Her smile encouraged him. He was ready to go.

The wedding was picture perfect, from the giving away of the bride to the photos of the wedding party. Lusan said nothing controversial, as he sometimes did, which was a relief to Leland. Perhaps his grandmother would be less critical of him.

The reception following the wedding was enormous, held in the grand ballroom at one of Manhattan's most exclusive hotels. It was here that the inevitable confrontation between Claire and Lusan was bound to occur.

Leland noted how the two young people who had come with his grandmother followed her around. It was almost as if they were afraid to wander more than a few steps from her. Others from the youth group tried to lure them away, but they resisted.

Leland also discovered, rather quickly, that the events of this day had not swayed his grandmother's opinion in the least. Indeed, she was more negative regarding Lusan than ever before. She declined to discuss the reasons, at least not here. She claimed that she needed to gather more evidence. Yes, those were her very words. Had she taken up detective work during the past few days?

It was almost two hours before Claire and Lusan finally came face to face. Leland made the introduction and then awaited the fireworks.

"It was so nice of you to send over Julio and Karina to assist me," she began. "They are such wonderful young people, and we have had such a nice chat. I know so much more about your organization now, so much more."

For a moment, Lusan seemed at a loss for words. "It was no trouble," he finally said.

"You know, I thought I might be angry with you at our first meeting," admitted Claire, "especially after this morning. But I'm not. I do have a word for you, though, a word from the Lord. You can do nothing beyond what He has permitted. You have no power beyond that which He has given you. Your destiny was written down from before the world began, ordained before your creation. I'll not stand in your way. However, you'll need to accomplish those ends minus these nice young people here. They are fellow inheritors with Christ. Just leave them in peace, and I won't trouble you anymore."

Lusan looked positively stunned. "I'm sure I don't have the slightest idea as to what you're talking about."

"Whatever," said Claire, turning to her grandson and his new wife. "Leland, I just want you to be happy with your new bride. Krissie seems like such a wonderful young woman. I'm glad you found her. He who finds a good wife finds a good thing." She focused upon Krissie. "Dear, you are a good woman. Never let anyone tell you different."

"Thank you," said Krissie, who also seemed at a loss for words.

"I would like to urge you two to run away as far as you can, while you still can," continued Claire. "Go to Italy. Find a new life there, if you can. Mr. Pagoni seems like such a nice man. I truly believe that he will help you when the time comes. Still, it will be more important for you to place your hand in the hand of the man who calmed the waters. He won't let you down. He never does. Still, you are both adults, you need to make your own decisions. The Lord will make clear the path for you, both of you. You will know it when you see it. Don't hesitate when that day comes."

"I won't hesitate," promised Leland, though he had no idea what he had just promised her.

Claire glanced at her watch, then at her two young escorts. "I really need to be going. It has been a wonderful wedding, a wonderful reception. Please, give my best to Mr. Pagoni."

"I will," said Leland.

Claire hugged Krissie, then Leland. She didn't let go for a long time. "I love you dear, don't forget that."

"I'll see you the week after next," said Leland.

"If the good Lord wills it," said Claire. She hesitated then walked away, with Julio and Katrina in tow. She disappeared into the crowd.

It was Lusan who spoke first, though his comments were brief. "Wow."

"I'm sorry," said Leland, his voice quivering and uncertain. "I didn't expect that. I think I might have something to confess to. I think I made a mistake."

"Like telling her how you met me?" said Lusan.

"Yes," said Leland. "I'm so sorry. I shouldn't have done it."

Lusan smiled, a somewhat frigid smile. "It's all right, Leland. I figured as much. I'm not angry with you. How could I be? You have been indispensable to me, both you and Krissie. Life is a learning experience. I suspect that you have just had one of those learning moments."

"Yeah," confirmed Leland.

"I'm not even angry with your grandmother," continued Lusan, glancing out into the crowded ballroom. "I'm just concerned. I think this trip to Italy is coming at a good time. You've been working nonstop for months. Don't worry, your job will be waiting for you when you return. This incident changes nothing. I assure you, even angels make mistakes. Let us speak no further of it."

Leland nodded. No doubt, he'd made a mistake telling his grandmother the story. He was thankful that Lusan had been so understanding about it all. Then again, this was the nature of angels. It had to be if they were going to put up with humans. This mistake would not be repeated.

Claire and her two escorts moved quickly through the crowded room toward the exit and the parking lot where their limo awaited them. It had been difficult for Claire to keep her cool, but she'd managed it. "He's a slimy one, that one," she finally said.

"I can't believe how you handled him," remarked Julio. "Weren't you afraid?"

"No, not really," replied Claire. "Maybe it comes with age. Maybe I was just too angry to be afraid. I don't know."

"But he's the Devil, Satan," said Karina.

"I'm not going to address him as sir, if that's what you mean," replied Claire.

Karina looked at Claire with a look of amazement and fear, only to see her gaze returned by one of mirth.

"He's just the Devil," said Claire. "I met Clark Gable in person when I was just a kid, got to talk to him. Now that was an experience."

"Clark who?" asked Karina.

"Oh you know," said Julio. "He was the lead guitarist for that hard rock band, The Flaming Skulls. They broke up about three years ago when their lead singer overdosed on meth."

"Oh yeah," replied Karina.

Claire shook her head. These kids had so much to learn about true American culture. "But even more important, I've met my Lord face to face.

I've been in the arms of Jesus."

"When you were there on the bed this afternoon," deduced Julio.

"Yes, Julio, that's right," confirmed Claire. "Eventually, I need to return to Him."

"No time soon, I hope," said Julio. "We're going to need you."

"No you won't," said Claire. "There is this friend of mine; I'm going to take you to him. He has a wonderful church not far from where the two of you live. He'll look after you, see to it that you get solid scriptural teaching."

"Won't we have to go into hiding or something?" asked Karina.

"Why?" asked Claire, as they stepped into the limo.

"Well, I mean, Satan's demons are going to come after us," said Karina.

"God has His hand of protection on both of you. He will never forsake or leave you. Go on about your lives. You were both going to school. Don't stop just because your demons left you. Surely, you've absorbed something from the classroom. Turn it to good. Julio, you were going into criminal justice; keep going. Become a police officer, maybe a detective. Work against Satan and his demons; expose his evil plans. Karina, you were studying business. Well, keep going. There is still a place in our society for good, Christian businesswomen. Satan won't bother you further, so long as you remain faithful to Christ. He wouldn't dare. He's been warned. There are certain lines that he just won't cross. This is one of them."

The kids would continue their lives at home as they had been these past months. But this time they would be in control. They would decide their destinies, not one of Satan's minions.

In the days that followed, Karina and Julio frequently visited their new friend. They helped her around the house, went shopping with her, and studied the Bible together. Claire was in her glory. How she loved these two gifts from God. Would that she could have had more time with them, but she knew her time was short.

It was on a Friday night, the night before Leland and Krissie were due to return. Claire sat in front of her old, venerable computer. She sent off a dozen or more emails to friends and family before falling asleep right there in her chair.

She was awakened by the sound of her name being spoken, even as she felt a hand upon her shoulder. She turned to see Jesus standing there at her side, a broad smile on his face.

"It's time, isn't it?" she asked.

"Yes, Claire, it is," confirmed Jesus. "Are you ready?"

"Yes, I guess so," said Claire, rising from her chair, literally rising out of her body. She looked back. It seemed so strange to be looking at herself from this vantage point. Yet, she looked so peaceful, like she was simply asleep. "I wish I could have seen my grandson one more time."

"You will," assured Jesus. "But for now, I need you more than he does. The Father needs you. We will be going there presently." Jesus motioned to the great glowing vortex that seemed to extend straight through the back wall and into eternity. It seemed so bright, so inviting. Jesus extended His hand and Claire accepted it. They walked together into the luminous gateway and vanished, after which the gateway too dissolved.

It was a chilly afternoon for so late in the spring as Leland and Krissie walked away from his grandmother's graveside service. If only he could have seen her one more time before her passing. He felt guilty to have been away when she died, when she might have needed him.

The turnout had been huge, over a hundred people. Her pastor had delivered a stirring eulogy for her. Normally, it would be a pastor's job to make the deceased appear larger in death than they had in life. With Claire that wasn't necessary.

Her young friends, Karina and Julio, had been at the service as well. Julio had been one of the pallbearers. They had sat together through the service in the very front row. Karina in particular had been almost inconsolable. That seemed strange to Leland. She and Claire could not have known each other for more than a few weeks. How could such a strong bond have formed between them during so brief a time? Indeed, how had they met at all? Word was that they had left the organization rather suddenly two weeks ago. What had been behind that? Right now, there were more questions than answers, and Leland wasn't in the frame of mind to seek them out, at least, not right now.

Lusan and Duras were conspicuously absent from the funeral. Maybe it was just as well. Lusan had seemed truly shocked to hear of Claire's passing. That in itself was strange. Nothing much seemed to shake Lusan, but that did.

It had been a second heart attack that had killed Claire. Leland hadn't even been aware of the first until just yesterday. Apparently, it had occurred right before his wedding. Yet, despite it, she had come, all smiles. It had been Julio who had called 911 during her first heart attack. His quick actions might well have been the reason she had survived that one. She had been alone during the second. Julio had found her that following morning, sitting in front of her computer. That was three days ago.

During the brief investigation, no one had attached much significance to it. Claire had given him a key to her house. That certainly said something about her trust in this young man. He visited her nearly every day, bringing her groceries and studying the Bible with her. A certain Detective Strom over in Manhattan had vouched for Julio's character, too. Julio had aspirations of eventually going to the police academy. No, it was just a matter of coincidence.

Following the service, there had been a reception at his grandmother's church. Leland and Krissie hadn't stayed at the reception very long. Neither of them were really up to it.

The odd events surrounding her death were still swirling through Leland's head as he and Krissie stepped through the door of their condo on Central Park West. It had been a rough three days.

Krissie placed her arm around her husband. "You need to get some sleep," she said. "You've hardly closed your eyes since you got back. You're going to see her again; you know that. Lusan said it."

"Yes," said Leland, "Lusan said it, so it has to be right."

"You doubt it?" asked Krissie, surprise in her voice.

"No, I don't doubt it," replied Leland. "She walked with the Lord during her whole life. Now she really walks with Him. I don't doubt that."

"Maybe you could go and talk to Lusan," suggested Krissie. "Maybe he could help."

"I'm sure he'd try," replied Leland. "No, I just need some time, that's all." There was a pause. "I need to check my email. I haven't checked it in days."

Leland logged onto his email account. There were several pages of messages. Many were sympathy emails from his friends. It was when he scrolled down that a chill ran up his spine. The title of the email was, "what I know now," and the sender was Claire James. Tears appeared in his eyes as he double-clicked to open it. It was blank, totally blank. He looked at the date and time it was sent, 11:03 P.M. four days ago.

The range of emotions that ran through his mind were indescribable. What had happened? He tried every trick he knew to retrieve the message; nothing worked. He was on his feet and heading for the door in seconds.

"What happened?" asked Krissie, as Leland practically stormed across the living room.

"I've got to go to Brooklyn, to my grandmother's house," said Leland, hardly turning toward her.

"Can I come too?" she asked.

Leland stopped, finally gaining control of his emotions. "Yes, that might be best."

"I'll drive," said Krissie, grabbing her purse and heading for the door.

On the way, Leland told Krissie about the email from his grandmother. "The computer from which an email is sent always saves a copy of that email. At least that's the way I set up my grandmother's system."

With late afternoon traffic being what it was, it took about an hour for Leland and Krissie to reach his grandmother's house. Leland used his key to go through the front door. The last time he had been here his grandmother was alive. It was really tough on him to see this place right now, to maintain his normally cool exterior. It all looked exactly the same. He made his way up to his grandmother's bedroom with Krissie following close behind.

He sat at the computer, turned it on, nothing happened. He checked under the desk to discover that the computer was unplugged.

"That's odd," said Leland. "Grandma kept the computer running all the time."

"Maybe one of the investigators unplugged it," suggested Krissie. "It would make sense to turn off things like that, wouldn't it?"

Leland nodded. "Of course. What am I thinking of?"

He reached down below the table, plugged in the computer, turned on the power strip, and booted the computer. After a few seconds, the message, "no hard drive," appeared on the screen.

"What?" said Leland, turning off the computer. He reached into the drawer of the desk and came up with a small screwdriver. He opened the back of the computer. Sure enough, the message was right; the drive had been completely removed.

"The police wouldn't have removed the drive during their investigation, would they?" asked Krissie.

"I wouldn't think so," replied Leland. "Something is very wrong here."

Leland and Krissie spent the next 20 minutes looking about the house. All was in order. There was no sign of a forced entry. Everything was organized just the way Grandma Claire liked it.

"I could find out what Julio knows about all of this," said Leland.

"Do you think he might have taken the drive?" asked Krissie.

"No," replied Leland, "I really don't think so. Then again, I really don't know him that well."

"Lusan says he quit the organization just after we left for our honeymoon," said Krissie. "So did Karina. I get the feeling that it wasn't exactly on the most pleasant terms."

"And they were both sitting with my grandmother at the wedding," said Leland.

"You think your grandmother convinced them to leave?" asked Krissie.

"I wouldn't be surprised," said Leland. "But how did they meet her? That's what I don't understand."

Krissie just shook her head. "Julio gave you his key to her house after the funeral, at the reception didn't he?"

"Yeah, he did," replied Leland. "I probably should have asked him a few questions about what happened then, but I was really out of it. I remember him saying something about her saving him from Hell. That was an odd comment, but

I didn't pursue it. Now, I think maybe I should have. I remember that he seemed a bit nervous around me."

"I guess you can't blame him," noted Krissie. "I mean, things being the way they are."

"I suppose, things being the way they were," replied Leland.

"So, what are you going to do?" asked Krissie, as Leland locked up the front door on his way out.

"I don't know," he admitted. "There is something really wrong here. Maybe I'm just not thinking straight. I need a few days. I don't want to go off and do something stupid."

They walked arm and arm to the car. Leland would try to sort things out when he got home.

CHAPTER 9

Lusan gazed out upon the group of humans, bat-winged demons, and barely detectable disembodied entities gathered before him. Here in his large conference room turned audience hall on the 32nd floor of the Davidson Building, he could be himself, as could his followers.

In a way, this audience chamber was not that different from the one in Lusan's dark domain. It was not nearly so large or ornate, of course. He had neither his robes nor his scepter, but that was OK. He wore a finely crafted, black business suit, one that was tailor-made for him. He sat in an expensive, black executive's chair behind his hardwood desk, and not upon a golden throne, but that was all right too. In this society, it served the same purpose and commanded the same sort of reverence, even fear. That was, after all, the whole point.

The agenda was full this morning, as it was every morning. His agents in the United States and across the globe had been making dynamic strides. For the moment, this was the hub of the operation, though that might soon change.

A young, heavily tattooed youth bowed low before Lusan. There was a terrible void in his eyes, a sort of soulless expanse that is all that remains when a downtrodden soul was locked up in the prison of his own mind. He was but one of four men and two women who stood before their master this Friday morning, all prisoners of the demons who ruled them.

"My lord," he began, "we searched through the home of this Claire James from top to bottom. Any evidence of what she knew about us has been removed."

"She had a considerable amount of time to communicate that knowledge to others," replied Lusan. "Still, who would believe her? She is but an old woman. Most humans tend not to value the words of their elders."

"She managed to send an email message to her grandson on the night of her death," noted a middle-aged man to the first's left. "I was able to delete its contents, but not the email itself."

"That might arouse Leland's suspicions," noted Lusan. "Still, there is nothing we can do about that now. I fear his grandmother has planted the seed of doubt within his mind. Let us hope that it does not germinate."

"It would be unfortunate if we had to terminate his employment," noted Duras. "He is not such a terrible sort, for a human that is. As for his new wife, she is really quite agreeable. I find it hard to believe that I would ever say such a thing about a human."

"Don't become too attached to them," cautioned Lusan. "The day is coming when we must cast them away into the fire, like the filthy rags that they are."

Duras nodded, but said nothing further.

"However, we have a problem," noted another. "The hard drive of the old woman's computer is missing. Someone has taken it."

"Perhaps it was Julio," suggested Lusan.

"We went through his apartment and found nothing," noted another man. "We went through it quite thoroughly."

"I wish we could just kill him to be on the safe side," said the tattooed youth.

"But it is not possible," noted Lusan. "The Father has made that quite clear. There is a hedge of protection around him.

"Could our program be hurt in any way by its contents?" asked Lusan.

"I can't be certain," replied the man. "Hopefully, we don't find out."

"I'll be going on the road in another two weeks," noted Lusan. "I will be speaking at auditoriums and even stadiums throughout the country bringing my message to the masses. I do not want rumor and innuendo detracting from my words. I must appear different, free from scandal. For a long time I have sent out minions into the field before me to tempt the ministers among the children of God. They have made these high-profile ministers of the Gospel their prime targets. So easy to tempt, they have been. Even you would be amazed, my friends. An affair here, the lure of wealth and power there, has unraveled their character. They even resort to tricks, to theatrics, to beguile their followers—to lead them to believe that they can perform miracles even as the spirit of God has departed them. They appeal to the greed that is within all people to lure them into supporting their false ministries. I shall allow them to weave their webs of deceit. Then I expose them for what they are, mere humans whose love for God is not so great after all as their love for the things of the world. No, I must appear different."

"And you will, my lord," proclaimed Duras. "You offer humanity what they might call the real thing, not just trickery. They want so much to believe in something, some power beyond themselves. You are that power, my lord."

Lusan chuckled. "Yes, I am that, aren't I? After this tour of the nation, a lot more people will know it." He turned to one of the pale skinned demons cloaked in black. "And what of our brethren who still seek entrance into this world? Has any progress been made in opening the gate for them?"

The gaunt figure stepped forward. He looked like a man in his eighties, thin of face and not in particularly good health. Yet this was an illusion. Health was an irrelevant term when it came to describing an immortal. The minions of Satan had long used this form when appearing in public. In Hell, this visage had served the purpose of striking dread in the hearts of humans. It reminded them of death and its dire consequences—their sentencing to the very heart of the realm of Outer Darkness. When it came to appearances, old habits were hard to break.

"A human filled with the Father's divine Spirit continues to block the only easily accessible avenue of passage into this world, an oil well in the Middle East," announced the dark being.

"We need that gateway opened," announced another. "Through it millions of our fellows, disembodied spirits, whose physical forms were utterly destroyed during the War in Heaven, could enter this world. They could be of great assistance to us if only the way could be made clear."

"I know that," said the first, who seemed a bit agitated by the comment. "Our agents went to great lengths to persuade the humans to drill a well in that exact spot. Now this foreman stands in our way, a foreman schooled and encouraged by that loathsome Serena Davis and her meddling husband, Chris."

"That human wench," cursed Lusan. "Her presence continues to be an affront to me. Would that she had remained within the Great Sea of Fire as I had intended. Yes, that is where she truly belongs, cradled within the searing arms of the fiery, black oil. Why she has found so much favor within the Father's heart I shall never know."

The group became silent. All of them knew that it was unwise to interrupt the master when he was in such a mood as this.

Lusan turned to the pale demon before him. "Remind me, Runar, why is this particular spot in the Middle East so important? Surely there must be other routes into this world."

"There are," replied Runar, "but they are too deep. Before the city of Sheol was destroyed by the humans and their allies, your minions could enter the world wherever they chose. Through the gates of that great portal we gained free access to this world, at least in spirit form. But times have changed. Now we must find weak spots, holes in the ethereal maze that were produced by the cataclysmic destruction of that once great city. Most lie deep within the Earth and are inaccessible, but not this one. This one lies but two miles down. Even a portion of the Great Sea of Fire has leaked through the cracks into this world. We have secured much of this precious substance. Securing this well is the key, and we do it by eliminating this foreman, Will Reinhart."

"But the Father has put a wall of protection round about him," objected Lusan. "He has forbid us to touch him."

"Technically," replied Runar. "But what I have planned is an act of random violence not directed specifically at him. He will become just one of many victims of a suicide bombing. We have studied his habits. It shall be easy enough to orchestrate. Kurdistan is becoming the site of ever-increasing violence. It sweeps across their borders from Iraq in an attempt to draw them into the sea of chaos that surrounds them. We have been influencing Muslims throughout northern Africa and the Middle East. We have been enticing them into committing acts of violence—jihad that will ensure them a place amidst the pleasures of heaven. Soon there will be another one. Will Reinhart will be, as these humans say, in the wrong place at the wrong time. After that, our brethren will be free to stream into this world."

Lusan smiled, though slightly. "Then I leave this project in your hands.

Don't fail me, Runar."

Runar bowed, as was the custom, leaving little doubt in the master's mind that all was under control. Soon they would be back on schedule.

Julio Mendoza shook his head sadly as he cleaned up the last of the broken glass from his bedroom floor. Someone had made a real mess of the apartment, and he didn't have to think too hard to figure out who that someone was.

Detective Strom had been here this morning, surveying the damage. Julio had been so tempted to tell him all that he knew. It had really started to eat at him, especially since Grandma Claire's death last week. How he missed her. But no, he couldn't tell Detective Strom. It would raise too many questions about what he had been doing these past months. Indeed, it might bring his very sanity into question. He couldn't afford that.

Nor could he tell his mother. She had seen the difference in him these past weeks, had even commented on it. She liked the new Julio. She'd said something about life getting better and better. That was good. Still, he couldn't tell her. He wouldn't risk putting her in jeopardy, and that is exactly what would happen.

Grandma Claire had said something about a shield of protection about him. She said that he was in the hollow of God's hand. Still, she hadn't said anything about his mother being protected.

Grandma Claire had said that he should grow strong in the Lord. She called the Bible his instruction book and his spiritual bill of rights all rolled up into one. She'd gotten him into a good church. But even his pastor didn't realize the full magnitude of what he'd been through. Only Karina understood that. They stayed close on the assumption that there was strength in numbers. They supported each other. After all, when two or more gathered together, Jesus was in their midst.

Claire had said that when the time came they would know what to do. It seemed to Julio that they should be doing something other than hiding, but what? He only prayed that she was right.

Serena and Chris had pulled their old RV into a park just outside of Little Rock, Arkansas, about half an hour ago. The summer heat had really started to set in, and their air conditioning unit was struggling with it. Serena wiped a bead of sweat from her brow as she sat down at the computer in their RV. Chris was still outside monkeying around with the water hookup. This place, with its heat and humidity, was a far cry from her beloved Oregon. She really missed home when they were on the road.

She opened her email to discover a message from their good friend Will Reinhart. It was unusually long, and its contents were nothing short of revolutionary. As she read on, a chill ran up her spine. He'd been doing some snooping around regarding the hellish oil that they had drawn up out of the well, and he had hit pay dirt. The verdict was in, and it was indeed disturbing. She thought back to her time in that terrible sea of agony. Back then, she had not been in a state of mind to evaluate the nature of this unnatural oil analytically. There were times that her confused mind had become convinced that it was a living thing. She had once compared it to a spoiled child playing with the many humans within its grasp, unwilling to release so many as even one of them. Maybe she hadn't been so crazy, after all.

"Alive?" she gasped. "The oil is alive?"

"What oil is alive?" asked Chris, closing the door behind him and sitting at Serena's side.

"The oil from the well in Kurdistan," replied Serena. "This is an email from Will. Their lab has finally analyzed it, figured out exactly how it works. When it was cool, it was inert, just like any other sample of oil. It was in a sort of hibernation. But when it gets hot, like it was in the Great Sea of Fire, it begins to grow, multiply. Chris, it feeds on living flesh or any organic matter it comes in contact with. That's what it was doing to all of the souls in the sea in Hell. It was feeding upon us. The only reason that we weren't totally consumed by it was our ability to regenerate. And as it feeds, it multiplies, grows. When I was in Hell, I remember Abaddon telling me that the Great Sea of Fire was rising with the passage of every year. Now I understand why. It was growing larger as it fed upon all of those poor souls cast adrift within it."

Chris looked at his wife incredulously.

"Well, read it yourself, Chris. It's all there."

And Chris did. He could hardly believe it, yet it all made sense. "It says here that when living flesh is added to it, the oil heats up. Not dead flesh, like meat, but living flesh. I wonder what kind of experiments they were doing with that stuff."

"Will didn't say," replied Serena. "It's too late in Kurdistan to call him tonight. I'll have to call him first thing in the morning. He did say that he had a friend in research who leaked this information to him. The company is keeping all of this from the public for the moment. They're going to release this information eventually, at a press conference, but not just yet. You see, to them, it is just a new form of life. They're calling it a thermophile, a simple form of life that thrives on the natural heat two miles down. They're hoping that National Geographic or the Discovery Channel might do a piece on this new find, give them some positive PR."

Chris read on for another minute before looking up from the screen. "In Hell this oil, or whatever you want to call it, fed upon the life force of the souls within it. At least that's the way Will has it figured."

"And now that horrible stuff is right here on Earth," deduced Serena. "If it gets loose, what kind of damage could it do?"

"But life on Earth doesn't regenerate," deduced Chris. "It dies."

"Then this stuff has the potential to kill millions, even billions," said Serena.

Chris pondered the situation for a moment. "That European corporation that bought all of this hellish oil from Will's company, oh, what was it called again?"

"Roan Chemical," said Serena. "I did a Web search on them a few months ago, but it wasn't particularly helpful. There was no mention of any research on a strange new oil. That's no big surprise. Will has been looking into it too. He hasn't had any luck, either."

Chris nodded. "You think this corporation has some connection to Satan?"

"I wouldn't be surprised," said Serena.

"What is he up to?" pondered Chris. "He's been here on Earth for what, nine months, maybe ten? We have a lead here, a clue there, but it just isn't adding up."

"He's probably involved in all kinds of mischief," replied Serena. "That might be why the clues lead in so many directions. He must have operatives all over the world. His plan is so vast that the clues seem unrelated, small pieces in a huge puzzle."

"I'm starting to wonder if we have any chance at all of stopping him," said Chris. "I mean, what can the two of us do?"

"But we have to try," replied Serena, determination in her voice. "No matter what the odds, we have to try." There was a pause; then Serena smiled. "That wasn't always your attitude. When I was in Hell and you were in Heaven, you were told time after time that you couldn't rescue me, that there was no hope. But you wouldn't listen to them. You just kept struggling with the problem. Now, here we are, together, with a second chance. You're going to figure this one out too. We're going to figure it out together."

It was later that evening, after dinner, that Chris made a discovery. He was browsing news items on the Internet when he came upon an article that caught his attention. It wasn't the article so much as the photograph that went with it, the face of a man. He studied it for over a minute. "I've seen you before," he muttered. "Yeah, but in a way different context."

Serena looked up from the book she had been engrossed in for the past hour. "Chris, what are you going on about?"

"Come and see for yourself," he said. "But be ready for a shock."

Serena came to the screen and looked at the face of the middle-aged man pictured in it. A sudden expression of horror swept across her face. "It's him," she gasped. "It's Satan. Who does it say this guy is?"

"He calls himself Lusan," said Chris.

"Yes," confirmed Serena. "He's that cult leader who has been making such a stir up in New York. People say he has an incredible healing ministry. I've had some suspicions about him. This is the first time I've seen a photograph of him."

"He has done his best to avoid being photographed up close," said Chris. "Maybe we now know why."

Serena nodded. She turned away from the screen. She could bear looking at that face no longer. "We've got you," she said.

Chris scanned the article one more time. "I've been doing a little research on this guy during the past hour or so. That's how I stumbled on this photograph. It's strange, Lusan's organization just sort of popped up about nine months ago. It says here that he lived in Morocco before founding this church. He'd become wealthy by brokering some sort of gold mine deal in the depths of the Sahara last year. It was then that the spirit of God fell upon him, right out there in the desert, and told him to establish this church. Now he's going on sort of an evangelical tour of the nation, being God's messenger to the world. He's going to be in Atlanta three days from now. Maybe we should drop in. Satan has never been very good at controlling his emotions. Maybe we should go to the stage when he has his healing service. Seeing you there might cause him to blow a gasket."

"It might work," said Serena. "Yes, I like that idea. Maybe we should rain on his parade. The least we could do would be to become a real pain in his side. He's in our backyard now."

"These healings that are spoken of, they look real," noted Chris. "So many people attest to them. Why and how could Satan heal someone?"

Serena laughed openly. "It's not that hard to figure out. Do you know what a gambit is in chess?"

"Sure," replied Chris. "It's when you give up a piece in an attempt to gain a real positional advantage in the game. You give up a piece and win the game. But it's risky."

"Right," said Serena. "Satan has lost the War in Heaven. He has even lost his kingdom in Hell. He is in the endgame. This is his last chance. Satan has resorted to casting out Satan. People who have been physically afflicted by demons, some for years, are being released at his bidding so as to give him a PR advantage here on Earth. He gives up a few so as to gain even more. Don't you see? It's a game."

Chris nodded. "That makes sense. Then at any of his revivals there will be demons in great numbers, manipulating all that happens."

"I'm not afraid of demons, not anymore," noted Serena. "And if demons are the problem, maybe we could do a little spiritual healing of our own, show old slewfoot for what he is—a charlatan—and do it in front of tens of thousands of people."

"I'm liking this better and better all the time," said Chris. "It says here that there are still tickets available for the event. Are you up to it?"

"I'm up to it," confirmed Serena. "Let's rock his socks off."

For the next three hours they made their plans. They looked at the layout of the stadium that the Changing the World crusade would be held in. They considered the best place to sit, the best way to proceed to the stage. They even viewed a video of the first crusade in Philadelphia two weeks ago. By the time they turned in for the night, they had a rough plan as to how to proceed. Maybe they could head off Lusan's worldwide crusade before it hardly got started.

Serena awakened to cool dampness. She opened her eyes to find herself in a cool, misty forest filled with the illumination of thousands of fireflies. She rose to her feet. She could only see about 30 or 40 feet through the fog. It all had the appearance of twilight, not total night. Some of the mists around her even seemed to be glowing a pale blue. It was so very strange. It had to be a dream, but it seemed so very real. She closed her eyes once more, tried to will her body to awaken, but she had the sense that she was already awake.

She looked upon herself. She wasn't wearing her nightgown, but the knee-length print dress she had laid out for today's book signing. Had she gotten dressed and headed out the door without realizing it? Had she been sleepwalking?

"Serena, where are you?" came a voice from out of the fog. She recognized that voice, and she was relieved to hear it. It was Chris.

"Chris, I'm over here," she replied.

"Just keep talking. I'll follow your voice," came the reply.

"This is so weird," replied Serena. "Are you a part of my dream, or are we having this dream together?"

"I could ask you the same question," replied Chris. His voice seemed much closer.

Serena turned in the direction of the voice. She saw movement in the fog. She was relieved to see that it was Chris. He had found her. He too was dressed for the book signing. Had they both been sleepwalking? They embraced.

"Nice morning for a walk in the fog," observed Chris, looking about. "I take it you don't know how we got here either."

"I don't have a clue," confirmed Serena.

"Chris, Serena, where are you?" came another voice out of the fog. It was the voice of a woman. It had a kind, concerned tone about it.

It took Serena only a second to make a decision as to what to do. "We're over here," she replied.

A few seconds later, another figure appeared out of the fog. It was a thin and pretty woman of African descent, who appeared to be in her mid-thirties. She was dressed in a long, white robe and held a simple walking stick in her hand. Her smile was absolutely radiant when she saw the couple standing there in the mists.

"Oh, I hope you haven't been waiting out here long," she said, her tone almost apologetic.

"Oh no, not at all," replied Chris.

"Oh good," said the woman. "I was afraid that I might be running late. My name is Claire, Claire James."

"I knew that," said Serena. "Though I'm not quite sure why." She looked over at her husband, who was grinning from ear to ear.

"I know," said Chris, "because this is Heaven." He looked about at the mixture of tall pines and poplars. "I'd say offhand that it was the second or third plane."

Clair seemed impressed. "It's the third, actually. Very good, Chris."

A thought suddenly crossed Serena's mind. "Claire, we're not dead, are we?"

Claire laughed at that comment. "No, of course not, dear. You and your husband are quite alive. As for me, well, that's another matter. Still, Mark Twain was right when he said that the rumors of my death have been greatly exaggerated. Death isn't such a big deal, really. To be honest, I like it." Claire paused for but a moment. "The two of you probably wouldn't remember me, but we met once back on Earth, about four years ago when you had a book signing at the Book Nook bookstore in Brooklyn. The next day you gave your testimony at our church. I spoke to you for several minutes. I looked quite a bit older then."

"I remember now," said Serena, shaking Claire's hand. "I remember the conversation too. We talked about the inevitable fate of the dead in Hell. You brought up quite a number of good points, Claire. They've stayed with me."

"Thank you," said Claire, who then turned to Chris. "Oh, lest I forget, dear, your mother said to send you her love and that she is looking forward to your reunion. Jennifer has quite a few tales to tell you. She has had several adventures since you last saw her; you can be very sure of that."

Chris laughed, though he was crying too. How much he longed to be with her again. "Tell her I love her and am looking forward to that day."

"Yes, of course," said Claire. "But, maybe I should get down to the point. I don't have all that much time. I can't keep you so far from your earthly bodies for too long. You'll have to excuse me, dear. I am still all quite new at this. I know that you're planning to go to Lusan's crusade in Atlanta. You want to confront him, but I tell you that you must not. It's not the time, not yet. Your plans, though well intentioned, will only make a mess of things. You'll just end up giving him ammunition, the chance to rail against the Christian community. Don't give him that opportunity. There are certain things that are destined to happen, I fear. Not every battle can be won. Believe me, it's been a difficult thing for me to accept too. You see, my grandson, Leland James, is under Lusan's power. He can't or won't recognize who he truly is. I wanted to expose him myself for who he truly was, but the Holy Spirit stopped me. I guess the Father had different plans for me. I've been kept quite busy since I arrived here."

Claire looked up for a moment; so did Serena. Yes, it was becoming noticeably brighter.

"The sun will be up soon," said Claire. "Time is so short. You need to try to stay out of Lusan's way if you can. Keep doing what you've been doing, spread the Gospel and tell others about your experiences. That is, after all, what you're on Earth for. Still, I fear Lusan—no, let's call him who he is, Satan—will eventually come after the two of you. There is great anger in his heart against both of you. You'll know when he's coming, and you'll know what to do." Again there was a pause. "There's something else. I really don't like to have to do this, but it is the best way, believe me."

A few seconds later, another form emerged from the fog; it was Will Reinhart. He wore casual clothes, the sort of things one might wear if he were going shopping.

"Will," said Chris, walking up to him and shaking his hand.

"Good to see you again, Chris," said Will, who then turned to Serena. He walked up to her and gave her a big hug. "And it's good to see you too, Serena. I guess you've read my email."

"Yes, I did," confirmed Serena. "We both did."

"What a way for us all to get together again," chuckled Chris. "So you were called out to this meeting, too."

Will hesitated. "Not exactly. You see, there was an accident. I went to breakfast with a friend of mine just a few hours ago, just like we usually do. We went to a little café not far from the drilling site, in a town called Ibil. We go there for breakfast once or twice a week. They tend to cater to the Westerners in the area. It's a great place to go, or at least it was. This morning, that café was the target of a suicide bomber. He was one of those Islamic extremists. I don't know how many innocent people he killed; the place was full. I mean, it's not the kind of place where you expect trouble. Kurdistan is not really known for its ethnic violence. I assure you, I never felt a thing. The bomb went off right beside our table. I suspect that I might have been the target." Will paused. "Chris, the trip here was just like you said it was in the book. The trip to Heaven, that is."

Tears appeared in Serena's eyes. "Oh, sweet Jesus, no. Oh Will, I'm so sorry."

Will placed his arms around her. "Oh please, don't cry, Serena. It's OK, really. I'm more concerned about my family. I'll be fine. I've met my Lord face to face; I've met Jesus. He assured me that everything was going to turn out all right." Will chuckled. "Actually, I got the royal treatment. Since Satan's fall to Earth, most of those who have passed from life have been allowed to sleep. They will be called forth at the return of our Lord or on the Day of Judgment. But I was brought straight to Heaven. I'm considered one of the new martyrs—imagine that! I've only been here a few hours, but I love what I've seen so far."

"Yes, I know what you mean," confirmed Chris. His voice was quivering. "Still, it isn't fair. Satan has really overstepped his bounds this time."

"Yes," confirmed Will. "That's what Jesus told me. And it's going to cost the Devil big time. I'm not sure how it's going to work or what's going to happen, but you can be sure of it."

Chris nodded. He looked at Serena. She was beside herself with grief. "Did you learn anything more, anything we should know?"

"Yes," replied Will. "All of that hellish oil has been removed from the site. Any new oil we encounter is to be contained in a specially designed underground tank and shipped immediately under refrigeration. I'm not sure to whom. But I have a bad feeling about it, Chris. There's way too much secrecy behind all of this. Our company is usually pretty open about things. But that just isn't true anymore. There are even rumors that our stock is slowly being acquired by a third party, but I don't know who. I was trying to find out when, well, you know. I wish I had more information for you."

"I'm sorry, but they have to leave now," said Claire. "Our time is up."

"Yeah," said Will, "I know. We'll be seeing each other again." He gave Serena a final hug and a kiss on the forehead. Then he turned to shake Chris's hand. "You can do this thing," he said. "My prayers will be with you, both of you."

Will and Claire walked away into the mists. Then the whole scene faded into darkness.

Serena awoke in her bed, Chris at her side. He was still asleep. She looked over at the clock; it was just before 2:00 A.M. Had it all been a wild dream? She got out of bed and went for her cell phone. She called Will Reinhart's number. After a minute she got an automated message that the phone was off or the user was out of the calling area. It wasn't an encouraging message.

A few minutes later, she was back in bed. Her mind was full of confusion.

"I just had the weirdest dream," said Chris in a sleepy voice.

"About Will Reinhart?" asked Serena.

That comment made Chris sit up. "Yes. And a woman named Claire."

"Then we really were there," said Serena. "Oh sweet Lord. Will is dead."

"Yes, he said that in the dream," replied Chris. "He is a good man, a good brother in Christ. I'm going to miss him." Chris paused for a moment. "I wonder just how much of this suicide bombing Satan has been behind over the years. As much as anything else, it has destabilized the Middle East, turned it into the powder keg it is today."

"And we're partially to blame," deduced Serena, tears streaming down her face. "We put it in Will's head to guard that well. We made him a target. Now we've gotten him killed."

"No, Satan got him killed," said Chris, taking his wife in his arms. "And he's going to pay, but not now. Claire warned us about all of that, remember? We can't go after him yet, but the time is coming, I know it. He's going to slip up, and when he does, we're going to nail him."

Chris and Serena discussed their plans for nearly an hour before going back to sleep. It was difficult not to go ahead with their plan to expose Lusan. Still, they had been warned. If they proceeded, they'd be doing it on their own. They couldn't afford to do that. So they'd wait for a time and place of the Spirit's choosing. If Will's sacrifice was to mean anything, they'd have to.

CHAPTER 10

A terrible melancholia had fallen over the drill crew at well number 14. Will Reinhart had been a good foreman and a good friend. Everyone felt the loss. It reminded them all of where they were. This wasn't the lazy plains of Oklahoma, though it sometimes reminded them of it. This was the powder keg of the world. The lack of violence in the area this past year had lulled most of them into a false sense of security.

It wasn't just Will who had been taken from them. Actually, four of their number had lost their lives in the suicide bombing. The other three were assigned to wells 12 and 17, further up the valley. They were all there to enjoy a good meal and good company.

Most of the well 14 crew didn't know the other three men personally, but they mourned their loss nonetheless. Their deaths were pointless, lives lost over a conflict that had been going on for over a thousand years. There were no winners in this war, only losers. The Kurds would retaliate, of course. They always did. They'd take the fight back to the Shiites. They'd set off a human bomb in a crowded marketplace or fire a rocket into a bus. They'd try to beat today's death toll. And the war would go on. And, of course, innocent people would be killed. That was the name of the game, wasn't it? But it wouldn't bring any of today's victims back. The irony to the crew of well 14 was that this wasn't even their fight. Will Reinhart and the others had simply been in the wrong place at the wrong time.

It was just past nine in the evening when the first of a string of bizarre events happened. All power to the well abruptly went dead, leaving the new drill bit hanging there above the well casing, and leaving the crew in the dark. It took only a few minutes to locate the problem. The entire breaker panel had blown simultaneously. The flip of six switches brought them back on line. Nevertheless, it gave the entire crew the willies.

Fifteen minutes later, with the drill just over 200 feet down the casing, the main gearbox froze up. Again work stopped. The engineer had hardly put a wrench to the access port of the box when it seemed to fix itself. Once more work resumed, only to be halted by another power failure three minutes later. But this time the breakers looked to be fried. It was when they went searching for a set of replacements that steam began to emanate from the well casing. It was the straw that broke the camel's back. The crew backed away from and then ran from the rig even as the quantities of steam increased.

A sound emanated from the well, like the crackling of electricity, even as a growing blue glow from deep within the casing appeared. Then all Hell broke loose, literally. In a tremendous explosion, over 300 feet of pipe, weighing many tons, shot skyward. It rained debris as much as 50 yards away, injuring three of the crew, one seriously.

Then came the cloud of glowing gas and the terrible noise. It was like a hundred sirens all going off at once. The clouds climbed hundreds of feet into the dark, cloudy sky before appearing to dissipate. Later, some observers would swear to seeing what looked like individual forms in the glowing clouds. The term *demons* was widely circulated in describing what they had seen, as were the words *ghosts* and *evil spirits*. They had witnessed something truly supernatural, and it didn't look good.

At the end of an hour, the fury of the event was spent. What remained of the well was a mass of twisted and contorted metal. It was like nothing any of them had ever seen.

That was the end for well number 14. It was capped and the area was fenced off. The books were closed on this disastrous chapter in the company's history. The company had lost enough money on the haunted well. It was time to cut its losses. A 24-hour-a-day security detail stood guard over the well so as to report on any events that might affect the surrounding wells.

In the months that followed, a silence fell over well 14. There were no reports of voices from the depths of the Earth, no talk of glowing mists or any of the other manifestations that had haunted the well for so long. Whatever force had plagued the well had apparently been released during that one terrible night.

It was Cal Wayneright, the flight engineer they'd gotten to know on their trip to and from Kurdistan, who broke the news of Will's death to Chris and Serena a few days later. The news had come in the form of an email and later a telephone call. The news was not unexpected, of course, but it caused Chris and Serena a great deal of distress nonetheless. No less distressful was the word of the seemingly supernatural pyrotechnical display that had engulfed well number 14 the night following Will's death. The company had done its best to keep the events of that night under wraps. However, news of the event was spreading rapidly. It would probably be just a matter of time before the story was picked up by the tabloids or, even worse, by the legitimate media.

Chris and Serena knew only too well what sort of entities had just entered the world. The only question was, how many? Would they significantly enhance Satan's ability to control the goings on within this world? They would soon know.

For now, they would stay the course, continuing their evangelistic and book-signing ministry. They would tell the world that the last days had come without disclosing any of the specifics. They would preach boldly the word of repentance and salvation to any who would listen.

All the while, they monitored the media, watching as Lusan's power and influence grew. At meeting after meeting, the word of miraculous healings became the hallmark of his ministry. The numbers of his followers swelled during that long hot summer, even as the number of people attending their services waned.

In the shadow of the onrushing comet, interest in things spiritual had reached a fever pitch. And the pathogen at the heart of that fever was Lusan.

The scientists and members of the press filed into the large lecture hall at NASA's Johnson Space Center outside of Houston, Texas. There was a real buzz in the air; there had been all summer. Comet Florence had now been tracked for nearly a year and a half. Its orbit was continually being refined as ever more positions were plotted. For the past three months, the Earth's orbit had placed the comet too close to the sun in the sky to be observed by Earthly observers. Now it was far enough from the sun's glare to be observed by space telescopes in orbit of Earth.

It had now been observed by the aging Hubble Space Telescope. NASA had actually overridden several safety protocols in order to point the telescope so close to the solar disk, but the risk had paid off. They now had in their possession images that would answer the question as to whether the Earth was still in imminent peril. On this October morning the world would know what, up until now, only a few scientists and high officials knew.

Four experts sat on the stage before the assembling crowd. One of them was Dr. Sam Florence, the comet's discoverer. Today was the day of truth. Were we still on the crosshairs of Comet Florence, or were we to be spared by an act of complex gravitational interactions?

This briefing was being carried by every major network around the world. Soon the world would know the answer to the most pressing question of the millennium.

The hall lights went down as Dr. Henry Brown, the new director of NASA's planetary exploration division, took center stage. He took a moment to introduce the members of the panel. He spoke of their contributions to the program. All the while, the tension in the room grew. Dr. Brown paused for just six or seven seconds. He would keep the crowd in suspense no longer. His growing smile was encouraging.

"Ladies and gentlemen, it is the unanimous opinion of this committee that we have dodged the apocalyptic bullet. Our best estimates give us a closest approach to Earth of Comet Florence of 183,000 kilometers, 111,000 miles, with a statistical margin of error of approximately 36,000 kilometers, 22,000 miles. That's places it about halfway to the moon at closest approach. In short, the odds of impact with the Earth as it currently stands, are one in 40 million."

The swell of relief that swept through the room was something to behold. It quickly broke into wild applause. People cried and hugged each other. Human civilization would go on. Dr. Brown went on to display a set of PowerPoint slides of the comet's path and how that path was derived, but to most of those present, this was of only secondary concern.

"We'll have ringside seats to one of the most incredible spectacles in human history. Now, there are still some concerns," cautioned Brown, "very serious concerns. Yes, Earth itself is safe; however, we are going to pass through the comet's outer coma, its tenuous atmosphere. How serious a problem this is depends largely on how dusty the comet's coma turns out to be. Certainly, it will produce a meteor storm the likes of which no one has ever seen. But it is highly unlikely that any of these meteors will reach the ground. Most will range from the size of specks of dust to grains of sand. It will be a spectacular display from horizon to horizon lasting several nights, but it will pose no hazard to those of us on the ground. The problem is that these particles might sandblast many of our satellites in Earth orbit. We could be looking at losses in the billions of dollars if Comet Florence is a particularly dusty comet, like Halley. Then again, it might be a comet like Temple 2, with very little dust, producing little or no damage to our network of satellites. We just don't know yet. But satellites can be replaced; our Earth can't. It might be noted that, as a precaution, the space station will be evacuated during that period of time. In addition, all commercial, government, and military space flight will be suspended for the time we are in the coma. We're just playing it safe, that's all."

"Does this mean that the comet intercept mission will be abandoned?" asked the MSNBC correspondent.

"In part," replied Dr. Brown. "The two deflection missions carrying large nuclear devices will be canceled. There is no need for them, and at this point, the risks outweigh the gains. They were by far the most expensive aspects of the project. However, a smaller vehicle, that shall be launched next year, will loop around Jupiter and use its gravity assist to swing it around and follow the comet on its path through the inner solar system. It will provide us with valuable information about the comet's structure. It will also warn us in advance if anything unforeseen happens."

"Like what?" asked the correspondent.

Dr. Brown chuckled. "Well, if we knew that, it wouldn't be unforeseen. No, seriously, what we are still concerned about is explosions of gas and dust on the comet's surface as it grows closer to the sun. This could increase the amount of dust in the comet's coma, increasing the hazard to satellites in Earth orbit. A worst case scenario would be an eruption just before the comet reached us, filling the coma with dust at the worst possible time."

"For a time, NASA would have had us to believe that the comet had us on the crosshairs," noted a reporter from the Post. "What has happened to change that?"

"Thoroughly evaluating the paths of astronomical objects like comets takes time," noted Sam Florence. "In many ways, we were in uncharted territory, observing the comet both from Earth and a satellite in deep space. There was a point when things looked very grim. However, tiny gravitational interactions have been playing with the comet during the past year, to say nothing of the inevitable inaccuracies of our own scientific measurements. We have gone from a Doomsday scenario to what may be the most spectacular sky show in human history. I suppose people need to wind down and enjoy the show."

The press conference went on for another half hour, but the atmosphere had changed. Gone was the dread of calamity, replaced by the excitement and exuberance of an incredible display of nature at its best.

Still, as Sam Florence left the building and made his way to his car, he was troubled. Something was wrong, though he knew not what.

Autumn turned to winter. Chris and Serena kept a close eye on the goings on at the New World Faith Center. That wasn't difficult; the center was increasingly in the news. Lusan had been called the greatest faith healer since the apostles walked the Earth. The comparison made Serena cringe. She knew the truth. It was a real smoke and mirrors act. Lusan's invisible minions brought about the poor soul's infirmity, and Lusan gave that spirit the cue to leave. Then they could oppress someone else, and the cycle repeated itself.

Lusan was about to embark on his second crusade, a tour that would take him to virtually every country in Europe. Using the Internet and armed with the Freedom of Information Act, Serena did her best to trace the Center's business deals. It had become a real spider's web on an international scale. Still, it perplexed Serena; what was Satan up to? He had his hand in government, biotechnology, and high technology electronics. There was so much going on. It just didn't fit together, at least, not yet. Most peculiar was his organization's purchase of a small South Pacific island that was to have become an exclusive resort. It had been the worldwide meltdown, and the great recession that followed, that had put an end to that project way back in 2008. Since then, the nearly completed structures had rusted and rotted in the damp tropical air, with no buyer in sight. Lusan had picked it up at bargain-basement prices. What would he want with a South Pacific island in the first place? That would be a difficult question to answer because his private island was off limits to outsiders. It was just another odd piece in the puzzle.

Winter held New York City in its icy grip. It seemed that this winter might be even colder than the last. Scientists were calling it a Maunder Minimum, the onset of a little ice age that was only partially offset by global warming. Snow filled the air, drifting through the great canyon formed by the tall buildings of the city toward the boulevard below.

Leland James glanced up from his computer, looking out across his large, well-furnished office and then out the window at the falling snow. Never in his wildest dreams had he envisioned such a life as he had now. When he'd accepted the job of chief financial officer for Lusan's ministerial organization over a year ago, he'd imagined a task much more limited in scope. Yes, he was equipped for the challenge. He held a degree in accounting and had significant experience in business administration. But now he oversaw the finances of a global corporation. Some of it was nonprofit, other aspects were not. Even with the assistance of his well-trained professional staff, Leland was easily putting in 50 to 60 hours a week. There was just so much to oversee. That and Krissie's demanding schedule gave him and his wife very little quality time together.

Krissie would be accompanying Lusan on his European tour next month. Again, they'd be apart. He would miss her terribly; he always did. Still, the show had to go on. There was a world to reach out there, and they'd all need to do their part to accomplish it.

Lusan had his hands in enterprises ranging from his ministry, to mining, to manufacturing, to scientific and engineering enterprises. An infrastructure that any other entrepreneur might have taken a lifetime to put together, Lusan had done in a little over a year. Then again, he wasn't just any entrepreneur, was he? He was an angel, as were many of the other administrators of his organization. To Leland's knowledge, he was the highest-ranking human in the corporation.

Leland could now spot an angel in a crowd of humans. Even when the angel was in disguise, as they always were, Leland could point them out. That fact had impressed Lusan. It was a significant accomplishment, requiring a degree of spiritual discernment that most humans lacked. Angels had an invisible aura about them that Leland could sense at a glance. Humans didn't have that aura. At least most humans didn't. There were some people in the organization that Leland couldn't figure. They didn't have the aura of an angel, but they didn't seem quite human either. They were something in between. They were an odd breed. They had a tendency to make Leland feel uneasy. As the months had gone by, Leland found himself dealing with an ever-greater number of these people. He'd even seen that aura appear virtually overnight in people who had previously not exhibited it. Leland had never asked Lusan about those people.

His attention returned to the computer spreadsheet before him. "Deuterated water?" he said, under his breath. "What are we going to do with 80 kilograms of deuterated water, build a hydrogen bomb?"

When Leland ran into a line item that was unfamiliar to him, he always looked it up. He'd been doing that a lot lately. Deuterated water was also called heavy water. It was used by nuclear physicists. This shipment was heading toward the island. That was another thing. What did Lusan need with an island in the Pacific?

Lusan had said something about the angels needing a place where they could be alone, among their own kind. Still, Leland suspected that there was something more to it than that. He'd authored the purchase of heavy equipment, dynamos, turbines, and all manner of electronics for the island. It seemed to him like this was a bit more than an island resort for angels.

"My friend, Leland," said a cheerful voice from the other side of the office.

Leland looked up from his spreadsheet to see Lusan all decked out in his finest business suit. "Looking good this morning, boss," said Leland.

"Thank you very much," said Lusan, stepping to Leland's side. "I need you and your staff to find me some items. They are items we shall need for our construction projects on the island. I need it to be expedited." Lusan handed Leland a computer jump drive. "I could have sent this to you by email, but I wanted to drop by personally. We rarely have time to talk anymore."

Leland smiled. "No we don't. Saving the world seems to be a full-time job."

Lusan laughed openly. "Oh, my friend, it always has been. I've been in the business for a very long time. It hasn't gotten any easier, I can assure you. But working with people such as you makes it all worth it."

Leland popped the jump drive in the USB port of his computer and scanned

Lusan's list. His eyes opened wide when he saw its contents: "1,845,000 metric tons of concrete, over five kilometers of heavy rebar, and enough lumber to build a small town. This is some order."

Lusan cocked his head in such an odd way, for a human, that is. "Is there any problem with the order?"

Leland hesitated. "Well, no. I can get these materials all right. The cargo and dock facility on the island is complete. The runway is also repaired. Still, it is only 3,400 feet long. We can bring in crews and light materials on it, but it won't handle large cargo planes. The existing roads into the interior of the island have all been repaired, no problem there. We can get these materials in there, and get them to the job site.

"That is good," replied Lusan. "It is important that we get the preliminary work done before the onset of typhoon season."

Leland nodded; then he could keep his silence no longer. "My heavens, Lusan, this is a huge investment. You have sunk over a billion dollars into this project already. The whole island only cost us 48 million. What are you doing out there?"

Lusan hesitated. "It's a secret, a project of great importance." Again he paused. "But no, not to you. Yes, I'll tell you what it is Leland. I'll tell you, but there is a provision. You must tell no one else. It must remain our secret. It is too sensitive a matter for the world of humans to know, at least for the moment."

"You have my promise," replied Leland. "It won't be like the last time. You can confide in me."

Lusan placed his hand on Leland's shoulder. "Oh, my friend, I hold no ill will toward you about what you told your grandmother. No, that is in the past; it is forgotten. Indeed, there was nothing to forgive. I understand why you did it. But back to the issue of the island—I am involved in a scientific investigation, a project that fuses the fields of physics and engineering. In very fact, that is what it is. I am prepared to demonstrate a practical nuclear fusion reactor that will produce limitless power for humanity. Think about it, my friend. What is the root source of human discontent and strife? I tell you it is want—want for energy, for food, for water. But energy can be the key to the other two. Indeed, fusion power will save the environment of this planet. It is totally nonpolluting. It leaves no carbon footprint."

"Yes," confirmed Leland. "But we humans have been trying to make nuclear fusion work for over half a century. We haven't had any luck."

"So, give us angels a chance," said Lusan. Leland looked at Lusan incredulously. "Do you actually know how to build one?"

Lusan shook his head. "Do I know how to build one? No, I don't. That has never been my purpose in God's Kingdom. I am not a builder. I am, and have always been, what you humans might call a manager. It is my task to coordinate the efforts of others. And, if I may be so bold as to say it, I am the best. That is why I was selected to lead this project. But there are others, angelic scientists and engineers, who do understand this thing. We will coordinate our efforts with those of our human counterparts to build a full-scale prototype of just such a reactor. They have been working on the design for nearly a year. We will build it on that island."

"But why there?" asked Leland. "The costs of the construction that we have undertaken on that island have been made even higher by its remoteness, its isolation."

"But that is just the point," replied Lusan. "It is because of its isolation that we build there. Understand, we have never built a unit exactly like this one. There are certain risks. We understand the theory, but that is just what it is, a theory. It is a far cry from actual experience. If something happens, something very bad, it might be best if it happened in a remote location. We can ill afford to place the general public at risk. Now, understand, the risk factor is low, but it is not zero. It is not in my nature to take risks when human life is involved. I'm sure you understand."

"Yes, I do," replied Leland. "I think I understand now. I assure you, your secret is safe."

Lusan laughed again. "I never had any doubts. Now, obtain for me a good price for those items. Though extensive, my resources are not unlimited."

"You got it, boss," replied Leland. "I hope, at some point, I'll get to see this wonder of engineering for myself."

"Oh, be assured you will," said Lusan, "you and your lovely wife, too. I'll see to it that you get the full tour of Lusan's island of wonders."

"Oh my heavens it's cold out there," remarked Sam Florence, stepping into the warm control room of the Discovery Channel Observatory.

Ken, the 62-year-old observatory assistant smiled. "Eight below zero, according to the thermometer. Welcome back to the high country, Sam. It's a far cry from Phoenix."

Sam smiled and sat down beside Ken at the control console. "Ten minutes until morning twilight. This observing run is just about over."

"You got two clear nights back to back," noted Ken. "You had no equipment problems this time around. We didn't even have to pray over the equipment."

"You might not have, but I did," noted Sam. "I do every night I observe."

That comment made Ken laugh. "It's probably not a bad idea. I reckon that you'll have a mountain of data to go through before you come back this way again in April."

"I only took three images of the comet," noted Sam. "Mostly I was searching for new snowballs beyond Neptune. I computed the position of the comet, got a new orbital solution. I think I can safely say that there is a zero percent chance of impact with Earth." Sam paused. "You know, Ken, I had really convinced myself that this comet was the Wormwood spoken of in the book of Revelation. You know, the flying mountain cast into the sea."

"You're not the only one who thought that," said Ken. "Still, the end of times, she is a coming, you mark my words. The Beast is already among us. He ought to be, oh, about 35 or 36 years old about now."

Sam looked at Ken with an expression of puzzlement. "Now how do you figure that?"

"Simple," replied Ken. "Every Christian is familiar with the Christmas star, the star the wise men followed to Bethlehem. It's only spoken of in the Book of Matthew, but we're given quite a bit of detail about it. All sorts of people have puzzled over what that star was over the years."

"It was probably a planetary conjunction," said Sam. "Two planets passed unusually close together in the sky. It means something to astrologers."

"Right," confirmed Ken. "But this wasn't just any planetary conjunction, not this one. It was a great conjunction, a triple conjunction between Jupiter and Saturn. I'm here to tell you, they're rarer than hen's teeth. Jupiter passed

Saturn in its orbit because it is moving faster around the sun. It has the inner track, too. Then Earth overtakes Jupiter and it seems to move backward, passing Saturn again. Then Jupiter moves forward again and passes Saturn a third time. It only happens about once in 1400 years. But those Zoroastrian priests, they were watching out for one. Their great prophet, better than a thousand years before, had proclaimed that the next triple conjunction would foretell the coming of a great king who would save the world. He said that that king would be born in Israel. So when it finally happened, off they went. Well you know the rest of the story."

"Right," confirmed Sam. "But what does that have to do with the birth of the Beast? I always thought the Beast was Nero."

"Well, he was, in a manner of speaking," said Ken. "But he was only the first. Jesus said that this generation would see it all, speaking of the horrors of the Beast. But he also said that in the last days that people would grow greatly in knowledge and wisdom. That's today. There was another triple conjunction back in 1981, and it occurred on the exact opposite side of the sky from the one in 6 B.C. Everything about it was opposite to the 6 B.C. event. You'd be amazed. That 1981 event was something to see."

"That was a bit before my time," admitted Sam.

"But not mine," said Ken. I remember it well. And with that conjunction, the Beast was born."

"I've never been much for astrology," said Sam.

"It ain't astrology," corrected Ken. "It is an example of signs and wonders in the sky. I reckon the comet will fit into that bill, too. When a charismatic leader shows up over in Europe, a leader who is about 36 years old, watch out, the end of days are almost upon us."

CHAPTER 11

"The sun will soon sink into the sea, my dear one," said 36-year-old Julien Devereux, looking through the open French doors that lead out onto the balcony overlooking the Mediterranean Sea. "Do you think that we shall hear it hiss as it hits the cool waters of the sea, my son?"

There was no response. Julien looked to the bed where his son lay. His head was propped up on the pillows, facing the double doors. His eyes were open, but they held but an empty stare. A trace of drool hung at the corner of his quivering lips. Julien placed another damp cloth on his 11-year-old son's head. Adrien was having another of his fevers. The doctor said that these would come and go as the disease progressed, but this one was the worst to date. His body was fighting another infection, though by the looks of it, his son's immune system was weakening.

"And on the other side of that great sea is Africa," he continued. "It's a place of deserts and jungles. There the sun shines down with all of its fury. It shines down on a land of camels and elephants, lions and crocodiles. Someday we must visit it, the two of us."

His son made a faint gurgling sound. Julien was unsure if it was but a random spasm or the whisper of a response from his son.

"Yes, we shall go there," he continued. "We shall travel up the Nile, from the land of the pharoses to a land of jungles hardly explored by people. When you are better, my son, when you are better, that is where we shall go."

Julien thought back to the other love of his life. His wife, Mira, had died from the complications of bringing his son into this world. But that hadn't diminished his love for Adrien. Oh no, that could never be. Adrien had his mother's eyes and her smile. When he was close to him, he felt close to her. Julien had never remarried. He hadn't felt the need to. Instead, he had built his world around his son.

For nine wonderful years Adrien had been such a vital child, the apple of his father's eye. Bright, inquisitive, and always on the move, he had been hard to keep up with. He'd excelled in school and he was a constant source of pride for Julien. Then the problems had started. Adrien began to tire easily and slept ever more. His grades declined, as did his coordination. Then came the first of those terrible seizures. It had terrified Julien. Adrien had collapsed right after breakfast in a grand mol seizure that sent him writhing on the floor for nearly two minutes. A coma that had lasted nearly two days followed. And that was but the first episode. More seizures followed. With each seizure, Adrien's condition worsened. The doctor's diagnosis was Sandhoff Disease, a rare neurological disorder. There was no cure. Indeed, doctors were not all that certain of the cause, no less where to look for a cure. Still, Julien had searched the world for one. He'd seen the best doctors from New York to Shanghai, visited herbalists in the Far East, a famous Christian evangelist in America, and even a tribal witch doctor in the South Pacific; nothing had worked. The conclusion was inevitable. Adrien's condition would steadily deteriorate. He would slowly slip away from Julien both mentally and physically. He would never see adulthood, and he would be a mental vegetable in a considerably shorter time. Indeed, his son hadn't spoken to him in months beyond a few grunts and groans. He wondered if he even recognized him anymore.

As he thought back, it had been his experience with that television evangelist from America that had left the bitterest taste in Julien's mouth. Come to think of it, he actually wasn't an American. He simply preyed upon Americans. Oh, he was a smooth talker that one. He spoke of faith and a God who could accomplish all manner of miracles. Yet, he was just as quick to ask for money from those who came to him. He spoke of the expenses of his ministry, the expenses of bringing a healing ministry to the world. He spoke with such confidence that Adrian would experience a tremendous miracle. But it hadn't happened. More than anyone, he had been a deliverer of false hope.

Julien had resigned his cabinet post in the European Union months ago just to be here with his son in what would likely be his last months on Earth. To many it hadn't made sense. Julien had one of the most brilliant minds in Europe when it came to things economic. As financial advisor to the French president, his financial strategy had pulled the country out of the global depression. As financial minister of the European Union, it was hoped that he might help the rest of the continent do the same. Surely there were others who could help take care of his son. But no, this was not a job for someone else; this was his responsibility. If the EU needed him, the EU would have to wait. Right now, he had more important things to attend to.

For the moment, he would remain here at his home just west of Marseille with his son and housekeeper, Joan, whose love for his son was second only to his own. Yes, they would see this thing to the end.

As the twilight faded, Julien and Joan got Adrien ready for night. It was the better part of an hour later before the task was complete. His IV bag was changed and Julian and Joan had eaten a simple meal. Then Joan sat down to read to Adrian as she did every night. She wasn't sure that Adrien heard her, but she read to him nonetheless. Hers would be the first watch. Julien would take over at 1:00 A.M. and see his son through to the morning. He went to his bedroom at the end of the hall.

It was late when Julien awoke on the sand. He looked about in surprise to see the ocean waves lapping up just a few feet in front of him, illuminated by the nearly full moon overhead. He was out on the beach. He must have been sleepwalking, gotten out of the house, across the road, down the trail leading to the beach, and then gone to sleep once more.

He rose to his feet to discover that he had somehow managed to put on his business suit. This just kept getting weirder and weirder. He'd never had a problem with sleepwalking.

"Good evening, Mr. Julien Devereux," said a voice from behind.

Julien turned to see a middle-aged man, also in a dark business suit, standing some ten feet behind him. He was smiling broadly.

"I'm sorry," he said. "I didn't mean to startle you."

"You know my name?" asked Julien. "Sir, have we met before?"

"No," replied the man, "I don't think so. However, I know you nevertheless. You are a well-known man, Mr. Devereux, a very good and noble man."

"Then you recognize me from the papers, from television," deduced Julien.

"Yes," said the man. "All of France owes you a great debt. But that is not why I'm here. I have a different matter, a more personal matter, to discuss with you."

Personal matters? The thought suddenly hit Julien. "Oh my heavens, I was supposed to relieve my housekeeper in watching my son. I was supposed to relieve her at 1:00 A.M."

"Relax Mr. Devereux," said the stranger. "It is not even midnight yet. What I have to tell you is more important."

"Nothing is more important than Adrien," objected Julien. "He is my whole life."

The stranger smiled all the more. "Of course, Mr. Devereux, I quite understand. In very fact, it is that very thing that I wanted to discuss with you. You have searched far and wide for a cure for your son, but you have not found it. But there is a cure for your son, Mr. Devereux. You just haven't been looking in the right place."

"I don't understand," admitted Julien.

"And that is why I'm here," said the stranger. "There is a man coming to Marseille from America. There is healing in his hands, Mr. Devereux. He will restore your son to health in the twinkling of an eye."

"I've been to spiritual healers," objected Julien. "None of them could do anything for my son."

"This one can," assured the man. "His name is Lusan. God has His hand on this man. Your son's health will be restored so that you may return to the task God has set before you. You must complete the task you have begun. You must return this world's economic health. For without economic health, there can be no spiritual health. Take your son to him, Mr. Devereux. Allow God to do something for you. Then you can do something for God. Remember, you have three days."

Julien was amazed when the man seemed to vanish into a mist. In that last fraction of a second, his body was transformed into the form of a winged angel in white. A second later, Julien found himself in his bed once more. He quickly sat up. It had been a dream, nothing more. Oh, if only it could have been real. He looked over at the clock. It was just a minute before midnight. He might as well get up.

Julien ran his hands through his hair. Flicks of white dropped to the bed. It was sand.

"Sir, it has to have been a dream," objected Joan. "I know you want it to be true. So do I. But it was a dream."

"But this Lusan that the stranger spoke of is real," objected Julien. "He is coming to Marseille the day after tomorrow. He will be speaking at the Stade Vélodrome. I'm convinced that he can heal my son."

Joan shook her head. "But Julien, how would we get him there? It would be dangerous to move him in his present condition. And from what I have heard, there would be so many people, so many chances for something bad to happen."

"He can be moved by ambulance," replied Julien. "I can arrange for that. It can deliver him right there to the field. If I'm such a great hero of the people, well, maybe it is time for them to humor me a bit, give something back to me. They will be setting up a stage in the middle of the field. I will be there right in front of it. I'll be there with Adrian."

Joan nodded. "I can see I'm not going to be able to talk you out of this. I'll help you get ready. What do you need from me?"

The two days that followed were hectic. Still, Julian was right; the authorities couldn't deny him this favor. It all went as he had asked. Two hours before that early evening crusade, an ambulance carrying Adrian and a limo carrying Julian and Joan rolled out onto the soccer field.

The authorities took every precaution. Security was very tight, and paramedics, nurses, and a doctor were right there on the field in the event that something unforeseen occurred. As evening fell and the field lights came on, Julien was prepared for a miracle.

The setup on the stage was very different from that of the evangelist in America. There were no elaborate props, no whirling metal globes or flashing lights, just a simple lectern, about a dozen microphones, and a single banner with the emblem of

Lusan's organization. It sort of reminded Julien of the flag of the United Nations. A camera linked to the stadium's large screen would allow the crowd to get a clear picture of the one they came to see, this worker of miracles.

The crowd was quickly filling in the seats of the gigantic outdoor stadium. It was estimated that there could well be 40,000 on hand tonight. The 20,000 chairs on the field represented about half of the stadium's capacity. But Julien had his mind upon just one, Lusan.

Julien and his entourage had attracted quite a bit of attention. Yes, there were other sick people here. There were people on crutches and in wheelchairs, but none in quite so serious a condition as Adrien. The area around them had been cordoned off for their safety, and an escape route had been cleared if a quick exit were required.

Julien knew only too well that his coming here had complicated an already difficult job for the police and stadium security. Few people in France would have had the influence to have pulled off this last-minute stunt.

When Lusan did arrive, he did so without any obvious fanfare. He walked with about 30 others from the far end of the field. The crowd watched in silent wonder as they approached. He wore a simple business suit, as did the other men in his company. All of the suits were identical. The 12 women who accompanied them all wore long pink dresses, also identical.

To Julien, they looked like members of some sort of fundamentalist cult. Already he was questioning his motives for coming here. It was all based on the fleeting dreams of a desperate father. Might doing this make matters worse for his son? No, he couldn't think like that. Belief was an important element of the healing event. That was what that evangelist had told him in America.

The program opened up with singing by Lusan's 24-member chorus. Their song selections were, to say the least, unusual for a crusade. They opened with "We Are the World," only to follow it up with the modern Christian hymn, "God is Love." All the while, Julien waited impatiently. He often glanced over to confirm that his son was stable. It had been a long time since he'd been out in the open air, and it was not a particularly warm February evening.

It was the mayor of Marseille himself who introduced Lusan. That in itself struck Julien as being strange. The mayor was a devout Catholic, and this Lusan was anything but. If any term described the nature of Lusan's beliefs, it was New Age.

Lusan was a dynamic speaker. There was no doubt about that. He opened with the traditional thanks to the mayor and the events committee that had made this rally possible. Then he spoke of the state of the world, the need to discard racial prejudices and ethnic hate. He spoke of their being many ways to God and of a new age of enlightenment.

One of the things that attracted the crowd's attention was the fact that he addressed them in fluent French rather than using an interpreter. Yet, quite abruptly, he stopped. What followed was a good 20 seconds of total silence, followed by growing rumbling from the crowd.

"Before I continue, before I speak further of the coming golden age or pray for God's healing power upon the multitudes of sick people among us tonight, there is a special blessing that God Himself wishes to bestow upon one of your number," said Lusan. "You see, there is one here among you that will be at the heart of the new and better Earth that is coming. He is a man who is touched by God's spirit, a man whom God has already used and will use again. But he has a need that must be met first. Our Heavenly Father is about to grant that need." Lusan seemed to be looking directly at Julien. "It is not just to clear the way for your own ministry, but to give this congregation of people proof of God's power. Please, come forth. Bring your petition before the throne of God."

Julian's actions were impulsive. He reached to pick up his son and carried him up the steps and onto the stage. He brought him directly to Lusan.

The cameras zoomed in on the gathering. The tension mounted.

"Julien Devereux, you have a task to perform," said Lusan. "God is with you, and as confirmation, so there can be no doubt, your son must be made whole."

Lusan touched Adrian's forehead. "Awake, young man," he said. "Awake and be whole."

The cameras zoomed in even closer. There was no sound of thunder, no flash of light, but Julien felt something. It was like a darkness had been lifted. Abruptly the boy coughed; then his eyes opened. His gaze turned to his father. Their eyes met. Yes, they really met. There was depth to those eyes, not a blank stare. The slightest of smiles came to Adrian's face."

"Daddy, the sun doesn't really make the sea boil when it sets, does it?" asked Adrien.

Julien looked at his son in total astonishment even as tears of joy flowed from his eyes. "No, Adrien, I was just making a joke, that's all."

"I thought so," replied his son. "I feel like I've been asleep for a long time. I've woken up a couple of times, but I couldn't move or speak. I remember you saying the thing about the sun and about the trip to Africa. I do want to go to Africa."

"And so you shall," cried his father, holding his son tightly. "We'll go there together."

The crowd's response was one of amazement. Yes, they'd heard about this boy, the son of a national hero. Word was that his condition was terminal, that his mind was gone. Now, here he was in his right mind and talking. It was a miracle like none had ever seen before. After a moment, a growing applause erupted from the multitude, and it continued for two minutes.

"It is the return of the Lord," cried a man in the front row, falling to his knees.

"No," cried Lusan. "I am not the Lord. I am just His messenger, a prophet, no more. I serve the living God, and so should you. Let me show you how, all of you. Let me bring power into your lives. I tell you this, the age of miracles has returned."

When Lusan was finished speaking, over 10,000 came forward for prayer and healing, and still more miracles were seen. Yet, to Julien, this was all anti-climactic. Julien had his son back. He was in Lusan's debt, and he intended to repay that debt.

The service had been over for nearly an hour as Julien waited for Lusan outside of one of the meeting rooms below the stadium. Lusan had requested to meet him, and Julien would not deny the request of the man who had given back to him his son. A security guard opened the door, and Julien headed in to meet Lusan one on one.

The room contained a long, wooden table with 12 comfortable chairs surrounding it. At the end of the table sat Lusan. He still wore his suit, though he had loosened his tie a bit.

"I want to thank you for what you've done for my son," said Julien. "Mere words can hardly express what I'm feeling right now."

Lusan smiled broadly, extending his hand. "I assure you, it was my pleasure to have been an instrument of the Eternal Father. Please, Mr. Devereux, sit here beside me. We have much to discuss."

Julien sat beside Lusan. There was something about this man. Julien had long prided himself on being able to read people at a glance, but he had never been in the presence of someone like this. What was he sensing in his presence, power?

"And how is your son feeling?" asked Lusan. "Is he experiencing any unpleasant side effects from his long illness?"

"It's strange," replied Julien. "He remembers very little of his illness. He knows that he has been sick, but he found it difficult to believe how much time has passed. He remembers only bits and pieces of the past couple of years." Julien chuckled. "You know, it's funny. The last thing he remembered was a funny little story I told him three days ago about the setting sun causing the ocean to boil with its heat. He thought I'd told him that story just a few minutes ago."

Lusan laughed openly. "I was wondering about that. It was such an unusual comment. Now it makes sense."

"Actually, I'm glad he doesn't remember," continued Julien. "Really, I am. There were so many unpleasant things that happened these past two years. He complains that his legs feel week. He is having a bit of trouble walking. But I'm surprised that he can walk at all after so long."

"I'm sure that weakness will pass," said Lusan. "God performs complete healings, not partial ones."

"But where did you get this power?" asked Julien. "I've never seen a true miracle, that is, until this evening. There is no other way to explain it. Look, I'm not a bad man, but I'm not a religious man either."

Lusan laughed, placing his hand on Julian's shoulder. "Oh Julian, I don't ask you to be a religious man; neither does God. You have it right, my friend. You need but be a good man, and you are that, a very good man. But now God does ask something of you. He asks you to stand bold and resume the course. Too many people in Europe have lost faith. It is my task to help them find that faith. It is your task to bring peace and prosperity to them. You know what this is leading to, do you not?"

Julien nodded. "Yes, I think so. For the first time there is to be a real president of the European Union. It will still be a figurehead position, really, the union is too loosely knit. But whoever holds it will have the eyes of the world upon him. You want me to run for the position, don't you?"

"Not me, but God," replied Lusan. "Indeed, before Adrian's sickness you desired it. Desiring it is not wrong; it is essential. You must pull this continent's people together, Julien. Europeans must be as one. You have a gentle and just heart. No one else can do this thing. A thousand years from now, your children's descendants shall point to this day and say this is when and where it started. This is when Earth's people began to act as one, act for the common good."

"You seem so sure of what I should do," replied Julien. "I don't even know."

"I think the time has come for me to reveal something to you," said Lusan. "It is a thing that only a handful of people know. But you must swear to keep my secret. It is a thing that humanity is not ready to know. But you must know it. You must know that the goal you strive for is a higher calling. Do I have your word, Julian?"

"Yes, of course," replied Julien.

Lusan rose from his seat and stood away from the table. In a second his form had changed from one of a middle-aged man to a winged angel in white. Never had Julien seen a being so beautiful. He sat there in stunned silence.

"Now you know how it is that I know of God's intentions in such detail. I have stood before Him, heard His words. I've been sent here to guide humanity through this dark time. You must take command. With the light of knowledge in hand, you must start humanity on the long journey into the light. No other man can do it. You are God's man, like Abraham, Moses, or Jesus."

"How can I be like Jesus?" asked Julien. "Isn't He the Son of God?"

"Yes," confirmed Lusan, "and so are you. You need to allow God to perfect you. You need to be sensitive to His will." Lusan assumed the appearance of a middle-aged man once more. "Are you ready to open the way to a bright future?"

"I am," confirmed Julien. "Let's get started."

By the next morning the airwaves and papers were filled with the events that had occurred in the Stade Vélodrome the evening before in front of tens of thousands of people. It was inexplicable. In addition, it had been watched by millions on television.

Julien and his son were mobbed by the media. In but 24 hours, Adrien had regained his equilibrium and was running about the house and on the beach as he had before the terrible affliction had befallen him. Doctors confirmed that he had suffered no ill effects from his bout with a supposedly incurable disease. They sought to find a logical and reasonable explanation for what had happened, but there was none—that is, none beyond the invisible hand of God.

Even the usually reserved Joan was proclaiming the greatness of the new messiah, Lusan. Lusan had found a pair of new converts.

A week later, Julien Devereux announced that he would be a candidate for the president of the European Union after all. As soon as he, Joan, and his son had an opportunity to go on an African safari, he would begin actively campaigning for the office. Even with his late entry into the race, the best polls showed Julien with a 15-point lead over his nearest rival.

And Lusan's European tour went on. Dozens of cameras had caught the miracle of Adrien Devereux. It was played again and again for the world to see.

In Paris, Lusan spoke to a packed house. In Hamburg, people practically fell over each other to get a glimpse of this man with healing in his hands. In each country, in every city where he spoke, the attendees did not walk away disappointed. Miracles followed Lusan even more so than they had during his American tour.

In a continent whose churches had been practically empty for so long, the new spiritual zeal was a thing of wonder to behold. Rumors and evidence of all manner of miracles spread far and wide.

By the time Lusan's European crusade was complete, he had become the most talked about spiritual leader in the past thousand years. He had filled stadium after stadium with people who shared one thing in common; they were searching for spiritual meaning to their lives.

And following Lusan came other people from his organization—church organizers who established congregations across the continent, some within the walls of previously abandoned Christian churches. This New Age faith was sweeping Europe like an unquenchable wildfire. Yet it was not a fire that was kindled only in the hearts of agnostics and atheists. It fed upon disenchanted Christians, Muslims, and Jews—those who could not find peace with the faith of their youth. Now, Lusan had given them something to believe in, and they would cling to it.

Yet the new faith had its detractors as well. The aging Pope denounced him for preaching that man could be saved by his own works, for failing to recognize that only through God's Son Jesus was there salvation. Yet nowhere was that opposition as strong as in the community of what many branded the fundamentalist Christians. To them, Lusan was a false prophet, perhaps even the false prophet spoken of in the Book of Revelation.

They even questioned the validity of the miracles he had performed. Perhaps Satan was casting out Satan. Perhaps his ministry was a gambit aimed at securing power and prestige for his kingdom. If this was true, it had been an effective strategy.

Many new converts believed the Christians were taking a sour grapes philosophy. The fruits of their great leaders paled in comparison to what Lusan had provided a spiritually hungry world. The great revival that had filled the Christian Church just two years ago was fading, overshadowed by this new ministry. Indeed, resentment was beginning to build against the Church even as congregations waned.

Lusan was in his glory. His plans were proceeding better than he had dared to hope. Perhaps he would never be a prince of Heaven, but he might well be a Prince of the Earth. Prince of this world—the Christians had long referred to him as such. How very ironic. It was an undeserved title until now. His physical form had been trapped in the middle of Outer Darkness on the world of Hell for thousands of years. He was unable to ascend to an earthly throne.

Prince of this Earth—he liked the sound of it. First he would need to see to it that Julien Devereux ascended to the throne of Europe. Then he would investigate the possibility of assuming an even higher office. Perhaps he would fulfill their prophecy yet.

CHAPTER 12

Chris and Serena were at a citywide revival at the State Coliseum in Jackson, Mississippi, when word reached them of the goings on at the Stade Vélodrome in Marseilles. They felt so helpless. They were certain that Lusan's miracles were not authentic. It was more like Satan casting out Satan. Still, he was producing signs and wonders for the people to see, and millions of people were moving into his camp, buying the spiritual snake oil he was selling.

During the eight years of their ministry, they had prayed with so many people. They'd prayed for their salvation, answers to problems, and even healing. Yet they had never seen the kind of miracles that Lusan was producing. They doubted that anyone had. Yes, the world was looking for miraculous signs and wonders, and if Lusan seemed to have a monopoly on them, the people would flock to him.

Tomorrow was the last day of the citywide crusade. There would easily be 5,000 people in attendance. If only God would move in that meeting in a mighty way. They needed a world-class miracle about now. Yes, they were seeing lives changed at this revival. They were seeing people giving their hearts to Christ for the first time, while still others were rededicating themselves to His service. These were the really important miracles. But they needed something more. Chris and Serena prayed for it night after night. They were watching their world plunge into a dark hole, a pit of ignorance, yet there was nothing that they could do, at least not yet.

The last days, the thing they had warned so many people about for so long, was finally coming to pass. If only there was some way around this tragedy, but there wasn't. It had been building for the entire history of humanity on Earth. Their only hope was to appeal to a higher power. There was no help to be found here on Earth.

Serena awoke from a bed of moss in a cool, misty forest. She looked about. In the high treetops she could see the light of the morning sun reflected in the branches. She rose to her feet. She was still barefoot and in her nightgown. She was hardly prepared for a walk in the woods. But wait, this place was familiar. She'd been here before several months ago.

"Chris?" she called out. There was no reply.

A moment later she heard a branch snap. Someone was moving out there in the mists. Serena grew very quiet.

"Serena," said a voice from the mists. It was a woman's voice and a familiar one at that.

"I'm over here," said Serena. "Is that you, Claire?"

"Sure is," said the voice.

Serena could see an outline emerge from the mists. Yet it was not one, but two people. A few seconds later, Claire stood before her. She was decked out all in white and had a young black child who appeared to be about 12 at her side. Like Serena, the young man was in his pajamas.

"It's good to see you again," said Serena.

"Oh, same here, dear," said Claire, giving Serena a hug. "Oh, and this is my good friend, Mark. He's from Mississippi."

"How do you do, Mark," said Serena extending her hand.

"I'm really good right now, ma'am," said Mark, shaking Serena's hand.

"But you weren't just a few minutes ago," said Claire, looking over at Mark.

"No ma'am, I wasn't," confirmed Mark. "I was hurt real bad in a bus accident when I was eight. My back got broken, and I haven't been able to walk ever since. But I'm better here in Heaven."

"That's wonderful," said Serena. "How long have you been here?"

"Oh, just a few minutes," said Mark. "But I gotta go back to Earth so I can meet you."

"So you can meet me?" asked Serena, who seemed a bit confused.

"Oh, he's still crippled," confirmed Claire, "at least for now. You see, like you, he's just a visitor here. We've had a real nice talk, haven't we, Mark?"

"Yes ma'am," confirmed Mark, looking toward Claire. "I like Heaven a lot. Especially if it has nice people like you in it."

"It has lots of nice people like me," confirmed Claire, but you're not coming here to live just yet. You have a few things to do on Earth first." She turned to Serena. "I've got news for you. Today is the last day of your revival in Mississippi. But it's going to end with a bang. The Father has heard your plea and has sent me to talk to you. Mark is going to walk again. The Father is going to use you as His healing vessel. Don't be afraid. Be bold."

Yes, be bold," echoed Mark. "Please, I want to walk again. I want to go fishing and playing with my friends again."

There was an almost pleading aspect to Mark's request. It brought a tear to Serena's eye. "You will, Mark. I promise."

"Well, time to go," announced Claire, looking to Mark. "I'll see you again, soon, OK?"

"OK," said Mark.

A second later, Mark vanished from their midst.

"Wow," said Serena.

"OK," continued Claire, taking a deep breath. "I didn't want Mark here when I told you this. You must understand that this precious gift from God carries with it certain consequences on Earth. Lusan is not going to like it one bit. He'll blow a gasket. He'll see you as trying to steal his spotlight. He may even come after you."

"Nothing new about that," confirmed Serena. "There's been bad blood between the two of us for a very long time. But, I guess you know that."

"Yes," confirmed Claire. "I know."

"I just want to serve God," replied Serena. "I'll do whatever it takes, no matter what."

Claire's smile broadened. "Oh, dear, I know you would, and so does the Father." She gazed up. "It's time for you to wake up."

Serena nodded. A second later, she was in the RV. Morning sunlight was streaming through the window. She looked over at Chris. For some reason, he'd been left out of this journey. She wouldn't wake him. Furthermore, she wouldn't tell him about this visitation, at least not yet. She would wait and see what this evening's service would bring.

It was the better part of an hour before Chris woke up. They had their morning devotions and then went shopping for groceries. The day went slowly, and neither of them seemed to be in very talkative moods.

The revival started at six, but they were there two hours early. A different evangelist or preacher had spoken each night. As the Lord would have it, Chris and Serena were scheduled to speak tonight. Following that, there was to be an altar call.

The people started arriving just before five. Serena scanned the crowd in search of Mark, but she couldn't pick him out, at least not yet. Still, it was a large place, and she could easily have missed him.

Never had she been so nervous before a meeting. She'd spoken to crowds of this size before, but never had so much been riding on a meeting. She scanned the crowd again. She figured that she had underestimated how many people would be in attendance. The place was nearly full.

At six sharp, the service opened with music. There was old-time gospel, country music, even rock, with the new Christian rock band Glory. Yet, all of it glorified the name of Jesus. The people were excited and that excitement was growing with every song. Something was in the air, and the people could feel it.

It was just after 7:00 when Chris and Serena took the stage. They spoke of their experience beyond this life, eight years ago. They spoke of the wonders of Heaven and the terrors of Hell. It was not so different from many of the other services they had had over the years, at least at first. It was near the end of their message that Chris spoke of a dream he'd had the previous night. It was a revelation that caught Serena totally by surprise.

"I found myself in what appeared to be the private quarters of the prince of a great nation," he began. "The prince sat at the bed of his beloved son who was gravely ill. He spoke words of comfort to him, though he knew that his son could not hear them. What he wouldn't have given to have his son's health restored. As it was, his life would surely end, and soon. Then a man in flowing robes entered the room. He had the looks of an ancient alchemist, or a wizard of some sort, dressed all in black. He told the prince that he could restore his son to health, but there would be a price. The day would come, once the prince had become king, that he would ask a favor of him; he would ask to be the advisor of the new monarch. He would ask him to accept his council in matters of spirit and state."

Chris paused, looking out over the multitude that listened in silence. He stepped to the very edge of the stage. His eyes seemed so intense.

"But you see, the prince was desperate. Nothing in this entire world meant more to him than the life of his son. He agreed immediately to this stranger's terms. With no more than a touch, the stranger restored his son's health. Then he departed. But all was not as it seemed. You see, the stranger, this evil wizard, had agents within the palace all along, agents who had been slowly poisoning the boy. It was they who were behind his illness. The sly wizard had administered an antidote to the boy. So, you see, he was the author of both the disease and the cure."

Again Chris was on the move, making eye contact with as many people in the crowd as he could as he walked along the edge of the stage. Serena was astonished. Never had she seen her husband so totally inspired. At meetings, he was usually the quieter one, but not this time. She very much enjoyed what she was seeing.

"Then, the time came when the prince ascended to the throne. And on that day, the dark wizard returned. He had the new king's ear when it came to matters of the spirit. He poisoned his mind when it came to dealing with God's own people. Though it was the king's words that ruled the land, it was the wizard's plans that he was promoting. An otherwise good king had become an unwitting pawn in the hands of this darkest of all people. Through the king's own popularity, the evil one beguiled all but a few people within the great kingdom. In the end, the people turned away from the light, preferring the darkness. Indeed, they held those who chose the path of light in great contempt.

"For a time, the kingdom was prosperous. Then a great natural catastrophe fell upon the kingdom. Yet rather than turn to the light in that hour, the people were plunged even further into the darkness. They hated God's people, persecuting them in ways that had not been seen since the light entered the world. Yet at the height of the persecution, the people of God vanished and no one could explain it."

Again, Chris paused. There was now an undercurrent that echoed throughout the arena. Did the people hear and understand what Chris was talking about?

"Then I found myself standing on a hilltop, overlooking a battlefield," he continued. "Two great armies were approaching the field of battle, one from the north and one from the east. There were trumpets blowing and drums rolling. It was like a battle out of the past, not the current age. The soldiers of the army coming out of the north were all dressed in the deepest blue uniforms, while the army from the east wore orange. They were huge armies, millions of men, and even women, marching in precision like a well-trained army might in a parade.

"It was then that I noticed an angel in white standing beside me. He was like any of the angels I saw in Heaven. I didn't recognize him, but he was clearly one of Michael's minions. I asked him what it was that I was witnessing. Who were these soldiers, and why were they going to war? He told me that the army in blue was led by the beguiled king, while the army in orange marching out of the east had come out of Asia. They were fighting over the few resources that could still be found on this dying, polluted Earth, an Earth that was reaping what it had sown—the judgment of the Most High God. Yet before the armies could unleash the last of their mighty weapons, the children of God, along with God's firstborn, returned. The days of terror had to be cut short before all life vanished from this world."

Chris returned to the pulpit, to his wife's side. Serena was so proud of him. Truly, his words had been inspired of God. Yet his final point was yet to be made.

"I tell you this," concluded Chris. "This path to the end of the age has already been set in motion. This Wizard of darkness is already among us. Never before has there been more of a reason to be strong. Walk close to the Lord; accept His council. People, the clock is ticking."

The words of this evening's speaker had been bold, bolder than any that had come before it. It left the crowd in shock and wonder. It was time for the altar call. Twenty-three pastors and evangelists took the stage to pray over the sick and to help those in need. A great multitude came forth. Yet Serena was looking for only one person, a young man by the name of Mark.

Then she saw him. He was in a wheelchair being pushed up the ramp onto the stage by a young woman who might have been his mother. Serena rushed toward him. Almost immediately their eyes met.

"You're really here," he said, tears coming to his eyes. "It wasn't just a dream; you're really here."

"Yes I am," said Serena, "Nice to see you again, Mark."

The woman pushing the wheel chair seemed surprised. "I'm Mark's mother, Martha," she announced. "My son has been saying all day that he had to come here, that he had to see you. The two of you haven't met before. I'm quite sure of it."

"No, we haven't," replied Serena, "at least, not exactly."

"We met in a dream," replied Mark.

"That's right," confirmed Serena.

Martha's eyes opened wide. "But that was just a dream," she objected.

Already, Serena had placed her hand on Mark's head. Never in her life had she uttered the words that she was about to say. It was bold, expecting a miracle. Yet, Serena had total faith. "Mark, in the name of Jesus Christ of Nazareth, rise up and walk."

Serena gazed up to see the cameras all focused on her. Her microphone had carried her words for all to hear. Well, this was it, the moment of truth.

Yet, if Serena had no doubt about the miracle to come, Mark had even less. He took a deep breath and pushed himself up out of the wheelchair. Serena took his hand and pulled him forward.

"No," said Martha, who reached out in an attempt to keep her son from falling.

But he didn't fall. He stumbled for two steps then stabilized himself. He was standing on his own two feet, a thing he hadn't done since the accident.

"I can feel my legs!" he cried, "I can feel them."

The whole house turned to the boy who now stood steady on his feet. He took a step, then another. His steps were steady and deliberate. He walked another five paces, turned around and went straight into Serena's arms.

"I can walk! I can walk!" he cried. "Thank you, Jesus! I can walk!"

At this point the entire crowd was turned toward the exuberant youth and the woman whose hand had brought about the miracle. Serena was unprepared as a young man of about 25 with a white cane in hand was led to her by a young woman.

"Please, ma'am, I saw what just happened. Lay hands on my husband, please," pleaded the young woman.

Serena realized that she should probably have anticipated this. What now? She hadn't seen this man in a vision. Would God honor her prayers for him? She had to believe that He would.

"I'm right here," she said to the blind man, touching him on the forehead. "Do you believe that God, through His Holy Spirit, can restore your sight?"

"I believe," confirmed the man. "Oh how I believe. I just want to see the world. I never have, but I've been told that it's beautiful."

Serena hesitated, and then touched his eyes. "In the name of Jesus Christ, see the world."

A moment passed. The man spun around, his eyes darting back and forth. "It's getting brighter. Everywhere, it's getting brighter. Oh my Lord!" He turned directly to Serena; their eyes met. "I can see you! Oh, praise Jesus!" He spun around. "I can see all of you!"

More people came to Serena—people with cancer and heart disease, people whose conditions had been diagnosed as terminal, people who knew they had only one chance to live. Serena laid hands on every one of them. Pain vanished immediately, limbs straightened and strengthened. She could not be certain that healing had occurred in all cases, but she believed it. By the end of the night, she had prayed for over a hundred people with ailments ranging from arthritis to broken bones. When it was all finished, she felt thoroughly drained, yet oh so good.

As the meeting ended, people were still singing as they filed out of the arena.

They praised God for his mercy and goodness. They had been witnesses to such miracles. Surely God had been in this arena tonight.

"We need to work on our communication," noted Chris, as they drove back to the RV. "No secrets, OK?"

"OK," said Serena, "no secrets."

Right now, Serena was on top of the world. Over the next weeks, she got word that no fewer than eight full remissions from cancer had occurred on that evening. In addition, doctors had confirmed the restoration of a defective heart valve, arthritis vanishing from joints, and broken bones mending by themselves.

Still more healings were documented at the hands of Serena Davis at a revival in Louisiana the following week and at three in Texas during the two weeks following that. Suddenly, the world had two great healers in its midst.

In addition, the bold prophetic words of Serena's husband also made the rounds in the media. Those in Lusan's organization were quick to pick up on the not-so-subtle innuendo, and they were not pleased. An official representative from their camp, a woman by the name of Krissie James, called it just another example of fundamentalist Christian prejudice.

"There are many ways to God," insisted Krissie. "Surely the miracles we are seeing in our time confirm this. God loves all who seek Him, regardless of their route to salvation. We don't need haters in our presence. We all need to pull together."

Haters in our presence—it was Krissie James who first quoted that phrase to describe the fundamentalist Christians who opposed their organization. The term would be used many more times. The world was weighing in on the happenings of the past few months, and they were far from united in their beliefs.

In America people were divided on the issue. Some thought all miracles were trickery, a huge and elaborate scheme designed to win over converts. Still, even more seemed to be coming down on the side of Chris and Serena Davis, the evangelists from Oregon. Their message was, after all, a traditional American message of faith in Christ. It was what this nation was founded on. Even in England, where Chris and Serena had toured a year before and would be returning again come spring, public opinion was leaning in their direction.

Yet on the continent, the viewpoint was somewhat different. There Lusan found greater support. The people of Europe had given Christianity a chance for nearly 2,000 years. Perhaps it was time to explore some other avenue to God.

From their viewpoint, they were surrounded by extremists. To the east and south were the Islamic fundamentalists who were determined to win the world for Allah by the sword if need be. To the west were the Christian fundamentalists and their equally radical agenda. These two factions were quite capable of destroying the world to keep the other from getting it.

In Rome, despite his impassioned pleas for people to remain loyal to the church, the Holy Father of the Roman Catholic Church now found himself on a continent where the support of the people for the faith of their parents and grandparents was waning at an incredible rate. In Northern Europe, he presided over essentially empty churches. Things in the south were not much better. His faith was the faith of a shrinking minority.

Still, it seemed that in a crisis the Christian community was pulling together like never before. There was word of other great healers rising up within the Christian community. A Catholic priest in South Africa was also performing miraculous acts of healing. Thousands were descending on his services every Sunday and Wednesday in hopes of being a recipient of a miracle from God. An elder at a Mormon church in Globe, Arizona, had also experienced a revelation from God, and the gift of great healing could be found in his hands as well. Then there was the Baptist preacher in China who had created a great stir with her miracles of healing.

It was at a large revival in Kansas City that two envoys from the Pope met with Chris and Serena. Chris and Serena were amazed to hear of the Holy Father's enthusiastic support for their work. Indeed, the Pope had issued an invitation to the couple to come to the Vatican for a visit, a private audience with him. It was an invitation that Chris and Serena quickly and graciously accepted. What an honor! Their current crusade would be ending in just another week. They would meet the Holy Father at the end of March.

"Keep in mind, the Holy Father is in remarkably good health for his age," continued Father Giavani, as he escorted Chris and Serena down the bright and ornate hallway toward the Pope's private quarters in the Vatican. "Still, he tends to tire easily. The past year has not been particularly kind to him or the Church."

"I can imagine," replied Chris, looking about at the magnificence of this place.

"Lord forgive me," continued Giavani, "but this Lusan is the Devil himself."

That comment surprised Serena. "You mean the real Devil, Satan?"

"I mean no other," replied Father Giavani. "These are dangerous times we live in, my friends. The Holy Father is only too aware of it." Giavani paused, then stopped right there in his tracks. He turned to face Serena. "Signora Davis, you of all people must surely recognize him."

Serena too hesitated, though for but a couple seconds. "Yes, Father Giavani, I do. He has the same face, the same eyes. Yes, it's him."

Giavani nodded. "I know it must be difficult for you, signora, after the terrible thing he did to you. Knowing that he is here on Earth must be deeply disturbing."

"Very disturbing," confirmed Serena.

They continued on. Again Father Giavani turned to Serena. "I am sure that I don't need to remind you that everything that the two of you and the Holy Father discuss is strictly confidential. It must never leave this place."

"Of course," replied Serena.

The three passed another security officer, the third that they had met on this journey. The security guard opened a double door, and they entered a large and beautifully furnished room. Three chairs sat in a circle near the far end of the room, and in the center chair sat the pontiff himself. An aide dressed in black stood at his side.

The aide assisted the Pope to his feet as Chris and Serena approached him. The Pope had a wonderful, beaming smile that made Chris and Serena Davis feel so much at ease.

"Oh my children, it is so good to finally meet you," said the Pope at the two drew still closer. "Please, sit at my side. We have much to discuss."

Chris and Serena sat on either side of the pontiff.

"Thank you, Father Giavani. You and Mr. Anderson may leave us now, I'll be fine."

"Yes, your eminence," they replied practically in unison, making their way to the door.

"We'll be just outside," said Father Giavani, as he closed the door behind them.

"I trust that the two of you had a pleasant flight," began the pontiff. "Rome is beautiful this time of year. I hope that the two of you get to spend some time here."

"Yes, a most pleasant flight," confirmed Serena, "and yes, we plan to stay five days.

"Very good," said the Pope, scanning his two guests. "I've read your book. I read it from cover to cover several years ago, and again just last week. I want to assure you that I believe every word of it. The two of you have had an incredible experience and returned to tell of it. Surely our Father has a grand plan for you."

"I'd certainly like to think so, your eminence," said Chris.

"Know so," he replied. "I have no doubt of it." There was a pause. "I understand that the two of you are members of the Pentecostal movement, that you are firm believers in the gifts of the Holy Spirit, having received the baptism thereof."

"We have," confirmed Chris and Serena simultaneously.

"As have I," replied the Pontiff. "The fact that you are not members of the Roman Catholic Church is of no importance to me. You are blessed children of God, a part of the Body of Christ, as am I. I wanted you to know that from the beginning." Again the Pope paused. "I had a visitation just over two weeks ago, a dream. My visitor was someone with whom I believe you are already familiar. Her name is Claire."

Serena was astonished. "Yes, we've met her, too."

"She explained that to me," confirmed the pontiff. "She told me something that I already suspected; I shall be the last pontiff of this church. There will be no more. The last days are upon us, my children, and the Beast is already among us." He turned to Chris. "You said it to the world when you spoke of your own dream, your vision, in Mississippi. You realize who Lusan is."

"He is Satan in human form," announced Chris.

"He is indeed," confirmed the pontiff.

"He has already tried to kill us at least once since his arrival on Earth," said Serena.

"That doesn't surprise me," he confirmed. "I also understand that the two of you are in possession of some remarkable letters, delivered to you by an angel two years ago. If the contents are not too personal, I would like to know what you were told. I need to know the score, as you Americans put it. I need to know what we are dealing with. What you tell me shall stall stay with me and me alone. Then I shall share with you an incredible secret that may be of help to you."

"We thought you might be interested in the letters," confirmed Chris, pulling a large envelope from his pocket. "These are copies of the originals. They are yours to keep and study."

"Thank you," said the Pope, opening the envelope and briefly scanning its contents. "Remarkable," he said. "We have many incredible documents within our library. However, I doubt that we have anything more precious than this. I shall treasure these words from beyond this life."

For over half an hour, Chris and Serena spoke of the War in Heaven, of the struggle of Abaddon and his followers in Hell, and of the fall of Satan to Earth. They spoke of their trip to the Middle East and of the oil well that was a gate into another reality. They held nothing back from the pontiff; they told it all. The Pope asked but a few questions during the telling. When it was all told, he was deeply troubled.

"Yes," he confirmed. "I suspected as much. Satan is a clever opponent. Do either of you play chess?"

"A little bit," said Chris. "But Serena is the chess player of the family. She is really quite good."

The Pope chuckled. "I'm not surprised. She has the mannerisms of a good chess player. I deduced that much from your book. I used to play. Not so much anymore. The demands of this office are considerable. But let me get to the point. Like a good chess player, Satan is maneuvering his pieces for the end game. There is a reason behind everything he is doing, every move. Yes, he is trying to gain converts, but there is more to it than that. We must somehow deduce what he is really up to. We have two means at our disposal."

The Pope reached down to recover a small book from the floor at his side. It had been placed in a protective plastic cover. He gingerly pulled the small yellowing document from the plastic.

"This is a one-of-a-kind document," he continued. "It made its way from a monastery in Switzerland to the Vatican back in 1681. It has been in the Vatican Archives ever since. It is written in old German. I wish to read to you a passage from its pages. I will do my best to translate it. It is important that you know its contents, you more than anyone else. Only a few people know about it."

The pontiff pulled out his reading glasses, squinting at the document. "In those last days there shall come a young maiden, fair of face and strong of spirit. Yet her heart will be hard, like unto her mother's. For this reason she shall be carried to the very depths of Hell, there to be thrown into a great ocean of fire to suffer for her transgressions. Yet she shall call out to the Lord, and He shall in time hear her plea and take pity upon her. He shall deliver her from the fires and hide her among the rocks, within a cave. He shall appoint His servant to watch over her. And in the passage of days, the Lord God will remember her again. He will return her to the land of the living and charge her with a solemn duty—to give witness to what she has seen and expose the ways of the dragon and his angels."

The pontiff paused, adjusting his glasses. Serena's eyes had taken on a wide almost unbelieving stare. It sounded like he was talking about her.

"Let me read on," said the pontiff, "She shall free many captives. She shall make the lame walk and the blind to see with but a touch of her hand. She shall turn many from the road to Hell, depriving the dragon of that which he desires. For this, the dragon will be greatly angered and shall strike out at her, the one who had escaped him. He will threaten her with her life, threaten her with the pains of Hell. Yet she will turn neither to the left nor the right. Her life will be an example to many, both the quick and the dead. Even the souls of the lost would come to her aid if it were but possible. In the fullness of years she shall, through her suffering, deliver many, opening the gates wide to paradise. The lost shall find peace." The pontiff put down the manuscript. "Does this woman sound like anyone you know?"

Serena was absolutely pale. Indeed, she was shaking.

The pontiff placed a gentle hand on her shoulder. "Are you all right, my dear?"

"Yes," she said, in a trembling voice. "It sounds like they're talking about me. But that was written back in 1681."

"No child, not in 1681. It was brought here in 1681. About 15 years ago, we decided to have a small piece of this parchment and many others carbon dated, as we did the shroud. The paper dated back to the ninth century. It was copied from a still earlier manuscript. The original manuscript may be much older. We believe that the original manuscript may have been written by John of Patmos in the first century, the author of the Book of Revelation. Serena, in all ways you fit the description of the woman spoken of in this manuscript. The events of the past month leave me no doubt whatever."

"It's incredible," said Chris.

"Perhaps," replied the pontiff, "but keep in mind God's time is not our time. Child, this task was set out for you long before you were born. Forgive the use of the word, but it is very likely an issue of destiny. You are a part of God's grand plan; both of you are."

"There is something I don't understand, your eminence," said Chris. "Why has this document remained hidden for so long?"

The Pope smiled broadly. "That is a good question. Why do you think it was so?"

Chris hesitated. "Was it because it was a prophecy about a woman being a deliverer?"

"To a certain degree," said the Pontiff. "But that is not the only reason."

"It almost sounds like it's saying that there might be hope for the damned souls of Hell," said Serena.

"It does sound like that, doesn't it?" said the Pope. "In the Apocalypse of Peter, we find yet another passage that seems to imply that some of those who now suffer in Hell might find some sort of release, perhaps even redemption in the last days. If you read the entire manuscript, you can clearly see where it might be controversial."

"But I thought that there were no complete copies of the Apocalypse of Peter in existence," said Chris.

"Aren't there?" posed the Pontiff.

"Before you leave, if you wish, I will see to it that you have the opportunity to read it from cover to cover," said the pontiff. "We have translated it into English. I believe you would find it enlightening."

"That would be wonderful," said Chris.

"Therein we find the problem," continued the Pontiff. "The Church has long proclaimed that there is no escape from Hell. Thus, we have the doctrine of Purgatory. It has given us a reason for hope for departed loved ones. The faith of the Church concerning purgatory is clearly expressed in the Decree of Union drawn up by the Council of Florence in 1031. Most Protestant denominations dismiss the concept of Purgatory as little more than wishful thinking, as did many of our church fathers. I once had strong reservations regarding the doctrine of Purgatory, but not anymore." He turned to Serena. "From what I have heard, you might indeed be the author of Purgatory, as surely as Abaddon is its ruler. Perhaps this place they call Refuge is just that. It is a way back to the grace of God. It is a difficult road, but it is far preferable to the alternative."

"Incredible," said Chris. "It all makes sense."

"But that doesn't necessarily make it true," cautioned the Pope. "Though we might like to believe it for the sake of so many lost souls, it might just be wishful thinking."

"I want to believe it, too," said Serena. "There are so many people I met in Hell, people that really deserve a second chance. Many of them are in Refuge now."

"As I'm sure Father Giavani told you, I tire rather quickly these days," continued the pontiff. "There is something else that I wanted you to be aware of. My head of security will give you a full briefing on it, but I wanted to touch upon it briefly before we part company. The Vatican is truly a separate country unto itself. As such, we have access to certain Interpol and FBI files. There are people keeping an eye on Lusan and his dealings. Did you know that he bought an island in the South Pacific?"

"Yes," confirmed Serena, "though I don't know why."

"We aren't sure either," said the pontiff. "He claims that it will be a training center for his people, but that doesn't ring true. You'll be given a detailed report on his comings and goings since he arrived here on Earth. It might be helpful to you. Also, my people here will keep you informed as to his movements as best we can. It is the least that we can do. It might allow you to keep one step ahead of him. Also, know that you can depend on my office for almost anything you need. Just contact Father Giavani. The two of you will be in my prayers constantly."

Before leaving, Chris and Serena joined in prayer with the pontiff. They held hands in a circle. It was a rare and wonderful experience. He was so full of Christ's love, so strong in the Spirit. He was the right man for this job, of that Serena was certain.

As they left the Vatican, they had a reason to be hopeful. They had a new friend in the struggle, a very powerful friend. Before this was all over, they might need his help.

Back at the hotel, Chris and Serena poured through the Vatican file on Lusan. There were more than a few surprises.

"That island that Lusan purchased is called Katafanga," noted Chris. "He has poured close to a billion dollars into it. Some of the things that he purchased are just plain weird. It says here that he sank hundreds of thousands of dollars into purchasing heavy water."

"Doesn't sound like something you'd buy for a training center," replied Serena, looking through the copy of yet another file from the Vatican archives.

"Sounds like something you'd need if you were doing scientific research," noted Chris. He hesitated. "Or if you were building a nuclear bomb."

"But that doesn't make sense, either," objected Serena. "Why would he want to build a nuclear bomb? Anyway, wouldn't he need enriched Uranium or Plutonium too?"

"Yeah, he would," noted Chris. "There are a lot of clues here, just no answers."

Serena hesitated. "But this ancient prophecy about, maybe, me, has me more disturbed. There is a copy of it here in the stuff that the Father Giavani gave us. I think I'm going to be martyred. I think Lusan is going to kill me."

Chris immediately moved from the desk where he'd been sitting to the bed where Serena sat. There was a tear in her eye. "You don't know that. This thing is worded almost like a riddle. Some of this stuff could have lots of meanings."

"I know," insisted Serena. "I know just like Jesus knew in the Garden of Gethsemane. I know. And there's more. I don't think it will be quick."

"You're just upset," replied Chris. "I don't blame you. What you learned today was a powerful shock. I don't think you'd be normal if you'd have reacted any other way."

"But it's all right," said Serena, wiping away a tear. "I feel honored to do it. I'd do anything for the Father after the mercy He showed me. If it weren't for God's mercy, I'd still be in Hell, broiling in that awful black ocean. This is a small price to pay for God's mercy." Serena sat there deep in thought. Chris placed her hand in his. "Oh, Chris, I'd do anything if it would win the freedom of just a few repentant souls in Hell. There are people there who truly deserve a second chance."

"Maybe you will," replied Chris. "Didn't the prophecy say something about lost souls coming to your aid?"

"If they only could," corrected Serena. "I'm not so sure they can. I worry about my mother a lot. Yes, I know that she is there with Abaddon; still, the odds are so against them. In the end, at the White Throne Judgment, what will happen to her?"

"I'm afraid that only God knows that," said Chris.

"What I wouldn't do to save her from that place," said Serena, putting the papers away and preparing to go to bed. "If anyone deserves a second chance, it's her."

CHAPTER 13

Debbie Bellows gazed with terrified gray eyes, through veils of faint, drifting smoke at the sharp, menacing stalactites hanging from the rocky ceiling, stalactites that reflected the harsh, amber glow from the liquid metal that was even now beginning to spread across the floor of this hellish chamber like a pool of fluorescent mercury. The glow was becoming steadily brighter even as the room grew hotter. She knew that it was about to begin all over again.

She was held motionless, laying there shackled by her wrists and ankles in spread eagle fashion upon a horizontal metal platform that took the rough form of a human figure. The platform sat upon six glistening metal cylinders that currently held it about three feet above the rapidly flooding floor and 20 feet below the ceiling of this rectangular chamber. Around her, the walls were composed of irregular stone blocks encrusted with sulfur and soot and set in gray mortar. It was like being within some terrible dark chimney.

Despite its size, eight feet deep and nearly a dozen feet wide, it was very claustrophobic. There didn't seem to be much oxygen in this horrible place, and the air was filled with sulfuric fumes. She often found herself gasping for breath, suffocating. Of course, she couldn't die; she had already done that once. It was the way of the universe, one death per customer. Hell didn't offer that option to its residents.

Satan and his minions relished the thought of tormenting those humans within their domain, so great was their hatred of mankind. It was like a narcotic, a pleasure to which they were hopelessly addicted. Like most of the condemned females of Hell, she wore a short gray skirt and tattered skimpy top, which left her belly, arms, and legs exposed to whatever torments this fiendish chamber delivered. Like their wearers, these rags were impervious to the harsh environment, yet they offered her little protection from the elements.

Debbie turned her head as a trace of reddish vapor and a cloud of dust emanated from the far corner of the chamber, some five or six feet beyond her securely shackled right foot. What was it going to be like this time? How were they going to hurt her? She pulled upon her heavy restraints with all too predictable results; they were fastened securely to this terrible platform. Like everything else here, they seemed unaffected by the harsh environment, as strong as the day they first clamped tightly about her.

Her gaze turned to the wall to her left. There was the now sulfur-encrusted metal ladder built into the wall, a ladder that had been used just once—on the day she had arrived in this place. Above the ladder, which ran a total of ten feet up the wall, was the heavy riveted metal door that, in turn, led to the fantastically long subterranean corridor beyond, a corridor lined with many other doors not unlike this one. Did each of those doors lead to places like this? She couldn't say. She had been in that corridor but once, on the day she had arrived here, and had not been afforded the grand tour.

From time to time, when the machinery within this place was silent, she heard muffled screams coming from beyond that door, probably from other nearby chambers. On those rare occasions, when she was not otherwise preoccupied by her own agony, she had cried out to them, but she had never gotten a response. Oh, to speak to someone else, anyone else, even at a distance, would have been such a blessing. The isolation of this place was but a part of the torment, a bigger part than one unfamiliar with that special pain of absolute solitude might imagine. This chamber was her entire world, her own little universe, and it would be for all times.

She focused once more on that door, now partially encrusted with sulfur and bits of cooled molten metal. Since the day of her arrival that door had remained closed. She remembered that day with incredible clarity. Two demons had dragged her into this terrible realm. She remembered their arching bat-like wings, their ancient gray faces, and their foul odor. After locking her in place upon this cruel table, one had seemed impatient to leave, but the other had not been like-minded. He had insisted upon staying. He had so wanted to outline for her the nature of her eternal agony, the forms it would take. He seemed to truly love his job.

How long ago was that? She had no frame of reference, and time had become a meaningless concept without it. Could it be measured in terms of the long cycles of torment followed by the all too brief reprieves as her body healed itself? Perhaps, but she had not attempted to make the calculation. Eternity was eternity. One could not, after all, count to infinity.

The demon had declared that this was Satan's ultimate masterpiece of engineering when it came to the dispensing of pain in all of its forms. He went into great detail about it. So many horrible scenarios could be played out within this ghastly room. And the methods of her torment were totally random. There were no demons at the controls of this insidious device of torture, no master torturer at the helm of this ship of pain. No, she was far too minor a player in the game to warrant such attention. This was a totally automated operation. This chamber sat in the midst of a volcanically active region in the depths of Hell. The actions of this device were governed by the subtle shifting of heat in the rocks below and the ever-changing route of volcanic gases through its several hundred yards of piping. He must have ranted on for ten minutes before leaving her to her fate. She remembered hearing the dead thud as that massive door shut, hearing the heavy deadbolts slide into place and lock. Then, amidst the hissing of gas, it had begun.

Who was she that she had been relegated to this place? A fate such as this belonged to some human monster, a brutal mass murderer or a sadistic serial killer. She was just a Chicago real estate agent, a struggling mother who had been forced to raise a daughter on her own following the death of her husband in the Vietnam War. What could she possibly have done to deserve this?

No, she hadn't been religious. But as far as she was concerned, God had abandoned her, not the other way around. But that wasn't His viewpoint at her judgment, was it? She had ignored Christ's plan of salvation, a salvation He had paid for on the cross. It would have been so simple to have avoided all of this, but she hadn't. She had been condemned to Hell, and Satan, in turn, had sentenced her to this place. What right did he have to do that? The power to do it, that's what gave him the right. Satan claimed that she would come to know untold suffering, knowing not what form it would take from ordeal to ordeal.

In the years since then, she had discovered firsthand the truth of his words. The wrist and ankle restraints she wore were all bolted to sliding metal plates that were in turn mounted to worm gears that allowed them to extend outward, literally ripping her arms and legs from their sockets. All it took was for the volcanic gases to be directed into the right set of pipes, into the proper turbines. And that was one of the milder forms of pain she had experienced on this nightmarish table. Another set of gears and rods allowed this table to fold upward in the middle, literally breaking her back in the process. She had been electrocuted for hours when the turbines spun the generator. The table had been raised to the ceiling, causing her to be slowly impaled by the multitude of spikelike stalactites. She'd been immersed in the scalding liquid metal below her and left to cook for but a few minutes, a process that burned the flesh from her bones and reduced her to little more than a living, feeling human skeleton. Yet no matter how desecrated, her body always reconstituted, ready for the next round of torments.

Apparently, the demons had great faith in the reliability of this device; they rarely checked up on her. The door above her did have a metal window of sorts. From time to time, there would come a clicking of the bolt, following which it was shoved to the side. A demon would briefly look in on her, apparently to confirm that this poor woman's torments were proceeding as the master intended. Then it would be shut once more and her total seclusion would continue. The whole process might last ten or twenty seconds at most. They had no real interest in her. Her tragedy continued to play out before no one, serving no purpose.

Debbie's mind returned to the present. She had come to the end of a healing cycle, a particularly long one. Her body had been fully restored for over an hour. During that time, her only torments had been in the form of the heat and her eternal burning thirst. But the sound of venting vapors and turning gears told her that her respite was over. Volcanic gas was flowing through the pipes once more.

There was a slight jolt as the table began to slowly rise upon its pneumatic cylinders, the heated gas within them expanded in response to the presence of the hot liquid metal below her.

"Oh God, no," gasped Debbie, her hoarse voice barely above a whisper.

The table was rising, and she knew where she was going. She had made this journey so many times. She gazed toward the wall above her, about halfway between the ceiling and the floor. Here, mounted from the stone and protruding from its depths, on all sides, were a series of large industrial sized drills, probes, and pneumatic cylinders, each with its own fiendish purpose. The demon had named them all, the router, the rib smasher, the spit, and the pear, just to name a few. They could do such unspeakable things to her. They were among the worst torments that the chamber had to offer.

She would have wept, if her body had contained enough moisture for her tear ducts to flow, or cried out, had her throat not been so dry. All the while the table rose amidst a cloud of venting dust and sulfurous gas.

A sudden jolt reverberated through the table as it came to an abrupt halt. To her left and right, three large drills, better than an inch in diameter, had emerged from shafts in the wall. With their large and menacing bladed tips spinning in unison, they moved toward her flanks. She knew this scenario only too well; these bits would drill into her bare sides, into her lungs, kidneys, and other vital organs. Once there, their tips would expand, literally routing her out, reducing those organs to mush, even as they dripped acid into the newly formed slurry. It was an excruciating ordeal that only an immortal could truly appreciate.

Yet even as the blades telescoped toward her, there was noise from beyond the door. The demons were back. It had been a very long time since she had seen them. There was a clicking of a bolt and the opening of the shutter over the window. Someone was looking in on her.

"We've found her," said a voice from beyond the door.

It was a familiar voice, yet one she hadn't heard in a long time. She gazed toward the window, into the face of a man, not a demon.

"Come on, we've got to get her out of there right now!" There was a sense of urgency in the voice, even as she felt the pull on her arms and legs. Her shackles were beginning to stretch her out. In a few minutes her arms and legs would be pulled from their sockets, rendering her body totally motionless for the drills.

"I'm working as fast as I can, sir," came the somewhat muffled reply.

There was a sound of flapping wings as a series of small flying creatures swept through the window and into the chamber. They looked like large locusts. Circling her for a few seconds, they descended upon her restraints.

There was a flurry of sparks as the creatures went to work on the manacles about her ankles and wrists. At about the same time, there was a glow at the edge of the door.

"Come on, hurry!" said the voice. "Hold on, Debbie. We'll get you out of there."

Her name. It had been years since she had heard her name.

The shackles were growing hot. The one about her left wrist burst open, freeing her arm, which had been stretched to nearly its limit. She held her trembling hand before her, touched her face. It had been a very long time since she had last done that. She looked to her left to discover that the tiny creatures had literally eaten their way through the metal of her shackle. They were like nothing she had ever seen. They were neither birds nor insects. They were about as large as her fist, with elongated tan bodies covered with fur. At the end of the body was a sort of nasty looking barbed stinger half an inch long. Each creature had six legs, and two pairs of wings, not unlike a dragonfly, though the wings had the appearance of gossamer. Yet their faces had an aspect that made them look almost human. Right now, those faces were covered with shavings of metal. Several of the creatures were cleaning themselves with their front legs, which looked almost like hands, with five digits on their ends. One moved toward Debbie, looking directly into her eyes. Its expression seemed to hold a sense of sympathy about it, not frightening at all.

"Thank you," said Debbie, in a low hoarse voice.

She was surprised when the creature nodded and smiled. Had it understood her?

A second later, the shackle holding her right ankle in place gave way. Yet, Debbie's situation remained grim. The six whirling blades were encroaching upon her from both sides, and it was taking too long for her rescuers to free her from her restraints. Soon they would be drilling into her sides, between her ribs. Several of the creatures apparently perceived the danger and attacked the shafts of the blades. However, they couldn't manage to sink their sharp teeth into the spinning cylinders. They were thrown from them; yet they tried again and again.

The insidious drills were but inches from her flesh when Debbie's right wrist restraint was sliced open. She tried to rise to a sitting position, out of the path of the drills, but had not the strength.

A second later, the door burst open to reveal a group of men in military attire. There was a flash as the shafts of the drills approaching her from both sides were violently sliced in two by a brilliant beam of light. The tips plunged into the growing pool of glowing liquid metal below even as a stream of acid poured from the severed shafts, producing a toxic cloud of steam as they hit the metal. A small spray of acid even reached the altar, running across it, caressing Debbie's side with its burning chemical sting. She winced in pain, but still lacked the strength to rise.

The shackle restraining her left ankle gave way, and she felt a shaking of the altar as the soldier she had seen from the window jumped onto the cruel metal slab and cautiously picked her up in his arms.

"I've got you, Debbie," he said in a soft, kind voice. "I'll never let you go again."

Debbie looked into this kind face. For the first time in many years, tears came to her eyes; it was the face of her husband. "Kurt?" she whispered.

"Yes, it's me," he confirmed. "I'm so sorry that your knight in shining armor has taken so long to rescue you. I'm so sorry."

The toxic cloud around them was growing thicker. It was time to go.

"Come on, we've gotta go!" said another man at the door. "Jump, we'll catch you."

There was an instant of flight. Then Debbie and Kurt were in the hallway beyond. They were quickly followed by the mysterious flying creatures that had aided in her escape. The door was then closed behind them and, along with it, the world Debbie had known for so long. Debbie was amazed to find herself in the midst of five soldiers, four men and a woman, whose uniforms bore the insignia of the United States Marines. Debbie's mind was reeling; it didn't make sense. Battle-ready U.S. Marines in Hell: how could that possibly be? Her husband had once told her that the marines were prepared to travel to Hell and back on a moment's notice if needs be. Maybe she should have taken his words literally.

"Very nice work, Kurt," said the woman, glancing down at the digital watch in her hand. "We're right on schedule." Then she turned to Debbie. "Debbie, I've heard so many good things about you from Kurt. I'm very much looking forward to getting to know you better. I'm Bedillia Farnsworth, project counselor. It's going to be all right. We're going to get you out of here in just another minute. We'll be taking you to a place where no one is ever going to hurt you again. The nightmare is over."

"She's right, Mrs. Bellows," said a young marine with blond hair and freckles. "I'm Sean, Sean Martinson. The captain has told us so much about you. I'm happy to finally meet you in person.

"So good to meet you, ma'am," confirmed another.

Debbie didn't respond. She just clung to her husband as best she could. She felt like she never wanted to let go. If this were a dream, she prayed that it would last forever.

Kurt pulled a canteen from his utility belt. "Here, Debbie, drink this. It will make you feel better."

Water—in Hell? This just kept getting better and better. Debbie literally gulped down the water in large mouthfuls. It felt so good. It was indescribable. For untold years the only liquid that had flowed into her body was acid or hot liquid metal. She had been certain that she would not taste this sweet nectar again.

"Easy, my love," said Kurt. "Not so fast. Your body isn't used to it."

Debbie looked up to see one of the flying creatures on her husband's shoulder. It had a face that looked almost like that of a woman, complete with long brown hair. The creature returned her gaze and smiled. Kurt looked over at the creature for but a second.

"I know, Drannon, it's time to get out of here." Kurt scanned the others. "Do we have everyone?"

"The five of us and twenty-four of Abaddon's children," said Sean. "We're ready to rumble."

"Ready to pull out, sir?" asked another Marine.

"OK, open the portal," said Kurt, putting the canteen away once more.

The Marine pulled what looked like a cloudy, white marble from his utility belt. Before them, the hallway was filled by glowing vapors and glistening stars. To Debbie it looked absolutely mystical. They advanced into them, followed by the small flying creatures. They vanished into the mists. The phenomenon illuminated the hallway for another few seconds before fading from view. The forever twilight environment highlighted by faint moans and muffled screams returned.

From the shadows a hundred feet further down the corridor, a dark figure emerged from his hiding place, his huge black bat-like wings towering over his form. A slight smile came to his face as he turned. An oval-shaped portal of brightness appeared before him, and he entered it. It dissolved behind him.

For a moment, Debbie seemed to be traveling through wonderfully cool, blue mists. It was like heaven to her. Then she was passing through a ring of shimmering metal into the middle of a large, well-lit room with walls that appeared to be composed of polished rock. There were more people around her. Debbie looked into the faces of two dark-haired young women dressed in knee-length brown dresses. One appeared to be Hispanic, the other Asian.

"My name is Julie," said the Hispanic woman, approaching her. "Welcome to Refuge."

"And I'm Kim," said the second woman. "You are among friends, I can assure you. You are safe here."

Bedillia turned to Kurt. "That went well."

Kurt nodded. "In and out in less than five minutes." Kurt hesitated, "Not like the other time."

Bedillia nodded. "Thank heavens, I could have lived without that experience."

"Yeah, I hear that," said Kurt, who turned to look into his wife's eyes. He had never seen a more beautiful sight. "Do you think you can stand?"

"I don't know," said Debbie in a soft, quivering voice.

"Let's try," replied Kurt. "Our mission isn't over. We've got one more objective to accomplish, and then I'll be back with you."

"You're leaving me here?" asked Debbie.

Kurt nodded. "Safer than where we are going."

"Please, don't go," pleaded Debbie.

"I have to," insisted Kurt. "We have another damsel in distress to rescue."

"My wife, Sue," said the freckle-faced young man. "Our mission today is a very personal one, and it has been a long time in coming."

"Amen to that," said Bedillia.

Debbie only nodded. She would not presume to be so selfish.

"We will all get together later," promised the young man. "We can take you gals out for dinner."

"Dinner?" asked Debbie, in a voice barely above a whisper.

"Sure," confirmed the young man, a broad smile coming to his face. "I know this really great place where they serve the best tossed salads."

"Sounds nice," whispered Debbie, who was now more confused than ever.

"But we won't be able to go there until you can walk," said Kurt, gently bringing Debbie into a vertical position. Her bare feet met the cool floor. Bedillia quickly produced a pair of leather sandals for her, helping her to slip her trembling feet in. The world went almost dark around Debbie. She struggled to remain conscious. How long had it been since she had been on her feet? She wasn't sure.

Slowly, her surroundings grew brighter. Somehow, she was still on her feet, with only minimal help from those around her. It seemed incredible to her that she had recovered so quickly.

Julie and Kim helped Debbie put on a long, tan robe. It was warm and comfortable.

"We can't have you walking around in those awful rags," said Bedillia. "This will do for the moment, till we can get you cleaned up and give you a new wardrobe. Satan might have found pleasure in humiliating women by dressing us in such filth, but he is not in command here. We call the shots here. Now, let's try to take a few steps."

And Debbie did. She nearly fell twice, but she was moving on her own power. Before her was a glowing sphere of light, nearly two feet in diameter, hovering in midair, and beside it stood a man dressed in a gray business suit whom she hadn't noticed when she'd first arrived. He had dark, curly hair, a narrow mustache, and such intense eyes. He looked almost familiar, though Debbie knew not from where.

"I rejoice with the others over your safe arrival," he said in a soft voice that held little emotion. "I am Nikola Tesla."

Nikola Tesla—yes, that name was familiar to Debbie. At least, she had heard it before. He was some sort of famous scientist or something like that, a genius almost certainly. She wondered if he was behind all that had happened to her this day.

Tesla reached over and adjusted a set of controls on a circular stand about a foot below the glowing orb. "We call it a telesphere," he continued, without looking up from his labors. "It allows us virtually instantaneous communication with any other telesphere at any point within the known universe."

For a moment, the sphere was full of static, like that of a television turned to a blank channel, except that this salt and pepper static was three dimensional, filling the sphere. An instant later, a holographic figure appeared within the sphere. He was dressed all in white, and his white-feathered wings arched majestically behind him. He was beautiful; no other words could describe his countenance. From his golden hair, to his azure blue eyes, to his perfect skin and mouth, he was the image of perfection and symmetry. The angel stood amidst shelves of books that looked like a library. At his side stood a young, handsome man who appeared to be in his early twenties. He too was dressed in white.

"The first part of the mission went without incident," said Bedillia. "We met with no resistance."

"I'm glad," said the angel in a melodic voice. He turned to Debbie. "I am so happy to see you safe and sound in Refuge with your husband. I am Aaron, and my compatriot is David."

"The David who slew Goliath?" asked Debbie, who, at this point, seemed a bit confused.

David laughed. "No ma'am, not that David. I'm from New York City originally. I was killed in the World Trade Center attack on 9/11."

"9/11?" asked Debbie. "What's that?"

"There will be time for that later," interjected Kurt. "How does our second target look?"

"We can't be sure," replied Aaron. "We just don't have enough information. Sarah is alone right now. That is to say, there are no demons within that room. I don't think she has much time before she is in serious difficulty again. You will need to make haste, my friend, if you are to spare her from additional pain and grief. May the Father guide your steps."

"Yeah, good luck, Kurt," said David. "We're pulling for you and yours on this side. Sorry we can't be more help."

Kurt only nodded as the image within the glowing sphere faded. The sphere itself dissolved into empty air, leaving only what looked like a fortuneteller's crystal ball on the pedestal before her. Debbie shook her head. This was all so surreal, a strange mixture of magic and technology. She couldn't be sure where one ended and the other began. Maybe they were one and the same.

"The coordinates are set," noted Julie, turning from a set of controls on a small marble pedestal not far from the nine-foot-diameter silvery ring through which the group had emerged just a few minutes ago. "You'll be traveling to a place about 1,400 miles southeast and 2,000 feet shallower than your last gate in point. Ready when you are."

It was at that very second that a metal door at the other end of the room opened and another being entered the room. He was tall and dressed all in black. His enormous black wings reminded Debbie of a gigantic crow. He had a short beard and indeed piercing eyes. Actually, he was quite handsome, very much unlike the demons she had encountered in the past. Perhaps he was no demon at all.

He scanned the room carefully and then focused his gaze on Debbie. "Well, people, are you going to introduce me to the new member of our community?"

For a few seconds there was only silence. Then Bedillia spoke up. "Abaddon, this is Debbie Bellows, Kurt's wife. Debbie, this is Abaddon, our chief administrator."

Abaddon approached Debbie. His smile reduced her apprehension somewhat. He gently took her hand in his. "I am pleased to meet you, Debbie. You are welcome among us. I assure you that the horrors of Hell are behind you."

Again there was an uneasy pause; it was Bedillia who finally spoke up. "We have one more rescue mission. It is very time sensitive."

All eyes were on Abaddon as he scanned the group carefully. Debbie was still trying to make sense of it all, but she couldn't.

"Continue the mission," said Abaddon. "However I need to speak to you, Bedillia, in my council chambers."

"Thank you," said Bedillia.

"I've gotta go," said Kurt, taking his wife's hand. "I've dreamed of being with you again for so long. I promise I'll be right back. Go with Julie. She will take you to a place where you can rest. You need to rest. I'll probably be back before you fall asleep."

"You'd better," whispered Debbie, caressing her husband's hand. "I love you so much. I thought I'd never see you again."

"I have a tendency to show up when you least expect it," replied Kurt. "Get some rest, OK?"

"OK," said Debbie, watching her husband and the others head for the ring as Kim placed her arm around her and helped her toward the large metal door at the far side of the room.

"Let's get you into a warm bath and into some nicer clothes," said Kim. "The nightmare is over. It's time for the healing to begin."

She led Debbie through the still-open door at the far side of the room; Julie made a few additional keystrokes to what looked like a small computer keyboard. All the while, Kurt's eyes were on his wife. She returned his gaze, then headed on down the hall beyond the door. At long last she was safe.

The four Marines gathered before the great ring, gazing into its depths, which had started to glow. A cool, blue mist was beginning to blow through the ring as the wall beyond vanished. What stood in the middle of the room was no longer just a large ring, but a portal, a corridor through hyperspace that led to another place.

"Our intelligence indicates that the corridor you are traveling into is very dimly lit," noted Nikola, walking toward the four Marines. "You'll need extra illumination."

The Marines had already removed the covers from their flashlights. They had the basic shape of a small flashlight at least, but held no batteries or even a bulb. They were each composed of a hollow metal tube at the end of which was set a small, but brightly glowing, crystal before a small curved mirror that concentrated the light into a beam.

"You gentlemen can step through whenever you're ready; the corridor is stable," announced Julie.

The team proceeded through the ring without delay. They appeared to be walking through a misty tunnel with clouds instead of stone or metal for walls. As Julie and Nikola watched, they vanished into the starry mists.

"Walk with me," said Abaddon, looking to Bedillia.

The two walked out into the busy hallway, leaving Julie and Nikola to await the return of the rescue team. The hallway had the appearance of some underground, high-security installation. A network of what looked like water and electrical conduits ran along the ceiling of the rectangular corridor of hewn stone. In the background, one could discern the sound of machinery. Here and there, both human and dark angelic sentries had been posted, guarding sensitive areas and important labs.

"Bedillia, what do you think you are doing?" objected Abaddon as they stepped into a less-traveled side corridor illuminated from the ceiling by light blue crystals. "You above all should realize the position these rescues could put us in. We have managed to broker a truce with the demons."

"Thanks to Cordon," interjected Bedillia. "As long as Satan is stuck on Earth and Cordon is in charge of the demons of Hell, we are relatively safe. I know, in his heart, Cordon would like to free those truly repentant human souls. He sees the advantage of us all working together."

"You don't know that," objected Abaddon. "Cordon is in a difficult position. Even I can appreciate that. So long as it serves his purpose to maintain a relationship with us, he will do so, but that might not always be the case. Actions like this, which are clear violations of the treaty, do not help our cause."

"But I can't stand idly by while good people suffer when it's within our power to rescue them," retorted Bedillia. "Look, there have been seven peace conferences since the war in Heaven, seven. In all that time, what have we accomplished? You've called off your ACs. They no longer attack the demons. They feed exclusively upon the non-repentant humans. You even ordered them to refrain from releasing those humans who truly deserve a reprieve from their torment. You've bent over backwards for the demons, Abaddon. But what have the demons given us in return?"

"They haven't attacked," replied Abaddon. "They leave us in peace. And they claim that some of the ACs are still attacking them, and releasing humans, an issue that I can neither confirm nor deny."

"And they've been using that excuse to exterminate the ACs you released into Hell," continued Bedillia. "And you've done nothing about it. You once called them your children."

"That was uncalled for," objected Abaddon. "I still love them, but in recent months, they have become ever more difficult for me to control since the alpha male was killed in battle in the Valley of Noak. This peace is fragile, Bedillia, and it could unravel on us if we provoke them."

"Where is the bold Abaddon I once knew?" objected Bedillia.

"Alive and well, thank you," said Abaddon, "and trying to keep our small community alive. May I remind you that the judgment of the demons who participated in the war in Heaven is well underway. Once the saints pass judgment upon them, they are returned here, swelling the numbers of the demons we must face. We must not give the demons a reason to attack us here. Abiding by the terms of the peace agreement is vital."

"And while their numbers grow, ours remain static," retorted Bedillia. "Every day their numerical advantage on us grows. Can't you see where this is leading? Even if you discard rescuing more of Satan's victims on purely humanitarian grounds, consider it from a military standpoint."

"But more people here, utilizing our limited resources, does not necessarily equate to an advantage," said Abaddon as they entered his conference room. "We need to have weapons for them and power spheres for those weapons. Heaven is the only source of those spheres. With our lifeline to Heaven cut off these past two years, our supply is nearly exhausted. Nikola Tesla has been working with David Bonner on that teleporter thing for over 18 months, but they still can't make it work. Maybe they will never be able to make it work. Unless we can open some form of supply route between Heaven and Refuge, we will find ourselves in a difficult situation. And there is another thing, how did you obtain the power sphere to bring Debbie Bellows back through the ring? I ordered the storeroom to be closed and placed under guard. Only I have access to those spheres."

Bedillia didn't respond, but she had a very odd expression on her face. She cleared her throat.

Abaddon stopped in his tracks. "What?"

Bedillia now had a Cheshire cat grin that was positively amusing. "I didn't get the sphere from the locker if that's what you're implying."

"Then where did you get it?" asked Abaddon.

"I don't want to steal Nikola's thunder."

Abaddon cocked his head in the way that only angels did. "Bedillia, what are you trying to tell me."

"You were going to find out at this afternoon's advisory council meeting anyway." Again Bedillia hesitated. "I got the spheres from Nikola Tesla, and no, he didn't take them from your storeroom. Nikola and David formed the first stable wormhole between Heaven and Refuge two days ago. They've teleported 800 power spheres through since then. That should just about triple your supply." By now, Bedillia was beaming. "They all work, Abaddon, every single one of them. Nikola tested them. That's how we got the spheres to teleport Debbie out of that chamber. In another few days you'll have to build a second storage facility to hold them all. Now do you see why we need more people here?"

Abaddon looked at Bedillia incredulously. "Yes, I see. That is wonderful news. I will make it a point to seem surprised when Nikola tells us at this afternoon's meeting."

"I'm sorry that we did this rescue behind your back," said Bedillia. "But, beyond the strictly humanitarian grounds, we had to know where we stood. We had to know that the teleported spheres would work in gating as well. They do. Our energy crisis is over. I think it's time we became a bit more assertive at the bargaining table. We have power in our corner now."

Abaddon smiled. "It's all right, Bedillia. Why don't we head back to the ring room and see how your team fared on their second trip out."

They arrived just in time to witness a swirling of mists and sparkling stars appear in the midst of the shimmering, metal ring. A few seconds later, the team stepped from the blue fog and into the room. The freckle-faced man, Sean Martinson, held a thin, young woman dressed in gray rags in his arms. She held onto him tightly, like she planned to never let go. Bedillia couldn't help but notice the condition of her left foot. It was badly scarred, and several toes were missing completely. How dreadful. Still, they would grow back within the next half hour. After all, this wasn't Earth; it was Hell, and for better or worse, everyone here was immortal.

Bedillia recalled this morning's briefing from their friends in Heaven who, through the resources of the Hall of Records, could view the current situation of every sentient being in the cosmos, both the living and the dead. This woman, Sue Martinson, had been condemned by Satan to be shackled to a sort of trestle within a chamber infested by hungry rats. Yet the rats had been only one of her concerns. The other was the large, loaded crossbow directed at her heart. Every few hours, the rats would eat through the cord that held it in check, and the bolt would be propelled into her heart, adding to her suffering. There had been some concern about reaching her before that event was repeated once more. By the looks of it, they had succeeded.

There were so many stories of tragedy in Hell unfolding all around them. Bedillia was anxious to alleviate the suffering of as many as she possibly could. She thought of this afternoon's meeting. She was certain that her team would have still more surprises for Abaddon. She hoped that he would take them well.

CHAPTER 14

The governing council of Refuge was gathering about the rectangular, white marble table in Abaddon's audience chamber. The walls of the large room were adorned with beautiful paintings of forest scenes, beautiful beaches, and a great city with streets of gold. In the far corner of the room, above a black marble stand, a large sphere hovered, seemingly without support. Within it one could see several figures, observers from Heaven, who would also take part in this meeting.

The governing council currently included six dark angels and seven humans. The seventh human was the famous Nikola Tesla, who was actually a citizen of Heaven temporarily marooned on this wasteland of a world in the middle of Outer Darkness. The rest of the committee was waiting for him. He would be the first speaker, and he was late, again.

Nikola Tesla walked into the meeting a full six minutes late. He took his place at the table. "I was unavoidably detained, sorry," he said.

Abaddon opened the meeting with the old business, specifically giving Tesla the opportunity to report on the progress of his project, allowing him to proclaim his success. But he didn't. He spoke of very encouraging results. He spoke of having conducted a series of successful transports of power spheres from their allies in Heaven, but he did not proclaim final victory. There were still many tests to run. Yes, he had more than tripled their available energy supply, but he was not as yet satisfied with their results. He would not announce final success until human transport was a reality. That proclamation brought its share of raised eyebrows among the council.

"Human transport?" confirmed Samiazaz, the original leader of the dark angels.

"Yes," replied Nikola.

"So that you can return to Heaven," deduced Samiazaz.

"In part," replied Nikola, who hesitated some seconds before continuing. He scanned the other human members of the council. "Understand this; I lived the vast majority of my life as you did, beyond God's grace. In my final years, I was plagued by demons pretending to be J.P. Morgan or George Westinghouse, people I had known in my youth, but who were now long gone. They hounded me, tormented me to the point of madness. I was dying when I finally turned to the Lord and called upon Jesus Christ as my Savior. I lived two more days and then died. In my life, I accomplished nothing for God, nothing. All of you have repented, yes, every one of you. Yet I dwelled in Heaven while you were sent to suffer in Hell. I cannot see the justice in that."

Tesla paused. He looked around the table at his human and angelic companions alike. He'd lived for two years among them—two years to discover firsthand what it was like to know that the demons might break the truce at any time and storm this fortress.

"What is it that you are implying, Mr. Tesla?" asked Abaddon.

"That it might be possible for the people of Refuge, both human and angelic, to escape Hell altogether," said Tesla. "For some time before my arrival here, Dr. Kepler and I had been scanning the cosmos for habitable planets, places that would offer the people of Refuge a fresh start. They deserve that chance. I don't believe that it would be possible for me to take them to Heaven, but to another world within the many galaxies that populate the universe, perhaps. Dr. Kepler and I personally know of no less than five good candidates, every bit as nice as the green Earth, but with no indigenous population."

"But we are still a long way from even considering human transport," cautioned Dr. Kepler, speaking through the telesphere. "There are still so many problems to overcome. The physical laws that govern Hell are very different from those that govern the rest of the universe or Heaven. Molecules, atoms, subatomic particles, all function under different rules. We must find a way to adapt the particles designed to function in the environment of Outer Darkness to function in the environments of Heaven or Earth. Right now, we don't know how to do it."

"Wait a minute," observed Bedillia. "Nikola came here from Heaven on the Spirit spaceship or whatever you want to call it. He's been here among us for nearly two years and has not suffered any ill effects from it."

"It's not the same," insisted Dr. Kepler. "He traveled from a higher plane of existence to a lower one. His body, the atoms and molecules that make it up, were able to adjust. But now we're talking about going from a lower plane to a higher plane. Each atom must absorb tremendous amounts of energy to be stable at the higher plane. In effect, they must become different types of atoms. It was for that very reason that we couldn't transport your daughter back to Heaven with us when we came to Hell over eight years ago. If we'd tried, the transition would have reduced her to little more than a ghostly entity, dissipating ever more with each passing minute. It is one of the most basic laws of hyper-dimensional physics."

"But it's just a theory, isn't it?" asked Bedillia.

"I'm afraid not," replied David Bonner, stepping into view in the telesphere. "Why do you think demons can only come to Earth as spirits? The Father uses this law of physics to keep them trapped in Hell. It also prevents any of you from escaping. I'm sorry to shatter your hopes." He turned to Tesla. "Sir, what you hope to accomplish is a feat that only the Father can perform using an instrument of His own creation—the great ring on the plains of Hell. It might take us generations to perfect it. We might not be able to make it work at all."

"That doesn't sound like the David I've come to know," observed Tesla. "It is possible, and it might take less time than you imagine. Cordon and I have been working on a device that might solve our continuing problem with phase alignment and subatomic particle transition. We have been making good progress."

There was a general rumbling among the council. This was a very sensitive project. It wasn't the sort of thing to be discussed in the presence of the ruler of the demons.

"Is Cordon aware of the teleportation project?" asked the dark angel Eleazar.

"He is aware of it," said Tesla, "though he doesn't know how far it has proceeded. What he and I have been working on is a separate project. It has Abaddon's approval. I have abided by all of the prerequisites he established."

"And what of these rescues earlier today? continued Eleazar. "Did he know of them, too?"

Tesla hesitated. "Yes, he did." Tesla turned to Kurt. "Cordon made certain that you would encounter no problems on your mission. In fact, he was observing you from the shadows. He did not wish his council to know of it, for they are indeed opposed to the rescue of additional humans. However, he has agreed to allow us to conduct a limited number of rescues."

Now Abaddon seemed truly annoyed. "And when were you going to tell me about this?"

"I'd planned to inform you at this meeting," replied Tesla. "If things went badly for one reason or another, I wanted you to have plausible deniability."

"What?" asked Abaddon.

"I didn't want it to seem that you had ordered the rescue," said Tesla. "It needed to look like a rogue operation. Then you could say that you had no knowledge of it. The blame could be shifted to me, a relative outsider."

"That seems reasonable to me," said Lenar, another of the dark angels.

"It is not uncommon in the CIA or KGB," confirmed Kurt. "A leader is not aware of every covert action certain elements of his government are involved in."

Abaddon just shook his head. "For the record, this is not the CIA or KGB. And, for the record, I am still in command here. If anyone wishes to challenge that leadership, do it now." Silence followed Abaddon's challenge for the better part of half a minute. "Very well then, if that is the case, no decisions that impact this place, no matter how beneficial or insignificant you think they might be, are to be made without me. Is that clear Professor Tesla?"

"Abundantly," confirmed Tesla.

"I know that you consider Cordon to be a friend," continued Abaddon, his tone less intense. "I can understand why. He saved your eternal existence during the operation to close that rip in space two years ago. You have worked closely together ever since. I can see where you might consider him to be a noble being. Maybe he is, but what I see is a demon, one of Satan's minions. I have no evidence that he has lied to us in the time since the signing of the treaty. Still, I can ill afford to lower my guard."

"May I continue to work with Cordon on this project?" asked Tesla.

"You may," confirmed Abaddon, "so long as you abide by the ground rules I set for you."

"I will," confirmed Tesla, "just as I always have in the past."

The meeting continued. Plans were made to transport the newly acquired power spheres from Tesla's lab to the central storage area. Plans for the establishment of a second storage area were also discussed. Their power crisis was over. Still, it became obvious that at least one of the demons knew far more about the goings on in Refuge than they would like. Yes, he had never gone back on an agreement with them, and it was clear that he had at least a few friends on the council, still, he kept poor company. He was a demon, plain and simple. Could you really trust a demon? To the dark angels, the answer was only too clear; no. Only time would prove their prejudice to be right or wrong.

Satan's old audience hall was strangely quiet. There had been a time when the atmosphere of this place was a continual circus. In those days, one human after another was brought through that shimmering metal ring that formed an ethereal corridor from the holding cells to the place of their sentencing in this very hall. From here, they would be taken to the place where their sentence would be carried out. The ring was positioned about 50 feet in front of the place where Satan's magnificent throne once stood. It deposited the shackled and often beaten victim virtually at Satan's feet.

The lurid atmosphere of this place set the stage for their eternity. Upon the walls of this grand cavern room were great murals depicting the terrible nature and torments of the realm of the damned. Within this hall, the humans would experience their last relatively pain-free moments before their eternity of agony. Satan had been determined to make it a memorable experience.

At any given time, there might be a hundred or more demons in this place to witness the festivities. They would assume a multitude of grotesque shapes so as to terrify their rag-clad prey. But now, those days were passed. In the two years since the war in Heaven, no new souls had come to this realm of the damned. Now, the grave would retain its dead until the final judgment. This chamber no longer served a purpose.

Yet, this place was not empty. Two bat-winged beings knelt before the great ring. In very fact, they had partially disassembled it and were now peering into its interior, which was filled with a multitude of different-shaped crystals linked by fine fibers of what appeared to be glass. One held in his hand a sort of tool that caused the crystals to glow when brought near it.

Unlike most demons, these did not have the countenance of pale old men. They had the appearance of men in their mid-thirties. They were handsome men at that.

"I never tire of the beauty, the intricacy of this thing," noted the demon who watched the other skillfully move the tool. "It is a pity that Satan forbid you to build any more of these. You created a thing of true wonder here."

"Thank you, Rolf," said the other, moving the tool still deeper into the maze of crystalline wiring. "It has been a very long time, over 6,000 years, since I last gazed upon it. I had nearly forgotten the principles involved. It is all coming back to me, however. Yes, I do believe that we will be able to build more of these all over this world. They will give our people greater mobility, the ability to reach a trouble spot more swiftly."

Rolf once more scanned the crystalline wiring. "Then you envision trouble in our future, Lord Cordon?"

Cordon withdrew the tool from the other-worldly circuitry. "My dear friend, Rolf, how many times do I need to tell you that I am not a lord or a duke or a master. I am simply Cordon. I am no different than I ever was. I have no ego to feed."

"Maybe not, my friend," said Rolf. "But you need to exhibit a more commanding presence before the others. If you do not, you simply enforce the opinion that you are a weak leader. They are used to being dictated to, accustomed to following commands. You tend to make suggestions, not commands. You are far too soft spoken."

"So am I to become a tyrant?" asked Cordon, a slight smile coming to his face.

"I don't know," replied Rolf. "It couldn't hurt." Rolf hesitated. "There is something else—the matter of the two women you allowed the humans to rescue. If the others discovered that you did this thing, they would be enraged."

"In that case, I did the right thing," insisted Cordon. "I need to throw these people a bone once in a while. At least they came to me and asked. They did not attempt to take the women from behind my back. I respected that. That very fact leads me to believe that I can trust them. They have a certain nobility, a nobility that many of our people have lost over the eons that we have been here. We need to give in to the requests of these humans from time to time. What they have asked of us is certainly not unreasonable. We need to be good neighbors. Perhaps it will not always be so, but it serves us well for the moment."

The huge, orange sun stood low in the sky as 19-year-old Tim Monroe knelt behind a large boulder, gazing through his crystal-viewing orb at the dismal procession of shackled, rag-clad humans making their way single file up the rugged, rocky canyon floor. From there they proceeded barefoot along a steep switchback trail up the 45-degree slope to the west that led out of the canyon and unto the long sloping ridge above. Inevitably, their route ended at the top of a towering cliff.

The Plunge of Desolation—yes, that was what they called it. It was a place where, one by one, the people in the procession threw themselves from the precipice to the valley floor hundreds of feet below. From there, the poor souls were compelled to drag their broken and mangled bodies from the base of the cliff, out of the way of those who would follow. There was no time of rest, no time to allow their shattered bones and ripped muscles to mend. They were expected to begin the long journey back up the canyon by any means possible, under the whips of their demon taskmasters, to repeat the cycle of regeneration and destruction again and again. It was barbaric—the fate of those who had chosen a homosexual lifestyle on Earth.

Tim knew their pain only too well. He was once counted among their number. How long ago had that been? Right now, he wasn't sure. It had been easy to lose track of time in the depths of that cave. It had been a place of healing, both physical and spiritual. That cool subterranean realm had become his new world, and he liked it. Indeed, he felt very uncomfortable out here in the open, in the sunlight. He longed to return to that twilight realm, but there was work to be done first.

Again he focused on the procession. He had endured the suffering for nearly a year before the invasion of the Marines and dark angels. Imagine that—U.S.

Marines in Hell. At least, that was what they looked like. They had swept into the valley through some sort of otherworldly portal, mowing down the demons like so much chaff with beam weapons and blazing swords. It had looked like something straight out of a science fiction movie. They had brought with them thousands of small flying creatures who did their bidding. Those creatures had descended on the demons, biting and stinging, giving them but a taste of the suffering that they had dispensed to others for so long. They had literally chewed away the ankle shackles of some, freeing them, while leaving others to their fate. Those released had been escorted through the otherworldly portal to a place they called Refuge.

He should have gone with them. The creatures had sliced away his shackles, too. He had struggled to get to the place from which the others were being spirited away, but it was so far, and the crowd of still-shackled people made the going slow. He had almost reached the head of the line, but he had been too late. The demons had returned, and his fleeting opportunity for freedom vanished as the last of the liberators fled into the mystical portal.

Yet in the pandemonium that followed, he managed to flee up the canyon in which he now stood. Those around him were still shackled, slowed down, unable to escape the wrath of the demons that were already in the process of rounding them up, but he was more fortunate. It was better than a mile up that canyon, in a place that he had never been before, that he found one of the small flying creatures, seriously wounded from the battle, laying amidst the rocks. It was there, too, that he found a cave, a cave large enough for him to slip into, but too small for a demon's massive wings. He had taken the small creature into the cave with him, nursed him back to health. He had become his friend. He had named him Goliath.

He glanced over at Goliath, who sat on his left shoulder, as he often did. He had helped Tim through the good times and the bad. He wasn't a pet; he was far too sophisticated a being for that. He was his best friend, and during the months that followed, an even more special bond had grown between them. Tim didn't have a word for it beyond telepathy. He could literally sense his tiny friend's thoughts, his feelings, and he, in turn, sensed Tim's. Over time, the link between them had grown stronger.

And as Tim had saved Goliath's life, Goliath had become Tim's provider. Tim still remembered the first time that Goliath had left the safety of the cave. He had returned with a strange artifact, a ring with the power to give forth light. It made it possible for Tim and Goliath to explore the cave, which was actually the entrance of a grand cavern system that extended for miles.

Yet Goliath had been but the first. In the months that followed, others of his kind had discovered the cave. They had been fruitful and multiplied. Now, their numbers were in the tens of thousands. They had become his companions, his friends. They made living in the caverns more of an adventure. Amazingly, Goliath seemed to have the ability to command the others, and they obeyed him.

Then again, Goliath was special. He wasn't just the first of these creatures that had entered Tim's life; he was one of the first 24 of these creatures to exist at all. And he had plenty of stories to tell, incredible stories. He related tales of the dark angel Abaddon, his creator, of his relationship with a human woman who had escaped from the Great Sea of Fire, and of their flight from Satan's wrath. There were so many adventures, and through them, Tim came to better understand the nature of Hell, better understand the grim world beyond the Plunge of Desolation. He came to understand what purpose these creatures, Abaddon's children, served. Perhaps, one day, they would help change the face of Hell. Perhaps, he could play a part in that change.

The creatures ventured forth from the cave to prey on the demons and on those humans whose hearts were still full of darkness. They traveled far and wide in their search for food. Often, they returned with things that he could use. They brought him literally thousands of brightly glowing crystals that allowed him to bring illumination to his subterranean world. They brought him the dark cloak and robe that he wore now, clothing to replace the gray loincloth that he had worn for so long. They had even brought him a demon's sword and scabbard. It had taken at least a dozen of the creatures, working together, to bring him such a heavy object. He had spent literally thousands of hours practicing with it, and he had become quite good.

Tim had even mastered some of the sword's hidden powers, such as the ability to project a sort of ball of fire. He had seen the demons do that trick many times, mostly to evoke fear among the humans under their command, to keep them in line. It was Goliath who had coached him in this art. It was a mental discipline, not unlike the telepathy they shared. The energy to project the strange fiery manifestation was found not in the sword itself, but within him who wielded it. Its wellspring was within his very soul. The trick was bringing forth that energy and infilling the sword with it. It had taken months for Tim to achieve some measure of competence in the art, though true mastery still eluded him. Nonetheless, firing it at the cavern wall 60 feet away had driven the rocks to a dull red heat. Not bad for a human. At least, that was Goliath's observation. To his knowledge it was a feat previously achieved only by the demons.

Yet these creatures had become more than his personal thieves and companions. They had chiseled out a great chair, a table, even a bed, from the rock around him, using their powerful teeth. They had turned this cavern into a home, even a fortress. They had become his loving subjects, his warriors. No longer was he just another helpless human at the mercy of the demons. Now, he had power in his corner, and today, for the first time, he would use it.

Again Tim peered through the fist-sized crystal that acted like a spyglass toward the shuffling multitude about 200 yards away. Where was she?

He had met Megan just a few weeks after his arrival here. She wasn't much older than him. She had ended up in the eternal line just ahead of him. The demons forbid it, yet the two of them had managed to strike up a conversation here and there, when no demons were in sight, when their pain had receded enough to allow it. It had helped them to maintain their sanity. They'd been lashed over it a few times, but it hadn't stopped them. He'd desperately needed someone to talk to; so had she. Most of those around him didn't even speak English, but she did. She was from Australia, of all places. He'd come to love her, and she him. It was a strange situation for a pair such as they, sentenced there for their unnatural affections, but there it was. They'd made a pact between them; they'd stay together, no matter what. They'd take the plunge together, wait at the bottom of the cliff until the other was able to travel, whatever it took. Occasionally they'd gotten separated, but not for long. One of those times was on the day of the attack. Megan had already gone over the cliff, he was left on top. That was the last time he'd seen her for a long time.

For so long he'd assumed that she had gone with the dark angels and the Marines. She'd never given up hope of being rescued, even here. She went on and on about it. Perhaps her hopes had been a prophecy of things to come.

For so long, he'd been afraid to venture from the cave, afraid of being captured and returned to the torments of Hell. Life was good in his cavern. He had light, fresh water, and good company. There was nothing out there for him, or so he thought. It wasn't until a month ago that he had once more stepped into the daylight, escorted by several dozen of his small friends. He knelt right here, behind this same rock, observing the tragic procession before him. He was horrified to find that Megan was still there. She hadn't been rescued. She'd been stuck there all this time. She looked so sad, so alone.

Tim had retreated back to the cave and cried for hours. He felt like he'd abandoned her. What could he do? He had to do something. Yet his grief was turning into something else. It was turning to anger and then into the desire for revenge. In the end, it turned into a plan. He would rescue her; no one else would. That dark angel, Abaddon, had vowed to return for the others. He'd said so, but he never had. Now the task fell to him. Tim had planned it for nearly a month. Goliath and some of the others had helped, but their brains weren't quite wired like a human brain. They were smart, yes, but they were designed to execute plans, not to engineer them, so most of the planning had been up to him. They'd gathered what he needed from the surrounding land, reconnoitered the region carefully, and reported back to him.

The plan was complex and the hours of planning were great. It had taken much time and effort, but now he was ready. All he was waiting for was Megan. He'd been waiting for what seemed like a very long time; then he saw her amidst the ragtag procession coming up the canyon. She limped as if her left leg were still not fully healed. It was time. He turned his head to Goliath. "Now," he said, in a voice of the mind, and Goliath understood.

Goliath shot into the air. His voice was hypersonic, like a dog whistle, a voice that only those of his kind could hear and understand. It was a voice that carried on the air, echoed across the canyon walls. All hell was about to break loose.

It had taken many hours for the creatures to move into position. Some had followed the many underground passageways that led to small cavern entrances here and there along the canyon walls. Others had flown and walked to their stations. Yet, the demons had taken no notice of them. Their full attention was directed toward the thousands of human victims remanded to their care. Now they swept in from their hiding places among the rocks by the tens of thousands, quickly overwhelming the demons. They never stood a chance. For the second time, pure pandemonium had broken out. The humans gazed on in wonder as the creatures literally darkened the skies in places. There was less fear than anticipation among them this time. They hoped that it spelled liberation for them.

Faced with the danger, most of the demons drew their swords, yet it was clearly the wrong weapon. The swift and agile creatures were able to avoid the vast majority of these attacks. They went instinctively for the demon's weakest point; their bat-like wings, tearing them to shreds, and rendering their adversaries unable to fly.

A few of the demons tried to make a break for it, taking to the air. Yet they soon discovered that the creatures were both swifter and more maneuverable than they were. Within a minute, they had come crashing to the ground, their wings in tatters.

With the battle in full swing, Tim rushed from his hiding place, and ran toward Megan, who stood motionless amidst the others. He couldn't risk losing her again, couldn't risk something happening to her in all of the confusion. Yet he could not have anticipated the obstacles he would have to overcome to reach her.

Tim saw the demon's shadow before he saw the demon himself, a dark form sweeping across the canyon floor. The demon was plunging headlong out of the salmon sky, three of the small creatures in pursuit. He was targeting the stranger in the dark cloak. Perhaps he sensed that this being was somehow behind the current attack.

Tim had but a fraction of a second to respond. He dug his sandaled feet into the gravel and stumbled backward. The demon swept across his path, missing him by a matter of inches. A second later, the demon's feet were planted on the ground. The creatures lit into him, but he quickly shook them off, creating a whirlwind with his bat-like wings.

The demon turned to the hooded stranger, and Tim came face to face with his nemesis. The demon's skin was almost gray, with facial features like those of an incredibly old man. He scowled as he looked Tim over.

"I know you!" he roared. "You walked this very trail not so long ago. You should not have come back. Now I will make you pay in pain." The demon drew his long, menacing sword.

The demon was surprised when Tim drew out his equally menacing sword from beneath his cloak. There was no fear in Tim's eyes. Instead, he saw rage.

"You boast way too much," said Tim, stepping forward. "You're brave enough when you're dealing with shackled and defenseless men and women. Let's see how you do against me."

"You're just a boy," said the demon.

"All I hear is talk," replied Tim. "I think that's all you are. That and stupid."

The demon was enraged. He charged headlong at the youth, who most certainly was no more than half his weight. Their swords clashed amidst a flurry of sparks. They clashed again and again.

The humans looked on in amazement. That cloaked figure was not a demon or an angel, it was one of them—a human being—and he was holding his own against a demon.

The demon had apparently been convinced that he would defeat this human within a matter of a few seconds, but the clashing of swords was going into its second minute. The demon had raw strength on his side, but this human had superior speed and agility. Tim lunged and slid from side to side, avoiding every thrust of his opponent. In fact, he had actually scored a hit at the base of the demon's left wing. There was a wild-eyed madness in his eyes of a sort the demon had rarely seen. The demon actually found himself on the defensive. How could a mere human be so good?

"Do you need help?" asked a telepathic voice that Tim recognized as Goliath.

"No, he's mine," replied Tim.

Tim knew this demon, or at least he thought he did. He'd applied the lash to him and to Megan more than a few times. Now, it was his turn.

"You're only delaying the inevitable," roared the demon.

"Then let's be done with it." Tim made his move, one both bold and foolhardy. He lunged forward. The demon swung his sword laterally, missing Tim by no more than two inches. Then Tim thrust forward and upward. His sword penetrated the demon's throat from below, and plunged straight into his spine. He went down, amidst a rush of pulsing blood.

The demon looked up incredulously, unable to move. Tim returned his gaze for but a moment. Then the demon looked around to see that no less than a hundred of the creatures surrounded him.

"Now, he's yours," said Tim, turning to Goliath and the others. "Have fun."

The creatures wasted no time; they tore into the helpless demon, and more were joining in the attack every second. Tim turned away, sheathed his sword, and proceeded toward Megan.

At first Megan didn't appear to recognize the approaching figure in the dark cloak. Then she began to walk toward him, her shackles clanking and rattling with each step. Could it really be? He stopped about ten feet in front of her, drawing back his hood to reveal his face.

Megan's eyes immediately teared up. "Tim?" she gasped. "I thought they took you."

"No, they left me behind too," he replied. "But I won't leave you behind, not again, not ever again. We're getting out of here."

Megan took several more steps forward and practically fell into his arms. She could hardly believe it. "I've missed you so much," she wept.

"I've missed you too," replied Tim. "I swear that no one is ever going to hurt you again, not ever. I'll destroy anyone who tries it."

Megan looked down, even as four of the small creatures lit into her ankle shackles. Within a minute, she was free.

Tim looked at all of the others who starred at him in stunned amazement. "I'm releasing all of you," he announced in a loud voice. "My name is Tim Monroe. I don't care what you've done in the past; it is the past. We're all here in Hell; none of us were angels in life, but we didn't deserve this. I'm giving you all a second chance. The rule of the demons is at an end. There'll be no more chains, no more whips, no more jumping off that cliff. I'm calling the shots now. Don't be afraid of my small friends. They will release all of you; just stay where you are. They're going to be your friends, too—just wait and see."

Hundreds of the small creatures moved into the crowd and started to work on the shackles. Sparks flew everywhere.

A bald man, released from his shackles, but still limping from his recent fall, stepped up to Tim and extended his hand. "I'm glad and grateful to see you again, Tim. I'm with you wherever you lead. What do you need me to do?"

"I am too," said a dark-haired woman several feet away. "I promise to do whatever you ask."

A general round of agreement arose from the growing crowd. Tim was the hero of their eternity. He was their messiah.

Tim turned to the bald man. "Karl, I need for you to go to the top of the ridge. Tell everyone that you see that they're free. They can go wherever they please, but if they want my protection, they should come right here. I have a plan for everyone." Then he turned to the dark-haired woman. "Silvia, you can go down the canyon and out into the plains, give everyone you see my message."

"I will," confirmed the woman.

Twenty minutes found not a single human in bondage in this place. And the runners took the word of the coming of a messiah to the Valleys of Noak, of a human who had defeated a demon in combat and commanded a vast army of creatures.

Within three quarters of an hour, the valley around Tim was full of grateful people. Some ran, some walked, some were carried, but all came to offer thanks to their liberator.

Tim had the limelight, and he took full advantage of it. He spoke of the difficult times ahead. For the moment, they would be living in the caverns; it was the safest place. But the day would come when they would live on the surface. They would build towns and roads. They would create a civilization, perhaps an empire. They would try to make peace with the demons if possible, eradicate them if necessary. But in the meantime, there was a lot of work to be done. There were a total of 64 demons assigned to the Plunge of Desolation—demons who had been literally ripped apart by his creatures. Still, given time, they would regenerate to become a threat once more. Tim had already arrived at a method of removing them from the picture, but it wasn't pretty. Then again, it didn't need to be.

Tim began to delegate responsibility to teams of people in his midst. They would be gathering up things they needed; swords, clothing, even shackles. They would raid a small cave that the demons used as a storage area for any materials they might use, and that might well be everything that was there. Then they were on their way.

The creatures had turned out to serve many purposes. They were warriors and builders, but they could also be excavators. During the past few days they had widened and leveled a previously unusable cave that led from the cavern system to the surface, about a mile up the canyon from what was previously the only entrance large enough for a human to pass.

Creating it was a risk, and Tim knew it. It became the Achilles' heel of his subterranean world, an entrance large enough for a demon or group of demons to enter. Still, he could ill afford to have an entrance so small as to prevent the passage of many of his liberated subjects. What was he now—a king, an emperor, or just a frightened youth? He really couldn't answer that question.

With thousands of the small creatures flying overhead, the once victims of the Plunge of Desolation moved the needed supplies and their former captors, now shackled hand and foot in a sort of hogtied position, up the canyon and into the cavern. The demons growled, snarled, and howled, for all the good it did. If anything, it only sweetened this moment for the humans. Many of those in the precession took this opportunity to brutalize these foul creatures, kicking and punching them savagely and throwing rocks at them. For much of the two-mile journey to the cavern entrance, that was the order of business: revenge. The demons were dragged into the subterranean twilight, into a maze of tunnels, and in the end, were hauled through a narrow passageway and into a cavern room dominated by a dark pit 20 feet wide and 50 or more feet deep.

One by one, the demons were tossed in. Their bodies were broken by the fall. The abyss echoed with their shrill cries of pain. Some ended up impaled on the scattered stalagmites that protruded from the rugged floor. Their bodies soon covered every square inch of the floor. Then bodies piled upon bodies. It was truly poetic vengeance.

Stones were piled up at the entrance of the passageway, leaving only enough room for the small creatures to enter. And so they would. No longer would they need to travel miles in search of prey that might just as easily kill them. No, now they would have a practically limitless supply of food close at hand in the form of these constantly regenerating demons, a supply unable to fight back. The demon taskmasters would now assume a new role: meat. Already, the tiny creatures were taking full advantage of this new resource, a fact attested to by the shrill cries of the demons within the pit. They swept in and out of the cavern room by the hundreds.

With their captured supplies stored, Tim allowed his new subjects to rest. The discovery of often-deep-pools of water within some of the rooms led to a gleeful episode of splashing and drinking among the former victims of the Plunge. Then, with their thirst quenched, they rediscovered the wonderful blessing of sleep, free of pain. Tim knew that if their experience was anything like his, they might be in for a rough few days. They would have to help each other through those difficult times.

The caverns had grown quiet once more as Tim walked with Megan amidst the crystal light, hand in hand. "They'll probably sleep for days," he said, motioning toward a particularly well-lit tunnel. "These are my quarters, my own private refuge, and yours."

They stepped into a cavern room aglow with crystal light. Its walls were exceptionally smooth and regular, and the light glistened off a floor, which had the consistency and texture of dark glass. "I created it using fireballs from my sword," said Tim, pride in his voice, pointing at the floor. My small friends shaped the walls and made the chairs, table, and furniture from the rock itself. I then melted the fine dust to create the floor.

"It's beautiful," gasped Megan. "It's almost gothic, and I love gothic things— or at least, I did."

"You can again," announced Tim. "This is your place too. It's our place. I can make you happy; I know it. Hell will never be the same."

"I hope you're right," said Megan, walking over to the far side of the chamber where an intricate pattern had been etched into the wall. "What's this?"

"It's a map," replied Tim, stepping to her side. "It shows the caverns I've explored. My friends helped me make it. Pretty cool, don't you think?"

"Yes," replied Megan, "it's pretty cool." She paused. "But how did it all happen? How did you get away from the demons?"

"I hope you have time," said Tim, "It is kind of a long story."

"I think I have time," said Megan. "I think that is about all we have."

Tim led Megan over to a sort of bed made of rock. It had several cloaks tossed across it to soften its hard texture. They sat down. Tim told Megan the whole incredible story. Megan asked only a few questions; mostly, she just listened.

When she had heard it all, she asked one final question. "Do you think it might have been God's mercy that saved you, brought Goliath to you?"

"No, I don't," replied Tim. "I don't think God gives a damn about us. The way I figure it, He threw us away. To Him, we're damaged goods with defective genes, so He threw us here in His garbage dump. I didn't ask to be born a homosexual; it just happened. I couldn't help the way I was, the way I felt. I mean, I only did it twice, you know?"

Megan said, "I'm afraid I did it a few more times than that. I had a steady girlfriend back in Perth. But it wasn't my lesbian lifestyle that killed me; it was my girlfriend's father. You see, she was only 16 and I was 20. He warned me to stay away, but I guess I wasn't smart enough to do it. He caught me in her bedroom with her, and in the process of throwing me out of his house, he threw me down the stairs. I broke my neck. I guess he had it figured that it was ok to kill one of us. I wasn't a bad person; I wasn't ready to die. Oh, if I'd only had a second chance, had the chance to invite Jesus into my heart." She hesitated. "But after today, I don't know. Maybe there is hope. I'm not so sure God is done with us. Maybe He's giving us a second chance."

"No," replied Tim, "I think Goliath gave us a second chance. Without him, I might have made it into the cave, but I'd have been living in the darkness near the cave entrance. I'd have been better off, but my life would have been empty." Tim hesitated. "It would have been empty without you. Strange, isn't it, that I should feel the way I do about you? I never felt this way about a girl, not ever."

Megan smiled. Never had Tim seen such a radiant expression on her face. "Then it's not just me? I've felt that way about you for so long, but I was afraid to say it. Anyway, what did it matter, you know? We were in that line at the Plunge. What did anything matter?"

Tim's smile now matched Megan's. "Oh, this is incredible. What a place to meet."

This time, Megan laughed openly, yet the weariness in her eyes was really beginning to show.

"You need to rest," said Tim. "I mean, how long has it been, three years?"

"Yeah," she confirmed, "probably about that."

Tim rearranged the cloaks on the stone bed, and helped Megan lay down. He gazed into her tired eyes. "You rest. You might have some bad dreams. You might feel sick for a time, but it will pass. It did for me. I'll be right here with you. I'll never leave you."

Tim kissed Megan on the cheek. It felt wonderful. She was actually here. His plan had really worked, at least so far.

It was but a minute later that Megan was asleep. He thought about what she had said. Did God still care about them? He remembered a preacher who had told him that Hell was forever. Once you were there, you never got out, no matter how you felt or what you did. Was he right? At this point, he didn't know. Now his mission was clearer than ever—to reshape Hell into a place less terrible. Perhaps it was impossible; perhaps, in the end, Satan would crush him, but he had to try. He found himself asking God for guidance. Strange, he'd never done that before. Perhaps some portion of Megan's sweet spirit was rubbing off on him.

CHAPTER 15

Bedillia Farnsworth pushed her white queen forward four squares in an uncharacteristically bold move. "Check," she announced.

Her good friend, Tom Carson, scanned the board. He hadn't expected that. It was a good two minutes before he moved, blocking check with his bishop.

It had been a dull duty in Abaddon's conference chamber. Their main task was to monitor the primary telesphere in case an unscheduled communication came in. There was no more scheduled communication on this shift. Unscheduled communications were relatively rare. The beeping sound that announced an incoming communication caught them completely by surprise. It was Bedillia who walked over to the black marble table in the corner of the room and activated the crystal globe. The globe vanished, to be replaced by a sphere of static, then an image. The face they saw was one of a handsome, middle-aged man. However, this man was dressed wholly in black and had a large pair of bat-like wings. Bedillia recognized him as the leader of the demon forces of Hell, Cordon.

"I offer greetings to you, Bedillia Farnsworth," said Cordon.

"Hello, Cordon," said Bedillia. "How can I help you?"

The look of concern on Cordon's face told Bedillia that there was trouble. She had a bad feeling about this.

"I must speak to Abaddon on business most urgent," said Cordon.

"I'm afraid that he is in the lower chambers conducting an inspection," replied Bedillia. "Is there anything that I might help you with?"

"Perhaps," replied Cordon. "I wish to request permission to gate over to speak to you directly. We do have a problem, a very serious problem. I prefer not to discuss it over the telesphere."

"Of course," replied Bedillia. "You can gate straight over from your ring to ours. How would ten minutes be?"

"Acceptable," replied Cordon, no emotion whatever in his voice.

Bedillia definitely didn't like the sound of this. Cordon was usually very friendly and outgoing, but not today. "I'll do my best to get Abaddon to the ring room in time to meet you."

"Very well," confirmed Cordon. "I will be in your ring room in ten minutes." The image immediately faded.

"Wow," said Tom, "who put a bee in Cordon's bonnet?"

"I don't know," replied Bedillia, "but can you get Bill to go looking for Abaddon? He should be in his lab. Abaddon said he would be down in area seven. Then come on back and watch over the telesphere in case we get another incoming call. I'll meet Cordon in the ring room."

"Right," said Tom, heading out into the corridor.

Bedillia paced back and forth across the conference room floor several times. She wondered if this communication had anything to do with the taking of two young women from their places of torment. He had agreed to it, hadn't he?

Abaddon arrived in the ring room just a few minutes after Bedillia. "Did he say what he wanted?"

"No," replied Bedillia. "I got the feeling that he didn't want to say anything over an open channel."

About a minute later, the ring filled with mists and Cordon stepped alone through the ring without fanfare. He turned to Abaddon. "We need to talk in private."

"Then we shall go to my conference chambers," said Abaddon.

"I'd like to be present at the meeting, if I may," said Bedillia.

Abaddon turned to Cordon. Cordon only nodded. The three proceeded down the hall. Cordon was uncharacteristically silent. Usually, you could depend on Cordon to be relatively cheerful and full of small talk, but not this time.

They hadn't even taken a seat before Cordon began. "My friends, there can be no secrets between us now. There are things I must know. Have you taken part in any attacks against any of our facilities, taken any humans from us since our last meeting?"

There was no hesitation in Bedillia's response. She turned to Abaddon. "Sir, may I answer that question?"

Abaddon only nodded. This would have to be an issue that Bedillia resolved with Cordon.

Bedillia turned to Cordon. "Sir, there were members of our security force that went into unguarded regions of Hell's underground and took their wives from their torments. They just couldn't stand the thought of their wives suffering any longer."

"Yes, yes, I am well aware of that," said Cordon, impatience in his voice. "I had assumed that Mr. Tesla had already conveyed to you my consent on that issue. Indeed, I was there during both rescues in the event of some unseen problems. I would have released them to you myself, but I am in a rather delicate situation. My people already view me as being soft on the human issue. If it became common knowledge that I had condoned the release of two human females simply because they were the Earthly wives of members of the Refuge military, matters would have become, well, complicated."

"I can see that," said Bedillia.

For the first time, Cordon smiled, though slightly. "I have been working closely with Nikola Tesla for many months on a variety of projects. We talk often and very frankly. I count him among my closest friends. He had spoken of the desire of some citizens of Refuge to rescue loved ones in Hell. He had sought to intervene with me on their behalf. We arrived at the plan that has already been carried out. Your people rescued them. For my part, I made sure that the books were altered in such a way that they would not be missed."

"We appreciate your efforts," said Abaddon. "It was very compassionate of you."

Cordon nodded. "It was an act of kindness between friends. However, that is not the incident I am referring to."

"Then I'm afraid you've lost me," admitted Bedillia. She looked to Abaddon who returned her puzzled look.

"Then you don't know?" asked Cordon.

"Don't know what?" asked Abaddon.

Cordon seemed to become more relaxed. "My friends, I think that I might owe you an apology. You truly don't know."

"Don't know what?" asked Bedillia, who had grown more frustrated by this whole state of affairs.

"About the incident at the Plunge of Desolation in the Valley of Noak," replied Cordon.

"You are correct," said Abaddon. "The last time we were there was shortly before the war in Heaven, two years ago."

"Very well, these are the facts, as we know them," replied Cordon. "Sometime between 7 and 29 hours ago, 64 of my people and approximately 3,000 of yours vanished without a trace from that place."

Abaddon looked on incredulously. "How could that possibly be?"

"That is the question I have asked myself: how?" continued Cordon. "I do know that there have been numerous attacks by your small creatures reported in that area, more than in most other regions of Hell. Your creatures attack my people and humans alike." He paused. "I truly do not see why you created them. What were you thinking of? They are a general menace."

"I created them for a different time, a different situation," said Abaddon. "I could not have foreseen this current age. My creatures have an instinct to feed; they are carnivorous. But they also have the ability to discern the contents of the soul. Their instinct is to attack and feed upon those whose hearts are filled with darkness. Others will be left in peace."

"That is curious," noted Cordon. "Rolf and I have encountered them on several occasions, but they always seem to leave us alone. Indeed, they have even alighted upon me on no less than three occasions, but they didn't attack; they simply flew off."

That revelation brought a smile to Bedillia's face. It confirmed what she had already suspected about Cordon's character.

Cordon turned to Abaddon. "Abaddon, is there nothing that you can do about these creatures of yours? They are a menace. We have tried to keep their numbers under control, but we are experiencing only limited success. I cannot dismiss the possibility that they are somehow behind the disappearances."

"But how could that possibly be?" objected Abaddon. Surely, you are not suggesting that they somehow spirited away so many humans and demons. They aren't capable of such a feat."

"No, I realize that," replied Cordon. "However, I suspect that there is a connection."

"My control over my creatures has faded with the passage of time," admitted Abaddon. "This is a consequence I had not foreseen. Only about a third of the children I released still respond to my commands. I lost their prime in the Valley of Noak two years ago."

"Their prime?" asked Cordon.

"Yes," confirmed Abaddon. "The prime is the eldest of the creatures, the father of the lineage of virtually all of them. It was with his assistance that I controlled the rest. With him gone, many simply follow their base instinct—to attack all of those whose hearts are dark and unrepentant."

"But they couldn't cause over 3,000 humans and demons to simply vanish," deduced Cordon.

"No, of course not," replied Abaddon. "And you have my word; neither I nor any under my command have returned to that place since then."

"Are you so sure?" asked Cordon.

"Yes, I am sure," replied Abaddon.

There was a long pause. "I believe you," said Cordon. "Which still leaves the question, who did this, and how?" He looked over at the chessboard on the conference table. "Checkmate in three for white. I fear that there is a new player in the game for power here in Hell, and that is not the worst of it. General Krell has returned. He has been judged in Heaven and sent back here by the Father. He will be expecting me to gate him to Satan's old audience chamber within the hour. I managed to delay him so as to speak to you first. I fear that he will not be pleased with me for many reasons."

"The least of which will be negotiating with us," deduced Bedillia.

Cordon nodded. "And this incident in Noak could not have come at a less opportune moment. Like all of the others who have been returned to us, he came through the great portal. That has never made sense to me. Rolf and I destroyed its internal mechanism, its circuitry, if you wish. It shouldn't function, yet it does. I examined its internal structure not long ago. All of its components were restored."

"The Father might have done that," suggested Abaddon.

The conversation was interrupted by yet another unscheduled telesphere transmission. Abaddon pressed the receive button to behold a momentary sphere of static before David Bonner and the angel Aaron came into focus.

"We have a problem," announced David. "General Krell was judged by the saints today. He is on his way back to Hell. I suspect that he might be there already. Tell Cordon that he may soon be deposed."

"Yes," confirmed Abaddon, "we just got the word."

"But how?" asked David. Only then did David see Cordon step from the background into full view. "Oh my."

"It's OK," said Bedillia, "he's a friend. David, Aaron, this is Cordon, leader of the demon forces of Hell."

Cordon cringed. "I prefer fallen angel, if you don't mind, and you are correct. I will not be their leader much longer. With his recent return, General Krell is now the ranking fallen angel of Hell. Within the hour, I will be compelled to turn over command to him."

"What might we expect from him?" asked Abaddon.

"I do not have that answer," admitted Cordon.

There was little more to say. Their worst fears had been realized. As Abaddon and Bedillia walked Cordon back to the ring room, spirits were low.

"Place your forces on high alert," warned Cordon. "I don't believe that General Krell will attack immediately. He doesn't tend to be impulsive, but I cannot rule it out. In the meantime, I'll try to negotiate with him on your behalf, but be ready for the worst."

"We all appreciate what you've tried to do," said Bedillia, shaking Cordon's hand as he prepared to depart. "I wish it had worked out better."

"Don't lose hope just yet," said Cordon. "I've always prided myself on being a good negotiator when I needed to be. The day may not be lost quite yet."

A field of misty stars appeared in the ring, and Cordon vanished into them. Abaddon and Bedillia walked back to the conference room.

"Maybe we could go somewhere else," suggested Bedillia. "There have to be other caverns."

Abaddon shook his head. "If we start running, then we'll be running until the day that the demons capture the last of us. We aren't putting plans like that on the table, at least not yet. We've got to know what we're up against. Then we proceed from there."

"But where do we start?" asked Bedillia.

"That's simple," replied Abaddon. "We start at where this conflict all started. We go to the Plunge of Desolation."

A glowing, blue cloud filled with shimmering stars materialized behind a pile of boulders along the narrow canyon. Out of the cloud stepped three figures, a dark angel and two humans. The cloud vanished behind them.

They ventured cautiously into the 50-foot-wide canyon. Normally there would have been a long procession of shackled, rag-clad people heading up this canyon, but not today. Bedillia looked about nervously. This place brought back bad memories. Two years ago, she had been a part of that procession for one complete circuit, even making the terrible plunge from the cliff. She caressed her particle pistol nervously.

"Are you OK, Bedillia?" asked Kurt, whose rifle was still slung over his shoulder.

"Yeah, I'm OK," she confirmed, scanning the length of the ridge to the west.

"Let's stay together," cautioned Abaddon. "There might still be demons here, searching the area. I'd rather not have to explain the reason for our presence here."

"According to the treaty, we have every right to be here," objected Kurt.

True," conceded Abaddon, "but our presence could place us in an awkward or even dangerous position. We don't want to create an incident."

"Well, whatever," said Kurt. "I wish we could have investigated this incident a few days ago, right after it happened, rather than wait five days."

"As I said, I didn't want to encounter any demons," said Abaddon. "I assume that they have completed their investigation by now."

The team moved southward, up the canyon, wary of any movement; there was none. There was a well-worn trail up the rocky floor, well worn by the feet of thousands of humans for just as many thousands of years.

Bedillia mulled over the reason for this place all the while, even as she scanned the barren landscape about her. She thought of the human tragedy it represented. She pondered the almost inconceivable pain and suffering. Where had all of these people gone?

For the next three hours the team searched for the sign of a struggle, dried blood, anything. They followed the trail up the side of the canyon and across the ridge to the very precipice of the cliff itself then backtracked their way to the place where the canyon met the four-mile-wide Valley of Noak, a place that appeared about as hospitable as Death Valley. There was never so much as a drop of rain here, not even clouds beyond those associated with the occasional dust storm. The bloated, red sun hung a short distance above the western horizon, forever stationary.

Out here in the open valley, the temperature was a very dry 90. There were certainly more unpleasant places in Hell, as far as the climate was concerned. Here the group concentrated their search. This was one of the places where the demons tended to congregate, the location where those who jumped from the cliff were at last reunited with the ground.

Over the two years since Bedillia had fallen from that cliff, she had tried to block this place out of her mind, but she particularly remembered this place. Still, it seemed strange that it was so quiet.

"I don't get it," admitted Kurt, taking a swig of water from the canteen. "There is soft sand and gravel all around, yet I don't see any footprints. It's like every inch of this place has been swept clean."

Abaddon scanned the cliffs behind them carefully as if looking for something in particular. "That is because it was swept clean."

"I don't follow you," admitted Kurt.

"This entire area was swept clean by tens of thousands of my children," continued Abaddon. "It is part of the instinct that I gave them—cover their tracks. You can see it in the scalloped texture of the sand. Oh yes, they were very busy. In this case they did the job too well. They not only removed their own tracks, they removed all tracks. They also removed most of the evidence, but not quite all." Abaddon pointed to the north side of a rock in front of him. "This blood, almost totally erased from the stone, is not human blood; it is demon blood. It has the smell of it. My children took a demon down right here. Then he was somehow removed. There are faint traces of blood that lead up the canyon. They are barely distinguishable, but they are unmistakable. Only a warrior angel would be able to track them, not one of Satan's brood."

"So, where to from here?" asked Bedillia.

"Back up the canyon," said Abaddon.

The group was on the move again. They went past the point where the procession normally left the canyon and followed the switchback trail to the west and proceeded even further up the canyon. All the while, Abaddon followed the scent of blood.

"Scan the canyon walls," said the dark angel. "Watch for any sign of movement."

"What are we looking for?" asked Bedillia.

"My children," replied Abaddon. "I assure you, they are here, and they know we are here. They've known it for some time."

The team was just over a mile up this previously unexplored region when Kurt turned suddenly to the left. He focused on a point about half way up the 300-foot-high wall of rock. "I'm sure I saw movement up there." He pulled his binoculars from their case and focused on a small cleft in the rock. "Abaddon, there's an AC up there watching us. No, make that two of them."

Abaddon took the binoculars and scanned the cliff. "I see them. They're watching us alright. I will try to summon them to come here."

Abaddon stretched out his hand, but his children did not respond. He seemed very troubled.

"They've gone feral, haven't they?" deduced Bedillia.

"Possibly," replied Abaddon. "Still, I can assure you that they will not attack us. That is their prime instinct."

"What now?" asked Kurt, who managed to catch sight of another AC in flight further up the canyon.

"We continue on," said Abaddon. "The blood trail continues. We should follow it."

They'd walked only another hundred yards when Bedillia saw a small cave to their right. She moved to investigate it. She looked into the quiet darkness.

"It looks pretty tight in there," noted Kurt, directing his flashlight into the opening.

"I think I could squeeze in there," said Bedillia, pulling the flashlight from her utility belt and sticking her head in.

"You'll do no such thing," said Abaddon. "You don't know what is in there. There are beasts within the subterranean depths of Hell that are indeed cruel and dangerous."

"I don't think I could get through that tunnel," noted Kurt, turning to Abaddon. "And you certainly couldn't."

"I'm convinced that our answers are in there," said Bedillia, leaning in still further. "I need to go."

"You're not going in there alone," said Abaddon. "There is no trail of blood leading in there anyway. It continues further up the canyon, and so we should move on."

And so they did. Along the way they saw many more ACs watching them from the rocks and flying overhead, but none of them would respond to Abaddon.

The floor of the canyon was wider here, perhaps 150 feet, but littered with huge boulders. They had traveled another 20 minutes when Abaddon came to a halt. He pointed to a particularly odd-looking rock formation.

"That is strange," noted Bedillia, approaching it. "It is so smooth, almost glassy. How would something like that form?"

"I'm not quite sure," said Kurt. "It looks like the rock was melted."

"The result of a fireball projected from the sword of a demon," said Abaddon, reaching out to the rock face, "quite a number of them from the appearance of it. There was an opening here, but it was sealed. The blood trail ends here."

"Well congratulations Mr. Holmes," said a brown haired young man in a black cloak, stepping out from behind a boulder, accompanied by about two dozen ACs. "Or should I call you Abaddon, ruler of the dark angels, king of Refuge?"

"I am not a king," corrected Abaddon, "I am its administrator."

"Same thing," said the youth, scanning the three explorers. "And to set the record straight, the sword was wielded by me, not by some demon."

"I stand corrected," said Abaddon, no emotion in his voice.

"So, you finally came back," said the young man. "A bit too late, however. I have already liberated this place. I've set the captives free."

"Where are they?" asked Bedillia.

"Safe," said the young man, "safe and in no pain."

"You have us at a disadvantage," observed Abaddon.

The youth smiled an indeed devious smile. "Yes, you might say that."

It was then that Abaddon focused upon the AC setting on the youth's shoulders. Suddenly, he understood. "The prime; he didn't perish."

"No he didn't," confirmed the youth. "When you abandoned him two years ago, I rescued him." The youth paused. "And no, you can't have him back. He and I have been through a lot together. I named him Goliath."

"An excellent name," said Bedillia, "but we still don't know your name."

"Tim," said the youth, still focused on Abaddon. "I was a part of that grand march once, that march off the cliff. Several of your children, as you call them, sliced away my shackles. Some human soldiers, Marines I think, told me where I had to go to escape this place, to come to this refuge of yours. I tried. Oh, how I tried, but you left me behind. You abandoned me, just like you did Goliath."

"It's him," said Bedillia, looking to Abaddon. "He is the young man that Private Higgins came to me about two years ago." She turned to Tim. "Higgins was very upset when he discovered that you had been left behind. He came in to see me for several counseling sessions after that. We didn't mean to leave you behind; please believe me."

"Well, I suppose it doesn't matter," said Tim. "I've survived on my own pretty well up to this point." His anger seemed to ebb slightly. "Look, I know what you're trying to do; that's fine. But we don't need you, OK?"

"Tim, we could help you and the others," said Bedillia. "You don't need to go this on your own. We really want to help you. We can accomplish more together than we can separately."

Tim nodded. "What are you suggesting, pretty lady?"

"My name is Bedillia."

Tim nodded once more. "Oh, I know who you are. You're the mother of Serena. Yes, I've heard of you. Goliath really liked your daughter. He said that she was very special, very brave."

"Thank you," said Bedillia. She paused before continuing. "Goliath knew my daughter?"

"Of course," said Tim. "He told me the whole story. He has told me many things about Hell and Refuge."

"He has told you?" asked Abaddon.

"Sure," replied Tim. "He tells me all kinds of things. Some of the others do too, but it's mostly Goliath that talks to me."

"Then you have bonded with him and he with you," deduced Abaddon. "I can never take him from you for that reason. He must stay with you."

Tim seemed impressed by that statement. "At least you understand that. I guess it's a start."

Bedillia moved back to the initial point. "Tim, we really need to work together. I was suggesting that we could provide you and your people with things: training, food, supplies, and weapons that you could use to defend yourselves against the demons."

"And in return, what would you want?" asked Tim.

"Friendship. That's all," said Bedillia. "We could stand together against the demons, if it came to that."

"We hang together or we hang separately," deduced Tim. "The founding fathers would have been proud. Still, I want to avoid foreign entanglements."

"Tim, we need their help," said a second voice from behind the boulders. A young and pretty woman dressed in a black cloak like the one Tim was wearing stepped out into the open. "It wasn't their fault," she insisted. "The demons came back. There were so many of them. I was right there. I saw it. These people had to leave."

Tim glanced in her direction, then back toward Bedillia and the others. "This is Megan, a very special woman."

"Hello, Megan," said Bedillia.

Megan only nodded. "Tim, we shouldn't do this on our own when there are people who can help us. We really don't know what we're up against. I love our place. I want to make sure it stays ours. I don't want to go back to the Plunge or some other horrible torture that Satan might sentence us to."

"Satan is no longer in control of Hell," announced Kurt. "He isn't even here. He is trapped on Earth."

"Much has happened in both Heaven and Hell during the past two years," interjected Abaddon. "It's important that you understand what you're up against before you start making plans for the future."

The team took a few minutes to outline the current situation in Hell, telling them about Cordon and the treaty. All the while, Megan in particular seemed to be growing more nervous.

"Tim, we need to get back inside," she said.

"You could come with us," suggested Bedillia, "see Refuge for yourself."

"A kind offer," said Tim, "but we will pass, at least today; perhaps later."

They began to make their way back down the canyon, and Tim and Megan accompanied them. Overhead thousands of ACs patrolled the sky. Bedillia did most of the talking, speaking of life in Refuge. Her words seemed most interesting to Megan. Tim seemed less impressed. Neither seemed too willing to discuss their plans or the nature of the world they were creating here, and when it came to the issue of the missing demons, they were very tight-lipped. However, it became only too clear that Tim was holding them as prisoners.

"The demons are very sensitive when it comes to the issue of us holding one or more of their own against their will," said Abaddon. "They will not allow this to continue."

"Oh," replied Tim, "then it is OK if they torture us for eternity, but if we so much as touch one of them, then they cry foul. You'll excuse me if I don't have much sympathy for them."

"It doesn't matter if you have sympathy for them," continued Abaddon. "They will eventually mount a search, and they will discover the hidden entrance to your cavern. I would be willing to help you broker an agreement with Cordon, one like we have. You could enjoy freedom from fear. If not, you'll have a war on your hands. And I assure you, they will come. I'm surprised that they haven't come already."

"There haven't been any demons around here for some time," said Tim. "They've given up the search. Look, I don't plan to go out looking for a fight, and if they come looking for one, then we will give them a beating that they'll not soon forget."

"Son, you don't know what you're up against," cautioned Kurt. "You have no real weapons and no military training. Your ACs would defend you for a time, but in the end, the demons would overwhelm them. They'd roll right over you."

Still, there seemed to be no reasoning with Tim. He was stubborn and perhaps just a bit mentally unstable. A few minutes later, they reached the small cave.

"Here is where we get off," said Tim. He pondered their situation for a moment. "I'll tell you what; we can talk about this later. The next time you come, send Bedillia, just Bedillia. Have her come to this cave. I'll talk to her and her alone. Maybe we can come to some sort of a deal."

"I'd be glad to come to meet with you," replied Bedillia.

"Good," said Tim. "Why not come tomorrow, whenever that is. With no night here, it's kind of hard to figure, but I'll meet with you then. I'll throw out the welcome mat. I promise you'll be safe."

As Tim and Megan climbed back into the cave, the group continued on down the canyon beneath a myriad of renegade ACs. There was much to discuss. Yes, they'd found a potential ally, but he was also a destabilizing element in their shaky relationship with the demons. Their situation had just become a lot more complicated.

It was hours later, and Bedillia found herself alone in Abaddon's audience chamber. It was time. She walked to the black marble table and switched on the telesphere. A few seconds later the sphere displayed an image of the angel Aaron standing among the books of a library. He held a black book in his hand.

"Good evening, Bedillia," said Aaron.

"Hello, Aaron," said Bedillia. "Looks like you're doing research."

"Yes, I am," confirmed Aaron. "I am studying the life of this Tim Monroe you encountered in the Valley of Noak." Aaron shook his head sadly. "He is a truly tragic character, cut down by a senseless act of violence. I do not believe that he is a violent young man, but I would exercise care in dealing with him. If you are to meet with him alone, have your escape well planned."

"Don't worry, Aaron," said Bedillia. "I'll be fine."

"I shall present a full report on Tim Monroe to Abaddon and the council in the morning," said Aaron. Aaron paused then smiled. "However, I suspect that you want a report on someone else, someone on Earth."

Bedillia smiled. "How is she, Aaron?"

"She is doing well, under the circumstances," confirmed Aaron. "Times are trying, but that is only to be expected." Aaron went on to give Bedillia a full report regarding the life of her daughter on Earth, as he had once a week for so many years.

Bedillia worried about Serena, her only daughter. She felt so helpless right now. When Serena really needed her, she couldn't be there. Oh, if she'd only made different choices. If only she could go back and change the past.

It was a full half hour before she signed off. "Oh Serena, how I wish I could hold you in my arms, defend you against the enemy." But of course, she couldn't. Refuge might be fairly comfortable, but it was still Hell. From here she was powerless to help her daughter. She went back to the table. She wept for many minutes before she was able to return to her job.

CHAPTER 16

Abaddon paced back and forth nervously in the ring room. He was noticeably agitated. "I should never have allowed her to go back there alone," he lamented.

"I don't think there was any stopping her," replied Lenar, his chief dark angelic warrior. "That Tim fellow wouldn't talk to anyone but her."

Abaddon turned to Kurt, who stood not far away, leaning on the great metallic ring. "How late is she now?"

"Almost 20 minutes," he replied, glancing at his watch.

"Do we go in after her?" asked Lenar.

"I wouldn't do that if I were you," advised Kurt. "Bedillia was very specific about that. She gave her word that she would go in alone."

Abruptly, Kurt backed away from the ring. A few seconds later, its interior was filled with glowing mists. Bedillia stepped from those mists, a distinct look of satisfaction on her face."

"You were a bit late," noted Abaddon. "We were becoming concerned." He paused. "I take it that the negotiations went well."

"Exceptionally," said Bedillia. "I believe Tim is coming around. I think we have Megan to thank for that. I would like to make a gift of a telesphere to them. That way we could have instantaneous contact with them."

Abaddon nodded approvingly. "I have no objection to that."

"I would also like to get some decent clothes to them," continued Bedillia. "So many of them are living in filthy rags. It's deplorable."

"Again, I have no objection," replied Abaddon. "I believe that it would be a humane gesture. It would strengthen our relationship with them."

"Their cavern is not nearly as grand as ours, but it does have potential," continued Bedillia. "However, there are a few problems that might need to be addressed."

"Such as?" asked Lenar.

"Such as what they have done to their old demon taskmasters," said Bedillia. "It might be poetic justice, but I believe it will be a problem."

Bedillia spoke of the function that the demons were serving—food for ACs. Though Lenar seemed mildly amused by the concept, it made Abaddon cringe.

"That is a problem," confirmed Abaddon. "I take it that Tim isn't negotiable on the issue of releasing them."

"Not likely," said Bedillia. "I'm not even sure if it would be a wise move on his part."

"Catch 22," noted Kurt.

"Pretty much," replied Bedillia. "And right now, I can't think of a way around it."

"Catch 22?" asked Abaddon.

"A no-win situation," replied Bedillia. "I can't tell you, given his situation, that I wouldn't have done the same thing."

"I will have to think on it," said Abaddon. "I suspect that there is a solution."

"In the meantime, we can continue to build a relationship with them," noted Bedillia. "Despite a rough start yesterday, he was quite a gracious host this time. I want to continue talks with them tomorrow. Tim and Megan have granted me permission to gate directly into their quarters."

"I will allow it, said Abaddon. "However, I will want a daily report on your progress. Indeed, I want you to give a full report to the council following each meeting, starting with the one you had today."

"Of course," replied Bedillia.

And so the negotiations began. It was only three days later that Tim and Megan came through the ring with Bedillia on a tour of Refuge. Tim's attitude was changing. They were winning him over. All the while, Abaddon pondered a way to give Tim the same level of security that they enjoyed. Still, a solution avoided him. How could he place Tim's community under his protection without jeopardizing the treaty with the demons? It was a thorny topic indeed.

In three weeks they would be meeting with Cordon and his committee once more. That was, assuming that the committee would convene again. He had heard nothing from Cordon since the return of General Krell. That as much as anything would impact how he would solve the problem of the captive demons.

It had been several weeks since Cordon had last been in Satan's old audience chamber. General Krell had taken it over upon his arrival. Cordon had been given but a few minutes to gather up his things and vacate the premises. On that day, Cordon had ceased to be the master of Hell. He had been given Governor Molock's old position as administrator of the region of Hell that included the Valley of Noak. It was a figurehead position, really. Still, it gave Cordon and Rolf time to work on their prototype of a new generation of teleporter rings. They had made significant progress.

Cordon had been surprised when he was summoned to General Krell's audience chamber. He was apprehensive as he awaited Krell in the anteroom. He had been kept waiting for over an hour before one of General Krell's aids conducted him into the presence of the lord of Hell.

In a way, General Krell did not fit the mold of so many of the other minions of Satan. He took the appearance of a middle-aged man with great bat wings. He appeared rugged, yet handsome, in his own unique way. He had a long reputation of being very unemotional and very slow to anger, not at all like Satan.

As Cordon entered his chamber, he found it little changed. It was practically empty, an indeed Spartan environment. Krell did not even look up to acknowledge Cordon's presence. He sat on a simple, black metal chair that acted as his throne, and seemed engrossed in a document that Cordon recognized as the one he had composed at General Krell's request, a report on his two-plus years of service as Hell's chief administrator.

At Krell's side was his lieutenant, a rather innocuous minion by the name of Min. Cordon didn't know too much about Min. He had been returned to Hell following his judgment by the saints. Like all of Satan's minions, he had been found guilty. Right now, Cordon felt like a defendant standing before the judge for sentencing.

Krell placed the report on the table to the right side of his throne. "So you discovered the exact location of the rebel base, but you have not moved against them? Indeed, you have developed a cooperative relationship with them."

"That is correct, my lord," confirmed Cordon.

"It says here that you have been involved in active peace negotiations with them for nearly two years now and that you have made progress to those ends."

"Yes, my lord," said Cordon, his tone totally without emotion.

"And you thought this wise?" asked Krell.

Cordon did not hesitate in his response. "Yes, my lord. Under the circumstances, I thought it to be the best course of action. We needed their help in solving a grave problem of mutual concern."

"Yes," said Krell, "a problem that their own actions precipitated."

"That is true," admitted Cordon. "However, it might be noted that we were at war at the time."

There was a long pause. Krell gazed deep into Cordon's eyes, a gaze that Cordon returned unflinchingly. Then he looked briefly at the stack of papers. "I am not unreasonable, Cordon. Nor am I unfeeling. I bear no ill will toward the humans. I approve of your actions. Under the circumstances, they were prudent. You gave certain assurances of safety to these humans and dark angels of Refuge. You claim that they have lived by the terms of the agreement up to this point."

"Completely," assured Cordon. "We have even embarked on several small ventures of mutual benefit."

The general nodded approvingly. "And you feel that they had no part in this incident at Noak?"

"I am sure of it," replied Cordon.

"Very well," said Krell. "It is my understanding that you have scheduled another round of negotiations to be held just five standard days from now."

"Yes, my lord," replied Cordon, who did his best to contain his amazement.

"I wish the negotiations to continue," replied Krell. "I wish for you to remain our chief negotiator, but you may dismiss our other delegates. I don't need them. Here I am the law."

"I understand," confirmed Cordon.

"I've outlined a few things that I wish for you to relate to the human delegation at the negotiations. They are not unreasonable. I do not believe that these humans will object. In essence, it establishes that they are dealing with me and not a committee of my minions. The opinion of our people regarding the worthiness or unworthiness of humans is irrelevant to me. I've proposed a procedure by which these humans may win the freedom of others of their kind—those who have (and I believe this was the term you used) *repentant hearts.*"

At this Cordon was truly amazed. "I believe that act in itself will make you very popular with the humans and dark angels of Refuge."

"That is not my intent," said the general. "My concern is preventing anarchy. I know this was your objective these past two years, though I do not completely agree with your approach. This is not a democracy, Cordon; it never will be. My unconditional rule over Hell is not negotiable. I want it to be understood that I am in charge. However, I am not a tyrant. I am not opposed to granting the humans some degree of autonomy. I am not even opposed to listening to their petitions, so long as they acknowledge the fact that mine is the final word."

"I am confident that they will be your loyal subjects," confirmed Cordon.

"I expect nothing less," said the general. "There is one additional item I wish for you to see to. Find out who was behind the incident at Noak. I want them dealt with and order reestablished. I will give you full authority in this matter and hold you fully responsible for its execution."

"Of course, my lord," confirmed Cordon. "I will see to it at once."

For the first time a slight smile came to the general's face. "I know you will. You have done a good job of managing things these past two years. I could not have asked for more. Serve me with the same dedication and enthusiasm you have shown up to now, and we will carry this realm into a golden age. Again, well done, you are dismissed."

Cordon bowed low before his new master and departed from the chamber. He thought of the relief this news would bring to the people of Refuge.

Abaddon, Lenar, Kurt, and Bedillia waited anxiously before the teleportation ring. Cordon had sounded very upbeat over the telesphere. He had spoken of favorable developments.

Cordon and his lieutenant Rolf stepped from the ring and into their presence. They both seemed very pleased with themselves.

Rolf turned to Cordon. "I do believe congratulations are in order," he announced. "Your new ring worked perfectly."

The others seemed a bit confused. "New ring?" asked Bedillia.

"Yes," confirmed Cordon. "Since I no longer have access to Satan's old audience chamber and his teleportation ring, I was compelled to construct my own. That is how we arrived here."

"Congratulations," said Bedillia.

"I have much news," confirmed Cordon, "good news."

The group proceeded to Abaddon's audience chamber, where Cordon told the group of General Krell's terms. Abaddon and the rest spent 20 minutes looking over the document that outlined the general's terms. It was relatively short and concise. It was quite reasonable, even generous. It gave them reason for optimism.

"The full council will need to vote on this proposal," said Abaddon, laying the document aside. "But I believe that I can assure you that we will ratify it. I will not challenge the general's claims of dominion over this realm. I believe that I can assure you that we will cooperate with him fully."

"Yes, we will," confirmed Bedillia.

Cordon smiled. "That is all that the general asks of you. I do believe that he will be pleased." There was a pause. "We need to move onto another topic. The general has asked me to investigate the mysterious disappearance of the humans and demons in the Valley of Noak. I am certain that you have also launched an investigation into this matter. Am I correct?"

Well, there it was. Bedillia cringed. What were they to do now? Only Abaddon could make that determination.

"You are correct," confirmed Abaddon. "Furthermore, you will not need to launch an investigation of your own. We have completed our investigation already. We have your answers for you."

Bedillia looked at Abaddon incredulously. The relative quickness of his response told her that he had indeed arrived at a solution, though she had no idea what form it might take.

Cordon cocked his head in surprise. "Indeed, my friend. Would you be willing to share your findings?"

"Yes," confirmed Abaddon. "To do anything else would not be an act of good faith. Your original thoughts on the matter were largely correct. Your forces were attacked and quickly overwhelmed by a large group of rogue ACs under the command of an escaped human. It is he, and those that he freed, who are currently holding your people prisoner."

Bedillia glanced over at Kurt, whose look of astonishment mirrored her own. Could it be possible? Was Abaddon going to sell Tim and his people down the river just to protect Refuge?

Cordon nodded. "How is it that you know these things?"

Abaddon's eyes seemed very cold. They showed no trace of emotion whatsoever. "Because we encountered them. Indeed, we are in the midst of negotiating with them. I believe that we can secure the release of your people without the need for force of arms. Furthermore, I believe we can intermediate a treaty between your people and theirs. I assure you, they have no aggressive intentions. They only did what they had to do. Now, they simply wish to be left alone. Grant them a small parcel of land within the valley and freedom from persecution, and they will accept the general's rule, becoming his loyal subjects. Their leader also has something to offer you, beyond the release of your people. He is currently in control of about half of the ACs in all of Hell. He is willing to command those ACs to cease their attacks on your people and feed only upon the more unrepentant humans of Hell, those too vile to ever be released."

Bedillia had never seen such an expression of amazement on Cordon's face. It was clear that he had been unprepared for this revelation. Now it was his move.

"You ask much of me," he finally replied. "Negotiating such a treaty will be difficult."

"Think of it this way," continued Abaddon. "In doing this, you not only recover your missing people, but you do so without spilling a drop of demon blood. You also save much time and effort. You do not need to burden your already overextended forces with the task of guarding additional humans. The humans in question will stay within agreed upon boundaries and will not interfere with the operation of the general's realm. In addition the problems you have experienced regarding the ACs will end. The general wants to restore order. This does it. If Hell is to enter a golden age of cooperation, as your master desires, this is a good first step. Many years ago, I witnessed a courageous human standing in Satan's audience chamber. She boldly and very eloquently proposed a plan of cooperation not unlike this one. Satan laughed at her and sentenced her to the Great Sea of Fire. He lost a valuable opportunity that day. Now that opportunity stands before us again. Shall we once more cast it aside?"

Cordon paused, apparently absorbing Abaddon's proposal. "And how do you know that these people will accept this proposal?"

"Because I spoke to their leader," replied Abaddon. "I knew that this day would inevitably come. I proposed such an agreement as this to him. I will tell you this; he does not have a great deal of trust for your people, but given certain assurances, he would agree."

Bedillia looked at Abaddon in amazement. Abaddon returned her gaze.

"I contacted them by telesphere two days ago and gated into their realm to discuss terms. After some hours, I was able to convince Tim and Megan to open a dialog with the demons if the opportunity presented itself. I said I would only do this if I felt there was a good chance for success. We would hold the negotiations on neutral grounds, here in Refuge."

"Why didn't you tell us?" asked Kurt.

Abaddon smiled, though slightly. "We all have our secrets."

"I take it that you care for these people," deduced Cordon.

"I care for all humanity," confirmed Abaddon, "I am, after all, an angel."

Cordon smiled, though slightly. "Of course," he replied. He paused for a moment, seemingly deep in thought. "Do you feel that these people, this Tim and Megan, are worthy of your trust?"

Abaddon didn't hesitate in his response. "Yes, I do. I talked to them at length. They are true prisoners of destiny. They hardly deserve the fate they have met here. It was but an error in judgment, an error of their youth."

Once again there was silence. Cordon scanned the faces around the table. "Very well. I will take this issue to General Krell. I do not know what his response will be, but I will speak on their behalf. I will advise the general that I think it would be in our best interest to pursue negotiations with them, with you as the arbitrator. I can be rather persuasive when I need to be."

For the next four hours, the group hammered out the exact terms and a timetable that they would propose. By the time that Cordon departed, they had a well laid out plan on paper. They were cautiously optimistic. Only time would prove if that optimism was founded in reality.

Cordon had been gone for less than half an hour when Abaddon, Bedillia, and Kurt stepped through the ring on their way to Tim's quarters in his subterranean fortress. They were met by Megan.

Kurt couldn't help but smile at discovering that Megan wore the nice print dress that his wife had made specifically for her. She looked so much better in it than she did in that somewhat oversized black cloak.

"Sir," said Megan, "please tell your wife that I just love the dress she made for me. It fits perfectly. It makes me feel, well, like a woman again."

Kurt's smile only broadened. "I'll be sure and do that. Debbie has a real gift when it comes to the matter manipulator."

"Oh, yes," said Megan, "that machine makes almost anything you can think about. I saw it on my trip to Refuge. It's blooming magic is what it is." Megan hesitated. "But you wanted to talk with Tim. I'll take you to him. He's teaching his class."

"His class?" asked Kurt.

Megan smiled. "You'll see. Be prepared to be amazed."

Megan led the group down a rocky corridor in which the regular walls and floor were glassy smooth. And within the glassy surface were a myriad of small glowing crystals that added to its luster. Abaddon and Kurt looked around in amazement. Never had they seen a subterranean passageway quite like this. It looked unnatural.

Megan took note of their wandering eyes. "Tim's small creatures carved this tunnel, and then Tim melted the walls to make them smooth."

"With his sword?" asked Abaddon, gazing about in wonder.

"You'll see," replied Megan, a twinkle in her eye.

Somewhere ahead of them they heard voices, many voices. They shouted in unison again and again. As the group grew closer to the sound, they heard and felt the rhythm of pounding feet.

They stepped into a great, nearly circular cavern room that was well lit by hundreds of small crystals. Along the walls, a large number of ACs watched the proceedings carefully. Tim stood before about 50 men and women, sword in hand. All of them wore black cloaks, and all danced about with swords in their hands, following Tim's lead.

"You must anticipate your opponent's move," said Tim, looking out upon his followers. "Demons are strong, stronger than you, but they're not faster. Keep on the move, confuse them; it's your greatest advantage. They have thousands of years of experience with the sword, but they don't practice much. They've gotten sloppy. I can tell you that from experience. Look for that moment when they are most off balance, right after they swing. Let them make the first move then go after them. That is when they are the most vulnerable. A short quick thrust works best. Don't draw back to swing, don't give them time to react." Tim turned to see his guests. "Pair off. Practice with your partner. Don't be afraid of getting hurt; you'll heal quickly enough. Pain will focus your determination. But don't take stupid chances, either. Let's go."

The group paired off and continued the exercise even as Tim sheathed his sword and approached his visitors. An AC that Abaddon recognized as the alpha male, Goliath, swooped over to sit on Tim's right shoulder.

"Very nice," said Abaddon, looking at Tim. "I've never seen a human with such experience when it came to the sword."

Tim smiled. "I'm mostly self-taught, though Goliath has given me lots of advice, too. Actually, I had some lessons on swordsmanship back on Earth too; that helped. In time, I will have an army of my own, an army that can defend my people. You see, we won't have to depend only on Goliath and his family."

"I can see that," said Abaddon. "That is sound thinking."

"But I suspect that you haven't come just to inspect my training methods," deduced Tim.

"You are correct," said Abaddon. "The thing that we talked about two days ago is coming to pass."

Tim seemed truly surprised by that revelation. "So soon?"

"Yes," confirmed Abaddon. "I am very encouraged. Things are going better than I'd almost dared hope. You will need to become involved in the negotiating process."

"Tell me more," said Tim, drawing closer.

Abaddon and the others spoke of the recent meeting with Cordon and the new treaty. Through it all, Tim remained unusually quiet.

The story told, Tim turned once more to his students. "Now, before we break for the day, let's show our visitors our best trick. Take your positions."

The entire group moved in Tim's direction, then turned to the far wall, about a hundred feet or so away. They raised their swords, then directed them to the wall.

"Take aim!" barked Tim. "Fire!"

Almost immediately, several dozen fiery beams erupted from the swords and struck the far wall. There was a great flash of light and a loud report. A few seconds later portions of the wall were glowing bright red.

"Better," said Tim, "better than yesterday. Now, my dear friends, stand aside."

Tim pulled his own sword and directed it toward the wall, even as his students stepped out of the way. His sword glowed with blue electricity as one fiery beam after another hit the wall. When he was finished, the temperature of the room had risen to well over a 100 degrees."

"In time, all of you shall be able to do that," announced Tim, sheathing his sword once more. "Just stay focused; you can do it. Then you will be ready. Class is dismissed until tomorrow."

The group headed quickly down a side passage. As they did, the ACs took flight. Many took up positions upon the shoulders of the students. Others flew around the group as they left. Soon, only Tim, Megan and his visitors stood in the room.

"Let's get out of here," said Tim. "It's only going to get hotter."

"I have never seen a human summon the power of a demonic sword," said Abaddon, true amazement in his voice. "Nor have I seen a demonic fireball look quite as that one."

"It's not a demonic fireball," said Tim. "I like to call it Timothy's fire. Goliath said it was unique. All of my students can do it to some degree. With time, they'll get better."

"Incredible," said Kurt. "That is some weapon."

"Very nice, Tim," said Bedillia.

Tim smiled. "Thank you all. We can talk in my chambers."

As they walked back, Abaddon realized how the walls of the cavern around them had been transformed into glass so easily. "A demon, in good form, might be able to shoot two or three fireballs before his strength is exhausted. Then he would need to rest for at least an hour. I just saw you shoot at least eight."

"Oh, I can shoot a lot more than that," said Tim, a sense of pride in his response. "But I didn't want to melt the wall. Goliath tells me that my fireballs are not as powerful as a demon's fireball, but I can more than make up for that in the number I can project. I think my students will be just as good, as long as they practice. Our problem is that we only have 84 swords here. I need more, a lot more. Goliath tells me that they need to be made out of a stuff called angelic metal."

"Yes, that is correct," confirmed Abaddon. "It is very rare in Hell."

"Not here it isn't," replied Tim. "There are lots of angelic metal deposits in the lower cavern. The walls are full of the stuff. At least that's what Goliath has told me. A little angelic metal in his diet makes his coat glisten. I have some samples of it in my chambers. I just need to know how to turn it into swords."

"I think I could help you there," noted Abaddon. "We could help you set up a forge right here in the cave."

"Yes," replied Tim. "I'd really appreciate that. Thank you."

Upon their return to Tim's chambers, he showed Abaddon samples of the metal. It was indeed angelic metal. It appeared to be of high quality. It was an incredible find.

"If the demons knew this was here, they might fight you over it," cautioned Abaddon. "For a long time they have scoured Hell in search of it, and here it has been, right under their feet all of this time. This is truly ironic."

For several hours the group discussed the treaty. It took some time to convince Tim to agree to give up his demonic captives, should the terms of the treaty be ratified. Tim didn't like the idea of his creatures being relegated to feeding on other humans, even if their hearts were filled with evil, but inevitably he agreed. In the end, they had hammered out an agreement. Now all that remained was to hope that General Krell would agree to it.

The negotiations began three days later. Cordon seemed amazed to discover that the person behind the release of so many humans and the capture of dozens of seasoned demons was little more than a boy. Yet Tim was sharp when it came to negotiating. He seemed to have a maturity well beyond his years. He was a natural born leader; there were no two ways about it.

Two weeks later, Tim and Megan sat at the great table in Abaddon's audience chamber with members of the governing council of Refuge and with Cordon. The parties involved placed their signatures on the final version of the treaty. Before the day was out, Tim would release his hostages. In exchange, he got a promise of peace and about 12 square miles of the valley as a sort of homeland, though he had no intentions of moving back to the surface just yet.

It had all gone better than Abaddon had suspected, perhaps too well. Abaddon had come to trust Cordon, at least to a degree, but he remained suspicious of General Krell's intentions. What did he stand to gain from all of these concessions? He suspected that, in time, he would find out.

CHAPTER 17

The clear autumn night sky gave way to the brilliance of day and the roar of thunder as the Atlas V-Heavy lifted from the Kennedy Space Center pad 41 above a 300-foot-long column of fire. Although it was a late evening launch, it was televised to the people of the nation and the world. Atop the *Centaur* B2 upper stage rode the Herschel Spacecraft that would study Comet Florence in unprecedented detail.

Never in the history of NASA had a mission been put together so quickly. It had been less than three years from concept to launch. The spacecraft would travel to the planet Jupiter in record time, 12 months. Then it would use a gravitational slingshot from the enormous planet, as well as its on board booster, to place it into the same trajectory as the comet, monitoring it with 11 different instruments, mostly spares borrowed from other past missions. Nonetheless, it was one of the most expensive unmanned missions ever flown.

Normally, an unmanned planetary mission could use a series of gravity assists and a few extra years of flight time to finesse its way to where it wanted to go at a minimum cost. This mission, however, was all power and boosters, a real muscle mission.

Sam Florence watched with a sense of awe as the spacecraft vanished into the east. He'd never been present at a launch, and this one would be studying his comet. In very fact, he was a member of the science team that would be using the spacecraft to unravel its mysteries. In particular, he would be studying the comet's atmosphere and dust content, determining just how much of a threat the environment around the comet posed to our satellites in Earth's orbit.

"We have confirmed booster cut off and ignition of the *Centaur* upper stage," announced mission control over the loud speaker. "Trajectory and speed look very good."

Sam thought back. He had heard complaints from other members of the team that they had too little access to the real nuts and bolts designs of the craft. Most spacecrafts were designed by major universities in conjunction with the Jet Propulsion Lab in Pasadena, but not this one. This one was designed and built primarily by the military, with only minimal input from the outside. Sure, many of the instruments on board were designed by universities, but it was the military that had incorporated them into the spacecraft's design. It was rumored that the spacecraft itself was actually a modified spy satellite, though that could not be confirmed.

Sam put those thoughts out of his mind. He stood there amidst the other honored guests and members of the science team, waiting to hear that the *Centaur* stage had done its job. He glanced at his watch expectantly.

"We have *Centaur* cut off at 23:54, right on the second," announced mission control. "We're on our way to Jupiter."

A cheer arose from the crowd. This was an encouraging start to the mission. In 23 months, the spacecraft would be passing by the Earth one last time, circling the comet's nucleus at point-blank range and giving humanity a three-dimensional view of the comet's structure. What a priceless opportunity.

As Sam prepared to go to bed in the wee hours of the morning, all was still looking good. The spacecraft was in good health, ready for its record-setting mission. Still, he was troubled. Something wasn't right, though he knew not what. He offered a brief prayer for the planet and its people.

From their home on wheels, now parked in North Carolina, Chris and Serena also watched the launch on television with interest. They were happy to see the successful lift-off, yet like Sam, they had a sense that something wasn't quite right.

In reality, things hadn't gone as well as Serena might have hoped these past months. The miraculous healings that had accented their ministry during the late spring and early summer had faded in the fall along with the summer heat. Serena spent hours in prayer every night, as did Chris. They had fasted for two weeks in late August, yet it seemed in vain. The gift of healing seemed to have passed from her. Yet now on his second U.S. tour, Lusan's ministry was blessed with incredible miracles at every service.

Her sense of dejection deepened as she opened her email. She hadn't heard from Mark, the young man who had been healed in Mississippi for over a week. Up until this point, he had sent her at least one or two messages a week. He spoke of running and playing, of studying the Word, and of witnessing of God's goodness to others. He had dreams of going into the ministry, of becoming an evangelist. Now here was an email from his mother. Her words were indeed dire. Mark was gone. He'd been killed walking home from school by a stray bullet from places unknown. How could such a thing have happened?

"Lord, why have you abandoned your people?" asked Serena, sitting on the edge of the bed weeping.

Her cries awakened Chris, who joined her in her grief. It just didn't make sense. Here they were in Earth's darkest hour, and God seemed to have turned His back on His own people. Chris held her, tried to comfort her, yet he knew not what to say. In fact, he seemed more frustrated than Serena.

Chris spoke of the day of the martyrs, of the Christians who had perished at Nero's pleasure. Had there been any miraculous and inexplicable acts that had spared them? Not to his knowledge. Yes, those martyrs had gone to Heaven; he had met some of them. Yet what message had God sent to the world in allowing them to die at the hands of a madman?

Some people might have lost faith in God, but that wasn't an option for Chris. He knew the Father like no one else. He had spoken to Him personally, had heard His voice time and time again. He had seen him. Still, he just didn't understand His reasoning. Was He just giving Satan enough rope to hang himself? He couldn't say. But with the passing of the days, Satan's plan was becoming ever clearer.

Chris and Serena had to move on, but their evangelistic ministry was starting to wane. There was more time between revivals, and the crowds were once more starting to shrink.

Yet another blow was dealt to them with word of the relapse of the man who had regained his sight in Mississippi. Indeed, his condition was even worse than before. What was going on?

Even worse, Lusan's people were taking full advantage of this series of events. They spoke of lasting healings at the hands of Lusan, of a god who will not abandon his people. Lusan's miracles, over a 100 of them, had been recorded on video. There could be no doubt as to their authenticity.

Lusan said it was the narrowmindedness of these Christians that was causing their miraculous acts to fail. God didn't like their judgmental attitudes, their audacity in suggesting that there was only one path to His presence.

Lusan's most vocal spokesperson was one Krissie James, and her beauty and grace were winning many over to Lusan's side. She now had her own syndicated talk show out of New York, and ever more television and radio stations were carrying it.

By November, the ballots in Europe had been cast, and Julien Devereux had been voted into the position of president of the European Union by a landslide. From the beginning, Julien made no mystery as to his religious convictions. He was a follower of the man who had restored his son to him. And he wasn't alone. Polls in Europe showed that fully a third of the continent's people were either members of Lusan's New Age religion or had their sympathies leaning in that direction, and that number was growing.

With his Southeast Asian crusade upcoming, Lusan was riding high. Even in the United States, his popularity was rising, though it lagged behind the rest of the world. Throughout the presidential campaign of 2016, Lusan's influence was felt. In the end, however, the candidate whom Lusan's people had unofficially endorsed was defeated in the election. The new president, who described herself as a born-again Christian, had her work cut out for her. She was finding her nation ever more at odds with the rest of the world, a world in love with a modern day messiah.

Never in recent memory had the world's people seemed so hopeful about the future. They spoke of a new light, an awakening. But it was not the light of Christ, but a false light that was leading the world toward disaster. Chris and Serena knew this, but there seemed to be nothing they could do about it. Still, their crusade moved on.

It was late February as they rolled into Brooklyn. They had been invited to hold a three-day revival at the Light House Church. Serena recalled that they had been there once before, about four years ago. This was where they had originally met Claire James. It seemed strange to be back, considering the circumstances. Indeed, it had involved a last-minute change in plans. Ron Smith, the pastor of this church for the past 20 or more years, had practically pleaded for them to come. It had been a long drive through harsh winter weather, but they'd felt the need to come nonetheless.

The Lighthouse Church had a large congregation, over 2,000, and it was known for its lively services. For this reason alone, Chris and Serena wanted to come. They were convinced that they would be encouraged from this revival as surely as the people who would be attending.

"I'm so glad you were able to come," said Pastor Smith, showing Chris and Serena to his study.

Pastor Smith was a gray-haired, African American man in his late fifties with the excitement and charisma of a man half his age. Chris and Serena remembered him well. While many Christian churches had experienced declines in their congregation, his had actually grown. Here, right in the Devil's backyard, his church had remained vibrant, even defiant. He had come out against Lusan's organization boldly and publicly. In the process, he had made enemies.

"You know, people have been calling me a hater," said Pastor Smith, leading Chris and Serena to his study in the parsonage. "After so many years of serving this community, I never thought I'd be called that."

"These are strange times," noted Chris.

"Don't I know it," said the pastor. "I'm very glad to have you back. You need to know something before tonight's service. What I'm about to tell you may seem incredible, but it is true."

As they entered the pastor's large and well-furnished study, they noticed that five folding chairs had been arranged in a circle. Sitting side by side in two of the chairs were a young man and woman. They were both Hispanic and appeared to be about 20 years old.

"Chris and Serena Davis, I would like to introduce you to two precious members of my flock," said Pastor Smith. "This is Julio and Karina Mendoza. I had the great pleasure of joining them in marriage just last week."

"Congratulations," said Chris and Serena, almost simultaneously, as they sat down beside them.

"They have an incredible story to tell you," continued Pastor Smith. "It is a story about this Lusan character. They were both members of his youth ministry before they came here. They were brought to us by one of our long-time members, Claire James, just a week or so before she went to be with the Lord. I believe you met her some years ago."

"Yes," replied Serena, barely able to speak. "We both know her."

Apparently, Pastor Smith picked up on Serena's reaction. "Is something wrong?"

"No," replied Serena, "Nothing is wrong."

Pastor Smith turned to the young couple. "Go ahead; tell them what you told me."

It was Julio who opened the conversation. "Grandma Claire was very special to me. If it hadn't been for her, I might be in Hell this very minute."

Julio had a tough time telling the story. He came to tears several times. Yet he unfolded a tale of his time with the Latin Kings, of an encounter with a couple in Central Park, and the beings who came to their aid. He related his experience of being possessed and of the terrible things he had done under the demon's influence. He spoke of the woman he had been sent to kill, only to be delivered by her healing hand.

Karina, too, told her story to Chris and Serena. Being possessed by a being so foul had been a horrible experience. Under his control, she had come to realize the depths of depravity that was the heart of a demon. Her release by Grandma Claire had been a release from Hell itself.

"But there's more," said Karina, fighting back the tears. "Less than a month ago, I saw Grandma Claire in my dreams. It was so real, like no dream I'd ever had before."

"We both did," interjected Julio. "It was so good to see her again. She told us that we had to get the two of you here, that there were things we had to tell you." Julio pulled a stack of papers from a large envelope. "The night she died, she sent out an email to several people. Pastor Smith was one. I was another. She also told me that, if anything happened to her, I should remove the hard drive from her computer. I didn't know why at the time. I do now." He handed Serena a flash drive. "Here is the thing that she wanted to keep from Lusan. She was convinced that he would come looking for it. It's a sort of series of prophecies. I don't know what else to call it. She didn't want to send it out on the email. This may seem crazy, but I think she wanted you two to have it. You are both mentioned several times."

"I know how all this must sound," said Pastor Smith. "But she appeared to me, too. She told me that I should believe what Julio and Karina were about to tell me. She asked me to contact you. Never in my career as a pastor have I experienced such a move of God's Spirit."

By now, Serena also had tears in her eyes. "I know it sounds, fantastic, but she spoke to us, too, twice. No, we believe you."

It was time for Chris and Serena to share information they'd shared with no one beyond the Pope in Rome. All present were only too keenly aware that the Spirit of God was on the move. These incredible visions had bolstered everyone's faith. No, God hadn't abandoned them.

"There was one last thing," said Julio. "No, two, really."

"Grandma Claire said that we should help you in any way we could. We intend to. I earned my associate's degree in criminal justice last semester. I'd like to earn my bachelors, but I don't think I have time. I don't think this world has that much time. Anyway, there are more important things to do. If there is any way, we'd like to help you in your ministry."

"We need to," confirmed Karina. "There are things we know; we could help."

"That is a very kind offer," said Chris, looking over at his wife.

A pause followed. It was Pastor Smith who broke the silence. He looked toward Julio. "There was something else, wasn't there?"

Julio looked back toward the pastor. "Yes, there was." He turned toward Serena. "There was something else that Grandma Claire told us, both of us. It's about you, Serena, and her grandson, Leland. I told you about him before. Leland is Lusan's chief financial officer. He and his wife, Krissie, were his first converts. Grandma said that you need to walk into the lion's den and bring him out. Those were her exact words. You need to give Leland the email she sent him the night she died. You need to tell him what and who he's dealing with.

You need to go in there alone."

"Now wait a minute," objected Chris. "She's not going in there alone. That's way too dangerous. Anyway, what makes you think that he is going to listen to her? For all we know, he might be possessed just like you were."

"He's not possessed," said Karina. "There are a lot of people in that place that are, but he isn't one of them."

"From what you've told me, Leland is totally dedicated to Lusan," noted Serena. "I doubt that he is going to listen to me."

"He will," replied Karina. "The Holy Spirit is going to make a way. I just know it."

Through the testimony of Julio and Karina, Chris and Serena gained new insight into the workings of Lusan and his organization. It was positively diabolical. It was all a lie, and as Serena had suspected, it was Satan casting out Satan. There were no real miracles playing out here.

The revival was, as Chris and Serena had suspected, a blessing to them as much as it was a blessing to the congregation of this great church. It had been a long time since they had seen people so full of God's Spirit. In their midst, Serena's gift of healing, both physical and spiritual, returned, much to the wonderment of the congregation. And she wasn't alone. There were members of the congregation who displayed marvelous manifestations of the Holy Spirit ranging from prophecy to healing.

After the meetings, late in the evening, Chris and Serena scanned the contents of the drive that Julio had handed them. It filled them with both shock and wonder. It reminded them of the ancient document that the Pope had shared with them. God had not abandoned them. In fact, their ministry was about to enter into a new phase; they were about to face Lusan, and they were ready.

By the end of that glorious weekend, Serena was uplifted. She was ready to step into that lion's den with total confidence.

It was a cold and snowy Monday morning as Serena stepped from Pastor Smith's car across from Manhattan's Davidson Building—Lusan's headquarters. Serena was dressed for success, like a professional businesswoman. "I'll call you on the cell phone when I'm ready for you to pick me up," said Serena to the pastor.

"I wish you'd let me go with you," said Chris, who sat with Julio and Karina in the back seat.

Serena smiled. "We've been all over this before, dear. I have to go in there alone. I don't know how long I'll be, so don't worry, OK? Daniel stepped from the lion's den unharmed, and so will I."

She gripped Chris's hand through the partially open window for but a second, and then she was on her way through the inch or so of snow down the sidewalk. There was nothing more to say. Pastor Smith pulled out and headed for a nearby parking garage. Serena was on her own. Serena crossed the street and entered the Davidson building.

The lobby of the Davidson building was indeed grand. It was accented by its 20-foot-high ceilings and grand décor. She headed through the metal detector and then toward the directory that was displayed on the wall. Never had she seen one so large. It took up a full 30 feet of the cultured marble wall. Amazingly, it didn't take long for her to locate Leland James.

"Thirty-first floor," she said, heading toward a hallway with four elevators on either side. She joined the growing crowd awaiting the next one.

As she entered the elevator, she noticed that access to the 32nd floor was by key only. She smiled. That wasn't surprising.

The elevator made seven stops before arriving at the 31st floor. She stepped out to come face to face with a security station with two rather large security guards manning it. There was something about these men that she sensed immediately, something wrong. Their eyes seemed so cold, so distant. If the eye was a window unto the soul, no one was home. She didn't have to ponder why. She was already deep in enemy territory. She stepped boldly forward.

"How may I help you today?" asked one of the guards.

Serena didn't hesitate. "I am here to see Mr. Leland James."

"Do you have an appointment?" asked the guard, who was now eying her suspiciously.

"No, I don't," replied Serena. "I was, however, a friend of his grandmother." She held up a manila envelope. "These are some documents that she wanted him to have, personal documents."

"I will need to inspect them," announced the guard.

"As I said, they are personal documents," replied Serena.

"I can't let you see him," said the guard, "Mr. James is a very busy man."

"Contact him, tell him about the documents," replied Serena. She paused. "Tell him that Serena Davis is here to see him. He will want to see me."

The guard, who had shown no emotional response up to this point, looked at Serena with a look of incredulity. No, it was more than that, it was recognition."

"Serena Davis?" he said.

"The very same," confirmed Serena.

There was a moment of hesitation, then the guard picked up the phone. He stepped away as if wishing not to be heard. A moment later he sat the phone down. He pointed to a busy hallway to his right. "It's number 3141 at the end of the hall. You are expected; go directly there."

"Thank you," said Serena, who immediately made her way into the corridor.

"So far, so good," she said under her breath.

This place had the look of any large business. There was nothing about it that might have given the average person any sense of what was really going on here, yet Serena was anything but average. She could sense the coming and going of the spirits in this place, and there were many.

It took about a minute for her to reach 3141. The door was open. She walked in to find an office with two secretaries. One of them looked up and smiled. "You must be Serena," she said. "Mr. James is looking forward to meeting you. Please go right on in."

Serena looked toward the door on the far side of the room. She took a deep breath and walked on in. Leland James rose from his desk the very minute she entered.

"Mrs. Davis," he said pleasantly. "I thought I recognized your name. I just took the liberty to look you up on the Internet. You are quite an accomplished writer. I remember my grandmother mentioning you some years ago. I didn't realize that the two of you had stayed in touch."

"Yes, we had, Mr. James," confirmed Serena. "Your Grandma Claire was a wonderful woman and a good friend to both me and my husband, Chris."

Leland quickly pulled up a chair across from his. "Please, sit down, Mrs. Davis. I'm very curious about what brought you here. It was a personal matter, or so said Officer Crawley."

Serena and Leland sat across the table from one another. Serena pulled out the manila folder and produced three pages. "I have an email here," she began. "Your grandmother sent it to you the night she died. I get the feeling that you never got it."

A look of pure astonishment swept over Leland's face. "No, I got an email, but it was blank. I never got to read it. You have the email, the one she sent me?"

"The exact same one," confirmed Serena. "Claire had concerns that something might happen so she entrusted a copy of it to several others as well. She really wanted you to read it."

"Oh heavens," said Leland, taking the three pages from Serena's hand. His own hand was shaking. "God bless you, Mrs. Davis. You can't imagine just how much I wanted to read this, how much I've thought about it since my grandmother's death."

"I'm just happy to give it to you," confirmed Serena. "Your grandmother told me that if you hadn't gotten it that I was to give it to no one else, I was to place it directly into your hand. Oh, and please, call me Serena."

"And I'm Leland. Please, you don't mind if I read it right here, right now?"

"I was hoping you would," confirmed Serena.

Leland put his reading glasses on and began with the document. He read it very slowly, very deliberately. Several times, tears welled up in his eyes, though he did his best to control his emotions. When he was finished, he once more looked to Serena.

"Serena, have you read this email?"

"Yes, many times."

"This is incredible," said Leland. "Lusan tried to have her killed? But I saw her at the wedding with Julio and Karina. They seemed like they were so close."

"Of course," said Serena. "Your grandmother drove out the demons that had possessed them. It was the demon within them that wanted to kill her, not Julio or Karina. It was Julio's fight with the demon within him that gave your grandmother the time to cast the demon out and free him."

"Yes, it says that here," confirmed Leland. "It also says that Lusan isn't an angel at all, not in the sense that you or I would..." Leland stopped in mid-sentence.

"It's OK," said Serena, placing her hand on his. "I know the whole story."

"But it says in the email that Lusan is Satan, the Devil," continued Leland. He paused as if to collect his thoughts. "You know my grandmother didn't approve of Lusan. She had issues with my working with him."

"Yes, I know," said Serena.

Again Leland paused. "But no, that can't be true. He's done so much good. I've seen him heal people right in front of my eyes. The Devil doesn't do that. Didn't Jesus say something about Satan not casting out Satan?"

"Well, yes, that's in the Bible," said Serena, "Jesus essentially said it would be counterproductive for Satan to do that. But time is running out. Satan needs converts. He's casting out demons from one person and sending them just as quickly into someone else, to give the illusion that he can heal. He needs to lead as many people astray as he can. He is doomed, and he knows it. He wants to pull as many people down with him as possible. He'll pull you down, if he can. Your grandmother doesn't want that."

Leland shook his head. "No, I just can't accept this. I know you mean well, Serena. I appreciate you're coming here to see me, really I do. But toward the end, my grandmother was getting some pretty strange ideas. I think this was one of them."

Serena reached into the envelope and pulled from it a small jump drive. "This is information that was on her computer's hard drive. A friend of hers pulled it from the computer to keep Lusan from getting a hold of it."

"Julio?" asked Leland.

"I'm really not at liberty to say," replied Serena. "But there is evidence here. I hope that it will make you a believer in what I'm telling you."

Leland took it in his hand. For a moment he just stared at it. In that moment, Serena gave Leland her card.

"I don't wish to overstay my welcome," said Serena, rising to her feet. "Feel free to call me."

"Yes," said Leland, "have a nice day."

As Serena left the office, she looked back. Leland hadn't even moved. She wasn't sure if that was a good sign or bad.

It was in the hallway that Serena was met by three very large and angry looking security guards. Without so much as a word, she was whisked down the hall to the elevator. She was surprised when one of the guards inserted his key into the panel. They were on their way to the 32nd floor.

CHAPTER 18

Chris tried for the third time to call Serena's cell phone without success. He was growing increasingly agitated. "I should never have let her go in there alone."

"And having both of you missing would be better?" asked Pastor Smith. "She might have turned it off herself."

"Or someone might have turned it off for her," retorted Chris. "It's been almost an hour and a half since she walked in there."

Again Chris pulled out his binoculars. From their vantage point on the fourth floor of the parking garage, they had a clear view of the main entrance of the Davidson building. Serena was nowhere in sight.

Chris looked up through the snow toward the 31st floor. He couldn't make out much from here, just offices with people milling about. He looked still higher to the 32nd floor. All of the windows on that floor were shuttered. From here it looked like one whole floor had been left vacant, but Chris knew better.

It was then that Julio stepped away from the edge and walked back toward the middle of the garage. He pulled out his cell phone and made a call. Chris glanced back for but a moment before turning his attention to the main entrance once more. How long was he supposed to wait? He and Serena had not discussed that issue. Certainly he hadn't expected her to take this long. No, he shouldn't have allowed her to go in there alone.

"She's going to be fine," said Pastor Smith. "If the Holy Spirit led her in there, then He is going to lead her out."

"OK, let's go over this again," said the uniformed security officer as he paced across the floor of the small, poorly lit room.

Serena sat in a metal folding chair, as she had these past 50 minutes, a security guard to either side of her. The only light in the room of any consequence was directed practically in her face. It reminded her of one of those old detective flicks, of an interrogation of the prime suspect by the police.

"It's like I told you, there's nothing to tell," she insisted. "I was a good friend of Mr. James's grandmother. This was a personal visit. There were things that I wanted him to know."

"Like what?" asked the interrogator.

"That was between him and me," insisted Serena.

"Then why didn't you visit him at home?" continued the officer

"Maybe I should," was the response.

"Don't think that we don't know who you are, Serena Davis," said the interrogator, a growing menace in his voice. "We know all about you."

"Do you?" asked Serena. "Then why don't you tell me."

Serena was surprised when her response was met with a hard slap to the face. She might have fallen from the chair had not the two officers grabbed her by the arms.

"Know this, Serena Davis. I'm not in the mood to play games," said the interrogator at point blank range.

He had a very bad odor about him, very disturbing. Serena could smell the demon within him. The other two guards were a different story; they were totally human. Serena could not be certain if this bully was a man possessed or a demon in disguise. Still, he smelled like a demon, despite what he looked like.

"Tell me what the two of you talked about," said the interrogator, his voice louder this time.

"It had nothing to do with your company, if that's what you mean," replied Serena, rubbing her mouth to find blood on the back of her hand. Yes, there was fear in her heart, but it was more than that. There was a sort of righteous anger in her heart. She knew what she was dealing with—this foul creature. He had no right to be here. Yet she curbed her anger. It might be a very bad idea to tip her hand at this point. If this being realized just how much she knew, she might not get out of this place at all.

At that very moment, the door to the hallway opened and in stepped yet another shadowy figure. He was dressed in black, and he was surrounded by a dark aura that matched the grim environment.

"Sir, this is the one who was talking to Mr. James," said the interrogator. "Her name is Serena Davis."

"Yes," said the figure, stepping into the light. "I know who she is."

It had been a very long time since Serena had last seen him, and that had been in another place in the universe altogether. He had made no effort to alter his facial features whatever. It sent a chill up her spine. "Hello, sir," she said.

Lusan smiled, though slightly. "Of all of the people I have ever known in my long existence, you are probably the only one that insists upon calling me sir."

"I do it out of respect for your position," replied Serena. "I take it that we are not playing charades here."

Lusan laughed openly. "And what purpose would that serve? It has been a long time, Serena. Why I do believe that you have some gray hairs on that pretty head of yours. I suspect that I put at least a few of them there."

"I'm sure you did," confirmed Serena.

"I have been looking forward to this little chat for a long time, little one," said Lusan. "And for all of that time you have been a pain in my side."

"It is my job, sir," replied Serena, doing her best to remain calm, at least on the outside. At this point, she was doing a pretty good job of it.

"Yes," confirmed Lusan, "I suppose it is."

"So, where do we go from here?" asked Serena.

Again Lusan smiled. "Well, I suppose that's up to you, little one. Garthang here has asked you a question. From my understanding, he has asked it several times. If you want out of here, you could start by answering it."

"It really bugs you, doesn't it?" posed Serena. "It is difficult to perpetuate a deception within a deception. Leland James believes that he is protecting your true identity from the world, but even what he believes he knows is a lie."

The interrogator prepared to strike Serena again, but Lusan stayed his hand. "Easy, Garthang, we don't want to damage her, at least not yet."

"You can't win this, you know that," said Serena.

"That is a matter of opinion," objected Lusan.

"Not to me," replied Serena. "Your downfall was prophesied thousands of years ago."

"By misguided humans," interjected Lusan. "I don't take their words very seriously."

Garthang touched the ear bud in his right ear. "Go desk," he said.

A scowl came to his face. At this point, Serena found herself wondering what this character would look like aged a bit and with black bat wings. The guard turned to Lusan.

"Sir, there is a detective and two patrolmen in the downstairs lobby, NYPD. They are asking for Serena Davis. They are very insistent about it."

Lusan shook his head sadly. "Too bad, this was just starting to get interesting." He turned once more to Serena. "I fear that we will have to continue this discussion at a later time."

"You intend to release her?" asked Garthang.

"I can do little else," replied Lusan, turning back toward his minion. "Escort her back downstairs, and don't harm her." Lusan paused and then turned once more to Serena. "Understand this, little one. You are not welcome here. Do not return. The time might come when I will call for you. Until then, our conversation is at an end."

The guards helped Serena to her feet and back out into the hall. A minute later they were on the elevator going down.

"I would take the master's words seriously if I were you," said Garthang as they passed the 11th floor. "You were lucky today; you might not be next time."

"I don't believe in luck," said Serena.

"Believe it or not," replied Garthang, "but yours is about to run out."

The door opened before them, revealing the brightly lit main lobby and the snow falling beyond the large windows. Before her stood two NYPD officers in blue, while behind them, stood two other men. Serena recognized one as Julio.

Serena turned to the security guards as she stepped from the elevator. "Thank you for your hospitality. I feel most enlightened."

Garthang and the others said nothing. A few seconds later the elevator door closed.

"Are you all right, ma'am," said one of the uniformed officers, glancing at the small slightly swollen gash at the side of Serena's lip.

"Yes, thank you," said Serena. "I am now."

The man standing behind the uniformed officers stepped forward. "John, Sergio, thank you very much for your assistance."

"No problem, Detective Strom," said the officer on the right. "We're just glad that everything worked out OK." He turned to Serena, "Have a good day, ma'am."

"Thank you," said Serena, as the officers departed.

"I think we all need to talk," announced the detective, "but not here."

The three headed on out into the snow where Chris and Pastor Smith were waiting. Chris and Serena embraced.

"I was afraid I'd lost you," said Chris. "I couldn't bear to lose you again."

"There is a nice coffeehouse about a block down that way," noted Detective Strom, "We can talk there. It's too cold out here."

"Thank you for your help, Detective Strom," said Julio, as the group walked through the snow.

"Yes, thank you," said Chris and Serena almost simultaneously.

"That's my job," assured Detective Strom. He paused for just a moment. Mrs. Davis, can you explain to me why you went in there if you felt that it might place your life in some risk?"

"Place my life at risk?" asked Serena.

"Yes," confirmed Strom. "Everyone else here seemed to believe you were in some danger. That's what Julio thought when he called me. Now, you're not going to tell me that you're the only one here who felt comfortable about it."

Serena hesitated. "No, I'm not. My going in there was a bit risky. You see, there is a bit of a history between me and Lusan. It goes about nine years back, long before he came to America. The relationship was quite a bit more painful for me than it was for him."

"I see," said Strom. "Not too many people can claim that they knew Lusan before he came to New York."

"I'm sure of that," confirmed Serena.

"So, let me ask you again," continued the detective, "why did you go in there?"

"I had some important personal papers to deliver to Leland James. He works for Lusan. They were papers from his late grandmother."

"And you thought they were that important?" asked the detective. "You couldn't simply have delivered them to his house after work or even mailed them to him?"

"No," replied Serena. "I felt led to deliver them to him here."

"Felt led?" asked Strom. "What do you mean by that?"

"I felt the leading of the Holy Spirit," replied Serena.

Detective Strom shook his head. "Look, I need to know all that happened to you in there, everything you remember. By the looks of you, someone in there gave you a rough time. Once I know what happened, we can figure out if you have the grounds for charges of assault against you."

Serena covered all of the details she could remember from her conversation with Leland to her interrogation and her conversation with Lusan. She left out how it was that she knew Lusan. She hoped that Detective Strom wouldn't pursue that line of questioning just yet.

"So, basically, you were just sharing some personal information with Leland about his grandmother," said Strom. "Not to antagonize Lusan or his people."

"Of course not," replied Serena.

"And your conversation with Leland James was civil?" continued Strom.

"Yes," said Serena. "We got along very well."

"Security's actions against you were unprovoked?"

"I didn't do anything to them," said Serena. "In fact, I was on my way out."

"Do you think what they did to you had anything to do with problems you and Lusan have had in the past?" asked Strom.

"I can't rule it out," said Serena.

The detective nodded. "I would say, based on what you've told me, we have grounds to file a charge of aggravated assault against this Mr. Garthang, but not against Mr. Lusan. If so, we need to photograph your injuries here within the next half hour or so. I have a camera to do that. That is assuming that you want to press assault charges. Still, it would be your word against theirs."

"I'm not sure what I want to do," admitted Serena.

Detective Strom shook his head again. "Folks, you'll excuse me if I tell you that this whole thing just isn't making sense to me." Then he turned to Julio. "Julio, if my memory serves me correctly, you were also a close friend to Clare James."

"Yes, we were very close," confirmed Julio.

"And that is how you came to know Chris and Serena Davis, through Claire James?"

"Yes," replied Julio.

For a while, Detective Strom said nothing. They were almost at the coffeehouse when he continued. "You know, something else has me concerned here. Lately, I've been doing quite a bit of work on a certain cold case. You remember it Julio, the murder of your three friends in the park two and a half years ago.

I've looked over hundreds of hours of video footage from all sorts of cameras around Central Park. So many businesses have security cameras, and nearly all of them have a cooperative agreement with the department, allowing us access to them via the Internet. I'd downloaded them a long time ago, but there wasn't time to go through them all. It was just two months ago that I finally got a break in the case."

By now they had reached the coffeehouse, but the detective paused at the door. He focused on Julio, who seemed visibly nervous.

"I was looking at the images from a security camera at a café on Central Park West," continued Detective Strom. "Just before ten I noticed four youths running across the street into the park. Then at about 11:15 P.M., I saw someone running across the street out of the park, he was practically stumbling over his own feet, as if the Devil himself were on his tail. From his clothes I suspected he was one of the four I had seen earlier. Sadly, the person was too far away, and the image wasn't clear enough to make a positive identification.

"Now, that was almost two hours after you told me that you'd left your friends at the edge of the park. Julio, don't you think it's about time you came clean about a few things?"

Julio looked over at the detective, yet he said nothing. Still, his expression said volumes. He seemed sad perhaps even ashamed.

"Julio, two and a half years ago, when your friends from the Latin Kings were cut down in Central Park, you were with them, weren't you?"

Julio looked down at the snow before him. "Yes, I was."

"And it was you running for your life, across Central Park West, wasn't it?"

"It probably was," confirmed Julio. "That was the direction I ran."

"So you saw the whole thing; you know who killed your friends," deduced Strom.

"Yes," confirmed Julio, who still hadn't looked up.

"They were your friends," Julio. "You saw who killed them. You even came forth to make a report, but you weren't being truthful about what happened. Julio, I just don't get it. Were you afraid that the killer or killers would have come after you if you testified?"

"They would have," confirmed Julio.

There was a long pause. Then Strom continued. "It's cold out here; let's go on inside."

The group found a table and sat down. Julio was shaking, though Serena suspected that it wasn't from the cold. The detective placed his hand on Julio's shoulder.

"It's OK, Julio. We're going to get through this. But answer me this: it was that Lusan character who was behind the killing of your friends, wasn't it?"

Nothing much surprised Serena anymore. She'd been through way too much. But this was one of those moments. This Detective Strom was either sharp or lucky. Maybe he was both. Oh, if Detective Strom could just make that charge stick, they'd finally have Satan on the ropes. She looked toward Julio, whose eyes had finally turned to the detective.

"Yes. But he wasn't just behind it, he killed them himself, at least he killed two of them. The third was killed by this guy called Duras" said Julio.

"Then, after all of that, you joined that cult of his? I think you'd better tell me the whole story from the beginning," said Strom.

"That's the problem," said Julio. "You won't believe it."

"Try me," replied Strom. "You might be surprised."

And so he did. Julio spoke of a game of toll taker in Central Park gone horribly wrong. He told of watching his friends butchered right before his eyes only to end up kneeling before Lusan as he awaited his own fate at the end of a sword. He had been granted mercy, only to face an even more terrifying ordeal several hours later atop a high-rise parking garage in midtown Manhattan.

There he had been offered a horrible choice. He could throw himself to his death or submit to possession by a demonic force. It was then that the detective stopped him.

"Wait a minute Julio," he objected. "Are you talking about demon possession, the exorcist, Linda Blair, type stuff?"

"Yes," confirmed Julio. "But the real thing, real demon possession, usually doesn't work like that. The demon first seizes your body; he takes full control. Then he uses it for whatever purpose pleases him. He uses your body as his own. You become a prisoner within your own body, unable to do anything but watch."

"Please believe him," said Karina. "It happened to me too. I know what it's like."

"It wasn't until Grandma Claire freed me that I became myself again," continued Julio. "Since then, I've had a new master, Jesus Christ. Believe me, He is a lot gentler."

"I'm sure of it," said Strom, not quite sure what else to say. "So who is this Lusan guy that he has this kind of power to control demons?"

"He is the Devil himself, Satan," said Julio.

"He's telling you the truth, detective," said Serena. "I saw him up close. Lusan is Satan. As I said I have met him personally. I'll never forget that face."

"Yes, I know who you are now," said the detective. "You're that woman who went to Hell and came back again. You wrote a book. My wife told me all about it. She's into that kind of thing."

"And you're not," deduced Chris.

"Well, no, not like that," said the detective. "I'm a Lutheran. I go to church and all. I go with my wife and son. I mainly go for them. I believe in Jesus, really I do, just not quite like that. Exorcism, demon possession, that's Dark Ages sort of stuff."

"I only wish it were," said Pastor Smith. "But I've seen it at work more times than I care to remember, especially since Lusan arrived."

With difficulty, Julio continued. He left nothing out. Detective Strom was attentive throughout. He nodded a few times, but asked no questions.

"You're asking me to believe an awful lot of incredible things on faith alone," said the detective, leaning back a bit. "I suppose that also explains why your original testimony was false. It all makes sense. The problem is, it sounds crazy. I doubt that a jury would see it any differently."

"Then you believe our story?" asked Pastor Smith.

"Reverend, I don't know what to believe," admitted the detective. "A couple years ago, I'd have dismissed the whole story as pure fantasy. But you haven't seen and heard the sorts of things I have down at the precinct these past couple years. And it all started around the time that this Lusan showed up."

"Believe me, I have," replied Pastor Smith.

The detective smiled, though slightly. "Yeah, I guess you have." The detective turned to Chris and Serena. "Are you folks going to be in town for a while?"

"Yes," said Chris. "We'd sort of planned on staying the week."

Detective Strom nodded. "OK, I might need to get back to you regarding a few things. However, I want you to promise me that you won't be visiting the Davidson Building again. That place is off limits, understand?"

"Certainly, Detective Strom, I promise. I won't go back there," said Serena.

The detective nodded once more. "Mrs. Davis, have faith in me. I'm going to be pursuing this investigation further, I assure you. I'll get back to you in a few days. Just stay safe, OK?"

"OK," said Serena smiling.

"Detective Strom, I'm really sorry," said Julio. "I feel like I really let you down."

"Don't feel that way, Julio," said Strom. "From what I'm hearing, the blame isn't yours. Still, what I told Mrs. Davis, I'm telling you and Karina too. Don't try to get involved in this investigation, at least not until you've graduated from the police academy and are a member of the NYPD."

"Sure," said Julio, smiling for the first time.

"I promise, I won't leave you out of the loop," said Detective Strom. "After what happened today, I think this cold case is about to open up wide."

Krissie looked at her husband incredulously. "Serena Davis visited you right there in your office?"

"Sure did," said Leland, finishing up dessert. "She had a hard copy of that email that my grandmother sent me the night she died. You know, the one that turned up blank. Apparently she and my grandmother were close friends."

"But do you really think that this email is the real thing?" asked Krissie. "She might have forged it."

"I don't think so," replied Leland. "There were just too many things, personal things that only my grandmother would know. She also sent me some files from the missing hard drive. I've had a chance to look at a few of them already. It's just the sort of thing that my grandmother would write."

"But you don't know this woman like I do," retorted Krissie. "She's a real witch. The things she has said about Lusan are horrible, just horrible. I'll tell you, some of these Christians are total haters. They are a big part of what is wrong in the world today." Krissie paused. "Your grandmother was a real exception."

"No she wasn't," corrected Leland. "She was very opposed to Lusan; you know that."

"I guess I do," said Krissie, "sorry."

Leland smiled but said nothing.

The conversation, such as it was, was interrupted by the ringing of the doorbell. Leland opened the door to discover two plainclothes police officers, Detective Strom and Lieutenant Stoddard.

As they all gathered in the living room, Leland wondered what this was all about. He had a bad feeling about it all, but was hoping for the best.

"We are here regarding two issues," began Detective Strom. "Do you know a woman by the name of Serena Davis?"

"Sure," replied Leland. "She was a friend of my late grandmother, or so she said. She seemed like a very nice person. She dropped into my office early this morning with some documents that my grandmother had written. I was very happy to get them. We spoke for 20 minutes or so; then she left."

"And you didn't see her again after that?" asked the detective.

"No sir," confirmed Leland. "Nothing has happened to her, has it?"

"No, she's fine," replied Strom. "It would seem that several of Lusan's security people roughed her up a bit. It wasn't serious, mind you; they just scared her a little, that was all. I was just checking up on her story."

"I didn't know anything about that," said Leland.

"Mrs. Davis didn't think you did," confirmed Strom. "I just wanted to hear your side of the story. If assault charges are filed and it goes to court, you might be called as a witness, that's all."

"There is another matter," said Lieutenant Stoddard, "a more serious one. It has to do with one of our cold case files, a murder that occurred about two and a half years ago."

"A murder?" asked Leland.

"Actually, a triple homicide," said Stoddard. "Are either of you familiar with a young man by the name of Julio Mendoza?"

"Why, yes," replied Leland. "He was in our youth group for a while, but he left almost two years ago for unexplained reasons. He was also a friend of my grandmother. They studied the Bible together along with a friend of his. I think her name was Katrina or Karina, something like that. The thing is, he was with my grandmother when she had her first heart attack. He probably saved her life that time. But then she had the second one when she was alone."

"Yes, that's the young man we're talking about," confirmed Strom. "He told me a rather incredible story this morning. The night that his friends were killed, that was the night of September, 11, 2014, do you remember where you were, what you might have been doing?"

Well here it was at last. Lusan had warned Leland that this day might come. Thing was, Leland had expected it to occur two years ago, if ever. Lusan had prepared them for this day.

"You remember that night, don't you Leland?" said Krissie. "That was the night we walked through Central Park on our way home from the Anderson's party on Central Park East."

"Oh yeah," confirmed Leland, "that was some night."

"How so?" asked Lieutenant Stoddard.

"That was the night we got stopped by those kids in the park," said Leland. "They were wearing the Latin King's colors. They wanted a handout or something like that. But I wouldn't give it to them."

"Then these two businessmen came up the trail from the other direction," said Krissie. "One of them hollered at the kids. I guess that kind of spooked them and they moved on."

"That was the first time we ever saw Lusan and Duras," said Leland. "To say the least, we were grateful that they'd happened by right then. We invited them to come on over to our condo for a nightcap. I guess you could say that the rest was history."

"It was about an hour or so later that we saw the lights of the police cars at the edge of Central Park," continued Krissie. "Those murders had occurred not far from where we had been walking. They must have occurred just after we left."

"But you never contacted the police about it," noted Stoddard.

"I didn't see any need," said Leland. "We didn't even know if the boys we saw were the same ones that got killed."

"Was Julio one of the kids you saw in the park?" asked Strom.

"I'm not sure," admitted Krissie. "It was pretty dark, and I'll admit to you right here and now that I was pretty scared."

"I can understand that," confirmed Strom.

"I'm not sure either," admitted Leland, "but I don't think so. I think I would have recognized him."

"And Lusan and Duras were with you every minute from the time that the boys ran off until you saw the lights of the police cars in Central Park?" asked Strom.

"Oh yes," confirmed Leland.

"We were up talking late into the night," interjected Krissie. "They ended up crashing in the guest bedroom till morning. Like my husband said, the rest is history."

"We'd considered the possibility that the kids we met in the park might have been the ones who were murdered, but there were four of them, not three," said Leland.

"I sure wish you'd come to us earlier with this information," said Detective Strom. "Still, I understand your reluctance, really. This can be a crazy place at times." Strom paused. "If there is anything else that comes to you, please feel free to call me directly." He handed Leland his card.

"We will," confirmed Leland, seeing his visitors to the door.

A minute later, both Leland and Krissie breathed a sigh of relief. They headed back into the living room.

"I didn't feel right lying to them like that," said Leland.

"We had to," objected Krissie. "What if it got out that it was Lusan who killed those thugs? Yes, he did it to protect us, but it would have made a real mess for his ministry. I, for one, had no problems with what we just did."

"We'll need to let Lusan know what just happened," said Leland.

"I'll make the call right now," assured Krissie. "Don't worry. I think this is the last we'll hear from those police officers. This cover story was perfect."

As Krissie headed into the bedroom to use the phone, Leland sat in his comfy chair. "What a day," he sighed, gazing out at the park. First there was the visit of Serena Davis, followed by what had apparently happened between her and security. Now the incident in the park had surfaced once more. It was a mess, and unlike Krissie, he didn't think this issue was over, no, not by a long shot. He felt for the flash drive in his pocket. He would be using his computer to examine its other documents tonight. For the first time in two and a half years, he was seriously questioning his loyalty to this new messiah.

Detective Strom and Lieutenant Stoddard stepped from the door of Leland's condo and into the frigid night air. A light snow was still falling, making the snowy park across the street look like a winter wonderland.

"What do you think about their story, Lieutenant?" asked Detective Strom.

Lieutenant Stoddard pulled his heavy coat around him. "It makes a whole lot more sense than that crazy tale you got from Julio this morning."

"But that alone doesn't make it true," noted Strom.

"No it doesn't," confirmed Stoddard. "Still, it looks to me like we're back to square number one."

"I don't think so," replied Strom. "They emerged from the park several minutes after Julio ran across Central Park West. That means that they were still in the park when the triple homicide occurred. They know more than they're telling."

"Maybe," replied Stoddard, "but I don't think you're going to get anything more out of them."

"Probably not," said Strom, "but they told me enough. They've pointed me in the right direction, perhaps without realizing it."

"Toward Lusan," deduced Stoddard.

"Right," confirmed Strom. "And there's something else. I've spent a lot of time examining video footage from all sides of the park. If the two people in black exiting the park with Leland and Krissie James are Lusan and Duras, when did they enter? At this point I can account for every figure that entered Central Park from eight in the evening on, except for these two jokers. I only have an image of them leaving."

Stoddard laughed. "Bill, I think you need to get out more often, find a hobby at least."

"Phil, this has been my hobby for the last two and a half years," admitted Detective Strom. "Call me compulsive or obsessive if you wish, but I'm not going to let this case go unsolved. It's become sort of personal to me. I will find out who killed those kids. I will get to the bottom of it. I will bring the perpetrator or perpetrators to justice."

"Tall order," noted Stoddard.

"True enough," confirmed Strom. "If Julio and the others are right, I'm facing off against the Devil himself. If I bring him to justice, I've just about got the world's problems solved."

It was 11 days later that Chris and Serena pulled out of New York City on their way to Memphis and their next revival meeting. For the moment, much to their disappointment, Julio and Karina would have to remain behind. There just wasn't enough room for them. Perhaps they would get together in the spring when they would be holding revivals in the northeast again.

Before they had left, Detective Strom had shared his findings with them regarding his interview with Leland and Krissie. This was something he rarely did during an ongoing investigation. The results had hit Julio and Karina pretty hard. They'd held out some hope that they might have Lusan on the run, but it wasn't to be. Still, the detective vowed to continue the investigation, keeping Julio in the loop.

Serena still wasn't sure if Strom totally believed their story. But maybe he would succeed where so many others had failed, checking Satan's progress here on Earth. Wouldn't it be wonderful to see Satan himself tried in a human court before a human jury? It was a nice dream, but for the moment, that was all that it was—a dream. Until then, she would combat the Prince of Lies in the only way she knew how, by winning hearts and minds for Jesus one soul at a time.

CHAPTER 19

Fifty-three-year-old physicist Dr. Les Geiger and his research team watched carefully as the enormous, shimmering ring was set into its yoke shaped base by the crane. It was a milestone in the development of this device. It was a matter teleporter capable of moving objects great distances through space. Yet unlike the more classical teleporter model, this one didn't disassemble an object atom by atom, convert it to energy, and then reassemble it somewhere else. No, this one created a tunnel through space and time—a wormhole that matter could pass through in one piece. The whole concept seemed like science fiction, and they had accomplished so much so fast.

Here on the Island of Katafanga, hardly more than a dot on the globe, they would accomplish two miracles almost simultaneously. Over in building three, another group of scientists and engineers were already testing the first economically feasible fusion reactor. Its design was like nothing any of them had ever seen. Never had anyone attempted to create a sustained nuclear fusion reaction this way. It transformed thermal and nuclear energy directly to electricity. At yesterday's trial they had cranked it up to over two million volts at a staggering 12 billion amps, and they claimed that was at just 20 percent capacity.

Les nodded approvingly as the 11-ton ring was guided into the base. It's electrical and control plugs snapped perfectly into place. Since college he had dreamed of such a device as this. It was he who had developed the theoretical model that proposed that just such a thing was possible. It had been his doctoral thesis back in 1991. His theory hadn't sat well at all with the review committee. It flew directly in the face of what was then the accepted model of the space-time continuum. In the end, he was granted his doctorate, but it was a hard sell. He'd ended up teaching undergraduate physics at a small four-year college in Wisconsin, but his dreams of quantum teleportation, as he called it, had never died. For the past 25 years he had refined his theory and written scientific papers about it. He felt at least partially vindicated to see scientific opinion slowly turning in his direction.

Then two years ago, he was approached to work on this project. Indeed, he would be the deputy director in charge of a dozen other engineers and researchers and over 30 technical staff. It had been just too good to pass up. He hadn't been off this island in all of that time. Then again, he didn't want to leave; this place had everything. His quarters were like a luxury resort suite with first-class service. He wanted for nothing. This place had some of the finest beaches he had ever seen, not that he took advantage of them very often. He worked an average of 60 to 70 hours a week, and he loved it. The amount of money needed for equipment was no object. He got anything and everything he asked for.

He had never in his wildest dreams envisioned seeing his theory actually demonstrated in his own lifetime, but if all went well, they would begin teleportation trials in less than two weeks. Right now it depended on the state of the fusion generator, and it was scheduled to be tested at full power sometime next week. That would pave the way for their research.

He thought of his wife, Ruth. He shook his head sadly. He thought of all of those years, through the bad times, when she had been the only one who believed in him, encouraged him. If only she had lived long enough to see this day.

The day after tomorrow they would be installing the second ring on the far side of the island. That would be their first teleportation destination.

Still, in many ways, this island was almost surreal. It was also the home of hundreds of what Les might have best described as cultists. The same Lusan who was bankrolling this scientific project had created his own religion, and the other side of the island was a sort of boot camp for the converts. The scientists and engineers didn't mix too much with them. Actually, they were instructed not to. It would impair their concentration or something like that. There was even an eight-foot fence between the two compounds. It wasn't electrified or topped by barbed wire, but it was a reminder that there was a separation between the classes. Indeed, Les had never even seen the inside of their compound. From some of the things he'd heard, he wasn't even sure he wanted to.

Nevertheless, some of his technicians came from the ranks of the converts. They were certainly a strange bunch, not very talkative to be sure. They seemed almost two-dimensional. Les didn't know how else to describe it.

Then there were the others, Lusan's people. They were even stranger, really cold. They were scientists and engineers, accountants and procurers, administrators and security people. The director of this project was one of them, Malnar. Not doctor or mister, just Malnar. He acted nice enough, though Les got the feeling that an act was all it was. He was all business, that one. In him there was a total absence of the social graces. He stayed clear of the other scientists and engineers outside of the workplace, yet he was positively brilliant. He had a level of insight into the topic of space-time the likes of which Les had never seen.

As for the other scientists and engineers, they'd become almost like family. Les figured that their isolation from the rest of the world had a tendency to do that. They were allowed to make phone calls to the outside world. They had email and satellite television, too. Still, they were ever mindful that they were working in a high-security facility. In email and on the phone they had to choose their words carefully. Everything they said might be monitored.

Lusan's people were pretty strict when it came to security. A month ago, an engineer had gotten into hot water after just mentioning the project in an email to his girlfriend back in Russia. Word was that he'd been reassigned to the other side of the island as a maintenance technician for the facility's computer network. That had to be a letdown after working on cutting-edge technology here. It had been a shot across everyone's bow. Everyone here was exceptionally careful about what they said to outsiders after Sergei had been escorted out of the facility by Lusan's security guards. The fact that big brother was watching was the only downside in paradise.

It was just before 11 that same evening. Les and his good friend Nabuko Yamura were sitting on his second-floor balcony staring out at the southern stars, each with a glass of red wine. Amidst the isolation of this island they had become kindred spirits. Nabuko was from Sapporo, on Japan's Hokkaido Island. She was a 45-year-old electrical engineer, and like Les, was alone after the death of her husband three years ago. They often met out here on the balcony for a nightcap or gazed at the stars through his telescope. Tonight found them talking shop, pondering a world with no energy crisis where transport from one place to another was virtually instantaneous.

Nabuko was speaking of the impact on the transportation industry when she suddenly went silent. She stood up, gazing out into the darkness. "Did you hear that?" she asked.

Les rose to his feet as well, standing at her side. "What did you hear, Nabuko?"

"I thought I heard a scream," she replied. "It sounded like a woman. It was coming from over there in the compound."

From the veranda, the compound was just visible, far to the right. It was tough for Les to make out from this distance, but something was going on.

There was another scream. It sounded like a cry for help. This time Les heard it. "What in Sam Hill is going on over there?" he murmured. He looked toward his telescope, which sat in the corner by the railing.

He rushed over to it and trained it toward the compound. In all of the time he'd been here, he'd rarely used it for terrestrial purposes. He'd always figured that what went on over there was their business, religious business.

It didn't take long for him to focus in on the source of the commotion, which seemed to be at the central building of the compound, the place they called the chapel. In reality it didn't look much like a chapel. It was a positively huge block building with few windows. It looked more like some sort of blockhouse. There was a young woman running away from it in this direction. The source of her distress soon became obvious. She was being pursued by no fewer than six of Lusan's guards.

"What's going on, Les?" asked Nabuko.

"I'm not sure," said Les. "Take a look for yourself."

Nabuko gazed through the small telescope. "What are they doing over there?" she gasped. She turned the eyepiece turret, zooming in on the scene. A second later, a spotlight from atop the chapel was directed at the poor woman. She tried to get out of the light, but it followed her.

About a minute later, the woman reached the fence. She tried to climb over it, but she didn't have time. The guards were on her before she was over the top. She screamed as they took her by the arms.

By now, Les was at the telescope again. "My God, they've handcuffed her!" he exclaimed. "They're dragging her back to the chapel, and she's not going quietly."

"What should we do?" asked Nabuko, coming back to the eyepiece again.

"I don't know," admitted Les. "I've never seen anything like this before."

A few minutes later, they led her back through the door of the chapel, still kicking and screaming. Then there was silence once more. Les looked around, to see if anyone else had witnessed what they had just seen. It looked like they were alone out here."

"What are we going to do?" repeated Nabuko. "We've got to tell someone."

"Who?" asked Les.

"I don't know," replied Nabuko.

"Neither do I," said Les, who noticed that the searchlight was moving outward toward them. "Quick, we need to get inside, right now."

Les turned the telescope away from the compound and, along with Nabuko, rushed inside. They closed the sliding glass door and drew the drapes nearly closed. Not 15 seconds later, the searchlight swept across their now vacant balcony.

"They wanted to know if anyone had seen what they'd done," said Les, looking through the slit in the drapes. "The light went right past us. I don't think we were seen."

"We can't call security," said Nabuko.

"Those are the last people we'd want to call," said Les. "For the moment, I think we'd better stay quiet about what we just saw. We can't tell anyone. We don't know what's going on. There may be a perfectly reasonable explanation for what we just saw."

Nabuko looked out of the sliding glass door just in time to see the spotlight go out. For a moment she seemed deep in thought. "Les, when was the last time you saw Sergei Urbanoff?"

Les had to think on that one. "I know that they moved him out of the resort when they demoted him. I heard he lives with the other workers on the far side of the compound. I don't think I've seen him since they escorted him out. Why?"

"I only know of one person who claims to have seen him," said Nabuko. "And she said she saw him working in a ditch down near the main well. He was shoveling dirt. They hollered at him, but he didn't even respond. Now, answer me this: what would an electrical engineer be doing digging a trench?"

"Putting in network cables?" asked Les.

"Not there," said Nabuko. "It made me wonder just what they had done to him. Look, he was in my department. I can tell you, he wasn't the sort that you'd find digging a trench."

Les just shook his head. He didn't know what to say, but he didn't like the sound of what Nabuko was inferring.

A minute later, Les heard heavy footsteps in the hallway. He cautiously made his way to the door and gazed through the peep hole. He was surprised to see two of Lusan's guards walk past the door. He was relieved when they kept right on going.

Two minutes later, he heard voices in the hall, then the heavy footsteps. The security guards walked past his door once more, only this time they had someone walking between them. Les walked back toward Nabuko.

"They just took Al Peltzer down the hallway," whispered Les, "and he looked pretty shook up."

"What should we do?" asked Nabuko.

"I don't know," admitted Les. "I'm out of ideas."

"Maybe Administrator Karr could help?" said Nabuko.

Les shook his head. "Aldo Karr is in charge of this island. Do you really believe all of this is happening without his knowledge? I don't think so. I suspect he's the one behind it all."

Nabuko nodded, but said nothing.

Les hesitated. "Look, I'd really like for you to stay the night with me. It's not safe out there, at least not now."

"I'd like that," said Nabuko. "Thank you, Les."

"I couldn't bear anything happening to you," said Les. "I'll sleep in here on the couch."

"You don't need to do that," insisted Nabuko, "I don't bite."

Les chuckled. "We'll figure something out."

The rest of the night passed without incident, and eventually, both Les and Nabuko got a good night's sleep. It was pleasant not to be sleeping alone.

Both Les and Nabuko were relieved to see a weary-eyed but otherwise healthy Al Peltzer drag into work the next day. He went on and on about being practically dragged out of his quarters and questioned by security for falling asleep on his balcony.

"The sound of the waves crashing on the beach at the bottom of the hill always puts me to sleep," he said. "I've spent many a night out there on the balcony. I don't know why they were so upset this particular time. They finally said something about mosquitoes and a concern for the health of the scientists and engineers and let me go."

Neither Les nor Nabuko commented on what they had seen. But the events of that night had them both scared. Nabuko spoke of beginning her own investigation into the matter, though she declined to comment just what that investigation might entail.

It was five nights later that Nabuko showed up at Les's quarters with a small modified FM radio. It didn't look out of the ordinary. She'd brought it with her from Japan. Still, it was unique.

"When these two buttons are pressed in sequence, it can receive and unscramble the radio traffic between Lusan's security people," said Nabuko. "I've been listening to them for the past three nights. What I've heard has been enlightening and frightening."

She placed the receiver on the dining room table and switched it on. At first, all they heard was a weak radio station out of Fiji. Then by making a minor adjustment, they were hearing the back and forth communications between

Lusan's people. It was routine for the most part, security patrols checking in at regular intervals.

"I've heard them talk about a ritual held at the chapel," said Nabuko. "They call it the union. I still don't know exactly what it is, but it is conducted late at night. They do it to their religious converts, usually just a few days before they leave to begin their ministry in the world beyond the island. It might be some kind of brainwashing procedure. I don't know how else to describe it. I believe that the young woman who was trying to climb the fence last week was about to undergo that ritual. I suppose that she liked her brain the way it was."

"It all sounds like something out of a B grade movie," said Les, who still seemed focused on the back and forth chatter over the radio. "This place must have more than one kind of mad scientists."

"Did you know that there is a cavern below the chapel?" asked Nabuko.

That caught Les by surprise. "No, I didn't."

"It must be quite large, from what I've heard," said Nabuko. "There is a lot going on down there, and it doesn't sound all that pleasant. They have created some sort of underground lake or pool within it, and I don't think it's a pool of water." Nabuko paused. To Les, she seemed a bit agitated. "Les, I want out of here. I'm scared. They talk about us, too. I don't think they much like us. No, I know it. We are a necessary evil to them. When we complete our work for them, we will be a liability. They don't trust us. I don't think they want the world finding out about this project."

"I thought that we were doing this for the good of the world," replied Les. "That was the main point in that grand recruitment speech we all got."

"What I'm hearing makes me doubt their sincerity," said Nabuko. "When they finish with us, we may all end up facing the union. I believe Sergei already has."

That didn't sound good. "So what do we do?" asked Les.

"I don't know," admitted Nabuko. "I am really torn. I don't think they'll do anything to us soon. We will be useful to them for quite a while, I think. Anyway, I might be reading this all wrong. I need to listen to their radio chatter, get a better idea what the story is."

So they had a quiet dinner and listened to the radio. They listened until well past 11 P.M. Nothing particularly troubling emerged from what they heard. They agreed to continue the vigil the following evening to gather more data, to get a better idea as to where they stood.

"Engaging safeties, current to the ring in one minute," said a voice over the loud speaker in the control room.

Through the thick Plexiglas windows the science team gazed out from the control room at the shimmering ring illuminated by the high-intensity lights. This was it, the first test. Could they form a stable wormhole joining two rings almost 4,000 feet apart? They would soon know.

Les and Nabuko stood side by side amidst the other members of the science team. Almost without noticing, Les had taken Nabuko's hand. She gave his hand a gentle squeeze.

"We'll begin with a million volts at 1.6 billion amps," announced Malnar, who stood near the back of the group, his arms crossed. "Mr. Wilson, watch for any power spikes in the flow. If you see anything at all that makes you nervous, hit the breaker. We'll sort out the data later."

"Yes, sir," confirmed Wilson, who sat at one of the three computer terminals before the observation windows.

"Engage," said Malnar.

Les was astounded. He could actually feel the power as it flowed into the ring over 50 feet away. The gasp from the crowd told him that he was not alone in that. Right now, he could just make out a faint aura around the ring. In the midst of the ring, a blue luminous fog was forming, even as the wall behind it rippled, as if viewed through waves of searing heat, then it began to fade. In the midst of the fog, a myriad of what looked like sparkling stars appeared.

A gasp of wonder arose from the group as the swirling clouds brightened. Never had they seen such a wonder.

Les glanced at the readouts before him then turned to Malnar. "I recommend we increase the current by 20 percent."

"Agreed," said Malnar.

The clouds within the ring brightened, even as what looked like daylight appeared within the heart of the ring. Les recalled the view from the ring on the far side of the island. It was out in the open air, perched upon a thick concrete slab covered by a sort of ramada. Was that what he was seeing through the ring? He wasn't sure. Still, something wasn't quite right. The image was intermittent, it twisted and undulated. Les moved forward to the center terminal. He made some quick adjustments. The image began to clear.

"Come on, think, what am I missing?" muttered Les.

"Adjust the phase discriminator," suggested Nabuko, "Narrow the band."

Les understood. The image became even clearer. Yes, they were looking at the beach. A cheer arose from the group.

"Let's give it a try," said Les.

"Go ahead with experiment one," said Malnar.

A research assistant stepped in front of the ring. In his hand were three silvery spheres, about the size of golf balls. Each was a miniature scientific probe that would record factors ranging from temperature to radiation intensity during their brief flight.

The assistant lined up, took aim, then tossed the first one underhand into the maelstrom. There was a flash of light as it passed through the mists.

Les followed its course carefully from the control room. He was certain that he saw a second flash still deeper into the mists.

"It came through!" said a voice over the radio. "Test sphere one just flew out of the destination ring. Man, was that something to see."

Again there arose a cheer from the team. The research assistant threw the second and then the third ball through the ring, after which the power was cut and the wormhole collapsed. The team was ecstatic. They had just created the first stable manmade wormhole.

Yet their triumph was short-lived. When the probes were recovered, they were found to be twisted and distorted. The trip through the wormhole had fundamentally altered their atomic structure. They had recorded no data that had survived. One could only imagine what the trip would have done to a human being.

"This was just the first step," said Les, examining the distorted sphere at a round table discussion some hours later. "We've weighed each one. No matter was lost in transfer. At least we got that part right. Now we have to figure out what happened, what went wrong."

"I don't think the wormhole was truly stable," said a woman at the far end of the table. "Space-time through the wormhole was twisted and undulating. We need to find a way to regulate the flow through the corridor, make it more laminar.

"Perfectly laminar is more likely," noted a man standing near the door.

Others around the table nodded in agreement. It seemed to make sense.

"Then let's get working on it," said Les. "We've made tremendous progress. We should celebrate. We will make this technology work. Once we review the data on the computers more carefully, we'll figure out what to do next. It's just going to take time."

There was a general agreement among the others. The concept was sound; today's experiment had proved that. It just needed to be refined.

Today's experiment was the center of conversation as Les and Nabuko had a quiet dinner in her quarters. They listened to the random security transmissions over her radio. They were only about half listening to it when one particular conversation caught their attention.

"These humans can be quite resourceful when they want to be," said a voice over the radio. "Their progress today with the ring was quite impressive. I was there; I saw it."

"I still think they look better burning in a fire pit, crying to me for mercy," said another, a sense of mirth in his voice. "I don't think I'll ever get used to treating them as equals."

"Enough," said a third voice. "I don't want this sort of talk going out over the airwaves in English, even on an encrypted channel."

Nabuko seemed to turn very pale. "What was that all about? Do you think it was a joke?"

"It didn't sound like it," said Les.

"Who are these people," said Nabuko, leaning forward on the table and placing her face in her hands.

"I don't know," admitted Les, "but they talked about us as if we were a different species altogether."

Nabuko looked up. "It was they who guided our work. They seemed to know a lot of the science, the ins and outs of the universe, but needed our help to make the technology work. Could they be some sort of aliens?"

"What about the comment about humans in a fire pit, pleading for mercy?" asked Les. "That almost sounds like some version of Hell."

"We have a form of Hell in my faith," said Nabuko, "but it's more like an enormous pot of boiling oil, not coals and fire."

"Lovely," noted Les. "To be honest with you, I'm really not religious. I believe in the big bang, evolution, not the creation of the universe by some powerful all-knowing being."

"Even after what you just heard?" asked Nabuko.

"Even after what I just heard," confirmed Les.

"What are these people?" continued Nabuko.

Les took Nabuko's hand. "Now we're not going to start making wild speculations based on a few sentences spoken over the radio. It could have been some sort of an inside joke for all we know."

For a while they spoke of escaping this place. This weekend they could take the shuttle to Fiji, on the excuse that they needed a weekend vacation. From there, they could fly to Australia or New Zealand, even Japan. Yet in the end they agreed to stay, to keep working. What they were doing was too important, too incredible. Perhaps it was their scientific curiosity overriding their common sense. And they would keep eavesdropping on Lusan's people too, gathering as much information as they could. Of course they couldn't tell a soul, because getting caught could be deadly, literally. They just hoped that they were making the right decision.

In Lusan's conference room in the Davidson Building, the usual gathering of his minions was assembled before him. Winter had given way to spring, and with it had come word of progress on his pet project, the ring. Yes, it wasn't fully functional yet, but they were making progress. Soon it would allow him to move his minions and the spirits of his minions back and forth between Earth and Hell. No longer would they need to squeeze through that tiny fissure in the ethereal realm beneath well number 14 in the Kurdish Republic. They would be able to pour through this gate by the tens of thousands. And when that time came, he would have them possess the souls of every last scientist and engineer who had made it all possible, thus keeping the secret of the ring from the world. These humans were such fools.

"We have another potential problem," noted one of his minions. "His name is Detective William Strom of the New York Police Department. He has been snooping into our business. My lord, he has been listening to that wench, Serena Davis. I fear that he is beginning to believe her story. He is attempting to prove that you are not who you say you are."

"He will have a great deal of difficulty on that score," noted Lusan.

"Perhaps," said the minion. "But I have been observing him nevertheless. He has not invited the Holy Spirit of God into his being so I am able to follow his movements without hindrance. He found the falsified airline records that show that you entered this country legally, but he didn't stop there. He located the row and seat that you supposedly occupied, 24B. He questioned the person in the seat beside it. Strangely, the woman in 24C remembered the flight perfectly. She claimed that 24B was vacant."

"How could that be?" objected Lusan. "That was almost three years ago."

"She remembered it because she had a long conversation with the man who had been sitting by the window in seat 24A. Apparently he had been quite remarkable.

"Pagoni's people provided you with a very convincing history. The paper trail is impressive, but it is not ironclad. If this Detective Strom follows the paper trail to Northern Africa or convinces some more significant organization such as the FBI or INTERPOL to take it up, they might find that you do not have a true life history on Earth. That might be difficult to explain. It might lead to your deportation or, worse, your exposure."

"Then eliminate him!" Lusan yelled in frustration. "Make it look like an accident or an incident of gang violence. I don't care."

The minion smiled. "It will be a pleasure, my lord."

"I will not allow a mere policeman to stand in my way at this point!" Lusan said, furious that he was being challenged by a mere man. "He should have confined his efforts to pursuing humans. He is not up to the challenge of confronting us."

CHAPTER 20

It was nearly dark by the time Detective Bill Strom reached his modest three-bedroom home in Montclair, New Jersey. It was quite a commute every day, almost an hour, but Bill wouldn't have had it any other way. Montclair was quiet, away from the gangs and the crime of the city. It was the kind of place that you could raise a family in, free of fear.

He pulled into the driveway. He would have pulled all the way into the garage if there had been room. But that was his weights room, the kid's playroom, and his workshop. After all of that, there wasn't room for a car.

He grabbed his briefcase, locked the car door, and headed toward the front door. He could see that the kitchen light was on, but that was about it. That seemed a bit odd. He wondered if the boys were home yet. He opened the front door and started down the hallway.

There was motion behind him, followed by a terrible concussive pain in the back of his head. He dropped his briefcase and fell to his knees. He tried to get up, yet a second blow drove him to the floor. He lay there in a semiconscious state. He was aware of motion around him, then nothing.

He awoke amidst a terrible headache. He found himself in the living room. He tried to move; he couldn't. He tried to speak; he couldn't. The room was lit only by light coming in from the kitchen. Before him he saw his wife Peggy lying upon the floor, her back to the sofa. Her hands were bound behind her back, and her feet were bound together with duck tape. Another strand of duck tape had been used to gag her. It looked like someone had knocked her around pretty bad. She had a black eye and several bruises on her face. To her left, his eight-year-old son, Willie, was similarly restrained.

Bill quickly discovered that he had been bound in much the same way she had been. Whoever had done this was a professional.

"Well, sleeping beauty is awake," said a bald, heavily tattooed man, switching on the living room lights.

Bill knew the look, the tattoos, and the colors. This guy was a member of the Aryan Brotherhood. Yet the young Latino guy who walked in directly behind him looked like a member of MS 13. The colors, the tattoos, it all fit. But their working together didn't. Their gangs were sworn enemies.

"You shouldn't have stuck your nose where it don't belong," said the second man, pointing an accusing finger at the detective. "The master is real upset with you. Now you're going to pay, you and your family."

"Now, let's see," said the bald man. "The boss said to make a statement with your execution. He wants it terrifying and painful. We have a lot of experience when it comes to that. Of course, fire is the worst, and the anticipation of its burning touch is the worst sort of fear."

Bill looked toward Peggy. Her blue eyes were full of terror.

"And you get to watch it happening to your family," said the Latino gang member, "even as it is happening to you."

Bill heard the back door slam, and a few seconds later, yet another heavily tattooed man entered the room. In each hand was a large, plastic gasoline container.

"Oh yeah, the good stuff has arrived," said the bald man. He looked toward his compatriots. "If you gentlemen would be so kind as to tie this family all together in the middle of the room, I think we can begin. Let's be sure and make them comfy. I'll get their home set up for a really hot party."

Bill, his wife, and son were roughly dragged into the center of the room. They were forced to kneel in a circle, facing away from each other. Ropes were looped about their ankles, joining them all together. Then they were looped about their wrists as well, forcing them into a most uncomfortable position.

The furniture and the floor were soaked with what smelled like kerosene, and the bald man set up a simple detonator. It was made of a short candle on a small plate. Through the candle ran a long fuse. The fuse then ran to a can that contained a mix of kerosene and some other chemical.

"In a few minutes, I'm going to light this candle," said the bald man, sounding ridiculously pleased with his explanation. "Then, you'll have about ten minutes before the candle burns down low enough to light the fuse. In, like, five minutes the fuse will burn over to the canister, which will go up like a torch, igniting the kerosene-soaked sofa. It's like science, dude." The man paused as if to allow his words to sink in, and then his voice got eerily serious. "My master is going to rule this world, but you won't be around to see it."

The bald man looked at the other two. They nodded. He lit the candle. The men quickly left the house through the back door, leaving the detective and his family to ponder their fate.

Detective Strom struggled with his bonds, searching for a knot that might be loosened, yet his search was in vain. There was no escape. He tried to get to the candle, to extinguish it, yet this too met with failure. Within ten minutes, his hands and wrists were bloody from his efforts, yet he had accomplished nothing.

There was a sudden flash of light as the candle lit the fuse. If only he could reach it. He heard his son's muffled cries. No, he had to do something, anything. With all of his strength he tried to move toward the fuse, but he could find no leverage. He gazed up and began to pray. From the almost-forgotten recesses of his mind, a jumble of phrases poured out of his heart in a desperate prayer: "Our Father in Heaven, hallowed be Your name…those who call on the name of the Lord will be saved…Jesus, save me! God, save my family!" Julio had been right; he knew that now. If only he had realized it earlier.

The sparks inched their way along the fuse toward that can. Bill made another valiant effort, yet he managed to move only a matter of inches. He tried again; nothing.

The fuse entered the can, and a second later, flames shot upward nearly to the ceiling. The sofa was ablaze. Within a minute the fire had spread around the room, and a thick smoke was descending from the ceiling. They had to get to the floor; it would be the last place in the room where there would be breathable air. Their bonds wouldn't even allow them to do that.

Bill heard his son and wife coughing on the thickening smoke. Maybe, if they were lucky, they would die of smoke inhalation rather than be burned alive. Yet the roar of the flames and the growing heat were already almost unbearable. Bill heard a crashing sound from somewhere else in the house. What was going on? Then something was moving through the smoke.

Three firemen in full gear descended upon them. One drew a large blade and started sheering their bonds, even as another removed his son's gag and placed an oxygen mask over his face. A few seconds later, the other did the same for Peggy. Then it was Bill's turn.

"Come on, come on," said the fireman who seemed to be in charge. "We've got to move, move, move!"

The next thing Bill knew, they were being led out of the room, toward the kitchen and the back of the house. They stayed close to the floor all the way. Then they were in the backyard, stumbling through the grass. The cool night air felt so wonderful. It was at the back fence that they stopped. Again, the three were administered oxygen.

"Am I glad to see you guys," gasped Bill. "How in the world did you get here so fast?"

"Don't try to speak, Detective Strom," said the lead fireman, pushing the oxygen mask back toward him. "Take a moment and get your breath. You still have a lot to do before this is all through. You need to join the battle. But for now relax."

"How do you know my name?" asked Bill. "Do I know you?"

The fireman shook his head. "No, not yet."

By now, the house was fully engulfed in flames. Bill just sat there, watching his dream home go up in flames. Yet, what was really important was around him—his family was safe.

The fireman attending to Bill rose to his feet, then stepped back. Then there was a flash of light. Bill turned around to find only himself and his family sitting on the wet grass. The firemen had vanished.

"What happened?" asked Bill, turning to Peggy. "Where did they go?"

Looking into Peggy's eyes, he could see her stunned amazement. Her eyes met Bill's, yet she said nothing.

"Mommy, you were right," said Bill junior, a broad smile on his face. "Jesus does hear us. I asked Him for help, and He sent us angels. They looked just like you said they did. Oh, their wings were so beautiful."

"You didn't see it?" gasped Peggy.

"See what?" replied Bill, trying to rise to his feet.

"I only saw it for a second," said Peggy. "Those three firemen, they turned into angels, all in white, then they just disappeared."

In the distance, Bill could hear the sirens. He and his family headed through the back gate and into the alley to get away from the growing flames. By the time they reached the street in front of the house, the Montclair Fire Department was on the scene. They immediately went to work trying to contain the blaze, but that was all they were going to be able to do. The house was a total loss.

It was past one in the morning as Bill and his family left the Montclair Police Department and headed toward his wife's parent's house. He had told them the entire story. His whole family had. Still, it defied belief.

The thugs had entered through the back door while Peggy was preparing dinner. They had subdued her and her young son. Then they had waited for her husband. Peggy gave the police a complete description of her assailants. She spoke of what they had said. They'd spoken of getting her prepared for the pains of Hell, of getting revenge on her husband. That aspect of the story was believable enough. It was the rescue by angels that they had trouble with.

The family had been nearly asphyxiated. An oxygen-starved brain could imagine all sorts of things. There were no firemen and certainly no angels. Sure, there had been three rescuers, but they were probably neighbors who saw the flames and rushed in to rescue them. They hadn't wanted to get involved with all of the publicity or the red tape that was sure to follow and had fled the scene. Sure, that had to be it.

A team of fire investigators would determine the cause of the blaze tomorrow. Until then, this family was just lucky to be alive. They'd experienced a miracle of sorts, just not the type they thought. Still, it was strange that they all experienced a common delusion.

As Bill and Peggy turned out the light that night, they both prayed. Bill invited Jesus into his heart for the first time while Peggy vowed to have a new and more vital relationship with their Savior. Bill recalled the last words of that angel. He spoke of joining the battle. Bill understood what he meant. It was how to go about it that had him mystified.

The next morning, Bill called in sick to work. Under the conditions, the lieutenant insisted upon it. However, Bill spent most of the morning with Pastor Smith, weighing his options. He also took some time to email Chris and Serena, filling them in on the crisis that had nearly killed his whole family. By noon he had developed a game plan; he would continue his investigation, but this time he would be fortified with the Holy Spirit.

In addition, Julio had practically insisted on getting involved in the investigation. Bill welcomed his help. The investigation would be conducted on the side, when he wasn't on the clock. That way he would have more liberties, free of some of the constraints of his office.

When the lieutenant finally heard the full story of Detective Strom's narrow escape the next day, he was left practically speechless. The fire marshal's report as to the cause and nature of the blaze supported the detective's story. It was the story of guardian angels posing as firefighters that made the story so incredible.

At the investigation, the detective made certain to emphasize the point that he had not actually witnessed the transformation of firefighters into angels. Those were claims made by his wife and son. He could only testify that they were there one moment and gone the next. Yes, he might have blanked out for a moment. They might have slipped out the back gate and into the alleyway in that time. But the firemen were real. They had saved his life and the life of his family. Perhaps they had been neighbors, perhaps firemen from some other department, but they were real.

In the end, the board accepted the detective's explanation. They were thankful to still have this fine officer in the department. For the next few months, he'd officially be assigned to look over the cold case files. He seemed to have a gift in that area. Also, it would keep him off the streets, in the event that whoever had orchestrated the first attempt on his life tried again.

All the while he was building his case against Lusan, gathering together the inconsistencies in his story, searching for damning evidence from his past. And he was making progress. With the lieutenant's permission, he would soon take his case to the feds, let them handle it from there. He had this guy; he was sure of it. Soon, he would be instrumental in toppling the empire of the great Andre Lusan.

It was late July, and New York languished in the midst of one of the most intense heat waves in its history. It was on this hazy, hot morning that Lusan's minions met in his conference room. What he was hearing from them only added to his foul mood.

"It would seem that the Father has placed a shield of protection around Detective William Strom and his family," said a heavily tattooed man. "We have tried to hinder his investigation, but have been only partially successful."

"If you'd just killed him and his family when you had the chance, we wouldn't be in this situation right now!" Lusan yelled.

"You insisted that their deaths be both terrifying and painful," replied the man in an uncharacteristically defiant tone. "A bullet to the head or a blade to the throat would not have accomplished that. I did as I was asked."

A sudden silence fell over the group. No one present could remember when anyone had spoken to the master in such a tone. They were even more surprised at his response.

"Yes you did," replied Lusan, his anger ebbing a bit. "Next time we will dispense with the melodrama, and I shall simply ask for a clean, quick kill."

The bald man bowed slightly. "Yes, my lord."

Lusan turned to another of his minions. "What of the island?"

The dark-skinned young woman stepped forward. "Our recruitment is ahead of schedule, my lord. Many humans have been subjected to the union and are now fully under our control. They spread your words on every continent, in every nation of the world."

"And what of the ring?" asked Lusan.

The woman hesitated. "The fusion power generator for the ring has lived up to and beyond our expectations. However, the scientists are still having problems with the ring itself. They are progressing, but it is slow."

"Give me a timetable!" Lusan snarled. "When will it be ready?"

"I'm sorry, my lord, I don't know," replied the woman. "There could be a breakthrough any day, or it could take years."

"Make it your top priority," Lusan ordered. "Within the week I will begin my Latin American Crusade, and after that I will return to Europe. We are going to make great strides in the next few months. I don't want any unexpected surprises surfacing, ruining my day. I need to be at my best. This audience is concluded."

The crowd bowed before their master. It looked like they had their work cut out for them. They began to file out of the conference room.

Lusan turned to Duras, who still stood at his side. "I would have a word with you, in private."

"Of course, my lord," confirmed Duras.

Lusan held his peace until the last of his minions had departed from the conference room. "I am concerned about Leland James. Ever since he had the visit from Serena Davis, he seems troubled and indecisive. He knows much about us. He bears watching."

"My lord, I do not think he would betray us," replied Duras. "I have come to know him well. He is completely devoted to you. And that sexy thing he's married to—well, she does your bidding as well. She is rather attractive, in her own human way."

"She is indeed endowed with certain gifts from the Creator," Lusan replied. "Still, Leland James bears watching—and who could watch him more closely than his own wife?"

Duras seemed confused. "Yes, she is most loyal to you, but is that loyalty greater than that she feels to Leland?"

Lusan smiled. "You do not understand, my friend. I might not have full control over her now, but that could be changed. If we were to invite her to the island, properly indoctrinate her, and subject her to the union, I believe that she could be made to serve us as a spy. The union would give us a far greater control over her than we would have through a simple possession. Her soul would be totally neutralized, yet we would still have access to all of her memories, all of her talents."

Duras seemed shocked by the suggestion. "Sir, she is, perhaps the most talented advocate of our cause. I cannot believe that she would be nearly so gifted following the procedure. My lord, your word is law, but I advise against this course of action."

It was incredible. For the second time in a single day, one of his minions had sought to oppose him. Duras was far more careful in the way he chose his words—still, it was an audacious move.

Lusan smiled. "I suspect that you have another reason for advising me as you just have."

"My lord, I don't believe I understand," asked Duras.

"You want the woman," said Lusan.

Duras hesitated. "Perhaps. I am sorry, my lord."

Lusan placed his hand on his minion's shoulder. "I understand, my friend. But there are times when we must make decisions that we are uncomfortable with. You might like her better once she has undergone the union."

Duras looked toward his master, regret in his eyes. "Yes, I am sure you are right, my lord."

Lusan smiled a final time. "You are dismissed, my friend. See to your duties."

Duras bowed low and then departed. Lusan walked to the window and drew the blinds back to view the hazy skyline. "Yes, Krissie, you were so frightened about going to Hell. Now your fears will become reality. You are about to walk into the eternal darkness."

Kristie practically ran into Leland's office. Leland looked up to see his excitable wife beaming like a searchlight. "I get to go to the island!" she said excitedly.

"The island," asked Leland. "You mean Katafanga?"

"What other island do you think I'd be talking about?" said Krissie.

"I don't know," admitted Leland, "maybe Staten."

"Cute," said Krissie. "Oh, I've been wanting to see it so badly, and now finally Lusan is letting me go."

"You're leaving *again?* When?" asked Leland.

"The week after next," replied Krissie. "I'd *think* you'd be proud. Lusan said that he's not too happy with the progress they're making there. He wants me to go there, see everything, the whole operation, and give him a full report. He called it a tour of inspection. He said I'd be gone for about ten days."

"Well, he must have great faith in your judgment," noted Leland. "I *am* proud of you." Leland rose from his chair and embraced Krissie. He sighed. "I just hate that you are gone so much. I love you. I don't know what I'll do without you while you're gone."

"Oh, you'll manage," Krissie chuckled. "I'm supposed to be interviewing a lot of people. I really don't know what to ask the scientists and engineers. I don't know the first thing about fusion power or nuclear energy."

"Well, read up on it," suggested Leland. "Really, Krissie, you're super intelligent when you want to be. You've got two weeks to learn as much as you can."

"I'll start tonight," vowed Krissie. "I'll do this tour of inspection properly."

As Krissie headed back to her office, Leland smiled. Never had he seen Krissie so happy. She loved her job here, sometimes too much. She didn't seem to have the doubts that he had. That was good. He returned to his chair and turned to the figures on the computer monitor once more.

During the next two weeks, Krissie did her best to learn all that she could about atoms, nuclear power, and fusion. She also looked over the program description for the converts who would be brought up to speed on the fundamentals of their faith. She wanted so much to make Lusan proud of her.

It was just two days before departure when Krissie awoke, lying amidst a bed of dew-covered moss in the depths of a great forest. It was misty, but she could see the early morning sun trying to break through the fog.

"Where am I?" she said, rising to her feet.

Krissie was still barefoot and dressed in her nightgown. How did she get out here? In fact, where was here? Had she been sleep walking? If so, this sure didn't look like Central Park. Maybe it was a dream. No, it was far too real for that.

"Krissie," said a voice from out of the fog. It was a woman's voice. It seemed so familiar.

Krissie debated if she should answer or not. She didn't know who was out there. "I'm over here," she finally said.

There was movement in the fog. A woman in a long white dress emerged from the mists. She had dark skin and was quite lovely. She looked to be in her late twenties, maybe 30, not much older than Krissie.

The woman smiled broadly. "Oh, there you are, dear. It's so good to see you again."

Krissie pondered her situation for a moment. There was something familiar about the voice, but the face was unfamiliar. "I'm sorry, have we met before?"

The woman laughed. "Oh my, yes, where are my manners? No, you probably wouldn't recognize me like this, but we've met many times. But I looked a lot different then, a lot older. I'm Claire James, Leland's grandma."

Krissie felt suddenly very uncomfortable. No, she didn't want to be here. She wanted to wake up. This was a dream, it had to be. "But you're dead."

Again Claire laughed. "Oh, my dear, death isn't what you think it is at all. And please, don't be frightened. I wouldn't hurt you for the world, not for the whole world. I love you."

Krissie closed her eyes; she was trembling. "Wake up, oh please wake up."

"I'm not here to upset you, Krissie," said Claire, stepping back. "No, I don't want to do that. You're going to wake up in just another minute, I promise you. But God sent me from Heaven to tell you something important. You mustn't go to Lusan's island. Bad things happen there, very bad things. If you go there, bad things will happen to you. Make up an excuse not to go."

"You can't be Claire; she's dead," said Krissie. "Please, leave me alone."

Claire seemed sad. "OK, Krissie, I'll go away. You're going to wake up right now."

The scenery seemed to fade around her. In an instant, Krissie found herself back home. The light of the early morning sun was shining through the window. Leland was still sound asleep. Krissie stumbled to her feet and headed for the kitchen. She just had to have a cup of coffee. She was still trembling as she poured the first cup. She thought about telling Leland about what had just happened. No, it would only upset him. She had been looking forward to this trip for almost two weeks. She'd spent so many hours preparing for it. What she'd just experienced was a dream; that was all. People didn't come back from the dead in your dreams.

"I'll be sure to call you when I get there," promised Krissie, as Leland pulled up to the departures drop off point at JFK International. "You don't need to stay with me; I'll be fine."

"Are you sure?" asked Leland.

"I'm sure," confirmed Krissie. "It's going to be a while before my flight leaves. There is no point in your waiting around. Anyway, they don't allow nonpassengers in the boarding area."

A quick kiss saw Krissie out the door, bags in hand. Leland hesitated; he clearly hated to leave her. After a moment he pulled out, leaving Krissie to get her bags checked in and get on the plane to Los Angeles. She had over two hours, more than enough time. From there she'd be catching the international flight to Fiji via Auckland, New Zealand. It was going to be a long flight. Thank heavens that Lusan had insisted that she fly first class all of the way. The last leg of the journey would be made using one of the organization's twin engine turboprops that transported supplies and personnel to and from the island. It promised to be an adventure and, since she'd be traveling westward all the way, the longest day of her life. From JFK to her destination would be better than 24 hours. Even with the amenities associated with the first-class passage, it was likely to be a grueling flight.

She'd traveled by air with Leland several times in the past. She'd traveled with Lusan and his ever-present entourage as well. However, this was the first time she'd traveled alone by air and was a bit nervous.

She checked her bags in, got her boarding pass, and headed on through the security checkpoint. It all went without incident. She had plenty of time, maybe too much. She thought back to the dream she'd had two nights ago. She hadn't been able to get it out of her head since. It seemed so real. Maybe making this trip was not such a good idea after all.

No, now she was just being foolish. The call came for the first-class passengers to board. She was on her way. She would put that silly dream behind her and enjoy the adventure.

CHAPTER 21

It was an indeed weary Krissie who stepped off the plane in Nadi, Fiji. It was just before seven in the morning, and she'd managed only a few hours of sleep during the past 24. She was happy when she saw the woman in the airport concourse holding a sign with her name on it.

Actually, Krissie recognized the woman. Her name was Lielani Lorenz, the young, bright-eyed executive secretary of Aldo Karr, chief administrator of the Katafanga Island facility. With the assistance of her escort, one of Karr's security guards, they picked up Krissie's luggage and made their way to a golf cart that took them to the small turboprop air freighter that would take them to the island.

"It's really not a long flight," noted Lielani as they got buckled in. "It usually takes less than an hour. And it's a gorgeous flight; you'll see."

A few minutes saw the last of the cargo on board and they were off down the runway. It was a bit of a bumpy ride, but the view out the window was everything that Lielani said it would be. Below them was a crystal-clear sea that ranged from very light to very dark blue. It was dotted with what seemed like thousands of green islands with golden beaches that stretched out to the horizons. Some were many miles across; others occupied but a few acres, little more than green dots in the vast Pacific.

Eventually, Katafanga appeared before them. It was not as large as Krissie had imagined. Most of the length of the island was taken up by a single runway.

Across its longest dimension, it was barely three quarters of a mile from beach to beach. The entire island was enclosed by a calm, clear lagoon. It looked like paradise.

The pilot circled the island allowing Krissie to see the Faith Compound as well as the research facility. They were such different realms squeezed together on this small archipelago.

"You'll be staying in the resort," said Lielani, pointing to the two-story structure on a hill near the research facility. "At least, that's what we call it. It has very nice accommodations. It is where our scientists and engineers live. It will give you a chance to interact with them, get a sense of what is going right and wrong there."

Lielani then pointed to a series of smaller buildings gathered about a large central building. By comparison, they seemed to be little more than shacks.

"We call that the village," she explained. "It's where those who want to become ministers of the faith live and study. As you know, we get tons of applicants for this program, thousands of men and women are touched by Lusan's message and want to spread the good news, but few are actually selected. We are looking for very special people indeed. For those few who come here, it's pretty Spartan. Mr. Lusan insisted on it. He said that in order to become truly holy, truly one with the spirit, one must put away the more lavish things of the world."

"I can see that," said Krissie, gazing out at the island over a thousand feet below them. "The apostles gave up an awful lot to follow Jesus."

"Yes," said Lielani. "Our modern-day apostles work here as well as study, and it's a rigorous program, 12 to 16 hours per day of labor and study. Lots of people can't cut it. But for those strong and dedicated enough to see it through, a whole new world opens up. You'll get a chance to meet some of our aspiring apostles, too."

"How long does it take for one to become a minister of the word?" asked Krissie.

"It depends," replied Lielani. "Some complete the program in as little as six weeks. Others take six months or more. And at the end of it all is a holy rite we call the union, where they become one with the spirit."

"Sounds interesting," said Krissie.

"Oh, it is," assured Lielani. "It's not like baptism or confirmation. No, it is more than just a ritual. They receive an infilling of the same spirit that flows from our master, Lusan.

"I think you'll find that he prefers the title founder, not master," corrected Krissie. "He really doesn't like being put up on some kind of pedestal."

Lielani smiled, though slightly. "Of course. However, my point was that we gain true knowledge and real power in the process. Krissie, after the union you are never the same; you see things in a whole new light."

"Sounds like you've learned a lot about it," observed Krissie.

"Yes, I have," replied Lielani. "You see, I've been through the program myself, climaxing with the rite of union. Now my eyes have been truly opened."

"I didn't know that. I'm happy for you," said Krissie.

"Be sure you have your seatbelts buckled for landing," announced the pilot over the PA system.

"We'll talk later," promised Lielani. "You've got to be exhausted after your flight. I'll get you set up in the guest quarters at the resort. Get a few hours sleep. I'll introduce you to our science and engineering staff this afternoon. Dr. Geiger, one of our chief researchers, will give you a personal tour of the labs and the instruments. He's been instructed to answer all of your questions. You've been given our highest security clearance."

"I'm really looking forward to it all," replied Krissie, "but a few hours of sleep sounds wonderful. I want to be alert when I see all of these science wonders I've heard about."

Their approach brought them around the fusion generating station, over a white, sandy beach, and down unto the wide, concrete runway. It seemed to Krissie that they decelerated rather rapidly. It was a fairly short runway for a cargo plane of this size, and it took a bit of finesse to put this aircraft down safely. When the plane finally came to a stop and turned off the runway, they had but a few hundred feet to spare.

As she stepped from the plane, she couldn't help but notice the couple dozen young people working in the fields about a hundred yards away, beyond the fence that surrounded the airfield. They didn't as much as look up from their labors.

"We grow a lot of our own food," explained Lielani, "tomatoes, corn, peppers, all sorts of vegetables; we grow them all here. Working with the earth builds character and an appreciation for the wonders of life."

The women stepped into a golf cart as the security guard placed Krissie's luggage in the back. They were off. They passed a sentry that guarded the airfield fence and headed toward the resort, which sat upon the rise to the north. It became immediately clear to Krissie that the island was divided into two very different societies by a fence. The fence separated the realm of science from the realm of faith. In the natural, it was only an eight-foot fence, hardly an impassable barrier, but in human terms it was a mighty wall, and the style of life found on either side was very different.

Krissie also noticed that the fence was patrolled by guards. That seemed odd to her.

Lielani helped Krissie carry her bags into the guest quarters on the second floor of the resort. This place was as nice as any five-star hotel Krissie had ever seen.

"We tend to pamper our technical staff," noted Lielani. "They work very hard, and when the day is through, we want them to be able to relax in luxury. We have a large pool, a recreation room, and a tennis court where they can unwind and recreate themselves. One day, the things they accomplish here are going to change the world."

"I can imagine," said Krissie, yawning.

"Oh, where are my manners?" said Lielani. "It's almost nine. You need to get some rest. I'll call you about one this afternoon. That will give you some time to rest and still give you time for the tour of the science facility. Tomorrow, you'll have time to interview some of the scientists, but now, rest."

This place was easy to relax in. Within ten minutes Krissie was sound asleep.

The afternoon saw Krissie touring this most wondrous of laboratories. The high point was watching a test of the teleportation ring. Krissie watched in wonder as several ball like probes were tossed into its depths, into what looked like some holographic projection of a seascape. It was almost magical. Yet she realized that this was no magician's illusion; it was real.

On the following day she talked one-on-one to a number of the researchers and technicians. She couldn't help but notice a certain tenseness that went beyond that associated with what some of them considered a performance interview. It was later that evening that she sat down to dinner with Les Geiger and Nabuko Yamura in Dr. Geiger's quarters.

"It was so nice to meet with someone who has taken such an interest in our work," noted Nabuko as they adjourned to the balcony and the warm tropical air. "I had not imagined that you would be so knowledgeable about physics or the nature of our research."

Krissie smiled broadly. She could not imagine a nicer comment. "Thank you. I spent a lot of time studying." There was a pause. "Nabuko, why is everyone here so tense? I hope it's not me."

"Oh no, of course not," replied Nabuko. "You've been a breath of fresh air, so friendly and open." She glanced over at Les, who seemed deep in thought.

"There have been some problems here," admitted Les. "Quite honestly, we've not known who to turn to. We don't know who to trust." He looked over at Nabuko.

"Doctor, I assure you, I'm here to listen," assured Krissie. "If there is a problem, we need to get to the bottom of it. I'll be honest with you. I've sensed some friction here ever since I arrived. I'm in a position to make recommendations at the highest level. Talk to me; let me help."

Les and Nabuko exchanged glances once more. They seemed hesitant. It was Les who finally told Krissie about the incident of the woman at the fence better than two months ago. They also spoke of some of the things they had overheard without referring to their modified radio. Through it all, Krissie listened intently.

"We knew we were taking a risk talking to you about it," said Nabuko, "but we had to tell somebody. We've considered quitting the project, but where would we go?"

"I'm glad you talked to me," said Krissie. "And I believe you. I will discover what is going on, and your names will not be mentioned, I assure you. If there is something going on at the compound, if people are being taken advantage of, it's going to stop. This organization won't condone that sort of thing. Mr. Lusan won't condone it."

"Be careful," warned Les.

"I promise you, I will," said Krissie. "My tour of inspection of the compound and its people starts tomorrow. Let me see what I can find out."

"But be careful," said Nabuko. "We've become rather fond of you. You're coming here has given us hope."

Krissie smiled. This trip was turning out to be so much more than she'd imagined. Perhaps she could make a real difference here, change things for the better.

Before retiring for the night, she spoke of what she'd discovered over the phone to Leland. She didn't mention any names, but indicated that there was a problem. Like Les and Nabuko, he too advised caution. As Krissie turned in for the night, she wondered what tomorrow might bring.

Krissie walked into one of the village dormitories accompanied by Lielani. The first thing that struck her was just how austere it was. It reminded her of a marine barracks—all spit and polish, but incredibly uninviting. Each of the villagers, as they were called, had a cot and a footlocker that fit under the bed for their personal belongings. On the far wall was a huge poster of Lusan behind a podium in a large stadium. Krissie recognized it as the Stade Vélodrome, the site of the first great miracle. Below it were the words, "Ushering in a new age of peace." Right now the dormitory was deserted.

"This is a woman's dormitory," explained Lielani. "There are four dormitories for the men and four for the women. Right now all of the villagers are working in the fields. They had breakfast and headed out at sunrise. In about two hours they will be heading to the chapel to begin their midday studies and prayers. They will be there for four hours. Then after lunch, they will be out in the fields again for about two hours. They conclude their day in service in the chapel."

"Sounds like a rough schedule," noted Krissie.

"But it builds character," interjected Lielani. "Actually, tonight most of the villagers will be getting some free time here in the dormitory. It will give them time to write to loved ones at home. We don't allow them to use phones or email. Isolation from the world is an important part of the experience here. Tonight we are going to have a union ceremony. Normally, only initiates and those who have already experienced the union will be in attendance. I've arranged for you to be there to see the entire thing for yourself. It will give you a better appreciation of what this whole thing is about. Prepare to be amazed."

"Sounds cool," replied Krissie. "I was hoping I'd get to see one of those."

"I guarantee you, it will be a life-changing experience," promised Lielani.

They next visited the chapel. Again, it was sort of an underwhelming experience. It reminded Krissie of a small country church. There were rows of wooden pews set before a slightly elevated pulpit. Off to the sides of the main sanctuary were a series of smaller classrooms and prayer rooms. What captured Krissie's interest the most was a large double door, apparently made of metal, behind the pulpit. It had the color and luster of gold and was engraved with symbols that Krissie couldn't identify. Upon each door was a keyhole of a size far greater than those used today. Krissie wondered just how large the key that fit it might be.

"That door leads to the holy of holies," said Lielani. "It is there that the ritual of union is conducted."

"May I see what it looks like?" asked Krissie.

"You'll see it this evening," promised Lielani. "It is a very special place for us. We can't just go barging in anytime. You'll understand why tonight."

Krissie only nodded. She would eagerly await tonight's festivities.

The afternoon was spent talking with the villagers. They were indeed a strange lot. Some were very animated, excited to be a part of the program, while others seemed exceptionally restrained. Still others were more troubling. They were like the walking dead, hardly acknowledging Krissie's presence. Krissie could easily see why these people and the scientists on the far side of the island had little in common.

Later that evening, Krissie again met with Les and Nabuko. She spoke of what she had seen in the village. The more she thought of it, the more troubling it all seemed.

"Perhaps you should back out on this ritual you speak of," suggested Nabuko. "It does not sound good to me."

"This is a fact-finding mission," replied Krissie. "I was sent here by Andre Lusan himself. They wouldn't hurt me. Mr. Lusan listens to what I have to say.

He respects my opinions. That's why I'm here. If heads are going to roll, mine won't be one of them."

"I hope you're right," said Les.

Krissie looked out from the balcony. She saw a vehicle coming up the road from the village compound. She glanced at her watch. "That's probably my ride," she announced. "I'll tell you all about this ritual when I get back. At least I'll tell you what I can. I'm sure it's not as sinister as it all sounds."

"I hope you're right," said Nabuko.

Krissie smiled, but said nothing. She made her way down to the front entrance just in time to meet the security guard driving up in the golf cart.

"You're right on schedule," he said pleasantly. "Miss Lorenz will meet you at the chapel."

"How long does this ceremony take?" asked Krissie, stepping into the vehicle.

"Not too long," replied the security guard. "It depends on how many people are being inducted. Tonight it will be just one. It will probably be just an hour if you don't stay for the reception afterward."

"Oh I wouldn't miss the reception," replied Krissie.

"Then I'll probably have you back here by 11," said the guard, pulling out once more. "I'm sure you will find what you see tonight enlightening."

It took just under three minutes to reach the chapel. Lielani was waiting for her under the light just in front of the entrance. She was dressed in a long white ceremonial gown of some sort with long-flowing sleeves. Down the front were some sort of golden letters that Krissie couldn't make out.

"Oh wow, Lielani, you're a real knock-out in that dress," said Krissie. "Very nice."

Lielani laughed softly. "Thank you, ma'am," she said, bowing slightly. "No union ritual would be complete without all of the pomp and fancy regalia. It is something that the master, I mean, the founder, insists upon. It makes the whole ceremony more memorable for the inductee and those who celebrate with them. It's like a graduation or a wedding. We all have to look the part."

"Oh, I fully agree," replied Krissie.

Lielani smiled broadly. "Well, let's head on in, shall we?"

Within the chapel, Krissie encountered four female villagers dressed in the same manner as Lielani, and four male villagers dressed in long white robes that seemed to be fashion coordinated to those of their female counterparts. They milled around, talking among themselves. What surprised her was the presence of four uniformed security guards.

"We need to get you ready," continued Lielani.

One of the villager women handed Krissie a white dress, and a pair of light tan slippers. She seemed a bit surprised as it was handed to her.

"Remember, we all play our part," said Lielani. "The dressing room is over there. We'll be getting started in just a few minutes."

Krissie smiled nervously. Right now she wasn't all that certain that coming here this evening was such a good idea. She headed into the dressing room. After a moment of hesitation she removed her sharp looking business attire and put on the white dress. It was rather becoming; there was no doubt of that, yet it didn't quite look like the one worn by the other women. It was only about knee length for one thing, and it lacked the lettering down the front. For another, it lacked the long flowing sleeves the others possessed—in fact, it was sleeveless.

Krissie paused at the door before taking a deep breath and stepping from the dressing room. The group looked at her approvingly.

"Very nice," said Lielani.

"Why is my dress different than yours?" asked Krissie.

"Because we have all undergone the union ceremony, but you haven't," she replied. "It is a symbol of passage." Lelani paused. "Well, let us get started."

Two of the guards brought forth a pair of heavy keys that were a good four inches long each. They had the color of brass. They approached the great door, one from the left and one from the right, and inserted the keys into the keyholes. A pair of sharp metallic clicks announced that the doors were now unlocked. The group approached it.

"Stay at my side," said Lielani to Krissie. "I'll show you what you'll need to do."

The massive doors, fully four inches thick, opened before them, and the group entered. Krissie discovered a wide set of steps that led downward through a stone block tunnel and then turned to the right. The way was lit by torches along the wall; the flames possessed a somewhat-strange, light-yellow color.

"Watch your step, Krissie," said Lielani, as she guided her along. "Sometimes the steps are a bit slippery."

Krissie looked back to see the doors close behind her. She was surprised to see two of the guards were following the procession several steps back.

Krissie was amazed to discover that the flames of the torches gave off no heat whatsoever. What sort of flame did that?

About 30 steps down, the stone block wall gave way to the rippling walls of a natural limestone cavern. Still they proceeded downward and then to the right with the curving tunnel. After over a minute, the steps led into a horizontal natural tunnel complete with shimmering white stalactites hanging from the high ceiling. It was pleasantly cool here.

"This is a natural cavern," said Lielani. "It is one of several here on the island, but this one is the most impressive."

Ahead the passage forked to the left and right. The passage to the left was dark and sloped rather sharply downward. A fairly weak, but nonetheless terrible odor emanated from it. It was like a combination of sulfur and tar, thoroughly disgusting. They bypassed it, following the illuminated corridor to the right.

After about another 30 seconds, they emerged from the tunnel into an indeed large cavern room, about 50 or 60 feet in diameter. The ceiling was at least 30 feet high, armored with five-foot-long stalactites. Like the tunnel they had just passed through, the floor of this cavern room had apparently been leveled and smoothed.

There were 13 torches mounted to the wall around the room, yet they were not the only source of illumination. The cavern walls themselves seemed to glow a dull green.

At the center of the room was a circular, white marble slab, about six inches high and 20 feet in diameter. Its surface was like glass. The whole way around its edges were golden symbols etched into the stone, probably some form of lettering.

"They are letters of the universal tongue of all angels," said Lielani, pointing to the glistening symbols. Apparently she'd anticipated Krissie's next question.

Krissie looked toward the center of the slab to see a heavy, black chair facing in their direction. She couldn't tell if it was made of wood or painted metal.

One disturbing feature of this chair was a series of leather straps that were apparently designed to restrain the occupant's ankles, wrists, and waist to the chair. It looked like something straight from death row.

"This is where it all happens," announced Lielani. "This is where it began for all of us." Lielani took Krissie's hand. "Come." She led Krissie onto the cool marble slab and toward the chair.

"What are you doing?" asked Krissie.

"I wanted this to be a surprise," said Lielani. "Or shall I say, Master Lusan wanted it to be a surprise. Tonight you are going to experience the union for yourself."

Krissie turned to see the two security guards step up onto the marble platform. A chill swept up her spine. "Look, I'm honored, but I'm not sure that I can accept this honor. I mean, I haven't gone through the program. I'm not prepared. I'm not worthy."

A swell of mirth swept through the entire group. It only added to Krissie's fear.

"Oh, don't be ridiculous," said Lielani, "of course you are. If anyone is worthy, you are. You welcomed the master into your home. You served him faithfully all of these years. It was you and your husband who made it possible for him to reach out into the world and who defended him from his enemies." Lielani motioned to the chair. "Please, have a seat."

"No," insisted Krissie, "I can't."

"You can and you will," said Lielani, her tone of voice more forceful. "Do you really think that you have a choice? We could compel you to sit in that chair, but it would be far better if you did it of your own free will."

Krissie looked about frantically. She realized that there was no way out.

"Sit down," repeated Lielani. "Sit down and I'll explain the whole thing as we prepare you."

With no real choice, Krissie sat down on the cold, metal chair, gasping in fear. Lielani stepped back. Within seconds the guards had forced her back into the chair and tightened the leather strap about her waist.

"Where should I begin?" pondered Lielani. "Well, at the beginning of course. When you met Lusan and Duras in the park, they were in flight, refugees from a war—a War in Heaven. Lusan should, by all rights, have been the ruler of the angels. Yet he was cheated by both men and angels. He retreated to Earth, where he saved your miserable life. But you have paid him back many times over. Now you are to be rewarded."

"I don't understand," wept Krissie, as her wrists were strapped to the arms of the chair. "Lusan was sent here by God."

Lielani shook her head. "I'm afraid not, sweetheart. God allowed him to challenge the archangels, Gabriel and Michael, but he did not send him here. He is on a mission of his own."

"Who is he?" asked Krissie.

"Oh come on, girl. I thought you'd have figured that out by now," said Lielani, caressing Krissie's cheek even as the security officers strapped her ankles in place. "He goes by many names—the Deceiver, the Prince of Darkness, Phosphorous, but the name by which he is best known is Satan."

"Oh God!" gasped Krissie, pulling upon her now secured restraints with all too predictable results.

"Yes," confirmed Lielani. "In a very short time he will be your god, your master, not the founder." She paused for a minute, watched the tears coming to Krissie's eyes. "Oh, don't worry, Krissie. You're not some sort of human sacrifice or something like that. You are far too vital to us for that. What you are going to be is a spy, an undercover agent, so to speak. You are going to spy on your husband, inform the master's minions of his every move. You see, we think he is starting to have second thoughts about serving the master. If he becomes a liability, well, you will be the one who terminates him. Killed by the one he loves most in the whole world—now that's irony."

"I'd never hurt Leland," cried Krissie.

"Yes you would, or at least your body would," replied Lielani. "Let me tell you a story. For thousands of years, the master has controlled people by having his minions control them. Usually it was just by appealing to their greed, lust, or avarice. But from time to time, stronger measures became necessary. You might call it demon possession. In that case, the demon's spirit enters his human victim and uses his powerful will to override theirs. Still, there is a downside to such a possession. Most humans fight their demon masters. The demon spirit expends much of his energy just trying to control his host. At critical moments, the host might even find the strength to keep his master in check for a few fleeting seconds. Sometimes that can make the difference between a successful mission and failure."

"That's crazy," replied Krissie. "That sort of thing can't be real."

There was a general round of mirth from the group around her. It only added to Krissie's fear.

"You are such a foolish girl," said Lielani. "Do you remember Julio Mendoza? He was one of the boys who attacked you and Leland in Central Park. He was the lone survivor. Does it not strike you as strange that he later became a member of Lusan's youth organization? It's all very simple, really. He was possessed by one of our lord's minions. But as I said, possession is a difficult task for a demon. At the critical moment, when he was to kill Leland's grandmother Claire, Julio fought against his possessor. He delayed him long enough that Claire James was able to cast him out, using the Spirit of God within her. Now Julio fights against us. This, and several other incidents, have made it necessary to explore a new alternative to the classical possession. We found it in the ritual of the union."

Krissie's eyes grew large and filled with horror. "I'm going to be possessed? No, I'll fight you. I'll fight any demon who tries."

"Yes," replied Lielani, "I'm sure that you would if you could, but you see, union is different."

One of the other women in white came forth with a large and menacing looking syringe in her hand. She approached Krissie's right arm, which had been strapped to the chair in two places to hold it more securely.

"We found a biologist who had the answer to our problem," continued Lielani. "We call it tetraflexis. It is a drug that attacks the neurons of your cerebrum." Lielani chuckled. "At least, that was the way it was explained to me. In essence, it kills your soul, severs the silver thread. It destroys all that it is that makes you who you are, yet it leaves an imprint behind. All that you knew and loved is still there. Your body is still quite alive, only you are gone. Then the demon comes in and forms a union with what is left. He takes the place of the soul that has departed. He rules the body without interference. It becomes his body, a body that he has to share with no one."

Krissie struggled as a security guard held Krissie's arm still, even as the woman with the syringe searched for a stout vein. "No, please, you can't; you can't!"

"Now don't become overly difficult," warned Lielani. "I wouldn't want to have to glue those pretty lips of yours together to keep you quiet. It's such a messy job to separate them later. The effects of the drug aren't painful at all. Actually, it's quite a pleasant way to go."

Krissie winced as she felt the sting of the needle, felt the horrible liquid entering her bloodstream. It took over a minute to unload the contents of the syringe into her. She tried to pray to God for forgiveness, but she didn't know how.

She thought back to that dream. Grandma Claire's spirit had warned her not to come here. If only she had listened.

"Grandma, help me," she gasped, even as the syringe was withdrawn from her arm.

"No one can help you," said Lielani. "Let us hope that all goes smoothly. Usually this technique is quite effective, but sometimes something goes wrong. Your memories become scrambled and you become something like a zombie. It was that way for one of the scientists, too bad. But I think you will be fine—at least, your body will. As for your soul, I have it on good authority that that part of you will find its eternal home in Hell's Great Sea of Fire."

"No," gasped Krissie in a voice no louder than a whisper.

Lielani stepped away from Krissie and joined the others in a circle around the outside edge of the marble platform. They chanted in some indecipherable tongue even as the world began to slowly whirl about Krissie. She felt so confused. She fought against the influence of the drug, but it was to no avail.

"We'll be leaving you now," announced Lielani, though her voice seemed far away. "It will give you and the new master of your body a little time to become acquainted before you leave."

The group departed. The light of the torches faded away, leaving only the faint green glow of the cavern walls. And in the faint glow, something stirred.

No, it wasn't just one thing, but a multitude. They were faintly glowing, almost transparent entities flying around her like plastic wrap in a whirlwind. Krissie was feeling weaker, more disoriented, by the minute. Were these apparitions real or imaginary? She practically jumped out of her skin when one of them abruptly moved toward her. Within seconds it was floating directly in front of her.

It had the face of an incredibly old man and was clothed in translucent robes that prevented her from seeing its entire body. It was like some sort of hologram, quivering and fading in and out of focus. It was terrifying. It reached out to her. Krissie could actually feel its icy touch. It was waiting for something, waiting for this body to be vacated so that it could take full control. Its arms and hands reached into her body then pulled up, only to repeat the cycle. And with each pass, those hands felt more real.

Others, whose appearance was like the first, gathered in close around her, reaching into her with their boney arms. Then, it happened, Krissie felt like she was being ripped out of her own body. A moment later she found herself looking down upon her own body from above, restrained by four ethereal beings. She was surprised when her head looked up at her and smiled.

"Go away, little Krissie," she heard herself say. "This is not your body anymore, it is mine, all mine." Her physical form looked to the demonic spirit to her left. "It has gone well. I'm in. Take this wench to the rift and see her through the corridor to the master's kingdom. You know the procedure."

The next thing Krissie knew, she was hurtling through the rocky ceiling and into the night air beyond, though to her, these things of the world appeared but phantasmal. The ethereal wasteland she found herself in was her only reality. The two demons that held her in their grasp and traveled through the nothingness at tremendous speed seemed far more real than the world.

They made no mystery of her fate. It would take seven hours to reach the rift, the only easily accessible route between Earth and Outer Darkness. From there, she would be taken to a holding cell to await the pleasure of the new master of Hell, and then she would travel to the Great Sea of Fire, where she would spend her eternity in agony.

Years ago, Krissie had spoken to Lusan of her greatest fear—being condemned for eternity to the realm of Hell. During the years since, that fear had faded away. Now Lusan had turned that long-dormant fear into a reality. He had betrayed her. Still, during that long flight into oblivion, Krissie's thoughts were of her husband as well. If only there were some way she could warn him, warn him about the intruder coming to their home, the intruder in her own body. This wasteland beyond life seemed so very cold. How could a spirit feel cold? Yet she realized that this was just the prelude to her eternity. The nightmare had just begun.

CHAPTER 22

Leland smiled broadly as he watched Krissie walking down the jetway toward him. He'd been so worried about her during those three nights she hadn't called. Then when she had, she seemed so cold and distant. Now, at last, here she was, home again. She smiled broadly when she saw him. A minute later they embraced.

"It's so good to be back home," she said.

It was when she drew back that their eyes met. For a moment they seemed locked. Then Krissie looked away.

"I want to get my bags and get out of here," said Krissie. "I'm sure that the work has piled up on my desk this past week."

Krissie was off toward the baggage claim area almost before Leland realized it. Leland took up the pursuit. Something was wrong. Leland could feel it. Looking into Krissie's eyes was like looking into a frozen lake—so cold, so distant. And there was more to it than that. There was an aura about her that he had never felt before, at least not emanating from her. He was tempted to say something about it, but decided against it. They picked up her bags and headed for the car.

"Krissie, do you know a woman by the name of Nabuko Yamura?" asked Leland.

"Sure do," replied Krissie, looking toward Leland only briefly. "She is a project scientist working on the ring project. I met her while I was on the island. Why do you ask?"

"She emailed me about three days ago," said Leland. "She seemed pretty worried about you. She said something about you going to some sort of mysterious meeting on the island and then never coming back. This Nabuko said that security had come and picked up your things the next day, but that you'd never returned to the resort. She wanted to know if I'd heard from you. I fired an email back, assuring her that we'd talked on the phone that very morning. She sent an email back to me a few hours later. She was very relieved. She was afraid that something might have happened to you."

Krissie laughed. "She is one high-strung chick. I don't know what she would do if she didn't have something to worry about."

Leland smiled. "Oh, that type."

"You got it," replied Krissie. "I'm afraid I'm not going to be able to write a very favorable report about her work on the project. It's a shame, really. She's smart, but not too stable."

"I see," replied Leland.

Krissie was unusually quiet as they rode home toward Central Park West. Her eyes were on the scenery all the way home. Leland had expected to hear her go on and on about her big adventure, but that wasn't the case.

"Did you learn anything about the union ritual?" asked Leland.

"Nabuko probably told you about that," said Krissie, shaking her head. "She had some crazy notion about it being some sort of dark rite. It's just a graduation ceremony. They hold it when someone graduates from their religious studies program. Actually, it was kind of boring. I'll tell you more about the trip later. Right now I'm pretty tired."

"Sure," said Leland. "That was a long flight. Lusan said that he didn't want you coming into work until Monday. That will give you the whole weekend to pull your report together."

"I'll need it," confirmed Krissie.

Leland and Krissie pulled into the underground parking garage. Three minutes later, they were in the elevator on their way to their condo. It was just after six in the evening as they walked in the door. Krissie put a few of her things away and headed straight to bed. She was asleep in minutes. Leland decided not to disturb her. He sat in the living room watching the nightly news. Maybe it was just the fact that she was tired. Maybe that explained the odd way she had acted this afternoon. Yeah, that had to be it.

It was just before ten when Leland stepped into the bedroom to find his wife still sound asleep. He slipped in beside her. He should let her sleep. She'd be more like herself tomorrow. He was sure of it. Then he'd hear all about her adventure. He faded off to sleep pretty quickly.

Leland awoke with bright moonlight in his eyes. He was confused. He gazed up to find himself at the edge of a forest. It was cool and damp. Here and there, a light, low fog hung over the high grass of the meadow and amidst the trees of the forest. The air was full of fireflies. It was like some sort of wonderland out of a storybook.

He stood up. He was surprised to find that he was wearing his business suit. Yet he was barefoot. The pieces of the puzzle that was this place just didn't fit together. It was then that he saw a light coming in his direction. It was not the light of flashlight, but an old style lantern.

"Is that you, Leland?" asked a familiar voice. Yes it was a familiar voice, yet he was convinced that he'd never hear it again.

"I'm over here, Grandma," said Leland.

A moment later, his grandmother stood before him. She looked positively radiant and years younger than when he'd last seen her—it brought back wonderful memories of when he was a teenager standing in her kitchen while she baked cookies and talked about his schooling, the neighborhood, and Jesus. He blinked in disbelief even as tears came to his eyes. Yes this had to be a dream, but it seemed so real. And he wasn't afraid. He was just so glad to see her. He walked toward her; they embraced.

"Oh Grandma, I've missed you so much," said Leland, holding her close. She was soft and warm, not like a ghost. She seemed so real.

"And so have I, dear," replied Claire. "I've wanted to come and see you for so long, but it just wasn't allowed until now."

"Wasn't allowed?" asked Leland, stepping back to get a good look at Claire.

"Yes," confirmed Claire. "God wouldn't permit it until now. Remember my email? I told you I'd be seeing you again."

"I remember," replied Leland.

"Oh, and my appearance," said Claire. "Normally I take the appearance of a 30-year-old, but I thought you'd feel a bit more comfortable if I appeared 60, about the way I looked when you were a teenager."

"Oh wow," said Leland. "This is incredible. This has to be a dream, right?"

Claire laughed. "Well, yes and no. You are asleep, but this isn't a dream." She stretched out her hands. "Welcome to the third level of Heaven, my home. You ought to see it during the day."

"But I'm not dead?" said Leland.

Again, Claire laughed. "Of course not, dear. You'll need to go back. You can only stay here for a few minutes. But there are things I need to tell you, and I'm afraid that they will be difficult for you to hear, but you must."

Leland nodded. "OK, Grandma, I'm listening."

"Leland, you're in great danger—the whole world is, but especially you. Understand, I was right about Lusan. He is the Deceiver; he is Satan masquerading as an Angel of Light, and he's done something terrible to your wife, something dreadful. I tried to warn her, but she wouldn't listen. Leland, you have to listen. I don't want you to be lost, too."

Claire spoke of the terrible fate that had befallen Krissie and why. It was almost too much for Leland to bear. "I know that you have a God-given gift to spot those that Satan's minions have possessed," continued Claire. "Can you tell me that you have not seen this thing inside of Krissie?"

"I felt it," replied Leland, "but I just thought that she was tired. She'll be better in the morning."

"Now you're deluding yourself," said Claire.

At this point, Leland was in tears. It was incredible, but he knew that his grandmother was telling him the truth. She always did. "Why can't we drive the demon out of her?" asked Leland. "In one of your letters, the letters that Serena Davis brought to me, you said that you did that for Julio and Karina. There must be someone here who can do that, maybe your pastor."

"I wish it was that simple," lamented Claire. "It's not. Her soul and spirit have been driven completely from her body. If the demon were driven out, all you would have left was an empty shell, and that shell wouldn't live long."

"Where did they take her?" asked Leland.

Claire's expression turned suddenly solemn. "Please, Leland, don't ask me that question."

"Grandma, please," insisted Leland.

"They took her through a sort of tunnel that leads out of our reality and into Hell," said Claire. "They want to condemn her to the Great Sea of Fire." Claire hesitated. "Don't dwell on it. There's nothing you can do about it, but maybe there is something I can do. I won't make promises, but maybe."

By now Leland had dropped to his knees. "What am I going to do?"

Claire knelt at his side. "First of all, you're going to pull yourself together. You're no good to anyone in this state. Second, you're going to make your peace with God. You are going to accept His plan of salvation for your life. You know who the author of that salvation is."

"Jesus," replied Leland.

"He is the light of the world," said Claire. "Now, make Him the light of your life."

"Then I should leave the organization," said Leland.

"No, that's the last thing you should do," said Claire. "Don't give the demon within Krissie any reason to suspect you. You need to gather information, and when the time comes, act upon it. The Spirit of God within you will tell you when. Concern yourself with your world. Let me worry about what is happening over on this side, OK?"

"But I helped bring this terrible thing into the world," lamented Leland. "I've been helping the Devil all along."

"Stop it," Claire insisted. "You are going to help bring about Satan's downfall. You will be God's man, not his. It's time for you to act the part. Will you follow Him?"

"Yes," said Leland, still sobbing.

Claire placed her arm around her grandson. "Be strong in the Lord, my love," she said. "Trust God's Word. It will be your guide. I've known all of my life that you were meant to do great things. Remember all I've told you."

"I will," replied Leland.

Abruptly, the scene dissolved around him. He awoke in his bed, Krissie at his side. He looked over at the clock; it was just past two. He got up and went to the kitchen for a glass of water. Had it all been a dream? Standing there in his home, it seemed somehow less real. As he turned, he noticed the telltale footprints leading into the room. He'd left wet, muddy tracks across his nice tile floor.

Krissie stood barefoot at the bars of her dismal eight-by-eight-foot cell, gazing out into the stone corridor. There were many other cells along this corridor, perhaps thousands of them, yet they all seemed to be empty. It was just as well. She preferred not to have people see her as she was now, dressed in this ragged gray top and skirt. She felt practically naked. The demons had called this a waiting cell, but they hadn't told her how long she was going to have to wait. How long had she been here? She wasn't sure; it was long enough for her to grow very hungry and very thirsty, that much was certain. She now knew that Hell was a very real, very physical place, not some sort of spirit realm. The worst was yet to come, of that much she was certain. This Sea of Fire that the demons spoke of was almost certainly worse than this cell.

She returned to the rear of the cell and sat on the floor. She cried. How could she have been so foolish? Yet in the midst of her sorrow, she noticed a faint blue glow in the middle of her cell. It brightened, becoming a foggy realm filled with stars. Then someone stepped from the stars, followed swiftly by another.

The appearance of the first man caught Krissie by surprise. He looked so much like her husband. He was dressed in a camouflage outfit that looked almost military. The second man had the looks of a battle-ready U.S. Marine with all of the necessary gear. In his hand he held some sort of rifle.

The first man approached her. "Don't be afraid, Krissie," he said. "We're your friends. We've come to get you out of here. My name is Leland, Leland Brown."

Now Krissie was confused. "Leland Brown?" Then it suddenly fell into place. "My husband's great-grandfather?"

The man smiled broadly. "Yes. You see, you're among family, and families take care of one another."

"You're not going to the Sea of Fire," said the second man. "There has been a small change in plans. I'm Kurt Bellows, commander of the military of Refuge."

"Pleased to meet you," said Krissie, not knowing what else to say.

Leland Senior reached down to Krissie, assisting her to her feet. "It's time to go, granddaughter."

The misty portal formed once more, and the group quickly walked through. Krissie realized where she'd seen a thing like this before. It was in a lab on a South Pacific island.

For a moment they seemed to be walking on a cloud. Then they emerged from a ring that, to Krissie, seemed all too familiar. The only thing was that this one worked.

They were in a room with about a dozen people. Two of them looked like some sort of dark angels, with gigantic wings like those of a raven. The entire group immediately broke out into a round of applause, as if to welcome Krissie. She smiled through her tears.

A pretty, dark-haired woman stepped forward and took Krissie into her arms. "It's OK, Krissie. You're safe now. No one is going to hurt you. Welcome to Refuge. My name is Bedillia. I'm a member of the high council here. Come, there are some people whom you will need to meet. They will be glad to see that you're safe."

Bedillia and Leland Senior led Krissie toward the corner of the room where a large, glowing sphere hung in mid air above a marble table. Within it, Krissie saw a three-dimensional image of Leland's Grandma Claire standing beside a winged angel in white. But this time she looked as she remembered her, a woman of 80. She smiled broadly as the group approached.

"Thank you for rescuing her, father," said Claire. "I'm very grateful."

"Family helps family," said Leland Senior, "just as I told you when you were a little girl."

"I remember," said Claire, turning to Krissie. "How are you, my dear?"

"Better now," said Krissie. "I wish I would have listened to you. I was being so stupid."

"Hush," said Claire. "Appearing to you as a young woman was wrong. Things might have gone better if I'd appeared as I do now." Claire appeared to look about the room. "These are good people Krissie; they'll help you, protect you."

"Grandma, is there any way for me to get home again?" asked Krissie.

"I'm not sure," admitted Claire. "That's up to the Father, and He has not revealed that to me."

Then the realization hit Krissie. "Leland, my husband—that thing in my body was sent to spy on him, kill him if she has to. We've got to warn him somehow."

"Be still, child," said Claire in a calming voice. "It's already been done. Leland knows what he's up against. Already he has accepted Christ into his heart. God has placed a hedge of protection around him."

"He's safe, then? He won't have to come here?" asked Krissie.

"Yes, dear, he's safe," promised Claire.

"Thank you, Grandma," said Krissie. "I love you."

Claire smiled. "I love you too, Krissie. Don't worry; things are going to work out, you'll see. We'll stay in touch. You just get some rest, OK?"

"OK, Grandma," replied Krissie.

The image faded. Krissie turned to Bedillia. She did her best to smile through her tears.

"You need to get some rest," said Bedillia. "You've had a pretty busy day.

We've prepared a place for you, as well as a better wardrobe. The demons might like to humiliate women by forcing them to wear clothes like that, but things don't work that way here."

Krissie was led by Leland Senior and Bedillia to her new home. As she walked down the stony corridor, she thought of how stupid she had been and how fortunate. But more than anything else, she worried about her husband. Apparently, she was out of the game, but he still had many difficult days ahead right there in the Devil's playground.

It was a little past eight in the morning when the woman who had been Krissie James awoke from a sound sleep. Leland had been up for several hours already. He had hoped against hope that Krissie would be more like herself. He hoped that what he'd experienced had been nothing more than a vivid dream. But it was not to be. It didn't take long for Leland to realize that the woman he loved was gone. Now she seemed cold. She tried to play the part of the loving wife, but a demon just wasn't all that good at playing the part. And this would be his life for the foreseeable future. He would live with the being who had condemned his wife to Hell. He would have to play the part of the loving husband. He prayed for the strength to see this thing through. Who could he turn to? His grandmother's pastor came to mind.

It was early that Sunday morning, long before the thing that occupied Krissie's flesh had awakened, that he had journeyed to Brooklyn. Pastor Smith was not difficult to find. He was in his study at the church. He seemed genuinely surprised to see Leland.

Leland was truly desperate at that point. His soul was so filled with the filth and spiritual decay he'd been exposed to the past few years. They talked for nearly two hours. He told him everything. Leland was, in turn, surprised to discover just how much Reverend Smith knew of this whole affair.

Before he was through, Leland had fallen to his knees in grief. "How can God forgive me for what I've done?" He wept. "I've given Satan himself the means to rule our world. Even before that, I was a pimp. I sold drugs, and I encouraged women to sell themselves for money. I'm a real piece of work."

"Christ died for sinners," said Smith. "He didn't come here for the righteous. You've just given Him your heart and soul; now comes the most difficult part.

You've got to serve him on a day-to-day basis in the darkest place in our world. God will give you a way to derail Lusan's plans. You, Leland, are in a unique position to do just that." The pastor glanced over at the clock on his desk. "I wish you would stay for service."

"It's just too risky," said Leland. "I don't want that thing in Krissie to get suspicious. Anyway, I can't chance someone seeing me here."

"I understand," replied Smith. "I'm glad you're finally with us."

Leland nodded as he headed for the door. He had a difficult journey ahead, yet he knew he had started down this road himself. Now he'd have to complete it.

By the time September had arrived, Lusan was on the road again. This time his travels took him to Europe. He was met like a champion of the people. In Berlin, a small and quiet demonstration by a group of local Christians protesting Lusan's arrival turned violent as counterprotesters clashed with them. Within minutes, 37 people, mostly the demonstrating Christian's, lay dead in the street. Public opinion had turned against them, and it was getting worse.

The mob had crossed the line, and they would cross it still further. Before the evening was through, they would burn churches and drag known Christians from their homes, beating them to death. Some would fight back, yet this only fanned the flames. Not since 1938 on the night of broken glass, had the likes of this been seen. Before order was restored, the death toll had soared to over a thousand.

In an impassioned speech, the new European Union president spoke with regret of the incident in Berlin. He asked the people of Europe to be tolerant. Yet at the same time, he spoke against a policy of hate, and he openly stated that the source of that hate was these evangelical Christians.

Europe, Germany in particular, had seen this whole thing before. Nearly a hundred years ago, in the midst of rising anti-Semitism, the value of the life of a Jew had become tragically cheap. They had become the focus point for a beaten-down nation's frustration and wrath. Now, with the memories of the great, global meltdown still fresh in the memories of the people, it was happening again. Humanity's memory was short indeed.

To the man of reason, the parallels were undeniable. The problem was—men of reason were in short supply these days. Now with over half of the people of Europe in Lusan's camp, things were likely to grow worse. Things were little better in Latin America and Asia. Despite China's efforts to stem the growing madness, its people revered Lusan's words over the rhetoric of the party. Christians there had become used to being treated with something less than respect, but now matters were worse.

Yet in England, the United States, and a few other smaller hold-out nations of the world, Lusan's message was met with skepticism. And these were the same places where another breed of miracle was being felt. These nations were in the midst of a Christian revival. Yes, Lusan had a hold in these nations, but it was not as great as in the rest of the world, and in some places he was starting to lose ground. In the American South and Midwest, there was a revival in progress like none the nation had ever seen. In the Middle East, another sort of rebellion against Lusan was taking place. Elements within the world of Islam were also rebelling against Lusan, though this rebellion took on a distinctly more belligerent flavor. Lusan was not bringing peace to the world. Clearly, the world was on a collision course with disaster.

Through the whole thing Leland was there, crunching the numbers from his office, gathering the information that might one day expose Lusan for what he truly was. And watching him every step of the way was Krissie. On the outside, she seemed so much like she had once been. The demon within her was doing a better job these days. At times she even seemed loving and caring, almost like herself, and for a time, Leland could forget what she had become.

Yet all too quickly, she could turn around and speak of the Christian blight on society. She spoke of the wonders that might be accomplished in their absence. Perhaps isolating or confining them was the answer. Perhaps more radical means of neutralizing them might be justified. It was language that seemed so foreign coming from her lips. When she spoke like that, Leland found ways to be out of the house.

And his grandmother appeared to him in his dreams. Through her, he knew that Krissie was safe, at least for the moment. That knowledge helped him focus upon what had to be done in the here and now.

Leland gathered information about Lusan, damning information. He passed it on to Pastor Smith who saw that it, in turn, was passed on to the proper authorities. Leland longed for an end to it all. Someone had to stand in Lusan's way. He only prayed that someone would step forward soon.

Detective Strom and Lieutenant Stoddard sat across the desk from the commissioner in his downtown office. The commissioner was still pondering the pile of documents set before him.

"You're serious," he finally said. "You want to charge this Andre Lusan with murder, accomplice to murder, money laundering, racketeering, and being in this country illegally. Have I left anything out?"

"Attempted kidnapping," said Strom.

"Oh," said the commissioner, "I missed that one." He leaned back in his chair. "My god, man, do you have any idea how well connected this guy is? I mean, he might as well be the Pope."

"We can prove every charge," said Stoddard. "Detective Strom has been working on this case for years. He and his family were nearly killed over it. This Lusan is a menace. No, he is even worse than that."

"From what you're saying, you'd think that he was the Devil himself," noted the commissioner.

Strom practically bit his tongue to keep from saying something foolish. No, he wouldn't hurt his case, not now.

There was a pause. "Look, I don't like this guy either," said the commissioner. "I'm a good Catholic. I go to mass every Sunday, but I sense something spiritually wrong with this guy. My priest tries to be politically correct, but he senses it too." Again there was a pause. "I'm sticking my head way out on this one, but I'll authorize it. Arresting the most popular religious figure since Jesus Christ—it almost makes me look like Caiaphas, doesn't it?"

"No," said Strom. "You're doing the right thing. Your children and grandchildren will thank you."

The commissioner shook his head. "My own son follows this guy. He thinks that Lusan is some kind of saint. I'll let history be my judge. Go ahead, do the paperwork; pick him up, but do it by the numbers, by the book."

"Yes sir," said Stoddard, as he and Strom rose to their feet. They headed out the door, through the secretary's office, and down the hall.

"Thanks, Lieutenant," said Strom, "I owe you big time."

"For what?" asked Stoddard. "It was good police work, some of the best I've ever seen. You've got your ducks in a row, Bill. Lusan is guilty all right. It will be interesting to see how he rules this spiritual empire of his from behind bars."

Lusan offered up no fight as he was escorted from the Davidson building in handcuffs. Despite every effort to make this as quiet an arrest as possible, an array of reporters were on hand just outside the main door. All were anxious to get a piece of the biggest story of the year.

Lusan was quickly led to the back of a squad car and was whisked away. There was no time for questions and only a fleeting moment for photos. There was rejoicing, crying, and even violence in the streets that afternoon.

By the following day, the news had spread to every corner of the world. In France, protests in front of the American Embassy turned into a rock-and-bottle throwing exhibition. In other European nations, the protests and violence against America and American citizens escalated.

When Lusan's bail was denied by a New York court, the outcries against America grew even louder. The European Union's President Julien Devereux spoke out angrily against the arrest of Andre Lusan, calling it an act of Christian American imperialism. He demanded the immediate release of Lusan.

All the while, Lusan sat in his cell on Riker's Island, a model prisoner, enjoying the show. His enemies had fallen into the trap. They had sewn the wind; now they would reap the whirlwind.

The issue of Andre Lusan was no longer a city issue or even a state issue. It had become an international incident. A week of political bickering and legal wrangling ensued as some of the nation's best lawyers hopped on either side of the argument. In the end, it was politics that decided Lusan's fate and not legal precedence. Neither the City of New York nor the United States could afford to put Lusan on trial, and as it turned out, the Country of France filed a request for extradition. It provided the American president with a way out of this political quicksand. She urged the powers that be to deport Lusan, to turn him over to the French authorities.

Ten days after his arrest, he was on his way from New York to Paris, in the custody of the French authorities, with first-class flying accommodations. He was greeted like a returning hero upon his arrival in Paris. A day later, he was cleared of any charges in France. He was free to continue his crusade in the place where his support was the greatest.

The Divine Light Foundation's offices in New York would be closed, and his offices in Paris would become the center of his spiritual empire. There was no purpose in having the capital of his empire in such a closed-minded and hostile nation as America. He would deal with her people soon enough.

Leland was clearing his desk in his office when he got an unexpected visitor. "Mr. Pagoni," said Leland rising to his feet.

Pagoni smiled broadly. "How are you doing my boy? It has been too long since we last talked. Please, sit down. The way you jumped to your feet, you'd have thought that his holiness had just entered the room."

Leland couldn't help but laugh at Mr. Pagoni's comment. He quickly pulled up a chair for his landlord and his friend.

"Bad business, all of this," said Pagoni sitting down across the table from Leland. "Will you be leaving us?"

"Yes sir," said Leland. "That's my understanding, anyway. Word is that I'll be relocating to Paris."

"Such a shame," said Pagoni, "and your lovely wife, too?"

"Yes," replied Leland.

Pagoni hesitated. "Leland, this is really none of my business. I am, after all, just the landlord. But something has been bothering me. I see a lot of Krissie in the conducting of my business. I've gotten to know her pretty well. Quite honestly, she has become almost like a daughter to me, the daughter I never had. I know that must sound overly sentimental, even foolish."

"No, sir, not at all," replied Leland. "I can understand completely."

Pagoni chuckled, placing his hand on Leland's. "Yes, I suppose you can. But she has me worried. Ever since she came back from that island, she's been different. Oh, she doesn't look any different, at least not until you look into her eyes. They're so empty, Leland. I don't know how to describe it other than that."

That caught Leland by surprise. Still, he said nothing.

"The two of you are getting along all right, aren't you?"

"Yes," confirmed Leland. "It's only that…"

"Only what?" asked Pagoni.

"She changed after the island," said Leland.

"Leland, she has changed," confirmed Pagoni, "and not for the better." Again he paused. "Leland, I've known you since you were just a boy. I know now that something is troubling you. It has been for a long time. There is something you're not telling me, something that I really should know. Leland, I'm on your side, I always have been. What's wrong?"

By now there were tears coming to Leland's eyes. He'd hidden his emotions for so long, but his willpower was at an end. He began to tell Mr. Pagoni the story. He told him everything. Pagoni turned out to be a good listener.

"Leland, if almost anyone else had come to me with a story like that, I would have called him a liar or worse, but not you. No, I believe you. Anyway, I've seen too many strange things this last year. I'm actually glad to see Lusan leave, the loss of a profitable tenant notwithstanding. I never did feel comfortable around him. Now I know why. But why go to Paris with him, to save your wife?"

"Yes," confirmed Leland.

"From what you've told me, I think you can do more for her here," continued Pagoni. "Look, I have a plan. I want you to stay here in New York and work with me. I'll make it an official request to Lusan. That will give us time to sort this whole thing out. The Holy Mother Church is in jeopardy, and I won't abandon her. Nor shall I abandon you and Krissie. You're a part of the family, as far as I'm concerned, and family sticks together."

Leland managed a slight smile. "You've always been good to me, Mr. Pagoni, thank you. Okay, I'll stay and work with you."

"Good," said Pagoni. "You know, there have been things I've done in my life that I'm not particularly proud of. I fear I'll have a lot to answer for on Judgment Day. Maybe it's time to clear the slate. Maybe it's time to fight on the side of God."

CHAPTER 23

The Herschel spacecraft glided silently a mere 4,000 miles above Jupiter's clouds of orange and yellow. It was just one minute from the closest approach to the planet. It was picking up ever more velocity even as it stole a portion of the mighty planet's momentum for itself. Right now it was being bombarded mercilessly by intense alpha and beta radiation, the penalty for its theft. This was the most dangerous aspect of the mission. If too many of those particles were to get through its shielding, hit a circuit in just the wrong place, the mission might well end there. Abruptly the craft was shaken by the roar of its main engine. Its velocity increased even more.

At mission control, they monitored the craft's progress. Everything was going as planned. At 13:42 hours the computer shut the engines down right on schedule. A few minutes later they had confirmation; they were right on course, and no further course corrections would be needed.

Dr. Sam Florence gazed approvingly at the telemetry on the screen before him. Once again, their hastily assembled spacecraft had performed beyond their expectations. They still had to pass through several hundred thousand miles of Jupiter's radiation belts. They weren't out of the woods just yet. Still they were hopeful. The most difficult maneuvers were behind them, and at the speed the spacecraft was moving, it would clear the worst of the radiation belts in a matter of hours.

Right now they were about a quarter of a million miles behind the comet, closing the distance at a rate of about 20,000 miles a day. Up to this point the comet had been incredibly calm—no gas eruptions, no odd changes in course due to venting, and no surprises. That was the way he wanted it, a quiet comet that would be positively dull if it weren't passing so close.

Their computations of its path had been right on. There was a zero percent chance of the comet hitting Earth. In reality, it would pass closer to the moon than the Earth, missing old Luna by a mere 40,000 miles. It would be an astronomer's dream come true. In the night sky they would see a comet with its enormous tail stretching across the gibbous moon. What a sight that would be.

It was mid-afternoon when the spacecraft returned the closest view of the comet to date. It still lacked a tail, and only a faint trace of an atmosphere enshrouded the almost naked rock and ice. Their view would steadily improve until they maneuvered into orbit 13 days from now. Then they could begin mapping this dirty snowball from the depths of the solar system. The stress associated with the impending fear of a collision had passed. Now the team could concentrate on the science. It promised to be an exciting couple of years as they followed the comet through the inner solar system and back out into the darkness.

Sam couldn't help but smile. If there had never been a danger of collision, this mission surely would not have been funded. Now, as it was, they would conduct the most detailed study of a large comet ever undertaken. Tonight he would have a mountain of data to analyze. He would love every minute of it.

"I wish you didn't have to stay behind," said Krissie as she prepared to head through security at JFK International.

"I don't have a choice, love," said Leland. "There's a mountain of paperwork to go through. Mr. Pagoni insists on getting it all cleared away before closing the books on this place. He's been awful good to us, you know."

"That's a matter of opinion, I suppose," said Krissie. "He made a fistful of money on this deal."

Leland held his peace. The real Krissie really loved Mr. Pagoni. She would never have said such a thing.

"How long will you be here straightening up this mess?" asked Krissie.

"Oh, Krissie, I don't know," admitted Leland. "It could be a month, maybe more. I don't like it any more than you do, but it has to be done."

"I suppose," said Krissie. "You'll call a lot, right?"

"Right," confirmed Leland.

The two kissed. Leland tried to imagine that this was the real Krissie, but it was tough to do today. She was in one of her moods. A moment later she was off down the jet way. He stood there until he could see her no more. Then he was on his way home. It was a long drive this afternoon; traffic was particularly slow.

Leland had pulled into his parking space below his condo and was on his way to the elevator when he saw a man in a dark suit.

"Hey Leland, over here," said the rather large man.

Leland recognized him immediately; he was one of Pagoni's men. He smiled. "Hello, Carlo."

"Leland, no questions, just follow me, OK?" said Carlo, pointing toward a dark-colored sports car.

"Sure," said Leland following his lead. A moment later they had pulled onto Central Park West. "What's up Carlo?"

Carlo smiled. "Sorry about the cloak and dagger stuff, Leland, but something has come up. It wouldn't be a good idea for you to go into your condo right now, at least not without being prepared."

Leland was confused. "Prepared for what?"

Carlo made the turn onto 97th Street, heading toward the river. "Mr. Pagoni had a bad feeling about it so he had some of the guys check out your condo, looking for bugs, and I don't mean the kind with six legs. They went over it from top to bottom; they found four. There was one in your bedroom, one in the living room, one in your study, and one in the dining room. Whoever put them there was pretty good—they were the high-tech kind, and they were hard to find. They were all microphones, no video cameras. That at least was a break."

"Lusan," said Leland.

"Yeah, that's what the boss figured," confirmed Carlo. "He's a slippery snake, that Lusan."

"So were they removed?" asked Leland.

"Come on man, use your head," said Carlo. "We remove them and Lusan knows we're onto him. We don't want him suspecting nothing. You're going to have to use common sense when you're home cuz you won't be alone, if you get my meaning."

"I got you," confirmed Leland.

"We might be able to use them to our advantage, feed that snake false information, but only so long as he thinks he has the drop on us. Frank is checking your car right now to see if we have any problems there. He'll let us know when we get back. Till then, just enjoy the ride and the pleasant company." Carlo laughed. "Sometimes I crack myself up. Anyway, Mr. Pagoni is going to send a car around for you tomorrow morning at seven sharp. You'll be meeting with him over at his place. He says to tell you he has the plan figured out. He said that you would understand."

"Sure do, thanks, Carlo," said Leland.

It was about ten minutes before they pulled back into the underground garage. Frank was waiting for them.

"There was one there, all right," said Frank. "They'd slipped it up under the dash. I arranged for it to develop a short. Stuff happens, you know? Whoever put it there will probably figure that it just failed on its own." Frank paused. "You told him about the ones in his condo, right?"

"Well, duh," said Carlo.

"OK," said Frank. "You be careful, Leland. Remember, you're on a party line."

"Sure, Frank," said Leland, heading for the elevator. He paused as the door opened. "Hey guys, thanks."

Carlo and Frank smiled, but said nothing more. The door shut and Leland was on his way up. "Not a moment of peace," he murmured.

Leland was in front of his building at seven, where Mr. Pagoni's limo picked him up. It wasn't a long drive, about 20 blocks to Pagoni's building. Leland was quickly ushered to the penthouse where he would be having breakfast with the godfather, as he had once before. Only this time, he was surprised to find Pagoni himself in the kitchen cooking omelets.

"You can't expect other people to do everything for you," said Pagoni in a jovial voice. "The Bible says that those who would wish to lead need to be the servant of all, or something like that." He glanced toward the large security guard behind Leland. "You can go ahead and leave us, Max. What Mr. James and I have to talk about is very private indeed."

The guard nodded and headed for the elevator, leaving the two men alone. A moment later, they heard the elevator close. It was only then that Pagoni spoke once more.

"I even gave Sylvia the day off," said Pagoni. "I decided to do for myself today."

"Very good, sir," said Leland, as Mr. Pagoni, placed a delicious smelling omelet on his plate.

They headed on into the dining room. After offering a brief prayer, Pagoni dug into the omelet. "Confession is good for the soul," he said. "There is something that you ought to know. When I saw that block of gold you brought in here that morning, I became very curious about this Andre Lusan. I mean, who with that kind of wealth doesn't have his own documents? And how did he get into the country in the first place? Everything you told me that morning was true. I had no doubt of it, but I also knew that you had left certain details out. So I took the liberty of wiring those floors of the Davidson Building. I made sure that my people were very discrete about it. After all, I didn't want my new renters to discover what I had done."

Leland looked on in amazement. Never had he even dreamed that Pagoni had done such a thing.

"Don't be so surprised, Leland," laughed Pagoni. "You know as well as I do that I'm no saint. Like most Americans, I pursue the almighty dollar. I just pursue it a bit more aggressively than most. I instructed my people to listen for any references to the gold. You see, I didn't buy Lusan's story about a Saharan gold mine. I figured that we might discover his source, claim a bit of the action for ourselves. We spent a lot of time listening, especially to conversations on the 32nd floor. Unfortunately, they didn't talk too much about it. What they did talk about was just downright strange. One of my people figured that they were talking in some sort of code. I mean, they had to be. After a few months we switched off the microphones. It just wasn't cost effective. Then, about four months ago, my youngest nephew got wind of what we'd been doing. He practically begged me to let him turn the microphones back on and take up the project on his own time. I agreed.

"He must have recorded thousands of hours of conversations. I remember him saying that some of what he heard really freaked him out. He also talked about hearing some really eerie sounds over the microphones. I'm here to tell you, it really shook him up. He asked me to listen to parts of a few of his disks. I told him that I really didn't have the time." Pagoni shook his head sadly. "In retrospect, I wish I had. One of the recordings was some sort of a meeting in which they talked about murdering a police detective and another was about their plans for your wife. I'm sorry, Leland. If I had listened to him when he first came to me, this horrible thing might not have happened to her."

"Oh, god," said Leland, leaning forward, his face in his hands. "It's not your fault, Mr. Pagoni; you didn't know."

"But we still have four months of disks," continued Pagoni. "I've got my nephew listening to them full-time. I'd like you to help him. Between the two of you, you might learn a lot about Lusan's plans. In the meantime, we have the bugs in your house. We might be able to feed him some false information, get him to slip up."

"But now he's under the protection of the French government," lamented Leland. "I doubt they would send him back to us."

"And keep in mind, this bugging I did was strictly illegal," noted Pagoni. "I fear anything we discovered using it wouldn't be admissible in a court of law anyway. But it will give us ammunition. I know what he is now, Leland. I'm not allowing him to desecrate our world. I have my own resources, even in Europe." He paused. "Especially in Europe. If no one else is willing to take on this unholy Monster, well, I'll do it myself."

"I'll help you, Mr. Pagoni," promised Leland. He glanced at Pagoni's ring. "You're a Knight of Columbus, aren't you?"

"I sure am," confirmed Pagoni.

"I think you've become a real knight now," noted Leland, "a knight on a holy quest. I'm proud to serve at your side."

Pagoni laughed openly. "Yes, I like that. Well, my friend, let us go forth and do battle with the dragon. I do believe that is what the Book of Revelation calls him. I'd like to add the title of dragon-slayer to my rather long resume."

As the two men parted that morning, they both knew that they had their work cut out for them. They had become noble knights on what was, perhaps, the most holy quest in all of history.

It was late November, and the Stade Vélodrome in Marseille was filled to overflowing. It was a big night. Both Andre Lusan and Julien Devereux, president of the European Union, would be speaking. It wasn't clear what the topic was to be, but the word was that it would be the announcement of the millennium.

Security was incredibly tight around the stadium. No one got in without going through a metal detector twice. Trouble and all kinds of threats surrounded these great men. They were considered enemies of both the Islamic and Christian fundamentalists. It was one of the few things that both groups could agree upon.

High above the upper tier of seats, a metal panel was lifted and slowly pushed to the side. From beneath, a thin and sweaty man emerged onto the roof wearing distinctly Middle Eastern garb. It had been the better part of a week since he had seen sunlight. That was how long he had been in the tight confines of that conduit. He drew out his sniper rifle.

Twice during the past week, Luis had nearly been discovered. If security had gone to the trouble of actually entering the ventilation duct rather than just glancing in with that mirror on a stick, his efforts would surely have met with failure.

Below him, in the stands, he heard the roar of the crowd as Lusan and Deveraux took the stage. Right now he was both hungry and dehydrated. His water and food had run out early yesterday. He knew that it was unwise, yet he stopped to rest. He scanned the enormous roof. Their intelligence was right; no security had been stationed on the roof itself. He scanned the skies. There was a helicopter far off to the west, but it was much too far away to detect him—at least he hoped so.

On the stage below, President Deveraux had stepped up to the podium. He was preparing to introduce Lusan to the multitude. Luis was almost sickened by the flattery the president heaved on Lusan. This was a murderer, a torturer, the greatest liar in human history he was talking about. You'd have thought he was describing a saint. "What fools," murmured Luis.

Far below, Lusan took the podium. It was the better part of a minute before the crowd quieted down enough for him to speak. "Fellow Europeans, you've been so kind, so much like God would have you to be. You've given to my ministry, you've given generously. Well, it is time for this ministry to give back to you. Tonight I announce where some of your money has gone. On a remote South Pacific island, scientists in the employ of the Divine Light Foundation have accomplished a feat that has been one of the great dreams of science for over half a century. I am pleased to announce the end of the energy crisis and the dawn of an age of clean, renewable power. For the past three months we have operated a full-scale fusion power plant capable of generating enough electric power to light every home in Marseille, as well as those within a 50-mile radius of this city."

On the screen behind him appeared the generator in operation on his island. It was quickly followed by a series of schematic diagrams of the unit. Lusan held up a small computer flash drive for all to see. "On this drive are the complete specifications of the plant. I am presenting them to the people of Europe. I seek no compensation. After all, it was your giving that made it all possible. Working together, you have accomplished a miracle."

Lusan proceeded to walk over to the president. He handed him the drive.

The crowd went wild, rising to their feet. Again Lusan had come through for them. He had delivered to them one of the Holy Grails of science.

"Global warming is over," he announced, "as is the era of high-cost electricity. Welcome to the future!"

Again the crowd exploded in applause, and in the midst of their moment of joy, an assassin took his stance at the edge of the roof and centered his sights on Lusan. His high-powered scope focused in. Yet Lusan was out of position, blocked by a metal pillar. He should have taken his shot ten seconds ago. He looked up; the helicopter was coming back this way, its searchlight shining brightly. A guard standing on a suspended walkway on the far side of the stadium had shifted his attention in his direction. Had someone seen him?

Time was running out. Luis made a split-second decision. He would target the president first; he had a clear shot. Then he would get Lusan with the second shot. He focused in on Deveraux, placing the crosshairs on his head. He placed ever more pressure upon the trigger. There was a sound like thunder.

The president reached for his head and went down amidst a cloud of blood. Luis turned to Lusan. He was in the clear, confused, trying to assimilate what had just happened. Suddenly, Luis felt a terrible cold surrounding him. He knew only too well what was happening. He had to take his shot. A second blast echoed through the stadium. Lusan reached for his stomach. He'd hit him all right, but was it a fatal blow?

People were scattering for cover all over the stadium. A shot rang out from the far side of the stadium, then another. His time was almost gone, and Luis knew it. He felt like he was being buried in a block of ice. He tried to get another shot. Lusan had found cover. There would be no more shots. It was time. He reached into his pocket for the detonator; he could barely feel it. He stumbled to his feet. He felt a searing burning sensation in his hip. A bullet had found him. At this point he was nearly blinded by the terrible, ethereal force around him. He searched for the edge of the roof; he found it.

"Allah Akbar!" he cried, in the loudest voice he could muster, as he stepped out into thin air. He fumbled for the button of the detonator and then pressed it.

He was still better than 50 feet above the stadium floor when the powerful bomb went off in a mighty flash. The people on the ground were spattered by hot blood and a hail of shredded clothes, flesh, and body parts.

On the stage, Lusan was in tremendous pain. It was a new experience for him, and he didn't like it a bit. He crawled toward President Deveraux. He'd been hit in the forehead by the bullet. The bullet appeared to have hit his skull at a relatively high angle and lodged itself somewhere within the brain.

"No," cursed Lusan, "it can't end this way. I've worked so hard." He looked about. He sensed dozens of his minions in ethereal form all around him. They had come to protect him if need be. But, for once, he wasn't worried about himself. He figured that he would survive. It was President Deveraux he was worried about. "Prevent his spirit from leaving his body," he commanded. "Give him whatever strength you have." Lusan thought and came up with a plan. "Push the bullet back from where it came. Reach into his skull and remove it."

By this time, paramedics were on stage. They tried to render assistance to Lusan.

"No," said Lusan, "Stand back. He is beyond human medical help. We must reach beyond the natural." Lusan placed his hand about two feet above the president's head even as his minions did their work.

The paramedics stepped backward as they witnessed the slug literally push itself from the open wound. It levitated then fell to the stage.

For a moment nothing happened. Then the greatest minion of the thousand among them descended into the body of the president. He took control, bringing order to the chaotic cascading of nerve impulses firing off of the dying neurons. All the while, Lusan's hands remained above the president.

One of the paramedics drew close, searching for the president's pulse. He found it, though it was very weak. The president was breathing now, though the breaths were shallow and irregular. A faint glow appeared between Lusan's hands and the president's body. It was a phenomenon witnessed by virtually everyone within a hundred feet of the stage.

"His pulse is growing stronger," said the paramedic, a sense of astonishment in his voice. "This is incredible."

All the while, Lusan knelt before the president, the glow growing ever brighter. Yet Lusan's own injuries threatened to end the show. His pain was tremendous and his consciousness fading. "Don't allow the president to die," he said in a voice that everyone on stage could hear.

It was but a few seconds later that the glow faded and Lusan collapsed to one side, blood spreading across his suit coat. By now, stretchers had been moved onto the stage, and the president and Lusan were placed upon them. The medical staff quickly moved the two dignitaries into two waiting ambulances. The president's young son and his housekeeper climbed into the ambulance with the president, and within a minute they were off.

The stadium was filled with screaming and crying. The two greatest men of the century might well die tonight. And what was that glow that so many had seen? Many claimed to have heard the assassin cry "Allah Akbar!" It was the cry of an Islamic suicide assassin.

Within an hour, the word was out that a militant Islamic group associated with Al-Qaeda had called the media, claiming responsibility for the assassination. Yet three hours later, a second phone call, allegedly from the same group, denied that they had anything to do with the attack and expressed sympathy for the families of both leaders.

But people were already reacting to the first message, and a night of violence against those of Muslim descent spread across Europe. By the next morning, it was anyone's guess as to who the responsible party was. Some theorized that it had been the work of a lone gunman, others a conspiracy.

Yet, the morning brought other news as well. President Deveraux was alive and conscious, speaking with both his doctors and his family. Lusan too had pulled through. The bullet had grazed his stomach, but had missed all of the other major organs.

Yet other rumors were emerging when it came to Lusan. There were stories of abnormalities associated with his anatomy, of too many ribs, an unusual arrangement of his vital organs, and a pair of strange growths on his back. Many dismissed these rumors as the sort of thing tabloid stories were made of, yet they persisted.

Within three days, the doctors announced that President Deveraux was out of danger. He would make a full recovery. So too would Lusan, who had become very quiet and reserved, avoiding the press.

Yet the paramedics who had attended his and the president's injuries had a great deal to say. They spoke of the incredible things they had seen, and with their testimony, Lusan's fame grew.

With these announcements also came an announcement as to the identity of the shooter. He was Luis Zapatta, a small-time thug out of Sardinia. He had no connections to the Islamic community. What he did have were shadowy associations with organized crime. There was also a rumor that he had once had some association with the American CIA, an allegation that the CIA flatly denied. Still little by little the story of the assassin was unfolding.

Back in the United States, Leland James followed the story with interest. He didn't like the direction the story was leading. Could Mr. Pagoni have had anything to do with the assassination attempt on Lusan? The thought disturbed him, but he couldn't dismiss it. How could he approach him about it? Should he even do so?

Leland was surprised when Pagoni canceled their regular Wednesday morning meeting. He even refused to see his nephew. It was as if he had shut himself up in his own world high above the street.

It was on the following Monday that the FBI came a calling on Pagoni, and on the next day, he was taken into custody. It was all over the papers; the great New York crime boss, Louie Pagoni, was being charged with masterminding the attempted assassination of the European president and his spiritual advisor. The French wanted him extradited to stand trial on French soil. However, after some days, the U.S. government denied the extradition order. Their view was that this American citizen could not get a fair trial in France or anywhere else in Europe, for that matter. If a trial was to be held, it would be held in America.

Relations between the United States and the European Union had turned distinctly chilly. In desperation, France turned to the United Nations for support of a resolution to extradite Louie Pagoni, yet they faced a threat of veto in the Security Council, not just from the United States, but from the United Kingdom, and the People's Republic of China as well.

And Leland had his own problems. The FBI considered him a person of interest as well. After all, hadn't he worked for Lusan? Now he was working with Pagoni. A search of his house turned up the four bugs that Lusan's people had placed there to monitor him.

In the end, the FBI determined that Leland was just another unwitting victim, not a suspect. He'd been a pawn, played not only by Pagoni, but by Lusan as well. Pagoni had told the FBI as much. In fact, Pagoni leveled countercharges at Lusan, claiming that he had not only been defrauded by him, but had been a target of an attempt by Lusan to take over his organization. Even more, he had the recordings to prove it.

The case was evolving into a murky quagmire of he said, he said. Yes, Pagoni had approved the hit on Lusan, but only to head off a similar operation by Lusan's people. And Lusan had brainwashed or murdered plenty of people during his stay in New York City. Still, Pagoni came short of calling him the Devil.

The weeks that followed were full of both legal and political maneuvering on the part of both sides. The U.S. attorney general suggested that extraditing

Lusan to face charges in America was warranted. Several cases of accessory to attempted murder could be brought against him, including one involving a police officer. All the while, Pagoni remained locked up, forbidden to have any visitors beyond his immediate family.

Nevertheless, Leland got a visitor, his wife. Krissie's return to the United States came as quite a surprise. She had resisted leaving Lusan's side, and Lusan dared not enter America if he had any intention of leaving again.

Leland was to meet Krissie at the airport. She would only be in the United States for a few hours. They met in the back of a little coffee shop. Due to the lateness of the hour, the shop was nearly deserted. It gave them a time and place to talk.

Krissie brought with her two messages, the first of which was that Leland was being dismissed as Lusan's chief of finance. His involvement with Pagoni had rendered him too high a risk for membership in his organization. Second, she brought a petition for divorce. If Leland was not a part of Lusan's world, he would not be a part of hers.

In that moment, Leland found a new boldness. "I would be truly upset by this if Krissie herself told me what you just did."

"And what do you mean by that?" asked Krissie.

"Oh, cut the game, will you?" replied Leland. "You don't seriously think I don't know who you really are, do you? And I know what you did to Krissie. And I'm telling you, you won't get away with it."

For a moment Krissie sat silently, then she smiled. "Very well, then. Let us dispense with the charade, if that is what you wish. For the record, I already did get away with it. I ripped your wife's spirit right from her body. You should have seen her. She was crying like a little girl. And she's not coming back, either. Souls in Hell never do."

That comment hit a nerve with Leland. He hadn't really expected her to be so bold. He kept his cool, but it was difficult. "That's not true," he said. "Some souls have escaped, and Krissie is going to be one of them."

"This conversation is over," said the demon within Krissie, rising to her feet. "Because you have been useful to him, the master has decided to allow you to continue to live; that is his message to you. But let me give you some personal advice. Stay out of our way, human. You'll live longer that way."

With those words Krissie departed. Leland didn't try to follow.

Well, that was it. He'd made a clean break from Lusan and his Divine Light Foundation. The road ahead had always seemed so clear. Well, not anymore. Now Leland had a different master; he wouldn't have it any other way.

In the months that followed, the old political fabric of the world seemed to unravel, making room for strange new alliances. Lusan's new faith had unified the people of Europe like no event in their history. Polls showed that fully 67 percent of the people of the continent had converted to this new faith. The churches and synagogues of their former faith became nearly empty and silent reminders of a way of life that had dominated the continent for centuries, but was no more.

The new faith had brought a unity that had even strengthened the bonds that held the nations of the European Union together. No longer would it be only a union of mere economic convenience. It would very soon bond the nations together under a single leader and a unified military. Its once individual nations would become the equivalent of states in the new and greater super nation. And at its head was Julien Deveraux.

Many long-established trade and security agreements between the European Union and the United States were declared null and void. The Americans were viewed as having both hindered and humiliated their spiritual leader. His would-be assassin had been tied to America as well, and now that same America refused to turn over the man who had masterminded the attempt. As a result, all American military bases were to be removed from European soil. They had six months to comply. The dissolution of NATO highlighted the severity of the political climate.

Yet Great Britain refused to abandon its longest and staunchest ally. Neither did the British have a taste for this new breed of what they viewed as European fascism. No, they'd been down this road before. They cut ties with the European Union completely, preferring to apply for membership in NAFTA, an application that was being seriously reviewed by all parties involved.

Across the Pacific, America and China, perceiving a common threat to their security, had signed several important trade and military agreements. Yet fearing the possibility of isolation, Russia had embarked on several new trade and military agreements with the European Union itself.

Most of the nations of the Middle East had also formed a more binding alliance than they had previously had, so as to secure their own interests. Yet, Egypt and Israel, leery of the growing Islamic fundamentalism gripping the area, and dominating the alliance, preferred to throw in lots with their old and trusted ally, the United States. The world was quickly polarizing, and the resulting fear and paranoia had created indeed strange bedfellows.

In Italy, the Pope's refusal to acknowledge Lusan as anything but a false prophet had isolated the Vatican from the rest of the new European nation. It had become a tiny nation surrounded on all sides by an almost hostile neighbor. It was a dark time indeed for the Church.

Indeed, just being a Christian of any denomination in the new Europe was a bad career move. It was a good way to find oneself out of a job, and President Deveraux was anything but sympathetic to the Christian plight. From his way of thinking, Christians were blind, intolerant haters of the truth. And his viewpoint was shared by ever more of his fellow citizens.

Lusan was making good on his offer to provide Europe with a new source of virtually unlimited and cheap power. Already 27 new fusion power plants were being planned for different countries in Europe. President Deveraux made sure that the technology remained a carefully guarded secret, for European Union members only. By his way of thinking, it was a gift from God, and it would remain in the hands of God's people, those who followed the teaching of Lusan.

CHAPTER 24

It was just after Christmas when a group of people, united by their struggle against Lusan and all that he represented, gathered in Pastor Smith's church in Brooklyn. They were a diverse group—two evangelists, a police detective and his family, two former gang members, a famous astronomer, a flight engineer, the nephew of New York's greatest crime boss, and Lusan's former head of finance. They sat in a circle, discussing their situation and options. Yet spirits were low, and a feeling of general helplessness ruled the moment.

"As long as I live, I'll never forget the things I heard on those disks," said 26-year-old Guido Pagoni. "The man is the Devil himself, of that I have no doubts."

"Yet everything we have done to trap him has failed," said Detective Strom. "I worked for years to get enough evidence to put him behind bars for life. I had him, and I had the NYPD behind me too, but he slipped through our fingers."

"My uncle thought to put an end to him in the only way he knew how," said Guido. "I don't think he'll ever see freedom again."

"But all he ended up doing was fulfilling Biblical prophecy," noted Chris Davis. "Revelation said that the Beast would recover from what seemed to be a fatal head wound. Now it's happened." Chris turned to Guido. "I mean no disrespect to your uncle, really. You're right; he did the only thing he could think of. I know his heart was in the right place."

"Lusan is like an irresistible force, pulling the entire world to its doom," lamented Leland. "I helped him get to where he is today. He took my wife from me because I couldn't recognize him for who he was. I'll have to live with that for the rest of my life. I don't know where I'd be without the love and forgiveness of Jesus."

"To say nothing of a praying grandmother," noted Serena.

Leland smiled, though slightly. "Her, too."

Pastor Smith turned to Dr. Florence, who had remained strangely silent throughout their meeting. "What about this comet? I can't stop thinking about the passage in the eighth chapter of Revelation: *'And the second angel sounded, and as it were a great mountain burning with fire was cast into the sea: and the third part of the sea became blood; And the third part of the creatures which were in the sea, and had life, died; and the third part of the ships were destroyed.'* That sounds like this comet of yours. Are you sure it's going to miss us?"

Dr. Florence nodded. "Believe me, Pastor Smith, if this comet were to hit us, it would do a whole lot more than that. It is over 27 miles long and 19 miles wide. It is far larger than the object that brought the reign of the dinosaurs to an end. It would probably annihilate 95 percent of all of the species on Earth. What has me concerned is its increasing activity. We've had to pull the Herschel spacecraft back away from it due to its violent outgassing. We hadn't expected there to be so much activity this early. The comet is still nearly 300 million miles from the sun. Debris from the comet could wipe out nearly every satellite in Earth's orbit if activity on its surface continues to escalate. No, believe me, we have a problem."

"So, what can we do?" asked flight engineer Cal Wayneright. "I've seen the Devil in action, seen what he can do."

"And you've seen what God can do too," corrected Serena.

"Yes," said Cal. "But right now, it seems to me that the Devil is on the offensive. He has a lot of political power in his corner. To be honest with you, I dread going back to Germany next week—with all that's going on. I don't see what any of us can do."

There was a commotion in the next room. A moment later, a tall, blond-haired man in a light blue jacket entered the room. "You all need to have faith," he said in a calm almost melodic voice.

"I'm sorry Pastor Smith," said the church secretary, standing behind the imposing stranger. "I know that you folks needed privacy, but this gentleman insisted that it was very important that he speak to you." She hesitated. "And, well, I just couldn't find it in me to turn him away."

"It's OK," said Pastor Smith.

At this point, Chris and Serena were practically beaming. Serena slowly rose to her feet and approached the man. She gave him a big hug, kissing him on the cheek.

"Hello, Serena," he said, his smile growing.

Pastor Smith rose to his feet as well. "Serena, would you introduce us to your friend?"

Serena looked into the man's eyes. He nodded approvingly. She turned to the others. "My friends, I have the honor of introducing you to my dear friend Aaron, a messenger angel in the service of Gabriel."

The silence that followed was profound. The group looked at Aaron in wonder.

Aaron nodded. "My friends, she is telling you the truth. However, to satisfy your curiosity…"

Suddenly, the stranger was aglow in a wonderful white light. In but a few seconds they were gazing upon a beautiful being with huge, white wings.

"It's another angel!" exclaimed Willie, Detective Strom's son. "I love angels."

Aaron smiled broadly. "And angels love you too, Willie. Angels love all of God's children."

"Holy Mother of God," gasped Guido.

"God does not have a mother," corrected Aaron, "though His Son does."

"This angel is different from the one I saw," said Sam.

"Yes, confirmed Aaron. "You encountered the dark angel Abaddon. He is just as much a servant of God as I am, loved by God no less. Still, he serves a different purpose in God's Kingdom." Aaron turned to Leland. "It is Abaddon who protects your precious wife, Krissie. I assure you, Krissie is well, and in good spirits, and, by the way, quite busy. She is working closely with Bedillia, Serena's mother. She is working for the same goal as all of you. She asked me to pass her love on to you, Leland. She looks forward to the day when the two of you will be together again. Have faith, you will."

There were tears of joy in Leland's eyes. "Thank you, Aaron."

Aaron then turned to Chris and Serena. "Both Jennifer and Bedillia also send greetings to you."

The thought of their mothers brought a smile to Chris and Serena.

"I never thought I'd see the day," said Pastor Smith. "Welcome to our church, Aaron."

"Very nice to be here," replied Aaron. "I wanted all of you to know that God has not abandoned you."

"Apparently," said Cal.

"But that thought has crossed all of your minds from time to time during the past months," said Aaron. "Satan may win a battle here and there, but he will not win the war. These are difficult times, my friends, but you must not give up hope." Aaron turned once more to Guido. "What your uncle did, he had to do. Prophecy had to be fulfilled. Don't think badly of him for what he did. He served the Father in the only way he knew how. What he did is but a single event in a string of events that will bring both Lusan and his followers down. The clock is ticking, and Satan's time is almost gone. He will turn his rage upon you, yet he will not succeed, for greater is He who is in you than he that is in the world. But I tell you this; things will get far worse before they get better."

Detective Strom nodded. "Look, Aaron, I know that you guys are all around us. Angels saved my family from that fire, and I can't begin to even tell you how grateful we are."

"We are," confirmed his wife, Peggy.

"I will pass your words of thanks along to Miless, Triffides, and Aroyoa, the servants of God who rescued you," continued Aaron. "Your words will fill their hearts with joy."

"Sir," said Karina, "I sure hope you have some advice for us. Right now, I'm pretty lost. I really don't know what we're going to do."

"I do have advice for you, and more," confirmed Aaron. "In a moment, I am going to lay my hand upon all of you. I tell you this; there is no power in my hand. I am just the servant. The power is with God. You will all be filled with an extra portion of God's Spirit today. It is He that shall guide you. Almost two thousand years ago, after his Lord ascended into Heaven, Peter felt lost. Yet he did what he'd been told to do. He and the others tarried in Jerusalem, waiting for the comforter, waiting to be endowed with power. Only then did he become the man whose shadow could heal the sick and whose voice could bring the multitude to repentance. That Spirit, that power, is still here among us, but you will be given a special infilling."

"Me too?" asked Willie.

Aaron laughed. "Especially you, Willie."

"And me?" asked the church secretary, who stood by the door.

"Of course, Marie, it's for you too," confirmed Aaron. "You also have a part to play in this ministry. You were here today for a reason. Please, all of you gather in a circle."

The group quickly cleared space and stood in a circle, Aaron at the center. They all joined hands. They were prepared to experience something wonderful. There was not a doubter in their midst.

"Father, we thank You for Your love," began Aaron. "Now fill these people, sanctified by the blood of Your Son. Fill these people who love You so much; fill them with Your divine Spirit."

Quite suddenly the room was filled with swirling winds, winds that you could actually see as streams of gold and orange vapors. They whirled about the heads of the people gathered in a circle, then descended on everyone. One by one, Aaron laid his hand upon them, and they felt the Spirit of God within them as they had never felt Him before. Within minutes, all doubts were gone. Each had a vision of what it was that they were to do. It had exceeded their wildest expectations.

They all began to glow with a white light. They spoke in foreign tongues and danced in the Spirit. Love and joy had become a tangible entity in their midst. By the time it was all over, Aaron had vanished from their midst, yet they had a new determination, a new conviction.

As they parted company they realized that they might never meet as a group like this again. Their work was scattered across the globe. They were ready for the year to come. Somehow they realized that, for them, it would be the last year of this life. Things were about to change.

"Increasing current to the coils," announced the technician. "One point nine billion amps and rising. We look good so far."

"Bring her up nice and slow," cautioned Les. "Let the field grow uniformly."

Again the ring before them filled with a sort of mist. Beyond the mists and the gleaming stars within it, Les could see daylight, yet as always, it was rippling and unstable. The time-space corridor was badly contorted, at least for now.

"Almost there," said the engineer.

At this point they could see the seascape of the receiving portal beyond the ring. Still the image twisted and contorted. He could see a person standing beyond the portal; it was Nabuko. It was time for the great experiment.

"OK, here goes," said Les. "Punch it."

The whine of the torus increased greatly in pitch as a second magnetic signature swept over the first, only this one was 90 degrees out of phase with the original. The image in the midst of the ring seemed filled with electricity, and then it stabilized to crystal clarity.

"Oh wow!" gasped one of the researchers.

"OK, let's try this again," said Les, picking up three probes and stepping toward the ring, toward Nabuko. It seemed like she was right there in front of him.

"Can you hear me?" she asked.

"Perfectly," said Les, who prepared to toss the first probe.

He tossed it gently underhand, and Nabuko caught it on the far side. She gazed at it in wonder.

"It still works!" she exclaimed.

Les tossed a second, then a third probe through. They all survived intact. For a few seconds he just stood there. What he was contemplating was crazy.

"No, don't even think it," said Nabuko.

But Les did more than that. After a moment's hesitation, he leaped forward into the open portal.

It had seemed like the portal was short, a direct connection between two places in space, but it wasn't. Les found himself floating weightlessly through a misty blue corridor. It was cool here, and he seemed to be breathing, but how? He looked forward; Nabuko seemed to be frozen in time. Behind him he saw the lab. Its people also seemed to be frozen. Maybe this wasn't such a great idea after all. Then, quite suddenly, his weight returned. His feet hit the concrete pad. He stumbled, but quickly regained his balance. He looked behind him at the others. He waved to indicate that he was OK.

"Les, what were you thinking of?" scolded Nabuko who wrapped her arms around him. "I couldn't stand to lose you."

The portal dissolved into the mists as several other researchers rushed to Dr. Geiger's side. Les just smiled.

"You guys have gotta try it," he said. "There's a lot more to it than you think."

"We've got to get you to the infirmary," said Nabuko. "We can't be sure what you went through in there."

Five hours of intense medical study, as well as an analysis of the spheres, confirmed what Les already knew. There had been some sort of time dilation effect in passing through the wormhole. The telemetry of the spheres confirmed that it took over 21 seconds to make the flight through the wormhole, though only a fraction of a second had passed for everyone else. In addition, the probe measured a temperature of about 52 degrees in the wormhole. Yeah, that seemed about right. There was only a small amount of radiation associated with the passage. You'd have gotten more from a tooth X-ray.

However, Les had suffered no ill effects from the passage. He would spend the night in the hospital under observation, but that was just a precaution. They had just pioneered a new mode of transportation, and it was safe. Several more weeks of tests confirmed that as still other people made the short journey through the wormhole. Now it was time to proceed on to the next phase— teleportation to a ring on another island, an atoll 27 miles to the south. Already, a smaller and more portable version of the fusion power plant had been developed to power this third ring. If all went well, by the end of the year, other rings in New Zealand and Europe would open the door to worldwide travel without the need of ever stepping on a plane.

It all sounded so wonderful—the sort of thing that Nobel Prizes in Physics were made of. Still, Les and Nabuko were troubled. When all was said and done and Lusan had his teleporter, what would become of them? They would no longer serve a purpose in his grand scheme—none of the project scientists or engineers would. Would he allow them to leave, knowing what they knew? And Les and Nabuko knew enough to be very frightened. Inevitably, they would have to share what they knew with the others, but not yet. They didn't want a general panic on their hands. That might hasten their demise. They knew enough about this process that the guards referred to as union to know that it was something to be avoided. They would keep their eyes open and look for a means of getting the entire team off the island before it was too late.

Lusan sat back in his large, comfortable chair in the conference room of his Paris office. He felt so much more comfortable there. The political environment of Europe was far more to his liking.

Word of the success on Katafanga had catalyzed Lusan's people in Paris. A key element of their plan's for Earth depended upon the development of a usable teleportation ring. Now they had one. If all went well, they would soon have an international network of them.

The next step would be more difficult, linking the ring in Katafanga with the one in his audience chamber in Hell. General Krell assured him that it was in working order. If he and his minions could move at will in their physical form between Hell and Earth, he might well be able to control both worlds. Being the leader of the angels of Heaven was beyond his reach. He knew that now. But ruling over both an infernal and Earthly kingdom might still be attainable.

Still there would be obstacles to overcome in reasserting his rule of his infernal kingdom. There was the issue of Abaddon, that muscle-bound, overly sentimental leader of the fallen dark angels. Lusan realized that he should have dealt with him when he had the chance to so long ago—the first time he tried to shelter humans from their well-deserved torments in Hell.

Still, for the moment, he had more pressing concerns. His plan to rule this pathetic Earth and her people was entering a critical phase. He needed to focus on consolidating his power. For now, Abaddon and his followers had about the same importance as a pack of rats scampering around within the walls of a once immaculate and well-run home. He would see to it that this pathetic excuse for an angel and his followers, both human and others, would spend the rest of eternity paying for the inconvenience they had caused him. Some of those others were, sadly, his own minions.

For the moment, he would allow them to feel a false sense of security. Let them believe that they were poised at the dawning of a new era. They would discover the folly of their own intentions soon enough.

His mind returned to the here and now. He would have a special guest this morning—Julien Deveraux, the president of the European Union. He would be meeting with his spiritual leader to seek guidance. The whole idea made Lusan chuckle.

Lusan rose to his feet and walked down the hallway to the reception area. There would be a brief photo op for the press, a few statements of support, then he and the president would retreat back here for their meeting.

The photo op was friendly enough. The European press loved Lusan and the American press had been barred from the event. After a few minutes, the two men proceeded down the hallway.

"It is indeed strange how all of this has worked out, my lord," said Julien.

"Yes indeed," confirmed Lusan. "When the bullet struck your host in the head, I feared that our well-laid plan had come to nothing." Lusan paused. "By the way, how is your host, Menlock?"

"Mentally, there is not much left of him," replied the president. "The bullet did indeed do extensive damage. The parts of his brain regulating his bodily functions suffered little damage, but his higher mental functions nearly perished. Without my intervention, he would have been little more than a child mentally, if he had lived at all. I still sense him, but he is confused, unaware of what is going on around him. The ritual of union would have availed little more than that bullet." Menlock paused. "Interestingly, he still recognizes his son. There is a very strong bond there. When I am around Adrian, I follow Julien's lead. It seems to pacify him, make Julien easier to control. If I treat his son well, and I do, he cooperates with me."

"Very good," said Lusan, smiling slightly, "and what of the investigation into the shooting?"

"That has worked in our favor, my lord. The person who assisted this Luis Zapatta, the man who would have been our assassin, was one Carlos Cappello, who has ties to the American CIA, though I suspect he no longer works for them officially. Still, we can make a credible argument that supports our accusations that the Americans were behind the attempted assassination. Their president is already very unpopular abroad. Her strong Christian heritage has become a great liability in Europe. This revelation will further weaken her standings in the world."

"That may be true," noted Lusan, "and it works to our advantage, but we still have to deal with Serena Davis."

"But, my lord, she is just some Christian evangelist traveling her country in an old, gas-guzzling RV," objected Menlock. "Of what real consequence could she possibly be?"

"Never underestimate that wench," said Lusan, anger in his voice. "I never shall. Serena and her husband have become all the rage in Christian circles. It is said that people flock from all around just to stand in their presence, to have their shadow cross them, especially Serena's. There are hundreds of documented miracles regarding her. She is at the forefront of yet another nationwide revival. Churches in America are packed with believers. And now Julio and Karina Mendoza travel with them, two more humans who managed to slip through my grasp. They have a gift of casting out my minions with a level of authority I have rarely seen in people so young. Now the four of them have started speaking out against me in public. Polls claim that less than 10 percent still follow me in America. And that number is still dropping. The situation in Britain is little different. She is holding revivals there even as we speak."

"What would you have me do, my lord?" asked Menlock.

"Look for an opportunity to remove her from the equation. Bring her to me. I wish to deal with her personally," Lusan snarled. "Get me the others too, if you can, but mainly I want her."

"Perhaps an accident could be arranged," suggested Menlock. "The American highways can be treacherous places."

"No, I want to deal with her myself," said Lusan. "I want to look into her terrified eyes when her last moment on Earth comes. Come up with a plan, Menlock. Bring it to me for my approval."

"I shall," confirmed the demon.

Winter was once more turning to spring when the first of a series of titanic eruptions on the surface of Comet Florence occurred. The Herschel Spacecraft had been forced to back away from the comet by another 20,000 miles, yet it still was taking impacts from ice and rock particles. Fortunately, those impacts came at a relatively low velocity, and its large Kevlar shield could be positioned in such a way as to protect it. However, any Earth orbiting satellite would not be so fortunate. It would encounter this same debris coming in at 20 or 30 miles per second. And that debris was not just in the form of sand and dust. Chunks of the comet the size of a small car had been blown off of its surface by the powerful steam explosions, especially on its daylit side.

Amazingly, the venting was changing the path of the comet, carrying it still further from Earth, but the debris cloud was drifting the other way, right into Earth's path. They had no contingency plan for this. Sam Florence was confident that friction with Earth's atmosphere would make short order of these chunks of ice and rock. But the damage they would wreak to satellites in orbit might be far reaching, not only destroying them, but creating a cloud of space debris that would hamper spaceflight for years to come.

It was only then that a terrible thought crossed his mind. No, this was an absurd concept, but he had to check it out. He looked at the projected orbit of the comet one week after it passed Jupiter, then he compared it to another projection from a month ago. Finally he looked at the latest data. Maybe it wasn't absurd after all. He threw in still more orbital data, then did a least squares plot. He sat there in silence.

Yes, the Earth was safe from the comet, but the moon, that was another matter. The comet would cross the orbit of the moon twice, once on its way into the system and once on the way out. But on the way out, a collision with Luna was now an actual possibility.

Oh sure, team members had spoken of the possibility of lunar impact before, almost jokingly. No one had taken the possibility too seriously. But the odds of impact were going up. It all depended on just how much the venting changed the comet's trajectory in the coming months.

Sam smiled. No, he was just being silly. The amount of venting needed to produce that sort of deviation in the comet's course was enormous. He saved the information and walked out into the backyard.

His new Queen Creek, Arizona, home offered him a much nicer view of the night sky than he had downtown from his old apartment just off campus. His eyes settled on the comet, low in the east. It was growing brighter, easily visible with the naked eye, and it sported a pretty nice tail. There was still a chance that the venting would subside and the dust around the comet would be driven away by the solar wind before the comet got here. The comet was still five months away. Predictions of doom for the halo of satellites around our planet were probably premature. He needed to turn in for the night. He needed to be at the university by nine in the morning to see the new ultraviolet imaging camera data. He headed on inside without noticing the sudden brightening of the comet in the east.

He heard the news over the radio on his way into the university and not from one of his colleagues. There had been a titanic explosion on the surface of the comet overnight, the worst one yet. Still, the radio announcer's details were sketchy. It wasn't until he walked into the Bateman Science Center that the magnitude of the event became clear. The explosion had occurred along a fissure that had been the site of several previous eruptions.

The massive amount of debris scattered by the eruption was currently obscuring the spacecraft's view of the fissure. However, it quickly became clear that some of the debris cast off by the explosion was the size of a house. A huge cloud of material was expanding into space, and mission controllers were currently evaluating any dangers the cloud might pose to the Herschel Spacecraft. The spacecraft might have to retreat still further from the comet, using valuable propellant in the process. Still, they could ill afford to lose this eye in the sky.

By late afternoon the debris cloud had cleared enough to allow them to see the fissure once more. It was now twice as deep and perhaps three times longer. The terrain around it appeared jumbled and chaotic, as though some powerful force was trying to escape from its prison deep below.

The comet had grown unusually quiet now, though the expanding debris cloud would make it a spectacular sight when it rose, around 11 that night. This wasn't a typical comet, if such a thing existed at all. This one had an attitude, and it would be passing within 150,000 miles of Earth. Sam wondered if this wayward comet had any more surprises in store.

CHAPTER 25

It had been a quiet time in the ring room of Refuge. There had been only one teleportation all day. It had been Bedillia, who had made a round trip from there to the new ring in the Caverns of Noak.

Although this subterranean realm had been established below a frigid land of eternal night, it was thought best to operate on a 24 standard Earth clock to make it seem as normal as possible to its human inhabitants. Right now, the standard clock they lived by read 2 A.M., and most of the citizens were asleep.

Bedillia had just used the telesphere in the ring room to communicate with her good friend David in Heaven. He had both good and bad news for her regarding her daughter on Earth.

"It sounds like the situation on Earth is deteriorating," noted the dark angel Lenar, turning to Bedillia.

"Yes," confirmed Bedillia. "Still my daughter is doing a great work for the Father."

"You must be very proud of her," noted Lenar.

Bedillia only nodded. Her attention had been drawn to the ring. A blue mist was forming in its depths. "We are about to have company," she said.

Lenar turned to the ring to see the wall behind it vanish. "There is no one scheduled to arrive at this time," he said, drawing his sword.

A dark angel and a human sentry quickly drew their weapons, not knowing what to expect. A second later a winged angel in white stepped through the portal.

"Aaron," said Bedillia stepping forward.

"Hello, Bedillia," said Aaron taking her hand in his. "It's so good to be with you again."

"But how?" asked Bedillia.

"With the Father, all things are possible," said Aaron. "I have been asked by God to bring Abaddon back with me. He is to have an audience with the Father of us all."

A minute later, Abaddon and others had joined the group in the ring room, including Nikola Tesla and Krissie James. There was excitement in the air. The ring had been designed to move passengers from one place in Hell to another, not from Heaven to Hell and back.

"I don't understand," admitted Tesla. "How was this accomplished?"

Aaron smiled. "I cannot tell you how God accomplishes a thing. His ways are beyond my understanding. I was simply told to bring Abaddon to the Father. We will be carried directly into his presence."

A cloud of blue appeared once more within the ring. Never had the sparkling stars within it seemed so brilliant.

"We must go," said Aaron, leading the way.

"Hey, Abaddon," said Krissie as he approached the very threshold of the ring. "Would you put in a good word for me when you speak to God? I think I need all of the help I can get."

Abaddon turned and nodded, then stepped into the blue mists of the ethereal corridor. He vanished from sight.

Krissie turned to Bedillia. "God has never called for him before?"

"Not as long as I've been here," said Bedillia, gazing into the dissipating mists.

"Any idea what it's all about?" asked Krissie.

"Not a clue," said Bedillia. She looked around the room. "Well, I don't know about any of you, but I'm going to get some beauty sleep. I'm sure we'll get a full report when Abaddon gets back."

"I don't see what beauty sleep is going to get me," said Krissie, shaking her head. "No matter what I do, I'm going to look the same come tomorrow morning, and the morning after that, and forever."

Bedillia placed her hand on Krissie's shoulder. "Good night, Krissie." With those words Bedillia departed, as did most of the crowd. They wouldn't hasten Abaddon's audience with the Father by milling around here. They had all of the time in the universe.

Abaddon and Aaron walked through the cool. blue mists. A moment later they found themselves at the edge of a meadow full of flowers. Behind them a majestic stand of tall pines towered toward a crystal-blue sky. Walking toward them, through the flowers, was a tall, golden-haired man with blue eyes. He wore a long white robe and leather sandals. He looked in all ways to be human, but Abaddon knew better. It was the Father. He knelt before his creator as did Aaron.

"Rise, my friends," said the Father, who now stood before them.

"I feel honored to stand in your presence once more, Father," said Abaddon.

The Father placed His hand on Abaddon's shoulder. It was soft and warm. "It is good to see you too," replied the Father. "Come, we have much to discuss."

They proceeded across the meadow side by side. Abaddon was not quite certain what to expect.

"Be at peace," said the Father. "I want you to know how pleased I am with your progress. You have learned so much, and you will learn more. For millennia you dwelled among Satan and his minions, yet not you nor a single one of your minions yielded to his will. You befriended Serena when she was very much in need of one. Because of your efforts, Satan has been denied thousands of souls, and just as many have been relieved of physical suffering. It was you who helped to reshape her character when she was at last ready to be remolded. Now, you have given thousands more a new life, a new purpose, in a land of despair. These are the acts of a noble angel. I am proud of you."

Abaddon was astonished. He only hoped that he was understanding the Father's meaning.

"Abaddon, today I tell you that you and your fellows have regained the status of angels in My service. The word fallen shall no longer apply to you. From this day forward your minions shall be known only as the dark angels, and you shall be their leader, answering only to Me."

For once in his long existence, Abaddon was without words. His greatest desire had been granted by the Father. He had been forgiven. "Yes, Lord," he finally said.

"The task ahead of you shall be difficult," continued the Father. "There is coming a day when your children will at last fulfill the purpose for which they were created. You shall send them on a mission to torment the followers of the Beast on Earth. They will be under strict orders not to kill them, nor to do damage to Earth's living environment. The Beast and his prophet will come to fear you and to fear the one who sent you. You will know when it must be done. You must be ready to send them through the gates to Earth at the right moment. You will need to work with others to that end."

"Yes, Father, I understand," replied Abaddon.

"Second, I give you this warning; do not trust General Krell, this new master of Hell. He serves Satan and none other."

Abaddon nodded. "Yes, I feared as much."

"But I tell you this," said the Father. "The day is coming when you shall face Satan on the field of battle. On that day it shall be your responsibility to defeat him that you might bind him in chains and confine him for a thousand years. You shall be his keeper. You shall become the master of Hell. You shall be challenged, but you shall receive help from Heaven. Remember, I am with you always."

Abaddon hesitated. "Lord, what of the people of Refuge? Is there any hope for them?"

The Father didn't answer immediately. They stopped in the middle of the field. "What do you think, Abaddon?"

"Father, so many of them, like Serena, were misled on Earth by the adversary. It is in their hearts to do right, but they never understood. Now they find themselves in Hell, beyond Your grace."

The Father smiled, though slightly. "Beyond My grace?"

"No, Lord," said Abaddon. "My words were poorly chosen. Perhaps I should have said beyond mercy and deliverance."

This time the Father laughed openly. "You still haven't answered My question, Abaddon."

"I suppose I haven't," said the dark angel. "I truly don't know the answer."

"Perhaps they have already found all three," suggested the Father. "When you freed them from the torment that Satan had inflicted upon them, you granted them both mercy and deliverance. In Refuge they have found a form of grace, a grace that you have granted them. It is not unlike the grace I have granted to you. My friend, grace and mercy flow from Me. I gave it to you, and you in turn have given it to others, who then pass it on to still others. So, you see, they are not beyond My grace."

"But do they have any chance of achieving Heaven?" asked Abaddon.

"You shall soon know the answer to that question," said the Father. "However, now is not that time."

Again Abaddon hesitated. "Before I stepped into the ring to come here, one of the citizens of Refuge asked me to make an appeal to You on her behalf."

"Yes," confirmed the Father, "Krissie James. Tell her this. I have not forgotten her. When the time comes, she will know what to do."

"Yes, Lord," replied Abaddon.

The Father placed His hand on Abaddon's shoulder once more. "You feel that I am being very vague in my answers to you. You are right, but it is necessary, I assure you. Knowing the future with certainty is not a blessing. If anything, it is a curse. Such knowledge dashes one's dreams and aspirations. Most often, it is in the race for the prize and not in the prize itself that one finds fulfillment and personal growth. I will not deny you the race."

Abaddon smiled. He now understood.

For over an hour Abaddon and the Father walked and talked. How Abaddon treasured this time with the Father. He had almost forgotten just how much he loved Him. By the time he departed, he had a new vision for the future. He didn't know exactly what the future held, but he was looking forward to the journey.

"Now, let me make sure I have this all straight," said Tim, looking across the large conference table at Abaddon. "God has pardoned the dark angels, but He isn't giving any of us humans any guarantees. As far as any of us are concerned, we could be damned for eternity."

"No, that's not what He was saying," interjected Bedillia in a gentle voice. "He was saying that our salvation is still being worked out. The dark angels have been here for thousands of years. They resisted Satan for all of that time. They have reached out to help us. They were in line first, so to speak."

"I think I understand," said Megan. "It makes sense to me. I wish He'd given us some rules to follow, told us what we need to do to get delivered from Hell."

"I think we already have the rules," said Tom. "We have the Bible as our guide."

"Still, it would be nice if we could somehow hedge our bets," said Kurt, looking toward Nikola Tesla. "How is that teleporter concept working out? Could we move the population of Refuge to some other Earth-like planet in the universe, start all over again there?"

Nikola shook his head. "It's an enormous problem. There are just so many variables, so many hurdles to overcome. It's not like teleporting from one place in Hell to another. The physical laws that govern matter in this place are different from those on Earth or any other planet in the known universe. The bodies we have here wouldn't survive out there. They need to be conditioned, altered on an atomic level. We have the whole science team working on it, but it's going to take some time. For the present, we are stuck here."

"And, from what the Father has told Abaddon, we can't trust General Krell," said Eleazar, one of the dark angels. "I question if we can even trust Cordon."

"We can trust Cordon," said Nikola. "Trust me on that one."

"I don't believe that he would purposely mislead us," said Abaddon. "Even my children are comfortable around him and his lieutenant, Rolf. He burned Satan's bridge behind him during the closing days of the war in Heaven. He is no friend of the Prince of Darkness. In fact, if Satan was to return here, and it looks as if he might, Cordon and Rolf would be among the first to feel his wrath, even before us."

"Back to the original point," said Tim. "You want me to gather up all of my creatures, these ACs, and send them through my ring on a few days notice."

"Yes," confirmed Abaddon.

"We only have a handful of particle rifles and pistols," said Tim, "and a hundred or so armed swordsmen and women who can command the power of a demon's sword. Our creatures are our best defense. If we sent them through the ring, we would be almost helpless if the demons attacked us."

"I realize that," said Abaddon.

"If I'm going to agree to this, I need something in return," continued Tim. "I want one of those machines that makes stuff by just thinking about it. I also need someone to teach my people how to use it."

"I think that could be arranged," said Abaddon.

"And I want enough particle weapons to arm all of my people," continued Tim, "and plenty of ammo for them too."

Abaddon nodded. "Of course."

"OK," said Tim. "I'll help you. I need to talk to Goliath, figure out how we could get all of his friends to my cavern when you ask for them. You just get us what we need and we're with you all the way."

Megan nodded approvingly, but said nothing.

Around the table there seemed to be a general agreement. This had gone better than Abaddon had dared to hope. When the time came, they would be ready.

By the time June rolled around on Earth, the political climate between the United States and the European Union had gone from chilly to downright frigid. Russia had signed a military alliance pact with the Union even as China signed a similar pact with America.

Few expected the political conflict to turn into a military one, but the two sides had practically irreconcilable differences. The Divine Light Church, as it was now called, had become the official church of the European Union. Neither the United States nor China could endorse such a move, though their reasons for opposing it were different.

In Latin America, a strange melding of Lusan's faith and Catholicism was taking shape. The church did not officially sanction this sect of Catholicism, but seemed unable to squelch it.

All the while the comet that continued to bear down on Earth had grown strangely quiet. It hung high in the evening sky, its bright and somewhat foreshortened tail pointing to the east. It was easily visible, even from city locations, and it was growing bigger and brighter by the day.

Minor gas eruptions continued on its surface, but no more than were to be expected. For the moment, the comet was behaving itself. The comet's tail was bright and full of debris, but Earth was not going to pass through the tail. Scientists were once again hopeful that Earth would experience nothing more than a day or so of minor satellite disruption. Still, plans were underway to evacuate the space station and ground all civilian and government spaceflight for the two weeks around the comet's closest approach in October.

Then on July 30, Sam came into the planetary science center to discover that the violent eruptions had begun anew, this time from the eastern edge of the rift. Concern for the safety of Earth's satellites was in the news once more.

The team carefully monitored the eruptions as tons of dust and debris were again injected into the comet's coma. Still, many hypothesized that, like the previous set of eruptions, this one too would subside. Once the venting released sufficient subsurface pressure, venting would cease and the solar wind would drive the dust in the coma back into the comet's tail and from there into the depths of space.

For weeks they monitored the venting. Its source seemed to be a vast chamber of liquid nitrogen and methane trapped some distance below the surface. As the comet had traveled from the frigid depths of the solar system ever closer to the sun, the growing heat was vaporizing this liquid, and the vapor was seeping through fissures in the icy crust, carrying ice and rock with it. Upon reaching the surface, it exploded into the vacuum of space. But now, after three weeks, the eruptions were subsiding once more. Perhaps the reservoir of volatile material deep within the comet was being depleted.

Then it happened. With but five weeks to go to closest approach, the fissure literally exploded. From Earth the brightness of the comet doubled in a matter of minutes as a great cloud of debris erupted from the sunlit side of the comet. Within an hour, all of the comet's surface was enshrouded within the dense expanding cloud.

It was only the quick response of mission controllers that had saved the Herschel Spacecraft once again from annihilation. It took much of the remaining fuel in the main engine to propel the spacecraft out to a safe distance.

Now they were operating blind. Astronomers resorted to using radar to penetrate the debris cloud. What they discovered made them cringe. They were picking up multiple echoes within the dense haze surrounding the comet. It became obvious that at least a part of the comet had been fragmented. Then the objects which would come to be known as Florence B, C, and D emerged from the cloud. The largest one, Florence C, measured nearly three miles in diameter.

Scientists scrambled to calculate the mass and trajectory of these new comets. The prognosis was not good. Florence C and perhaps Florence B were on a course that would bring them frighteningly close to Earth. Then there were the several dozen smaller fragments blown out from the explosion, any one of which had the potential to wipe out a city if they survived their plunge into the atmosphere.

It was at a closed-door session five days later that the verdict was finally announced. The science team sat anxiously in the lecture hall as the project science director, Clyde Mayfield took the podium. "I have some disturbing news," he announced. "Comet fragment Florence C will impact Earth. The impact will occur in the Eastern Pacific on October 9 at 22:16 hours universal. Seven other significant fragments are projected to impact Earth as well. Most of these impacts will also occur in the deep waters of the Central Pacific. However one impact may occur in Alaska, and two along the Western Pacific rim, perhaps in China. Florence B has a trajectory that makes it too close to call. It might bounce off of the top of our atmosphere and head out into space if we are fortunate. But the consequences of the impact of Florence C will be catastrophic. We might well be looking at a tsunami wave a thousand or more feet high, sweeping inland hundreds of miles, and a blast wave that would destroy all life for a radius of a thousand miles. Cities like Mazatlan, La Paz, Tijuana, and San Diego may well be within that blast radius. I suspect that Los Angeles will fare little better."

Dr. Mayfield paused to give the group a moment to digest the information they had just heard. "General Cutler, who headed the development of the propulsion system and the section of the craft housing the classified payload, has a few words for you."

The general took the podium. He gazed out onto his audience of scientists and engineers; they seemed visibly shaken. "Ladies and gentlemen, you've heard what our situation is. Can we destroy this comet fragment? Can we deflect it? Given all of the resources of our military, what can we do? Give me some options."

"Options, what options?" blurted out one of the engineers near the back of the room. "The world's arsenals of ICBMs are old and antiquated. They were never designed to reach that far out into space; they were designed to destroy targets on the surface of the Earth. Look if you retargeted them for a point in space, depending on the launch point, I seriously doubt that they could reach a point more than five or six hundred miles out."

"And that is if they could get through the debris field that almost certainly surrounds these larger fragments," said another.

"Deflection is out of the question," said yet another. "We've thought about that. Even if you had a heavy launch vehicle on the pad today with a massive nuclear device in its payload, you couldn't launch. You don't have a good launch window. The comet is currently behind us in its orbit. By the time a launch window opens it would be too late."

Others nodded in agreement. Still others talked among themselves.

"You might be able to destroy the smaller fragments," suggested still another. "If you could set off a nuclear detonation directly in their path, maybe three or four hundred miles up, you might vaporize them into so many fragments that most if not all would burn up in the atmosphere."

"But you'd end up with serious nuclear fallout," objected another. "Those smaller particles would be contaminated with radioactive decay elements from the bomb."

"I disagree," said the first.

"What we need is to deflect Florence C now, while it is still relatively far out," interjected Sam. "That is the only real hope." He hesitated. "But we don't have that capability, do we?" He looked at the general intensely.

"What could you do with four 100 kiloton nuclear devices and a delivery system, if you had them?" asked the general.

"Devices on the Herschel Spacecraft?" asked Sam.

"Yes," confirmed the general. "Would it be enough?"

"Describe them," asked Sam.

"We call them moles," said the general. "They were originally designed to deliver a bomb to an underground bunker. They can be dropped from a plane or, in this case, a spacecraft. They rocket into the surface at a moderate rate of speed, secure themselves, and start drilling. They have enough power to drill full bore for about an hour. In tests, they penetrated about 200 feet into cold Antarctic ice. You could detonate them in space or deep within the comet, whichever you choose."

"Yeah, but would four be enough?" asked another. "That is a mighty big object, over seven cubic miles of ice and rock. It weighs about 12 billion metric tons."

"It has to be," said the general. "It's all you've got."

"We'd need to detonate them just below the surface," said another. "Fifty to a hundred feet down would be good. The vaporized rock and ice would act like a powerful rocket engine. If we were to detonate them on the leading edge of the Florence C, one at a time, we might be able to slow the comet down enough to allow Earth to slip by in front of it."

"Suppose Florence C fragmented?" said another. "We'd be worse off than before."

"It won't fragment," objected another. "It survived being blasted off the surface of the parent comet; it's a solid ball of ice. It has to be."

"You hope," said yet another.

"Whatever we do, it has to be done soon," noted Sam. With every passing minute, it takes more thrust to make this work."

Under Mayfield's direction, they broke up into workgroups. They were given 48 hours to develop a plan. No one got very much sleep.

Meanwhile, the public gazed in wonder as the now fragmented comet grew ever brighter. Even a small backyard telescope revealed what had happened. The government did their best to keep a lid on it, but inevitably the word was out; the largest of the new fragments was on a collision course with Earth.

To stem the rising panic, the Herschel Spacecraft team released the details of their plan. Now the public also knew that the craft had been equipped with a series of four nuclear warheads. Two of those warheads would be placed 50 feet below the surface of the comet, some two miles apart. They would be detonated three hours apart, imparting a thrust to the comet to throw it off course. The remaining two warheads would be held in standby should the first two fail to produce the desired effect.

As a last backup, a battery of Earth-based nuclear missiles would be used to pulverize whatever was left of the comet just an hour before it hit our atmosphere. Officials spoke confidently of success, yet they had grave doubts.

Just 11 hours after the finalization of the plan, the world watched as the Herschel Spacecraft moved into position to launch the first two moles. The spacecraft's own cameras captured the launch. A mere four hours later, the moles were in place.

The first detonated with a flash so bright as to be seen from Earth. It left a huge crater in the small comet and a cloud of expanding vapor. The comet hadn't fragmented as many had feared, but it had slowed down on the order of several dozen feet per second.

The team was ecstatic. It had worked nearly twice as well as they had dared to hope. The second mole might just be enough to allow Earth to escape disaster.

Again the comet brightened as the nuclear bomb reduced the terrain around it to super hot vapor. For over an hour the small comet was shrouded in a veil of dense mist.

As the mist cleared, they were dismayed to discover that the comet had indeed fragmented. Instead of a single object, they were now looking at six large objects and a myriad of smaller ones. Still the news was not all bad. After another day of tracking, it was determined that only two of the six larger fragments were still on a collision course with Earth. The rest would miss by a narrow margin. They had two targets and two nukes.

The Herschel Spacecraft used its dwindling fuel supply to maneuver into position to deliver its last two stings. It was within a thousand miles of its larger target when all telemetry was lost.

"No, not now," lamented Sam. "We almost have it."

But it was over. The signal did not return. Apparently, the spacecraft had been hit by some icy fragment of the comet. They had realized that this was a possibility. They had been playing a risky game. They had lost. Now their last best hope would be a sea-based missile barrage. It would be launched just hours before impact. The objective would be to pulverize the remaining two cometary fragments to dust. Still, it was a daunting job. Both fragments were large, one over half a mile across, the other closer to a mile. As soon as they were able to refine the orbits of the two remaining fragments, they would make final plans.

On Katafanga, Les and Nabuko followed the progress of the comet mission. Neither one of them had an extensive background in astronomy, yet they realized the gravity of the situation. As the days passed, reports of the most likely impact points of the two remaining fragments were steadily refined.

One impact point would be in the Mid Pacific, about 500 miles south of Midway Island, the other was far closer to home, about 600 miles to their northwest.

"We have just over five weeks until impact," observed Les. "If that fragment isn't destroyed, we could be looking at a tsunami wave that would sweep everything on this island away. We wouldn't even be safe up here in the heights."

"So why aren't we evacuating?" objected Nabuko. "If we started now, we could salvage almost all of the equipment, even the fusion generator. A year from now we could be set up in New Zealand or Europe."

"That's not the way Lusan has it figured," replied Les. "He is confident that this comet fragment can be stopped."

"If worse came to worse, we might escape through the ring," suggested Nabuko.

"Maybe," said Les. "But we still need to form a stable wormhole between here and New Zealand."

"We might have that as early as next week," said Nabuko. "I've heard Lusan's engineering team is even building a ring just outside of Paris. We might become world travelers before you know it."

"I hope so," said Les. "Still, New Zealand is almost 50 times further away than any link we've tried to establish so far. Europe, that's several hundred times further. We may be stretching our luck on that one."

"But if we do succeed, I wonder what then?" posed Nabuko. "Will Lusan give us a still greater challenge, or will we have outlived our usefulness?"

"I'm not sure," admitted Les. "But I think it's about time we came up with an escape plan. I think that ring is our ticket out. I believe New Zealand is our best bet. The ring there is not so well guarded. We could take the whole team through, at least anyone who would come with us. I haven't worked out all of the details yet, but I will."

Nabuko nodded. At this point she was really afraid. She was becoming convinced that being drowned by a tsunami might not be the greatest of their worries.

CHAPTER 25

Chris and Serena were involved in a citywide revival at the Minneapolis Convention Center when word of the loss of the Herschel Spacecraft reached them. Sam Florence filled them in on all of the details, details they wouldn't have heard on the news. As Sam saw it, they were looking at a near apocalyptic event any way you sliced it.

Yes, the nukes might stop the comet fragments from hitting the Earth, but the resulting nuclear fallout might make it a dubious victory. And there was more. The breakup of the comet had left them with literally thousands of fragments. Perhaps many would simply sublimate to nothing in the vacuum of space during the five weeks until impact, leaving little more than a puff of ash to hit the upper atmosphere. But some would make it through. It would be impossible to stop them all.

An incident like this had no precedent. It was virtually impossible to predict the ecological consequences of this event. And there was more. The comet was still venting material that was altering its course. Sam could not discount the possibility of the main cometary body hitting the near side of the moon. Such an impact might rain down lunar material on the Earth as well, with as yet unknown consequences.

As Serena hung up the phone, she realized that their mission here on Earth was almost at an end. They would need to double their efforts during the days that they had left. They would be here another three days, and then they would be on to Madison, Wisconsin, then Chicago. Leland James would be joining them in Chicago, and from there, traveling on with them to Shelbyville and St. Louis. That would take them right up to the day of impact, assuming there was an impact.

It would be most ironic to have the financial architect of Lusan's spiritual empire with them on this revival. Leland would be giving his testimony as part of their next four revival meetings. They were unsure as to just how much information about Lusan he would reveal, but they had already agreed not to hinder him. If the Holy Spirit led him to reveal all, that was fine.

It was just before Lusan's regular morning meeting at his conference room in Paris that he heard the news. The science team on Katafanga had formed a stable wormhole between the island and New Zealand on the very first try. Already, members of the science team had made several trips through the wormhole to the new ring in their research facility just outside of Christchurch. The next step would be to make the journey from the island directly to the ring in the basement of this very compound.

Finally, they would attempt to establish a link between the ring on Katafanga and the one in his audience chamber in Hell. At that point, the science team would have outlived their usefulness. Perhaps he would send them through to his audience chamber, grant them a journey into the final frontier.

But that would be an experiment unto itself, wouldn't it? Would the passage into his kingdom profoundly alter their physical structure? Would they become immortal beings, just another group of damned souls within his dark realm? He wasn't sure. He would send them through just before the impact of this comet thing. He would promise them escape from the impending cataclysm. He chuckled. He could hardly wait to see the expressions upon their faces when they discovered where it was that they had escaped to.

His minions were filing into the conference room; their meeting was about to begin. The first order of business would be Serena. At last he was ready for her. With the group assembled, the minion Dolgrin, one of those who had fled with him through the ring of the Great Hall of Angels, rose to his feet.

"My lord," said Dolgrin, "we have carefully followed the movements of Serena and her husband these past weeks. We have studied her schedule and have found our golden opportunity to strike. Only five days before the impact of the comet, they will be traveling to an out-of-the-way church in the town of Shelbyville, Illinois. It was a revival they had set up many months ago, before they became so popular. They will be away from the crowds on a country road. That is where we shall strike. In addition, that traitorous Leland James will be with them. It will be our opportunity to take them all at once, in a single operation."

Lusan sat back in his chair. He liked the sound of this. "Tell me of this operation."

And Dolgrin did. He and his associates had been working on this intricate plan for months. And the more Lusan heard of the details, the more he liked it. It would be almost poetic in its execution. The presence of Leland James would only sweeten his long awaited victory.

In all of his existence, few humans had raised his ire more than Serena Davis. Within Hell's broiling Sea of Fire, he had afflicted her with horror and agony on the grandest of scales. He had done it for months. No human on Earth knew the meaning of pain as she did. But this was not enough. His thirst for revenge was still not quenched. He would partake of it once more.

Chris and Serena met Leland at Chicago's O'Hare Airport. They were encouraged to learn what the team back in New York had accomplished over the past month. They had been working with the FBI and the attorney general's office to build a case against Lusan. At this point, their case was strong indeed. Racketeering, money laundering, murder, conspiracy, and kidnapping were but a few of the criminal activities that Lusan had dabbled in while he was living in the United States.

Still, possession was nine tenths of the law. Lusan was in France, and neither the French government nor the European Union would recognize America's right to extradition. Still, the accusations themselves had brought some degree of discredit to his ministry and organization. That at least was a start.

Leland had been a part of that organization and had been involved with Pagoni, too. Still, the government viewed him more as a victim than a perpetrator. His only real error was his unwavering faith in this Andre Lusan. In the course of the investigation, he had told all to the FBI and the state and federal prosecutors. It was a puzzling story indeed, filled with gold from Heaven, demons, and possession. Most of the investigators who heard his incredible story agreed that he was not being intentionally deceptive. They were convinced that he had been the victim of some sort of elaborate smoke and mirrors illusion. Perhaps it had been a trick of the spirits, spirits of a different kind. After all, he had admitted to drinking in excess at the party that night. That certainly wasn't a crime, but it was an explanation.

Normally, as a potential witness for the prosecution he would not have been allowed to divulge any details of his testimony. Nonetheless, the authorities knew only too well that it would be unlikely that they would ever get Lusan before a judge. Therefore, in a very uncharacteristic move, they had granted Leland wide latitude with only a few restrictions.

When Leland finally stepped up onto the stage at the evening revival meeting in the Chicago Convention Center, he stood before an audience of nearly 10,000. All eyes were upon the handsome, well-dressed man before them.

There was anticipation in the air. Few people knew much about this enigmatic figure. Most knew of his wife, the long-time spokeswoman for Lusan's organization. But Leland had been in the background, in the shadows, though from all accounts, he had wielded significant influence within the organization. Serena had introduced him as Lusan's former head of finance and closest human confidant.

It seemed strange to Leland that she had used the phrase human confidant. Apparently she had sensed what was to come, knew what it was that he had to say.

"I may be the greatest sinner this modern world has known," began Leland. "My wife and I helped bring the current darkness upon the land, though many may refer to the darkness as light. And I humbly ask for your forgiveness for what I have done."

Leland's voice was certain and powerful, the sort of voice that commands attention from its very nature alone, notwithstanding the message. Never had anyone come forth with such an incredible eyewitness account regarding Andre Lusan. Particularly riveting was the telling of the events of that first night, the night he and Krissie had met Lusan.

Leland softened the blow of the events of that first night by openly admitting that he had been drinking. Perhaps some of what happened had been a sort of illusion, though he doubted it. Still, the deaths of those kids in Central Park were only too real, and it had been Lusan and Duras who had killed them.

Half an hour later, when it was all said and done, he left his audience in shock. He had just confirmed their worst nightmares. He could only imagine what they truly felt inside. Did they even believe him?

Believable or not, his comments made the religious section of both the Chicago *Tribune* and the Chicago *Sun Times* the next day. He had started a firestorm of controversy. More incredible still, there were eyewitnesses to many of the incredible events of which he spoke.

Lusan supporters picketed the revival meeting the very next day, and within an hour, clashes were reported with the police and with attendees of the meeting. Leland's comments had brought to the forefront a fear that had been only murmurings a few days before. His words spread quickly across the map as more news agencies latched onto it.

On the second night of the conference, Leland spoke again. He seemed very unyielding. No, he meant every word of what he had said. The Devil himself walked among us.

Before leaving Chicago, he had been interviewed by a talk radio station, three newspapers, a television talk show, and three television news programs. If people did view him as some sort of religious nut, nuts were apparently popular.

By the last night of services at the convention center, Leland was exhausted. The experience had been both physically and mentally draining to him.

"And you two have been doing this for almost ten years?" asked Leland as he and his hosts got back to the RV.

"That's about right," confirmed Chris, preparing for their departure tomorrow.

"You don't get home often?" asked Leland.

"No," said Serena. "We have this wonderful rock house in Oregon. Oh, how I love to be there. But we seldom are. What we do on the road is too important."

"The same home you mentioned in your book?" asked Leland.

"You've read our book?" asked Chris.

"Absolutely," confirmed Leland. "I read it just a couple nights after your wife came to my office with my grandmother's electronic journal."

"The same house," replied Serena. "I can't tell you how many times I thought of that house and my garden in the back when I was in Hell. How I longed to be there."

"But most of the past ten years have been spent in this RV?" asked Leland.

"Oh, heavens no," replied Serena. "Most of that time was spent in our old RV. It was barely half the size of this one. We got this one when Julio and Karina started traveling with us."

"It's hard to imagine," noted Leland. "It sounds like the life of a gypsy."

"I suppose it is," said Chris. "But you have to set priorities. Our experience ten years ago was very good at helping us do that."

Leland nodded. He tried to imagine the life these two spiritual vagabonds had been living. Their lives were so focused. Then again, having lived a part of your life in Heaven and in Hell might have a tendency to do that to you.

Chris looked at his watch; it was just after ten. "Well, I'm calling it a night. I'll be getting up at four to unhook the cables and pull out. You folks sleep in. I can do the driving. The next crusade starts tomorrow evening at six. I want to be there early."

Leland shook his head. "Chris, I don't see how you do it."

"You just need to know what is at stake, that's all," he replied. "We could have a matter of weeks before the Lord calls us home, maybe less. I plan to take advantage of every minute of it."

"It's been this way for us for ten years," confirmed Serena.

"I feel like I'm entering the fight so late and after all the mistakes I've made," lamented Leland.

"Don't beat yourself up over it," said Chris, heading for the bedroom. "Now that you're with us, just make up for lost time."

"I will," confirmed Leland. "Thanks for having me along."

"Oh, we've loved having you," assured Serena. "It's great to have you on our side. You really made the people think these past evenings. Who can say how many people your testimony touched." Serena wished Leland a good night and headed for the bedroom.

As Leland settled in for the night, he considered all that he'd seen these past few years. What a rollercoaster. Yet he suspected the roughest ride was yet to come.

No one else in the RV had yet stirred as Chris pulled out of their spot and onto the road.

Maneuvering through the light early-morning traffic, it wasn't long before he caught Interstate 57 south. They were on their way to Shelbyville.

This would be an unusual revival, a small church in a town of 5000. This meeting had been arranged the better part of a year ago. Actually, they had been there four times before and had made some good friends. This revival would be like the old days, before these huge citywide meetings, when things seemed so much simpler.

It was almost sunrise when Chris pulled off of the interstate and onto State Route 16. He remembered the lake just north of town. This might be his last opportunity to get in some fishing with Pastor Dave.

By now, both Serena and Leland were up. Serena was fixing breakfast for the group. The smell of bacon filled the RV.

Chris hadn't noticed the police car trailing him until his lights popped on. He glanced down at his speedometer; he was right on the speed limit. Chris pulled over, hoping that the officer would pass him by. He didn't. He pulled in right behind him and stepped out of his car. Chris could tell that he was a county sheriff's deputy.

"License and registration, please," he said, as Chris lowered his window.

Chris complied. The deputy looked them over carefully. "Mr. Davis, the reason I stopped you this morning is that you have a flickering tail light, probably a loose wire. It makes it look like you're trying to make a left turn. Where are you heading this morning?"

"Shelbyville," replied Chris.

"Well, this is nothing serious," said the deputy, "just a repair order. You'll be fine till you get to Shelbyville. Garage ought to be open by the time you get there. You can get it fixed there."

"Yes sir," confirmed Chris, "I will."

By now Serena and Leland were watching the goings on from behind the passenger's side captain's chair. The deputy glanced over at them, smiled, but said nothing.

"Let me head on back to the car and do the paperwork," said the deputy. "You'll just need to get the repair order signed by the mechanic and mailed on back to us."

"Oh, sure," said Chris, "no problem."

The deputy walked back to his patrol car. For a moment, he got on his radio, looked back toward Chris, then began to fill out some form attached to a clipboard.

"We have a bad tail light, that's all," said Chris, turning to Serena and Leland.

Leland hesitated. "There's something wrong about that guy."

"Like what?" asked Serena.

"It's something about his eyes," said Leland. "They're lifeless. I used to see it a lot back at the office. My wife's eyes were like that after, well, after they did what they did to her."

Serena seemed confused. Apparently, she hadn't noticed anything in particular, but she'd only seen the deputy for a couple seconds.

It was about two minutes later that another patrol car pulled in behind the first, even as a sheriff's van pulled in front of them, cutting them off. The deputy was once more approaching Chris.

"Mr. Davis, we need you to step out of the vehicle, along with your passengers," he said.

"Is something wrong?" asked Chris.

The deputy looked at him, his eyes cold and impassionate. "The sooner you folks comply, the sooner you can be back on your way."

"Sure," said Chris, stepping from the RV.

Serena and Leland quickly followed. They were surrounded by four other officers.

"I'd like your permission to search your RV," said the first deputy.

"Search all you like," said Chris.

Two deputies headed on into the RV while Chris and the others watched nervously. What were these guys looking for?

"There's fresh coffee in the coffee maker and cups on the counter," said Serena, glancing back into the RV. "You're welcome to some, if you like."

"Are you trying to be funny?" asked one of the deputies, hostility in his voice.

"No, she was just trying to be friendly," said Chris, who at this point had about enough. Still, he managed to control his frustration and anger.

"I've been through this sort of thing before," grumbled Leland, practically under his breath, "but it's been a while."

It was about two minutes later that the deputies emerged from the RV. One of them had in his hand some smoking paraphernalia and a small plastic bag filled with white powder. "You have an explanation for this?" he asked.

"Of course we do," replied Leland. "That's the stuff you planted in the RV. Who you working for anyway?"

A second later, two of the deputies had drawn their weapons. In that moment, Leland seemed to understand.

"So, it's come to this," said Leland. "Yeah, I know who you work for."

"We will need to take all of you into custody until we can sort this thing out," announced the deputy. "I need your legs spread, hands in front of you, leaning forward on the vehicle."

"Yeah, yeah, I've been through this whole thing before," grumbled Leland.

Still, Serena hadn't. There was fear in Serena's eyes as she turned to Chris.

"We'd better do what he says," said Chris.

A moment later they had all assumed the position, only to find themselves searched and handcuffed, with their hands behind their backs. They were then herded into the sheriff's van for transport to they knew not where.

The van was flanked by the two patrol cars as it proceeded up the main road for about five miles, only to make an abrupt turn down a dirt road on the left.

"I wonder where they're taking us," pondered Chris, trying to draw as close to Serena as he could.

"One thing's for sure—it isn't to the police station," said Leland.

"Pipe down back there," said the deputy on the passenger's side, looking back through the grill that separated the two compartments.

"Or what?" said Leland. "Or you'll kill us? I think you'll do that either way. You're all a bunch of losers anyway. You're gonna lose this fight no matter what happens."

The deputy chuckled, but said nothing more.

"I don't think that helped our situation," noted Chris.

"Maybe not," replied Leland, "but you know I had to say it."

It was about three minutes later that the caravan pulled up in front of an old barn of what appeared to be an abandoned farm. The barn door was unlocked and opened by one of the deputies. The three prisoners were then roughly ushered in.

The inside of the old barn was a clutter with wooden boxes, yet it lacked the dust and decay one might associate with an old abandoned building. In the very center of the barn was a cleared stretch of floor, immaculately clean. What Chris saw there made his jaw drop. It was a shimmering metal ring not unlike the one that sat in the middle of Satan's audience chamber in Hell; he had seen it through his wife's eyes ten years ago, using her book in the Great Hall of Records. He looked over at Serena. Her amazement matched his own.

"What is that thing?" asked Leland.

"It's a teleportation ring," said Serena.

"Very good," said the deputy, who seemed genuinely surprised. "But this one was fashioned by the hands of man, guided by the master. It is a supreme achievement."

Chris scanned the ring, doing his best to seem unimpressed. "It's OK, but it's hardly the first time that human hands have built such a thing. Johannes Kepler and Nikola Tesla built one years ago."

"That might be," said the deputy, "but the master is going to make great use of this one."

"Is that a fact?" asked Chris, defiance in his voice. "Kepler and Tesla used theirs to help defeat your master in the war in Heaven. I think your boss developed this little gem just a few years too late."

One of the deputies took an angry step toward the bold evangelist, yet one of his fellows stopped him. "The master wants them delivered unharmed," he said. "His orders were very specific. Let's get them out of here."

A few strokes on a keypad setting on a nearby box caused a blue, starry mist to appear in the aperture of the ring. The deputy that seemed to be the leader motioned to Serena. "Ladies first. You are expected on the other side."

Serena took a deep breath and stepped into the mists, vanishing from view.

"Holy God," gasped Leland, "where did she go?"

"There's only one way to find out, big man," said the deputy. "Off you go."

Leland was roughly escorted to the threshold of the ring by two of the deputies and forcefully pushed in. He vanished into the haze.

"And then there was one," laughed the deputy. "Do we need to drag you in kicking and screaming?"

"No," said Chris, gazing into the mists. "I've done this hundreds of times before." Without hesitation, he stepped into the mists.

Yes, this was very much like the gates he had formed in Heaven to travel from one place to another. There was a sense of pleasant coolness within the misty corridor. Yet he wasn't walking; he was floating. It felt as if about half a minute went by before he saw light up ahead. They looked like some sort of flood lights illuminating a sort of circular exit from this tunnel. Almost certainly it was another ring. He could see Serena and Leland in the hands of uniformed guards. Yet everyone looked as if they were frozen in time.

Two pairs of large hands grabbed him as he stepped through the ring on the far end. It was warm and humid here, and in the background, he could hear distant breakers on the shore.

"Welcome to the Island of Katafanga," said an Asian appearing woman who stood in the background. "I am Lielani. We are so honored to have the great Chris and Serena Davis in our midst. I can assure you that the master has been looking forward to this day for a very long time." She turned her attention to Leland. "And Leland James, what an unexpected surprise. Why, it seems like only yesterday that your lovely wife was my guest. Now all that made her the woman you loved is gone, condemned forever to the master's kingdom." Lielani smiled. "Oh, but don't worry, Leland; your separation will not last much longer. You are about to join her." Lielani then turned to three guards standing to her left. "See to it that he is prepared at once. His body and memories may be of use to us yet."

"Greater is He that is in me, than he that is in this world," proclaimed Leland as he was literally dragged away. "This isn't over! These are the words of the Lord, God. Your eternity is coming, Lielani. It will be an eternity spent in unquenchable fire along with your master."

Lielani only laughed. "Men—they make such promises, and they never keep them."

"Don't be so sure," said Chris.

"And why not?" retorted Lielani. "Your God had abandoned you. Can't you see that?" Lielani paused. "Well, you will soon enough. You see, the master has prepared something very special for you, a fate befitting your crimes. I assure you, he has spared no expense where you are concerned." Lielani turned to the four remaining guards. "See to it that these two are properly outfitted and seen to their special quarters. I shall be visiting them presently. But first, I shall see to Leland James."

The guards dragged the husband and wife away as Lielani looked on approvingly. As Chris was dragged down a dark, forested path with his wife, he prayed for the strength to see this thing through, whatever the outcome.

It took four of Lusan's guards to force Leland into that terrible chair in the subterranean room beneath the chapel. Leland wondered if the Christians in Nero's arena had put up the fight he did. Should he have submitted quietly? No, that just wasn't him.

They'd had to rough him up pretty good to get this dreadful white tunic on him. He felt practically naked in it. Now that he was strapped in securely, Lielani approached him, dressed in a long white gown, a large and menacing syringe in her hand.

"I know you, Lielani," said Leland, anger in his voice. "Or shall I call you Coraster? That's who you are, really. Lielani is gone. She wouldn't have done the things you have done to others."

"You talk too much," said Lielani, squirting a trace of the tetraflexis from the deadly needle. "I think this will silence you. It will stir your brain up like cake batter in a mixer, preparing you for the minion who will rule this body of yours."

Leland winced as the massive dose was introduced into his vein. He gazed deeply into Lielani's eyes.

She stepped back and raised her hands in praise to her master. *"Lu katu, indu es kalani. Durch entel es adaranda,"* she chanted.

"Vera kanta su lak," said Leland.

His words brought Lielani's chant to an abrupt halt. "How could you possibly know that?" she said. "How could you know anything of the angelic tongue?"

"I don't need to know it," replied Leland. "The Holy Spirit of the Father knows it, and He, in turn, has given it to me."

"In another ten minutes you won't know anything," retorted Lielani angrily. She and the others departed even as the lights went down, leaving only the faint green glow of the cavern.

Leland gazed out into this twilight realm. He continued to pray in an indecipherable tongue. He felt the growing confusion authored by that dreadful drug, but he focused on his Savior, on his newfound faith. No, Satan couldn't take that away from him. No drug could take that from him.

Among the stalactites near the ceiling and amidst the columns around the walls, the phantasms came. They were but glowing puffs of smoke at first, but they were becoming ever more distinct, growing ever closer. The fear they authored tried to overcome his spirit, but he wouldn't allow it. He continued to pray.

Then one of the spirits approached him. It was a dreadful thing to behold. Others gathered around it. It reached out to him. In that moment, Leland knew what to do.

"Sandazer, is your soul not dark enough?" asked Leland, focusing upon the hideous apparition. "Do you desire to do still more evil?"

The wonder of his words were not that he called the demon by name, but that he had done it in the demon's own language. The being drew back, only to move forward once more.

The demons surrounding Leland tried to reach into him with their ethereal hands. Leland could feel their icy touch upon his skin, yet their reach could go no further. They pushed harder, yet to no avail.

Leland knew what they were trying to do, though he knew also that that realization came from a higher source. "There is no room inside this flesh for you," he said, still in the angelic tongue. "Greater is He that is in me, greater than you."

Quite suddenly, the cavern was filled with a light invisible to the natural eye, but almost blinding in the spiritual realm. The demonic entities seemed to dissolve in its radiance. Indeed, they seemed in great pain as a result of it. Within a minute, Leland was alone once more. His mind was clear, free of the effects of the drug.

"Thank you, Father," he whispered.

It was the better part of an hour before the lights came up once more and Lielani and her escorts returned. Leland gazed upon her with tired eyes. "Not this time, Coraster," he said.

Lielani looked upon him incredulously. "How can this be? No human, no one, has survived the union."

"You need to adjust your thinking," said Leland.

Lielani turned away in anger. She said something to the guards, though Leland knew not what.

A minute later, Leland was surprised as the guards unbuckled the straps restraining him. He was so tired, too tired to resist whatever they had planned for him. If he was about to die, he doubted that he would be awake to witness it.

CHAPTER 26

Nikola Tesla pulled back the brown drapes at the entrance to his Refuge living quarters to discover his friend Bedillia in tears. "Oh, my dear, what is wrong?" he asked. In a highly uncharacteristic move, he placed his arm around the weeping woman. "Please come in."

Nikola's quarters were somewhat larger and more sophisticated than most of those in this subterranean complex. Like the others, it had been carved out of an existing subterranean cavern room. It contained a table and three chairs composed of a gray, plastic-like material. The bed was made from a block of stone with a thin yet soft covering that made it more comfortable.

Yet it also contained his personal telesphere for his own private communications and a very sophisticated talking computer that had been manufactured by one of his compatriots in Heaven and then teleported there.

Tesla pulled up his most comfortable chair for Bedillia, and a moment later they sat across his round table in the middle of the room. "Tell me, my dear, what has happened?"

"I've just gotten off the telesphere with Aaron," began Bedillia. "You know, I talk to him about once or twice a week about goings on back on Earth, checking in on my daughter. I'm so proud of her. The Father has granted her a miraculous gift of healing. From Heaven, Aaron has been keeping tabs on her." Bedillia wiped the tears from her eyes. "But you know all of this; you've met my daughter."

Nikola smiled. "Yes, I have, a most remarkable woman."

"Satan's people have abducted her," said Bedillia, starting to cry all over again. "They took her and Chris to some island in the South Pacific. They've locked them in cells apart from one another. Nikola, Satan has tried to duplicate Hell on Earth in that place. I don't know what he plans to do to her. Maybe he wants to send her back here to Hell."

"No," replied Nikola, "I don't think he could do that. First of all, I don't think the Father would allow it. Second, he would have to have a matter reformater. The Devil and his people are not so talented. Only the Father Himself holds that secret." Tesla hesitated. "Until four days ago."

Bedillia's eyes brightened. "Oh please, Nikola, please tell me that you've built one."

"I've built one," confirmed Nikola. "Years ago, in Heaven, Johann and I managed to teleport angels from Earth to Heaven, but we had to cheat to do it. We tied directly into the particle stream of one of the rings that had been fashioned by the Father Himself. In essence, we allowed that ring to do the reformatting for us. But when Abaddon traveled out and back from Refuge for his audience with the Father, I monitored the functioning of the ring. In doing so, I got an idea. I think the Father intended to give me that clue. Four days ago I managed to access one of the rings Satan has had built on Earth. For over 20 seconds I formed a stable wormhole with it."

Bedillia watched carefully as Tesla rose to his feet and walked over to what looked like a small box with a cloth over it. He picked it up and placed it on the table. He lifted the cloth to reveal a small cage and, within it, a small colorful bird—a living bird. Bedillia's eyes grew wide with wonder. It had been so long since she had seen such a thing.

"I don't know the species," said Nikola. "It's some sort of South Pacific variety. By sheer coincidence it happened to fly into the ring, into the open wormhole. I'd thought to collect only oxygen and nitrogen molecules, perhaps a trace of pollen. Instead, I got this. I discovered that he likes apple seeds. Eventually, I plan to send him back. Hell is no place for him."

"And he made it through OK," confirmed Bedillia.

"See for yourself," said Nikola. "He seemed a little bit disoriented when he first emerged from my ring in the lab. But he recovered after a few minutes. That is how I captured him."

"Does the door swing both ways?" asked Bedillia. "Could you send someone from here back to Earth?"

Nikola's expression was not encouraging. "I don't know. I haven't tried it. Matter in Hell is far less substantial than matter on Earth. Still the transport should be possible by reverse formatting. I had half of the equation right, the other half should also be correct. But it hasn't been tested. When the Father consented to my experimenting with inter-dimensional transport, he established one provision, one rule. Personal transport to and from Earth was forbidden. We could go anywhere else."

"Except Hell," noted Bedillia.

"Yes," confirmed Nikola. "The Father gave us that provision later. He sent His own son, Jesus, to deliver that message to us, as well as get us out of one terrific mess."

"You've already broken that rule," noted Bedillia.

"Yes, I have," noted Nikola.

"I need you to send me to Earth," said Bedillia. "I need to go to that island, Katafanga. I need to get my daughter and her husband out of there. I'll need to go there heavily armed. Perhaps I can take some bad guys out in the process. I could use that new-powered armor that Tom and Kurt developed."

"And you might need that armor to hold your body together too," replied Nikola.

"What do you mean by that?" asked Bedillia.

"I mean that we've never teleported matter from here to there," said Nikola. "It's all theoretical. Bill Wang has been looking at the problem, and he sees a danger. It's called atomic cohesive failure. Basically, you would begin to fall apart at the atomic level. You'd be fine for a while, but eventually you'd begin to massively hemorrhage inside. It would be like lethal exposure to radiation and just as painful. I could not even guarantee that your soul and spirit would survive, and if they did, they would be adrift forever in the ethereal wasteland."

"You're saying this might happen, not that it will happen," retorted Bedillia.

"Yes," replied Nikola, "but do you really want to take the chance? Look, Abaddon is mobilizing his children. He has had a visitation from the Holy Spirit. The time is upon us. Tim has sent the alpha male, this Goliath, out to gather them up from every corner of Hell. Abaddon has called still others to come. Within the week they will be dispatched, over 50 million of them. They will be entering Earth through the 20 or so rings Satan has had built, as well as through an oil well in the Middle East. I am sure that they could rescue your daughter. Indeed, I don't think you could keep Goliath from doing it."

"But they will arrive too late," objected Bedillia.

"And you plan to go alone," deduced Nikola.

"No," said Bedillia. "There are others here in Refuge with family in jeopardy. Satan is also holding a man by the name of Leland James."

"Wait," said Nikola, "I heard that name. We have a Leland Brown here in Refuge. He has spoken of a Leland James on Earth, his great grandson."

"It is his great grandson that Satan is holding," confirmed Bedillia. "Our Leland will be going with me. And so will Krissie James. The demon who has taken her body may be on the island as well. It might be possible for her to take it back. We are just waiting for the right moment." There was a moment of hesitation. "And Tom Carson is going too. He refuses to allow me to go alone."

"You all realize that this may be a one way trip," said Nikola.

"They'll know," confirmed Bedillia, "but I know it won't change their decision."

"And Abaddon has approved it?" asked Nikola.

"Not yet," said Bedillia. "I will ask him—plead with him, if necessary. To undertake this mission without authority granted from God through his servant here would be disastrous."

"And your timetable," continued Nikola. "When?"

"I don't know," admitted Bedillia. "A few days. Aaron will tell me when. We want Krissie's mortal body to be there, but we must do it before Satan has his way with my daughter." Bedillia hesitated. "I'll tell you this, Nikola. If the opportunity presents itself, I plan to blast Satan's physical form to atoms."

That raised Nikola's considerable eyebrows. "So, it's about revenge?"

"No," said Bedillia. "It's about family. It's about redemption, my redemption. I have never been a real mother to Serena, not like I should have. Now I have my chance. I won't fail her this time."

Abaddon listened as Bedillia presented her plan to rescue her daughter. Still, he didn't like what he was hearing.

"Perhaps Satan will delay whatever he has planned for her," suggested Abaddon. "It might be possible for me to rescue her when I lead my children in."

"When will that be?" asked Bedillia.

"Five days," was the reply. "It will take that much time to gather them all together."

"I don't think we have five days," replied Bedillia. "Look, Abaddon, I've got to do this."

Abaddon shook his head. "Yes, I know. I love her too."

"I know you do," confirmed Bedillia.

Abaddon paused, seemingly lost in thought for a few minutes. Then he smiled at her. "Go, with the Father's blessing," said Abaddon. "But take some of my children with you. They might come in useful."

"If you can spare them," said Bedillia.

"I can," replied Abaddon. "The four of you need a plan. You can't just go in there, guns blazing. I'll have Kurt work with you."

"I've been on enough rescue missions," said Bedillia. "I can handle myself."

For the first time in the meeting, Abaddon smiled. "I know you can. I just need you to return safe. Good counselors are hard to find."

The following days found the team planning their assault. They had a plan to get the prisoners out as well as a variety of contingency plans should something go wrong. Each of them would wear powered armor. It was amazingly light. It would cover them from head to toe, much like a skin diving suit, but this one would offer them a degree of protection from bullets and other weapons that might be thrown at them. Still, like so many of the devices they would be depending upon, it was experimental.

All the while, the number of Abaddon's children gathering in Refuge and the caverns of Noak grew. They would be ready when the time came. Abaddon only hoped that they would be ready to save Chris and Serena.

Serena gazed out through the bars of the eight-by-eight foot cell far below the chapel. After two days without food or water, she was very hungry and thirsty. There was not a stick of furniture in this cell, and most of the available light came from what looked like a series of glowing crystals built into the rocky ceiling beyond the cell. She suspected that they were actually fluorescent fixtures, but Lusan had gone to great lengths to make this place look like an authentic waiting cell in Hell—even down to the gray ragged skirt and top they had dressed her in. It brought back most unpleasant memories, memories that had haunted her dreams all too often over the years.

Still, what lay beyond those bars was not quite like the corridor she remembered from her first day in Hell. It wasn't a corridor at all, but a circular subterranean chamber about 40 or so feet across. Along its walls were cells, one after another, all the same, and at the center was a great pit, about 20 feet wide. A foul stench arose from it, a stench she knew only too well. Fifteen feet below the rim of that pit a black liquid bubbled and churned, a liquid she had once been most intimately associated with during her months in the Great Sea of Fire. Occasionally a brief pillar of flames arose from the black oily surface.

Of all of the things that could have been presented to her, this was the most frightening. She supposed that was the general idea.

"Serena, are you awake?" arose a voice from the next cell.

"I'm awake, Chris," she confirmed. "I sort of wish I wasn't."

"I managed to sleep a few hours," said Chris. "Has Leland moved?"

Serena moved to the bars and gazed five cells down, where the guards had tossed Leland almost two days ago.

"I'm awake," said Leland, his voice low and faltering.

"Thank God," said Chris. "We've been praying for you. You've been in some sort of coma. What happened to you?"

"They tried to do me like they did Krissie," said Leland. "They didn't have much luck. The Holy Spirit in me was a bit more than they could handle. I tried to tell them, but they wouldn't listen. Stupid demons, anyway." There was a pause. "Don't much care for wearing a skirt. Old slewfoot doesn't have a lick of sense when it comes to fashion. He doesn't know much about room service either. He's not getting a good rating from me."

Serena had to smile. From the short time she'd had to get to know Leland James, she'd come to respect him. He seemed almost fearless.

Leland took some time to share his experience in that chair with Chris and Serena. There was no doubt in Serena's mind; he'd come a long way in a short time.

It was about an hour later that Lielani walked into the chamber. She placed a cup of water just outside of each of the three cells.

"The master has been unavoidably delayed," she said. "He is such a busy man. Anyway, I didn't want you to die of thirst before he arrived. He'd never forgive me for that, after he had gone to so much trouble to provide you with the proper atmosphere. We've all been busy. Word has it that one of the larger comet fragments will strike less than a thousand miles from the island. We're under a general evacuation order. Just another three days and this island will be under a couple hundred feet of water, or so they say. It will be the greatest disaster in human history." Lielani laughed. "They don't know what disaster is. They will."

Serena grabbed for the water and took a drink. It was warm, but it tasted all right. It came well short of satisfying her thirst. She figured that was the general idea.

"Still, I don't think you'll need to concern yourself with drowning in the tsunami," continued Lielani. "Your deaths will not be nearly so merciful." She turned to Serena. "Two days, wench. That is all you have. You'll go first, but the rest won't be far behind."

"You're wrong," said Leland, who now had risen to his feet. "Hear me and hear me well, demon. You have been weighed in the balance and found wanting.

I tell you that you won't live to see the death of Serena or any of us. You shall be reduced to ashes, too few to even be buried. Your evil spirit shall wander the ethereal wasteland until the judgment, when an even more dire fate awaits you."

"You're dreaming," laughed Lielani.

"Time answers all mysteries," continued Leland. "It shall answer this one as well."

Lielani gazed at Leland in anger, then stormed away.

"You got under her skin," noted Chris.

"Because she fears that I am telling the truth," said Leland. "I am."

"Two days," said Serena. She gazed out into the room. Her eyes settled upon a narrow metal cage sitting on the edge of the pit about 20 feet to her left. It was shaped in such a way as to accommodate a single standing human. It looked like something straight out of a medieval dungeon. It was attached to a chain that, in turn, was attached to some sort of winch that ran along the ceiling. It gave her the chills. She reached through the bars of her cell. "Chris, please take my hand."

Serena stretched as far as she could. Eventually she found the tip of her husband's fingers. They intertwined. She seemed to draw some strength from him.

It couldn't end like this. Her life had to be worth more than this.

She thought back to the stories of the Christian martyrs. They too had died seemingly cruel and pointless deaths. She understood the lengths and depths of pain better than any woman alive. She doubted that would be of much help when the time came. She prayed for courage, hoped that her example would be pleasing before the Lord.

Bedillia and the others gathered about the telesphere in the ring room for their twice-a-day briefing from the angel Aaron. At this point they had a target date for their rescue mission, two days from now. It was a full day before Abaddon would be ready to lead his children and most of the dark angels through the ring, a full day before they could expect any reinforcements.

There were still so many unknowns, and once they were over there, there would be no more updates. They would be on their own.

For the past two days they had been getting used to wearing the power suits. They were truly amazing. They were black as night and weighed only ten pounds, but they were better than steel armor at deflecting a sword's blow and better than a bulletproof vest for stopping a bullet. The rubbery fabric actually moved with the wearer, adding both support and, amazingly enough, strength. It was powered by the same sort of energy sphere that powered their weapons and made site to ring teleportation possible. Walking around in it took some getting used to, but once you did, it was of great benefit.

If possible, they would teleport under cover of night. Still, it depended on the schedule over there, not here. Until then they would practice all elements of the mission. They weren't, after all, a military unit with years of military training; they were all civilians. They only hoped that they could pull this off.

"I don't see why they haven't evacuated us yet," complained Shane Gray, one of the electrical technicians at the fusion power plant.

It was the morning meeting, and all of the scientists and engineers were in attendance. The atmosphere of apprehension and, yes, fear was growing by the day.

"Most of my technical staff left yesterday," complained another. "I haven't seen anyone around that village of theirs since the day before. Apparently getting them out was the priority."

"We've developed a transportation system that spans the world," said a woman near the back of the room. "Now they won't allow us to use it to leave ahead of this predicted tsunami."

"Dr. Malnar left too," said still another. He turned to Les. "That makes you the ranking member of administration. Have you heard when we're getting out of here and to where?"

"No, I haven't, Ben," said Les. "I've been assured that it will be soon. If worse comes to worse, we could teleport to New Zealand through the ring.

New Zealand is three times as far from the projected impact site and at an elevation of almost two thousand feet. We should be safe there."

"If they allow us to use the ring," said still another.

"Of course they'll let us use it," replied Les. "Why wouldn't they?"

There was no response, yet the group was nonetheless uneasy. As the meeting broke up and the staff went about their duties, Nabuko approached Les.

"I think they plan to keep us here," she said. "We know too much. What I've been hearing over the radio at night makes me all the more certain. They are guarding the power plant. I've even heard talk of them disabling it before they leave. Les, they want to get rid of us. We've outlived our usefulness to them. We've even lost our Internet and telephone link. We're cut off, Les."

Les took Nabuko's hand. "Look, word is that Mr. Lusan will be teleporting in tomorrow. I'll convey our concerns to him."

"They won't let you anywhere near him," objected Nabuko. "He'll teleport in on the other ring. We won't even see him."

"I hope you're wrong," said Les, "I really do. But if we haven't heard anything by tomorrow night, we'll need to take things into our own hands—overpower the guards at the power plant if need be."

"But they have guns," objected Nabuko. "We're unarmed. Also, there are usually three or four of them over there. I don't think we would stand much of a chance."

For a moment, Les seemed deep in thought. "OK, talk to some of the members of the team you trust, see if they have any ideas."

Nabuko nodded then walked off, leaving Les to his thoughts. They were in trouble, he was sure of it. Still, right now, he didn't have a clue as to what to do.

It was mid-afternoon of the next day as Lusan and Krissie stepped from the misty ring on the south end of the island. They were met by Lielani and her entourage. They bowed before their master.

"Is all in readiness?" asked Lusan, gazing about at his tropical paradise.

"It is, my lord," confirmed Lielani.

Lusan smiled broadly. "I have waited long for this moment. I intend to savor it, draw it out as long as possible. We shall do that wench Serena first. See that she is placed in the cage around five this evening. See that she's made uncomfortable. My time is valuable, but this is a thing I must do. We must conclude the proceedings by first light. Then we must be off. When is the predicted time of impact?"

"Just after three o'clock local time," said Lielani. "If there is one, we should see the tsunami here on the island about 40 minutes after that, around 3:40."

"I want you and the last of your people out by two at the latest," Lusan ordered. "See to it that the power plant is rendered inoperable after you leave. An explosive device on a timer should suffice."

"Lielani smiled. "It has already been seen to, my lord. All shall be as you ask."

Lusan placed his hand on Lielani's shoulder. "You have done well, my loyal servant. You have accomplished all that I have asked of you. I will see you at six in the chamber. Until then I wish to take a last look at my island."

Lielani bowed once more before her master. "It has been an honor to serve you, my lord."

Lielani watched as the master headed for the administration building. The rest of the administrative staff, except her, had left this morning. Aldo Karr, the chief administrator of this facility, had actually departed several days ago. Chief administrator? Now that was an amusing title. Karr was a good example of a union gone wrong. His demon had been left with a mental mess to manage. As a result, Karr was indecisive, forgetful, and sometimes incapacitated for days. She had been the real administrator of Katafanga for the past year and a half. She suspected that the master knew it too.

Lielani smiled. Well, it was time for more amusing pursuits. She too was looking forward to this evening's festivities. None of them were likely to get any sleep tonight. But that was all right. Come tomorrow afternoon, she would be safely in Paris, far from the devastation these comet fragments were sure to bring. There she could glean a few well-deserved days of rest. She glanced at her watch. It was already after four. She couldn't keep Serena waiting.

Serena and the others looked on nervously as Lielani and four burley guards entered their subterranean prison. Lielani stood before Serena's cell, grinning from ear to ear.

"Well, I hope that you are well-rested," said Lielani. "Tonight is your big night. I expect you to put on a good show for the master." Lielani turned to her guards. "Now be gentle with her. We don't want to damage her just yet. Place her in the cage."

Serena felt suddenly very ill as her cell door was unlocked and she was escorted out, one guard on either arm. She stumbled barefoot across the rocky floor. To her right she could see down into the slick, black oil, frothing and bubbling. It didn't seem nearly as hot as the Great Sea of Fire. In fact she could barely feel the heat coming off from it. What was going to happen? Were they going to drown her in it? She figured that she was going to find out soon enough.

Ahead of her, one of the guards unlocked the oblong cage. The other two then forced her into it. It was anything but roomy. There was barely enough room for her to stand. The cage was then locked.

Well, I hope that you're comfy," said Lielani. "The master will be here soon. Until then just relax, get accustomed to your new home."

With those words, Lielani and her escorts departed. Serena rattled the bars, seeking any means of exit; there was none. She looked over at her husband for the first time in days. There were tears streaming from his eyes, and he was sobbing.

"Hush, my love," said Serena. "We've run the good race, fought the good fight. This won't last long, but our joy will be for eternity."

"Don't give up hope, either of you," said Leland. "Help is on the way. I'm sure of it."

"Help?" gasped Chris. "Help from where?"

"You might be surprised," said Leland. "Just don't let the Devil beat you."

Serena nodded. She wasn't about to doubt Leland. He'd been right way too often for that. She only prayed that he was right.

Kurt turned from the telesphere toward his four students. "Ok folks, this is it. You've heard what's going on. This is your cue. I need you to say your good-byes and suit up; you leave in an hour."

The group dispersed. They were as ready as they were going to be. Actually, things had worked out better than they had hoped. They would be going in less than 12 hours ahead of the troops, and some of them would be going to Katafanga.

Just beyond the door, Abaddon watched as the team headed for their quarters to make final preparations. This was it.

"I don't like the idea of Goliath going on this mission," said Tim, who stood with his wife, Megan. On his shoulder sat the tiny creature whom he loved so dearly.

"He's been over this all before," said Megan. "Serena was the first human Goliath ever bonded with. His instincts will be critical for this mission."

"He won't be going alone," said Abaddon. "He will be leading 23 others. Mostly they will be lying in reserve, scouting out the land. In 12 hours, he will be joined on Katafanga by a hundred thousand more."

"I understand that," said Tim. "I'm just worried, that's all."

Goliath rubbed up against Tim's neck as if to comfort him.

Abaddon drew closer. "Goliath, I owe you an apology. I should never have left you behind all those years ago. But that is in the past. I need you now. I need you to help rescue Serena."

Goliath turned to Abaddon then nodded. Yes, it was clear that he knew what needed to be done.

It was 50 minutes later that the group reconvened in the ring room ready to go. Kurt checked their equipment individually; all was in order. In the telesphere image they could see David and Aaron.

"There are presently no guards in their ring room," began Aaron. "However, there are two human scientists. They seem in no hurry to leave. I believe that they could be an asset since one of your main objectives is to make contact with a member of the science team. One of them is the leader of the science team. His name is Dr. Geiger."

Tom Carson stepped forward. "Geiger? Les Geiger?"

"Yes," replied Aaron. "I take it that you know him."

"I do," confirmed Tom. "We worked together for years. I know him very well, or at least, I did."

"This might be rather awkward," noted Abaddon. "He knows that you are dead?"

"I assume so," said Tom.

"Tom, perhaps I should lead the way," said Bedillia. "It might make things a bit easier."

Tom nodded. He had a sort of Cheshire cat grin on his face that was memorable.

"OK people, time's a wastin'. Let's get to the ring," said Kurt.

The group quickly moved into position, along with their ACs. Bedillia's own AC, Mirinda, had taken up a position on Bedillia's right shoulder. They were ready to go.

The ring before them had been somewhat modified in the past several days. The new electronics were in place. Nikola Tesla stood at the new control console. He would carefully monitor every aspect of their transit.

"OK," said Nikola. "You've never made a hyperspace jump like this one, and it's likely to feel strange. You might even feel a bit disoriented when you emerge, but it will pass."

"Your power suits should compensate for any temporary weakness in your muscles," said Kurt.

"But the weakness will pass within a minute or two," said Nikola.

"Our prayers are with you," said Megan.

"We'll be there with you in less than 12 hours," said Abaddon. "May the Father be with you."

"Amen," said the group, almost in unison.

The ring before them became a starry, misty wonderland. Bedillia took a deep breath and stepped forward, vanishing into the haze. One by one the others followed. The rescue mission was on.

CHAPTER 27

Serena's legs were growing very tired and her feet sore when the Prince of Darkness at last arrived. Gone were any attempts at disguise. He appeared as he had on that first day she had seen him in his audience chamber. Minus the traditional horns, red complexion, and tail, he was the classical image of the Devil. In his company were Lielani, Krissie, and two of his guards, though they now took the form of bat winged demons in black with the gaunt pale faces of incredibly old men.

"Well, Serena, what do you think of my little piece of Hell on Earth?" asked Satan. "Does it bring back memories?"

Serena looked directly into the Devil's eyes. She did her best to control her fear. "Yes, it brings back memories. It is what made me what I am today."

"I'm sure it does," replied Satan. "Before we begin with the unpleasantness, allow me to offer you a way out. If you were to fall down on your knees and worship me, I would show mercy, granting you and your compatriots a quick and relatively painless death. Think carefully, for I shall make the offer but once."

"I don't need to," said Serena. "The answer is no. You're pathetic."

"Very well," said Satan. "Then we shall begin. I don't need to tell you what that lukewarm mass below you is. You and it were very intimate at one time. But do you know what it is? No, of course you don't. It is the very essence of evil. It is a living breathing entity. It feeds upon all of those within its grasp, all of those who call it home. Over the millennia it has grown because it has fed and continues to feed. The damned souls within it cause it to multiply, and their life force is the very source of its heat. Allow me to demonstrate."

From the tunnel behind him, two of his minions brought forth goats, two of them. Without hesitation they threw the animals into the viscous black liquid. The beasts cried out as they struggled in the tar like mass. Yet even as they did so the black liquid around them began to froth. A moment later flames erupted all around them, quickly consuming the flesh and muscle from their bones. But it didn't stop there. The entire pool erupted with violence. Serena could feel the growing heat.

A minute later, this pool had been transformed into a seething, turbulent pool erupting with flames. It had become what it truly was, a piece of the Great Sea of Fire. Serena gazed at it in wide-eyed terror. The heat, the smell, it was all as she had remembered it. She tried to remain in control, yet her lips trembled and tears came to her eyes.

"Oh God, teach me how to die as I lived, for You," said Serena.

It was then that the cage shook. The heavy chain connecting it to the winch above had become taut. Then the cage rose into the air. All the while Serena prayed silently, her eyes closed, her hands clasped. For her, this wasn't just a death by torture; it was a death by terror, by the one element that most filled her mind with total, unreasoning panic.

The cage rose to a point about ten feet above the floor before coming to a jarring halt. All the while Serena quivered uncontrollably. Then it was on the move again, amidst the squeaking and clanking of gears and cogs. It was moving over the roiling black liquid of the pit.

In her mind, Serena was standing on the precipice of that terrible cliff that jutted out above the Great Sea of Fire. She'd managed to control her emotions that time. This time it was more difficult.

"How does it feel, Serena?" laughed Satan. "Does it bring back memories?"

"The Lord is my shepherd, I shall not want," whispered Serena, in a trembling voice. "I'll dwell in the house of the Lord forever."

Again there was a shutter, as the cage came to a halt directly above the center of the turbulent black liquid in the pit. Amidst the heat and horrible smell, the cage swayed. Then there was a sense of falling followed by an abrupt halt. The cage had only dropped about a foot, but it was enough. Serena was crying openly now, unable to stop.

"Child of God, don't despair," shouted Leland. "This is not the end for you. This will be your finest day. Remain strong for your Father, for He shall not abandon you."

Satan looked over at Leland and laughed. "You've become a raving lunatic on your last day on Earth."

"If you only knew," laughed Leland. "I'll let it be a surprise."

Satan turned once more toward Serena, watched her total terror. He seemed most satisfied. "No Serena, you are not going to die yet. You will plead for death, but it won't find you. You will be in pain, but it won't grant you death."

"So be it," shouted Leland. "You have pronounced a sentence upon yourself. You seek to torment Serena but five hours, but I tell you that the Lord will torment you and those who follow you for five months. They shall feel Serena's pains, but they will not be able to die."

"So melodramatic," said Krissie.

Again Satan turned to Leland. "Shut up human. Your mad ranting is beginning to annoy me."

"Very well," said Leland. "I shall say no more than this. Today marks the beginning of the end for your Earthly empire. Your ambitions shall lead you to a thousand years of dark imprisonment, chained hand and foot to a wall. And that will be but the beginning of your downfall. Still, I don't want to spoil the surprise."

Satan turned to his heckler, anger in his eyes. "We'll see how you boast when it's you in that tiny cage."

Leland didn't respond. He returned Satan's intense gaze unflinchingly. Satan broke eye contact first. He focused once more upon the poor damsel before him. The night was still young.

"This is our last night, Les," said Nabuko. "If we don't escape tonight, we will drown tomorrow afternoon."

Les turned to the teleporter ring just 15 feet away, then back toward Nabuko. "Right now, I think the ring is our only way out. But without power, we're going nowhere."

Nabuko's eyes had suddenly turned toward the ring. A blue glow emanated from its depths, even as mists began to form. "Les, the ring is active."

Les turned to see the wall beyond the ring vanish in the billowing haze. "But the power is off, how can this possibly be?"

They both stepped back as the glow brightened. It was accompanied by an uncharacteristic hum. Then a dark-haired woman dressed in black emerged from the mists. She wore some sort of dark visor over her eyes, and held a menacing looking rifle in her hands.

To Les, she looked like some sort of a cross between Barbarella and Emma Peal of the Avengers. She gazed about the room then focused upon the two humans before her.

"A space alien?" posed Nabuko, who seemed really shaken.

The woman lifted her visor, revealing her bluish green eyes. She certainly looked human enough.

"Dr. Geiger, Dr. Yamura, don't be afraid," said the woman. "I mean you no harm. I'm here to help you."

As Les and Nabuko watched in wonder, a second figure came through the ring dressed very much like the first. This one was a black man in his thirties. He lifted his visor and looked toward the people before him, a broad smile on his face. "How are you doing, folks?"

"Good," said Les and Nabuko almost simultaneously.

Then the third figure emerged from the mists. It was another woman. She lifted her visor. Her presence seemed to bring a wave of relief to Les and Nabuko.

"Mrs. James," said Nabuko. "Ma'am, it is really good to see you."

Krissie smiled. "Good to see you too, Nabuko. You too, Les. We need to get you and the rest of your team out of here. Bad things are about to happen."

"Yes, we know," confirmed Nabuko.

Then a fourth figure emerged from the mists, a man. He carried some sort of pack in his hand. He set it down on the floor and lifted his visor.

Les looked at him in stunned amazement. No, it couldn't be. "Tom, Tom Carson?"

"How you doing, Les?" said Tom.

"But you're, well, dead," gasped Les. "I mean, I went to your funeral almost five years ago."

"Was it a nice one?" asked Tom. "I always wanted a nice funeral."

"Tom, it was a funeral," said Les. "How could you possibly be here? You had a heart attack; you're dead."

Tom smiled. "Do I look dead, Les?"

"Well, no, Tom. You look good," said Les. "Looks like you've lost some weight too. But how are you here?"

Tom chuckled. "Les, it's really a long story, one for another time. Right now I need to see where your main power relays tie into your teleportation ring."

Les still seemed confused. "You know about our research?"

Tom just nodded. "Les, I just walked through your teleportation ring. What do you think? The power relays, please."

"Yeah," said Les, "they're over here."

Tom picked up the case and followed Les. Les was startled as about two dozen small creatures flew from the ring, following which the mists vanished.

"The power relays," said Tom, placing a hand on his old friend's shoulder. The two old friends continued on.

Nabuko stood there staring at Bedillia. "Ma'am, there is one of those creatures setting on your shoulder."

"Yes," confirmed Bedillia. "Her name is Mirinda; she is my friend."

"OK," said Nabuko, her voice uncertain.

Krissie walked up to Nabuko. "Look, you've got to go to the resort and tell everyone there to come here as soon as they can. Bring only what you can carry. You're all going to teleport out to Christchurch, New Zealand. You should be safe there. The teleporter ring there is way above sea level. You'll be safe. You'll all have to find your way home from there, OK?"

"OK, Krissie," Nabuko confirmed.

"Now, move, move, move; we need to get your team out of here within the hour."

"But the fusion generator is shut down," objected Nabuko. "It might take hours to bring it back on line."

"Go," repeated Krissie, "let us worry about that. Run!"

Nabuko didn't have to be told again. She ran out the door and toward the resort.

Meanwhile, in the power transfer room, Les and Tom were disconnecting the main power couplings. Tom moved the portable power supply into place.

"You're not going to power the ring with that," objected Les. "You can't even imagine how much power is required."

"If you were doing it efficiently, you could get away with using a third of that much power," said Tom, connecting the positive lead to the power supply. "But I don't have time for a tutorial tonight. The connectors of this supply have been custom made to fit your teleportation unit. I made them myself."

"Doggone it Tom," objected Les, "where have you been these past five years?"

"You really want to know?" asked Tom. "You might not believe me if I told you."

"Try me," insisted Les.

"OK," replied Tom connecting the other lead to the power supply. "I've been in Hell. I mean the real Hell, a place of wailing and gnashing of teeth. And believe me; during my first 18 months there I did plenty of both. Then I was rescued by a dark angel by the name of Abaddon. Since then I've worked for him, worked for the day that we would overthrow Satan."

"You realize how crazy that sounds?" objected Les.

"Sure," said Tom. "So explain how I can be here."

"I can't," said Les. "But you're asking me to believe in the Devil. I don't think I can do that."

"You should," said Tom, plugging a power sphere into the power supply, "you work for him."

"What are you talking about?" asked Les.

"I'm talking about Lusan," said Tom. "Come on Les, you've studied this guy. You know there is something sinister about him."

"Sinister, yes, but the Devil, I don't know about that."

Tom rose to his feet and turned to look Les right in the eye. "Look, Les, it's this simple; place your faith in Jesus Christ, God's only Son, and you can avoid all of the problems and pain that I've been through. I'm your friend; I want you to avoid my mistakes. Here is your chance."

"Tom, it's just too much for me to handle in one sitting, that's all," said Les.

"OK," said Tom, "take some time to think it over, but don't take too long. I don't know how much time you have left. OK, you've got power, let's get to your control room and get ready to establish your link."

Krissie and Leland Senior moved cautiously toward the fusion power plant. Darkness was falling, but it wasn't dark yet. They were almost there when a security guard emerged from the main door. He turned toward her.

"Who are you?" he demanded.

"Take a look," said Krissie. "Who do you think it is?"

"Mrs. James," he said awkwardly. "I'm sorry, ma'am. I thought you were at the pit with the master."

"I'm not," replied Krissie. "I hate to miss all of the fun, but I have other assignments. I need to inspect this power facility, make sure we're ready for tomorrow."

By now a second guard was at the door. "Ma'am, we weren't informed of any inspection. You don't have authorization to be here. And where did you get that outfit and that weapon, it's almost like…"

The rouse was over, they knew. The second guard went for his weapon; he never had a chance. A blast from Leland Senior's particle rifle literally dismembered him in a terrible blast, scattering body parts all around.

The first took a blast from Krissie's rifle. His fate was no better than that of his partner.

"There were supposed to be three guards," said Leland Senior.

He ducked into the building. He heard the sound of running somewhere down the corridor.

"We can't let him sound the alarm," said Leland Senior, rushing down the corridor.

A few seconds later, Krissie was in pursuit. She was amazed at how effortless running was in the power suit. She was gaining a real appreciation for its utility.

Yet that appreciation grew when she felt the sudden jab in her side. She turned toward a dark hallway to her right. She flipped down her visor. There he was, as clear as day, hiding at the next turn. She turned and fired, taking out the guard and a sizable portion of the wall that he must have assumed was protecting him.

"Stupid demon," she said. She glanced at her power suit where she'd taken the hit. It had sustained very little damage, barely a scratch, though she suspected that she would bruise by morning.

"Sorry, Krissie. I ran right past him," said Leland Senior, rushing to her side.

"I almost did too," said Krissie.

Leland looked on the floor to discover the round deflected by Krissie's suit. "My heaven's Krissie, that suit deflected a 45 slug. That's something else."

Krissie chuckled. "Forty-five, twenty-two, they're all the same to me. All I understand is particle rifle stream density and capacitor power. I never fired a gun that uses bullets. They're a bit too primitive for my taste. I think we need to turn the power down a bit. These weapons are more effective on Earth than they were in Hell. Let's try a setting of 65."

Leland went for the dial on the side of the weapon. "Right, 65." He turned back to Krissie. "I need to deactivate the detonator of that time bomb. It's supposed to be in the control room. There's not supposed to be anyone else here. You wait for me at the door and let me know if anyone shows up. That last guard may have gotten off a distress call. I'll meet you at the door in ten minutes?"

"Right," confirmed Krissie.

The two split up. Both were mindful of the possibility that there might be other surprises awaiting them, like an extra security guard.

Leland had been briefed on deactivation of the detonator of the bomb by Kurt. It happened to be out in plain sight. It was not a complex device. It didn't need to be. The throw of a switch and the cutting of a couple wires insured that there would be no explosion come tomorrow afternoon at two thirty. Ten minutes saw them back at the rendezvous point.

The group was remaining in contact with each other through low-power digital communicators. From the looks of it, the mission was going like clockwork so far. Bedillia had taken up a position in the forest halfway between the resort and the labs while Tom continued to work with Les on setting up an escape route for the scientists and engineers.

Bedillia in particular was very nervous. Yes, she knew that Satan planned to drag out the execution of her daughter for five hours. He'd try to frighten her before he put any serious hurt on her, but just the thought of him hurting her was driving her to despair. Once the scientists were at the ring, she, Krissie, Leland Senior, and 18 of the ACs would move toward the compound to rescue her daughter and the others. Tom would see the scientists safely to New Zealand and then return to cover their own escape route. It was totally dark when she saw the headlights coming up the road. At about the same time, the scientists were coming toward her from the resort.

"Great," she said.

She alerted the others, hunkered down, and hoped for the best.

Two security guards in a golf cart stopped by the growing group of scientists. "What's going on here?" demanded the driver.

It was Nabuko who stepped forward. "We are traveling up to building one, to the main conference room. We are going to have a general meeting to discuss some of our concerns."

"Concerns about what?" asked the officer.

Nabuko pointed toward the heavens, which were already filled with meteors, the most intense meteor storm anyone had ever seen. "We're going to discuss that, sir. Our time is running out. Sometime tomorrow afternoon a much larger fragment is going to hit the ocean to our northeast. Is this not reason enough for a meeting of this island's scientists?"

The officer looked at the scientists for a few seconds before responding. "You are going to a meeting with suitcases in your hands?"

"Too much time has been wasted already," continued Nabuko. "At this point, any other means of evacuation will be virtually impossible. Our only way off this island is going to be that teleportation ring. We are going to have our most valuable items on hand when the evacuation is finally called."

The security officer pulled out his radio and informed the central office of the situation. It was a minute later that he responded. "OK, here is what you are going to do. You are going back to your homes. Have your meeting in the recreation room or the hallway if it pleases you. But consider yourselves under house arrest for the night."

"Officer, since when has it been a crime for us to gather together?" asked Nabuko.

"Since martial law was declared," continued the officer. "I'm asking all of you to go back to your homes. I will not ask nicely again."

"We're going to be left to die on this island, aren't we?" arose a voice from near the back of the group. "We know too much."

"Everyone else has been evacuated but us," said another.

"Return to your homes!" demanded the guard.

The situation was quickly escalating out of control as one of the security guards went for his sidearm. What happened next in the darkness was unclear. A large rock hit one of the guards in the back. Several gun shots followed, and a scream rang out. Then pandemonium ruled the moment. When it was all through, two of the scientists lay wounded, one seriously, and one of the security officers was dead by a blow to the back of the head. The other had retreated about 20 yards from the crowd, his pistol drawn.

"OK, you're all under arrest!" he yelled, pointing his gun wildly about. "You think you're special; you're not. Your lives aren't important. You're just here to serve the master."

Bedillia aimed her weapon and tried to get a clear shot, but she was still just too far away. She racked her brain for a plan, but it wasn't there. Then she heard a small voice within the depths of her mind.

"You don't need to fire," it said. It was the voice of Mirinda.

Bedillia lowered her weapon.

A few seconds later, the guard started to flail about wildly, pointing his gun in this direction and then that. He fired shots into the air. Something was attacking him, something in the air. They were hard to see in the darkness, but there were many of them. The guard cried in pain. Apparently, whatever they were, they were either biting or stinging him.

The scientists seemed confused. One of them had retrieved the dead officer's gun, but he didn't use it.

"Come on, let's go," urged Nabuko. "Help each other. You've got to help each other."

The group picked up their wounded comrades and backed away from the screaming security officer, who seemed to have something other than the errant scientists on his mind. They'd been walking about a minute when a dark figure stepped out in front of them.

Folks, don't be afraid. My name is Bedillia, and I'm here to help you. There's not much time. We're getting all of you out of here."

It was about three minutes later that the group gathered on the main floor in building one before the ring. Tom stood before them.

"Everyone is here," confirmed Nabuko. "We're ready to get out of here."

Tom nodded approvingly. "Ok folks, some of you have already been through the ring; most of you haven't. There is nothing to fear. I've been through many times. Help each other as you go. Just step through boldly, don't hesitate." He turned to the control room, where Leland Senior and Les stood behind the glass. "Ok, power it up Les."

The blue, starry mists formed in the midst of the ring. A matter of seconds later, they were looking into the corrugated metal wall of what looked like some sort of warehouse, presumably in Christchurch, New Zealand.

"I've never seen the wormhole form that quickly," noted one of the scientists.

"Yeah," said Tom. "I had some time to tweak your software, improve your power distribution. I think you'll find that the ring works much better now."

By this time Les had joined the rest of the group. They all gazed in wonder at the scene beyond the ring. Never had it seemed so clear.

"OK, let's go," said Tom, stepping through the ring.

With the new improvements, it seemed only a few seconds before he stepped out onto the concrete floor on the far side. A few seconds later, the group followed one by one.

The air was rather brisk here. Apparently the building was not heated.

Tom turned to the left to see an unarmed security guard, an older man, step through a door to the left. He looked somewhat confused.

"We weren't expecting a transport this evening," he said. "Where are you folks coming in from?"

"Katafanga," said Tom. "We're evacuating the scientists as a precautionary measure."

"Oh, OK," said the guard, looking at Tom. "That's some suit."

"It is pretty nice, temperature controlled," said Tom. "It's experimental—you know, classified, that sort of thing."

"Got ya," confirmed the guard. "Mum's the word."

With the last of the scientists through, the wormhole closed behind them. It was then that the guard noticed the two injured scientists. "What happened?"

"We had an incident; bullet wounds I'm afraid," said Tom. "Sorry, I can't say any more than that until we finish the investigation."

"You want that I should call an ambulance?" asked the guard. "It would only take about five minutes to get from here to Christchurch Hospital."

"Yes, thank you," said Tom.

The guard made the call on his cell phone. Tom listened carefully to make sure that this guy wasn't calling backup instead. He didn't.

"They're on their way," said the guard, "We can meet them up front.

"Thank you," said Tom.

"They're talking about this bloody wave that we might get tomorrow night," continued the guard. "They're saying that it could be 10 or 20 feet high. Areas within a couple miles of the waterfront have a mandatory evacuation, but the hospital is on high ground, the safe zone they're calling it. So are we."

"Good to hear," said Tom.

It turned out that this facility was maintained by only three men. They were talking to the head of security. No, there would be no problem here. Already transport for the scientists to a local hotel on this side of the city was being arranged. Once this crisis blew over, these people would be able to arrange transportation back to their homes. Tom wondered what sort of life they would be returning to.

Tom and Les headed over to the hastily constructed control room in the corner of the warehouse. In a few minutes, Tom would need to be on his way back to Katafanga to resume the fight. Les powering up the small scale fusion plant and entered the coordinates into the computer.

"I think we did a better job on this one," noted Les. "The power plant is smaller, more efficient. It takes only five minutes to fire it up. One man can operate the whole system. It's the image of future transportation. That is, if we have a future."

Tom shook his head. "I've seen a lot during the past five years, both incredible and horrifying. Now, Satan's right here on Earth. I don't know if I envy you your future."

"So, where will you go now, Tom?" asked Les. "Will you be heading back to this Refuge place, back to Hell?"

"I might have to," said Tom. "We don't know how long our bodies will survive here. I still feel OK, but I don't know how much longer that will last. We don't belong here anymore."

A green light appeared on the control panel before them. "We have power for transport," said Les. The pressing of a single button brought the mists into the depths of the ring. He paused. "It was good to see you again, Tom. I'll consider what you've told me. My God, it's hard to believe. I can't imagine what it must have been like for you out on that altar."

"Do yourself a favor," said Tom. "Accept Jesus Christ into your heart. His way, God's way, is better than man's way. I had to learn it through the ultimate school of hard knocks. Learn from my mistake."

"I'll try," promised Les, "I really will."

The two men briefly embraced. Then Tom was on his way. He stepped from the control room and into the ring. He vanished like an apparition.

Les powered down the system and stepped from the control room to find Nabuko. He smiled.

"Has he left?" she asked.

"Yeah, he's gone," confirmed Les.

"Back there on the island you said something about him being dead," continued Nabuko.

"Yes," confirmed Les.

"You will need to explain that to me on the way to the hotel," said Nabuko, a smile coming to her face. "I suspect there is an even more amazing story here than I know. I've seen so many things tonight that I just can't explain."

"One could almost call it a miracle," noted Les, gazing toward the empty ring. "Yes, I'll tell you all about it."

"The van is waiting," said Nabuko. "I got one room for the two of us. I hope that will be ok."

"That will be fine, my dear," said Les, taking Nabuko's hand. "Let's go."

The two walked toward the front door, to the waiting van. They would have much to share tonight. What they might gain from the sharing was up to them.

CHAPTER 28

Serena clung to the bars, gasping for air amidst the sulfurous smoke. Her lungs burned and she was beginning to cough up blood. She had been lowered about ten feet during the past hour, and now the bottom of the cage was about level with the edge of the pit.

The cage itself, especially the bottom had become exceptionally hot. Her bare feet were scarred by its terrible touch, and the state of her dehydration was causing her body to overheat. No, it was not the equal of the terrible pains of Hell, but it was about as close to them as this world could provide.

Amidst her suffering she prayed. "Lord, don't let me seem to have lived in vain," she gasped. "You gave me life again. I gladly give it back to you."

Through it all, Satan watched intently. Indeed, he was in his glory. "Was it worth it, Serena?" he asked. "Were all of your years of reaching out to the lost worth this?"

Serena looked toward Satan. She could no longer see him clearly. "Yes, it was worth it," she gasped. "And I'd do it again. I'd do it a thousand times. To deprive you of so many souls, it was worth it. I've won. Admit it, I've won. And you hate me for it."

"Should I lower her still further my lord?" asked one of the demons.

"No," said Satan. "She will suffer longer, more exquisitely, if she remains right there. I want this moment to last. I want to wring the life out of her slowly. I want her to pay. And when I'm done with her, I'll do her pathetic excuse for a husband."

"You should know all about pathetic," said Chris.

Satan turned to Chris and laughed. "Your time is coming, I promise you."

From the corridor, one of the security guards summoned Lielani. She drew back into the darkness.

"Ma'am, I fear that something is amiss," he said. "We have been unable to make contact with our sentries at the fusion power plant. Another patrol reported that the scientists had left the resort and were trying to make their way up to building one. They were ordered to round them up and confine them to their quarters. We haven't heard from them since."

"How long ago?" asked Lielani.

"The sentries at the fusion plant missed their hourly report nearly an hour ago. The other report, the one regarding the scientists was 43 minutes ago. There was even a report of shots being fired."

"And you're only coming to me now?" said Lielani, anger in her voice.

"Ma'am, over half of our security personnel left for Europe through the ring this morning. We're working with a skeleton crew," said the officer.

"We either have our scientists in revolt, or we have uninvited guests on our island," said Lielani. "Contact our main security office in Paris; inform them of our situation. I want 20 armed security people on this island within the hour. Tell them we are looking at possible hostile forces on our island. Now, move."

The officer quickly departed, and Lielani returned to the chamber. She was not about to inform the master. Not now, not in his moment of glory. She would see to this problem herself.

Bedillia, Leland Senior, and Krissie had reached the perimeter fence surrounding the compound. Unfortunately the area beyond here was illuminated by security lights. This was the tricky part of the plan. Leland took the wire cutters and began to cut their way through the fence. It would be better than a one hundred yard run across open country to reach any cover. Bedillia was amazed that they hadn't encountered any further resistance. She'd seen a single sentry by the chapel door about ten minutes ago, but now he was gone. Perhaps the security was lighter than they had at first thought. If only they were so lucky.

But they had another problem; Bedillia was beginning to feel ill and achy. The others were beginning to feel it too. Tesla had said that this would be the first sign of cohesive deterioration. They didn't have much time.

"That's it," announced Leland Senior, "we're through." He tossed the pieces of fence to the side.

They were about to take off across the open field when they heard the sound of a vehicle engine. They dropped into the high weeds.

It was less than 20 seconds later when two jeeps with four heavily armed security guards each shot past on the road, 80 feet away, at high speed. They were on their way toward the resort and the science facility.

Immediately Bedillia went for her communicator. "Tom, can you copy?"

A second later she heard his voice. He had only just returned from New Zealand. Now he would have to face eight armed security guards on his own. Should he try to hold the building, cover their escape, or retreat into the woods?

On this mission, Bedillia's word was final. She ordered Tom to retreat into the woods. Lusan's people knew something was going on. Right now they didn't know what. The team would need to remain invisible for as long as possible. Tom complied. He would wait in the woods until further orders. Perhaps the security forces were spread thin. Perhaps they wouldn't choose to occupy the science facility.

Now Bedillia's team made the run across the open field. Bedillia was thankful for the power suit. She doubted that she could have made very much speed without it. She wondered just how much time she had before her body simply fell apart. "Lord God, give me strength," she whispered.

The team reached the shadows of one of the dormitories. They moved cautiously forward until Bedillia could see the front entrance to the chapel. She ducked back quickly. Then she turned to the others. "There is a guard at the door," she announced. "And it's not just any guard, it's a winged demon. I don't think he saw me."

"Why don't we just blast him?" said Krissie.

"Because we'd lose the element of surprise," said Bedillia. "We lose that, it's all over. Satan will kill the prisoners."

"So, what do we do?" asked Leland Senior. "Our time is running out."

"We wait," said Bedillia. "I feel like I'm being told to wait. Trust me on this one."

"OK," said Krissie, "but I'm feeling worse by the minute. If we wait too long, we won't be able to pull this thing off."

Bedillia didn't need anyone to tell her that. She didn't know how much longer she would be able to hold out either. Still that voice within pleaded for her to wait. She would follow its leading.

Yet in the distance, she heard the unmistakable sound of a particle beam blast, then another. Their element of surprise was gone.

Lielani slipped back out of the chamber of fire and into the corridor, summoned by the radio on her belt. The news was bad. One of the patrols had found the bodies of two of their fellows, both dead. And now, from the woods just beyond building one, they were under fire. But it wasn't just any sort of weapon; it was a beam weapon of a type they knew only too well. The last time any of them had seen it was during the great war in Heaven. They were being invaded, but not by any Earthly force. These invaders were from beyond, most likely saints from Heaven. They were in serious trouble. Lielani had to tell the master.

By now the cage containing Serena had been dropped to within ten feet of the black maelstrom. The flames were licking at her heels, yet she was too weak to move. Serena turned her head, blood oozing from the side of her mouth. "I want my mommy," she gasped, tears flowing from her eyes. Then she collapsed as far as was possible within the cage. Satan eyed her over carefully. Yes, she was still breathing, but the entertainment was almost certainly coming to a close.

Chris was on his knees, weeping bitterly. He had never imagined it coming to this. How could he live without Serena? The answer was that he wouldn't, at least not long.

It was then that Lielani broke the news to her master. He was positively livid. "Always interruptions," he raved. "No, I shall see her last breath, but I will not rush it, I will not be deprived! Raise the cage, move it off to the side for the moment. We will allow Serena to regain a bit of her strength, then continue later."

Satan and Lielani departed even as Serena was raised once more from the pit and moved to the side. A moment later, the cage had been set down at the edge of the pit. Still Serena barely responded.

The physical body of Krissie walked over to Leland. She smiled at her former husband. "I'm looking forward to seeing you in that cage, my love. It will be just so thrilling."

Leland was leaning against the back wall. He looked into Krissie's eyes. "You'll never live to see it."

Krissie continued to taunt him, but he wouldn't respond. It was an attitude that made her all the more belligerent. He just didn't seem interested in listening to her.

From the shadows of the dormitory, Bedillia looked on in amazement as Satan and his entourage emerged from the chapel. He didn't appear to be in a good mood. She found it difficult to resist the temptation of taking him out here and now. Yes, it was a long shot, but she'd made tougher ones. No, she couldn't; she'd stick with the plan. A minute later, the coast was clear. She felt the compelling urge to head out. The team was on the move.

They were somewhat amazed to find the chapel door unlocked and even more amazed to find the door to the inner sanctum ajar. No, this was just too easy. Could Satan really be that stupid? When he was angry, he certainly could. The team moved on through the chapel door.

Bedillia turned to the open air, reaching out with her mind. A minute later 18 ACs entered the chapel. Bedillia locked the door from the inside. Then she thought better of that decision. She unlocked the door, leaving it just as it was. Then they made their way through the great inner door and down into the depths.

They moved silently, yet their strength was failing them. They reached the branch in the tunnel, taking the left route. The smell was growing ever stronger, the smell of a sea only found in Hell.

They made their final plans. This was their ultimate goal. They could not falter now.

Within the terrible chamber, Leland rose to his feet and approached the bars of his cell. He gazed into Krissie's eyes. "The moment of deliverance is at hand, wife."

A fraction of a second later, a particle weapon beam hit one of the two demonic guards, tossing what was left of him back into the infernal pit. It erupted with flaming fury as it accepted yet another sacrifice.

Then the real Krissie burst into the room to encounter herself. She rushed headlong into her, pushing her against the bars of Leland's cell. Immediately Leland wrapped his arms around her, trapping her between the two people who most wanted the body freed of this demon.

The ACs lit into the other demon viciously. He tried to defend himself, but it was a futile effort. His adversaries were far too fast and numerous. Yet it was Bedillia who dealt the final blow. Drawing out her dagger, she plunged it into the demon's chest and then pushed him backward. He too plunged into the now flaming maelstrom. For a minute he flailed around wildly. Then he sank quietly into the depths.

On the other side of the chamber, Leland Senior had joined in the family circle about the possessed body of Krissie. A family circle encompassing a full century prayed together.

"Demon, we cast you out in the name of Jesus," commanded Leland Senior. "You have no place in this woman."

The others in the circle agreed. Then there came the terrible shriek from the woman in the center. A green glowing mist seemed to rise from her even as a gentle, white glow passed from the one Krissie to the other.

Both Lelands felt Krissie's hand grow limp; then she was gone. All that remained was her black power suit and her equipment, but she was gone. The other Krissie looked into Leland's eyes; tears appeared in hers. She embraced him. There were tears of joy all around as the family was truly united.

The ACs had now gone to work on the bars of Serena's cage and on the bars of the cells. A moment later, Bedillia pulled her daughter from her cage and laid her on the floor. For a time, Serena lay motionless; then she opened her eyes.

"Mommy?" she said in a quiet voice.

"Yes sweetie, it's me," said Bedillia, going for her canteen. "Here drink this."

Bedillia helped Serena raise her head and take a sip of the water. Serena took a few gulps before coughing up a grotesque mixture of partially clotted blood. She seemed to be struggling for every breath.

"I knew you'd come," said Serena. "When I was in that cage I cried for you. Now, here you are."

By now, the ACs had eaten away the lock upon Chris's cell. Chris rushed to Serena's side.

"Hello, Chris," gasped Serena. "See, she came, my mommy came."

Tears were streaming from Chris's eyes. "Yes, she came."

One of the ACs landed on Serena's shoulder. She looked over at him. Somehow she recognized him. "Hello, you," she gasped. "I've missed you."

The AC seemed so sad. He nodded and then rubbed up against her affectionately.

Now Leland also was free, joining the circle about Serena with his wife and Leland Senior. He looked at her closely. He shook his head, but said nothing.

"We need to get her out of here," said Krissie.

"I'm not so sure we can move her," said Chris.

For a moment Bedillia turned away, holding her hand to her right ear. "It's Tom. He made it back to the ring. He'll try and cover us from there." Bedillia paused. "He got one of their radios and has been listening in on them. Satan has just brought a bunch of reinforcements through the gate on the other side of the island. Tom is not sure how many. But if we're going to move, it's got to be now, while they're still getting organized."

"So, what do we do?" asked Leland Senior.

Bedillia glanced at her watch. "We can't wait. It will be almost another nine hours before we can expect any help, and that's assuming that the main gate doesn't get captured or disabled. We have to go now." She turned to Leland and Chris. "Get some water from the canteens; you'll need it."

Bedillia turned back to her daughter. "We're going to get you out of here, sweetheart. I promise."

"No, I don't think so," gasped Serena. "You need to leave me behind. I'll just slow you down."

"Don't talk that way, dear," said Bedillia, stroking her daughter's forehead. "I came all the way from Hell to rescue you. I'm not leaving you behind now. I'll carry you myself if I have to."

"No, I'll carry her," said Leland Senior.

Krissie picked up her power suit. She'd have to put it on all over again. Examining it, she discovered that there was not so much as a trace of her previous body to be found. The whole concept gave her chills. She was also thankful to be free of that sick, feverish feeling that had plagued her for the past hour or so. Then the realization hit her. "Bedillia, how are you feeling?"

"Not too bad," was the reply. "Not much worse."

She turned to Leland Senior. "What about you?"

"I've felt better," he said.

"What's going on?" asked Chris. "Why should they be sick?"

"Because there was a danger that our bodies wouldn't adapt or something like that," said Krissie. "I feel fine now, but we need to get Bedillia and Leland Senior back to Refuge, and soon. They can't survive on Earth for very much longer. If they die here, their spirits could be lost forever."

Serena's eyes grew big. "Mommy, you came here to save me even though you knew it could be the end of you?"

Bedillia nodded. "You're my daughter, Serena. I would give up anything to save you. But I'm not going to die here. We're all going to get out of here. The four of you are going to New Zealand, and the rest of us will be heading back to Refuge. We have a lot of work to do."

"You mean going back to Hell," said Serena.

"Yes, dear, it's where we belong." Bedillia unholstered her particle pistol and handed it to Chris. "Your good friend, Nikola Tesla, developed this weapon for us. Here you will probably need this. The power setting is here on the left side, the safety on the right. It's all set; just release the safety and pull the trigger. This model should give you about ten rounds before reloading. I have plenty of ammo for it."

"Even if we're all armed, there is a lot of open country to cross to get to the ring," said Leland Senior. "Just getting to the other side of that fence is going to be a challenge."

"We can't stay here and hope to hold out until the cavalry arrives," said Bedillia. "If we've got to fight them. I'd rather that it be on the outside, not here."

"Makes sense," confirmed Chris.

"So, what are we doing?" said Krissie, who again was wearing her powered armor. "Maybe I should carry Serena. I think I'm feeling better than anyone else here. Anyway, this suit will make her seem very light."

"I say we wait," said Leland, stepping forward. "Satan doesn't know what's just happened down here. He doesn't realize we've been rescued."

The others stood there silently.

"Well, don't you see?" continued Leland. "He'll come down here planning to finish what he started. If we could pop him right here, destroy him, this whole plan of his would fall apart. Maybe we could rewrite future history."

"How could we possibly do that?" objected Chris. "What is going to happen in the last days is recorded in the Book of Revelation. It doesn't say that Satan gets blasted into a billion pieces by a Tesla death ray. After tonight, after what he did to my Serena, nothing would make me happier, but I don't think we can get away with it. It's just not in the book."

"Maybe not, but I'm up to trying," said Krissie.

"I still don't think that's such a good idea," objected Chris. "If we get trapped in here, there is no way we could hold out. There's only one way out of this place."

"No, that's not true," said Krissie. "The demon who occupied my body knew another way out of here, and now, so do I. There is a whole network of caverns beneath this island. One of them leads to a cave by the sea, just below the building where the ring is. It's difficult, but we could do this. At least we should try. Maybe we can buy this world more time. I could sure use it."

"But we need to get Serena to a hospital and quickly," objected Bedillia. "I'm not willing to sacrifice my daughter's life for some crazy plan."

"Mommy, I'm going to die anyway," gasped Serena. "Maybe we should try Leland's plan."

"No, don't talk like that, dear," insisted Bedillia. "You're going to make it."

"You seem to be sensitive to the Spirit of God," said Chris, turning to Leland. "You've been right so far. Now, tell me truthfully, are you really that sure we should stay here and do this, or are you just looking for revenge?"

"I won't deny that I'd like some payback," admitted Leland. "Lord, forgive me, but it's true. But I also know we need to stay. Call the rest wishful thinking if you like. If things start to go bad, we can always try the caverns."

Bedillia hesitated. She figured that they wouldn't have much of a chance crossing that open field. It was well lit and in a direct line of sight with the other ring. Their odds of success were indeed slim. "Krissie, are you positive you can find your way through those caverns?"

"I'm positive," confirmed Krissie. "I also know that there are very few of the demons who know it as well as my demon did. It will take hours, but we can make it."

Bedillia pondered their options. She really didn't see any others. She prayed that her daughter could survive that long. "OK, we stay."

They came up with a game plan. There were so many things that could go wrong, but it was their best hope. Bedillia told Tom to withdraw from the building housing the ring. He should make his way through the forest toward the beach. Krissie told him just where the cave was. It was well hidden and not easily accessible. It would be particularly difficult to find at night.

Strangely, Tom's symptoms were not nearly so bad as Bedillia's or Leland Senior's. He wasn't feeling quite himself, but it hadn't slowed him down. It was an effect for which Bedillia had no explanation.

Now, all that they could do was to wait. They didn't have to wait long. Scarcely ten minutes later, they heard footfalls upon the steps above. They took their positions. The footfalls grew louder.

"Serena," called a voice from down the corridor. "Are you ready for the finale? It is time to bring an end to this thing called your life."

Yes, it was Satan's voice all right. Bedillia took aim at the point where the corridor met the chamber. She might have only one shot at this; she couldn't blow it. She'd dreamed of a moment like this for years, but she'd hardly believed that the opportunity would ever present itself. Now here it was.

Bedillia saw an advancing shadow on the wall. Then Lielani stepped from the shadows. No, this was all wrong, what could she do. She fired.

Lielani literally never knew what hit her. She exploded into a cloud of red vapor as shattered and burned body parts scattered for 20 feet around.

Bedillia didn't think twice. She rushed headlong toward the corridor. A large demon stepped into her way, drawing his sword. It barely cleared the scabbard before he was cut down by the pistol wielded by Chris. Apparently he had set the pistol at a low power setting. It merely blew a football-sized hole through the beast's chest.

For a second the dark warrior looked in shock at the gaping hole that penetrated his entire body, leaving a web of sizzling connective tissue around the periphery of the wound. Then he collapsed forward.

Bedillia leaped over his quivering body, propelled by the artificial strength commanded by her own deteriorating muscles. Before her she saw a single dark figure in a flight of panic. It was Satan. She wondered if he had ever fled in panic from a mere human. The ACs swarmed past Bedillia, attracted by the greatest evil in the universe, prepared to serve the function for which they were created.

Satan stumbled around a corner and up the stairs even as several of the ACs lit into him viciously. He screamed for his guards. Bedillia wondered if she would encounter any guards along the way. Right now she still didn't have a shot at her primary target. She had to move faster.

She heard footfalls behind her. She was sure it was Krissie. Between the two of them, surely they would have him.

Satan burst through the huge brass doors at the top of the stairs. It was but a matter of about six or seven seconds before Bedillia emerged into the chapel to see Satan almost to the outer door, several ACs swarming around him. Here, too, were two armed guards standing on either side of the door with menacing looking military-style rifles. Bedillia's heart sank. They took aim and fired even as several ACs lit into them as well.

Bedillia had taken half a dozen rounds before she could react. The rounds hadn't penetrated the armor of her suit, but the tremendous force of the impacts was very painful. She fired, but missed the guard to the left. Still the blast of the weapon ripped a gaping hole in the wall.

She stumbled forward and to the side, taking another shot. This one hit its mark, destroying her foe beyond recognition. Yet the other continued to fire, even with five ACs attacking him. Her left knee stiffened up. He'd hit a critical microcircuit. She fell to the floor.

The guard stumbled toward her, but he didn't get far. A powerful beam of high energy particles from Krissie's rifle dismembered him.

Bedillia looked toward the open door. She could see Satan's dark form fleeing in the distance, amidst a swarm of attacking creatures.

"No, you don't!" she cried. "You're not getting away from me." With all of her strength she struggled to get to her feet. Krissie grabbed her arm and pulled her forward. She was on the move again. Now she was at the door. Over a dozen security guards and demons caught her eye. Several of the demons were in flight, closing in on her. She blotted them all out of her thoughts. To her, there was only one figure out there. She took aim.

Krissie fired again, taking out a demon in flight, who, in but another few seconds would have been upon them. All the while Bedillia centered on her quarry. He was so far away. She'd have but one shot. It had to count. She squeezed back on the trigger. The weapon erupted with a loud report and a beam like fire. Her target was blasted violently to the left amidst an eruption of blood.

"I got you!" she cried.

He flailed wildly like a fish that had been hooked by the expert angler and now flopped around upon the bottom of his boat. He tried to crawl away, but he seemed stunned, disoriented. All the while, he suffered under the relentless tormenting of the creatures.

Bedillia took aim for a second shot. "One more and it's all over, Slewfoot," she said. "One more and your world, you ambitions, your empire comes to an end."

"Fireballs!" cried Krissie.

Bedillia saw their red glow, but she didn't waver. She took her shot.

Krissie pushed her out of the way, behind the last pew at the back of this unholy sanctuary. A fraction of a second later a raging firestorm of three fiery projectiles rained in on them. Krissie tried to shield Bedillia amidst a heat like that of a blast furnace. Had it not been for the protective qualities of their suits and the fact that the fireballs had exploded on the far side of the room, they would surely have perished.

"I'm sure I got him," said Bedillia, crawling from the smoking rubble. "I must have."

"Is that all you can think about? Come on," urged Krissie. "We can't stay here."

The two women retreated toward the inner door amidst the intense flames that roared about them. Krissie covered Bedillia's retreat, firing several particle beam blasts behind them.

They literally stumbled down the stairway. They had just completed the first turn when Bedillia turned and fired two blasts into the ceiling about thirty feet behind them. The ceiling collapsed amidst a cloud of billowing dust.

"That should slow them down," said Bedillia, continuing on down the corridor, fighting with her failing power suit. It was at the fork in the tunnel that they met the others. Chris held his wife in his arms.

"I got him," said Bedillia, in a breathless and pained voice. She looked toward Serena, but there was no response.

"She's passed out," said Chris, turning to Krissie. "It's up to you now. Take us out of here."

Krissie took the lead as Bedillia filled the rest in on what had happened. They wondered if they could be so fortunate.

They passed through the cavern room where so many unfortunates had met a terrible fate, giving up their bodies to a dreadful demon. On the far side there were a series of tunnels fanning out in different directions. Krissie led the way through one that sloped steeply downward. She drew out her crystalline flashlight so as to see her way through the growing darkness.

It was a rough and apparently seldom used route. The floor was littered with rocks, and at places, it was a tight fit. It was especially tough going for Chris and Leland, who were walking barefoot. This place seemed like an impossible maze. Chris only hoped that Krissie knew where she was going.

*

CHAPTER 29

Satan cried out in agony as his minions gathered about him, scattering his small tormentors. He'd been indeed fortunate. The beam of the particle weapon had barely grazed his left arm. However, the resulting cellular disruption had been far more widespread, rendering his arm practically useless, capable only of producing wave after wave of searing pain.

Satan's second in command, Governor Molock, had just come through the ring and now examined the injury. Like many of the others about him, he was in human form.

"My lord, you were most fortunate. This injury will heal, but not as quickly as it would in your kingdom. It may take a week for regeneration to become complete. In the meantime, you will likely be in considerable pain. May I suggest that we take you to the infirmary and administer to you something for that pain? I understand that the humans have a number of effective potions."

"I will not submit myself to any human contrived medications," roared Satan. "It will not only dull my physical senses, but my reason as well."

"Please, my lord, it is for your own good," insisted Molock. "I do not wish to see you suffer. I am here. I shall lead our forces. You know that you can depend on me."

"He is right, my lord," said Duras, standing at Molock's side. "Please, my lord, I do not wish to see you suffer needlessly."

"Very well," replied Satan, "but I want these intruders caught and executed. From the weapons they wield, I assume that they are saints from Heaven, perhaps members of Johann Kepler's group. Only they would be so bold as to do this. But now they are here on Earth. They are fair game."

"But why would they come here?" asked Molock. "Why did not the Father send His angels if He wished to rescue this wench, Serena Davis?"

"How should I know?" roared Satan. "Just get them. And destroy that ring the scientists built. If they did use it to come to this place, I shall cut off their escape route here and now. Use fireballs, RPGs, C4, whatever it takes, just do it."

"I shall, my lord," confirmed Molock.

Satan was assisted to the infirmary by Duras and another of his minions. Molock looked toward the building on the hilltop, illuminated by the rising moon. As the Earth had rotated away from the comet fragments, the meteor storm had waned to just a few sporadic bright streaks every minute. Only the great main body of Comet Florence remained, its foreshortened tail stretching off to the northwest. It was like some great celestial finger pointing to the world that would soon feel the wrath of God. Its brilliance rivaled that of the moon. Its presence reminded Molock that his time was limited. He needed to complete this operation by early tomorrow afternoon. He didn't want to be around when the predicted tsunami wave swept over this tiny island.

Yet even as Molock contemplated his next move, the ring in research building one filled once more with glowing mists. From its depths stepped a dark angel, then another and another. After a minute, 12 of the dark beings and 300 ACs gathered before the ring. The one in the lead pulled a communications device from his belt.

"This is Abaddon calling rescue team. Speak to me."

"Abaddon, I'm sure glad to hear your voice," was the reply. "This is Tom Carson."

It took but a few minutes for Tom to apprise Abaddon of the situation. The rescue mission had succeeded. They had Serena and the rest, but the rescue team had become trapped. They had been forced to return by some subterranean route. They were too far underground for him to communicate with them. Still, he knew that they were sick, and their condition was growing worse by the minute. Up until now he seemed to have fared better than the rest, though he could not explain why, nor did he know how long that would last.

As Abaddon turned from the radio his heart was filled with uncertainty. "Our mission just became considerably more complicated," he lamented. "It will not be the quick round trip I had hoped it would be."

"So, what shall we do?" asked Lenar.

"We wait," replied Abaddon. "We wait until we are in contact with Bedillia and the others once more. Until then, we guard this ring." Adaddon's force took up defensive positions.

"It's official. The main body of Comet Florence is going to impact the moon in a glancing blow somewhere in the Sea of Serenity," announced Dr. Mayfield. "This impact will occur just three hours after the remnants of Florence C strike Earth."

The scientists within the lecture hall had been prepared for this news; still, it hit them hard. Somehow, they'd been hoping for a miracle. No one knew what the implications of such a lunar impact would be. The moon hadn't experienced an impact event of this magnitude since the creation of the crater Tycho a hundred million years ago. How would it affect Earth? Would the Earth be pelted by still more space debris, this time from the moon? They were about to find out.

"At least Florence B will miss us by better than a thousand kilometers," continued Mayfield. "Still we've already lost three geostationary satellites to the bombardment of smaller particles, and we will lose more, perhaps all. The nuclear barrage orchestrated by the military is our planet's last line of defense."

"I still fear that mission is doomed to failure," said Sam Florence. "Those missiles are going to have to run a gauntlet of millions of high speed projectiles traveling along with the larger comet fragments. I'm afraid all we'll manage to do is make matters worse."

"You'd prefer we did nothing?" asked Mayfield.

"I don't know," admitted Sam. "I hope you're right, I really do."

"We're a bit over nine hours to the first launch," noted Mayfield, "about ten hour after that, I suppose we'll know."

As Sam Florence left the meeting, he was indeed troubled. So much was happening so fast. He'd been trying to get in contact with Chris and Serena for days, but had been unable. Then two days ago they were no shows at the big crusade in St. Louis. Their abandoned RV had been discovered along the shoulder of a back road in central Illinois. Since then an exhaustive search for the popular evangelists had turned up nothing. It was as if they had fallen off the face of the Earth.

Sam had a real bad feeling about it all. There were a lot of people out there praying for their safe return. They had given so many downtrodden and frightened souls new hope. But would all of their prayers be enough? Perhaps by tomorrow, hope, like the blue sky overhead, would vanish into the darkness of an unprecedented global catastrophe. He prayed that he was wrong.

It was shortly after midnight local time when the last of Satan's new troops stepped through the ring on the rocky hill at the south. Some took the form of heavily armed humans. Most of these were demon-possessed humans or demons who had gained human bodies through the rite of union. Others were winged demons in physical form.

Satan hadn't been seen since he had headed off to the infirmary an hour ago, and for the moment, Governor Molock was calling the shots. Molock made no claims of being a military leader. That honor had always fallen to General Krell. Still, he prided himself on having a clear and methodical mind. He wouldn't approach this operation like a bull in a china shop, sending the troops out into the jungle and firing at whatever moved. That might be the master's way, but it wasn't his. He would gather the facts first.

"My lord Molock, we have cleared the tunnel below the chapel of rubble," reported one of his lieutenants, a very human-appearing warrior. "But we have found no sign of Serena or those who rescued her. Those familiar with that area tell me that there are natural caves under the entire island. Some lead to other exits along the shoreline. They have to have followed one of those natural tunnels. I've dispatched warriors to search the tunnels for them."

"Very good," said Molock. "Do we know who they are, these rescuers?"

"No, my lord," replied the warrior. "All of those who have gotten close enough to identify them have perished. But, from their weapons, we know that they are not local. They are either saints from Heaven or warriors from the place called Refuge, in Hell."

"That's a thought," noted Molock. "I find it far more likely that they would be Abaddon's people rather than Kepler's. But how would they get here? Humans in Hell are unable to leave Outer Darkness in physical form."

"Perhaps that has changed," suggested the lieutenant. "They are quite resourceful."

"They are," confirmed Molock. "Here is what I would have you do; send a team of eight up to the building-housing ring. Select them personally. They are to exercise extreme caution. We don't know who or how many hostiles we are dealing with. I don't wish to lose still more of our people in a foolish expedition. They are to scout out the land, attach an explosive device to the ring, detonate it, and return."

"It shall be as you command," said the lieutenant, bowing slightly.

Molock took a pair of binoculars and scanned the area around building one carefully. He didn't see anyone. He hoped that was an indication that they were dealing with a relatively small force and not a well-hidden, larger one.

Within ten minutes, the lieutenant was leading an all demon force toward building one, spreading out across the jungle rather than following the road. Little did he realize that Abaddon had adopted a similar strategy and had scattered his limited forces into a defense perimeter surrounding the building and their only easily accessible route back.

The dark angel Lenar had moved out a bit further from the building than most of his fellows. He sat crouched among some bushes scanning the dimly moonlit scene. It was nearly two in the morning, and he was getting anxious to pull out. In but another seven hours, he would be accompanying a force of over three million ACs that would stream out of the ring in Lusan's headquarters in Paris. In reality, he was very much looking forward to it.

He was actually amazed that the growing army of Satan's minions down there in the valley had not made their way back up here. Perhaps he and the team would get out of here without a fight. Now wouldn't that be just too bad?

His sensitive hearing detected the sound of soft footfalls on leaves. He directed his attention toward the growing sound. He pulled out his radio. "We have company," he whispered, "coming up through the jungle."

Then he saw them, two winged demons. He drew his sword. It was show time.

They saw him just seconds before he was upon them. The demon in the lead barely had time to raise his sword before the dark angel's sword swept toward him. The blades clashed, and the force of that clash threw him to the ground.

Lenar immediately went for the second demon. The crossing of their power endowed swords again and again filled the jungle with flashes of illumination.

Lenar kicked the first demon back to the ground even as he thrust his sword at the second. His agility and strength were superhuman. He was a being created by the Father for combat; these demons were not. Though he was outnumbered two to one, it was he that was on the offensive.

The first demon screamed in a shrill voice as Lenar's sword was thrust into his side through an opening in the unseen armor beneath his cloak. At least it was unseen to the human eye, but Lenar knew exactly where to strike. Then he withdrew the sword again and swung it with unbelievable speed, cutting across the demon's throat. His body and head parted company. Now Lenar could concentrate on his one remaining adversary; but alas, he had already fled into the jungle.

"Coward," cursed Lenar, though he doubted that the demon took note of his insult.

It was but a moment later that two other dark angels arrived to offer assistance. The presence of the decapitated demon told them that they had missed out on the fight.

"Rank amateurs," said Lenar, kicking the disembodied head to one side. "You would think that, after several thousand years, their fighting skills would have improved at least a little bit."

"And there won't be any rapid regenerating for the demons here, not on Earth," noted another dark angel. "It gives us a distinct advantage."

"Almost too easy," noted the other.

"Let us make sure that they don't attempt to flank us," said Lenar. "We need to protect that ring until the humans reach us."

"If they reach us," said another.

"Think positively," urged Lenar. "I know Bedillia well. She will bring those captives out."

The dark angels spread out once more, leaving Lenar alone with his thoughts. He suspected that the demons would try a second attack, perhaps from the air. But as the minutes passed, nothing was happening.

An hour had passed when the sky was lit in amber luminance as a fireball hurtled overhead. It struck the forest near the building housing the ring. Then came another, and another. Satan's forces were trying a different approach, an aerial bombardment.

"I should have anticipated this," Lenar said, as he went once more for his radio. "My friends, we must take wings and stop them," he cried.

Seconds later, Lenar had taken flight. From the air he could see the others bursting forth from the forest, and ahead of him, an armada of demons, 50 or more of them, preparing to launch fireballs.

Another fireball roared past Lenar to his left. He spun around and drew his sword. From its tip a beam of bright blue light erupted. It was like a bolt of lightning. It hit the fireball and detonated it in midair. Then Lenar turned his sword toward the gathered demons. He discharged a second bolt, narrowly missing one of his adversaries. He fired again, this time hitting his mark. The demon tumbled toward the forest below.

Lenar was astonished. He had fired three lightning bolts in rapid succession. Normally he could summon up only one or two of these potent weapons without resting. He should have been exhausted, but he wasn't. Then he realized why. He and his fellows had been restored to God's grace. Now they were able to pull strength from the vast well of power that was God's Holy Spirit. He felt like he might be able to throw several more bolts before expending his strength. It was a source of strength that only they possessed. Still, they were badly outnumbered.

Clearly, the dark angels were on the defensive. They did their best to take down demons and detonate fireballs. But some of the fireballs were getting through.

Lenar was surprised when several fireballs seemed to detonate on their own just seconds before hitting the building housing the ring. At first he was puzzled, and then he understood the terrible truth. It was the ACs. They had moved into the path of the fireball in an attempt to detonate it before it did any damage. Their selfless determination might just have preserved their route home.

Another group of over a hundred of the tiny creatures swept past, just below him, on their way to engage the demonic forces. Their presence here was becoming a real blessing, perhaps the pivotal element in the battle.

Then a brilliant beam of energy erupted from the forest below, striking a demon and scattering his body parts across a vast area. Apparently, Tom had joined the struggle.

Several fireballs were projected in the general direction from which the particle beam blast had erupted. A second later, another beam shot forth, barely missing yet another demon. This resulted in the launch of a second volley of fireballs toward the dense forest. This volley was not answered.

For several minutes the heavens were ablaze with angelic and demonic weapons, yet in the end, both sides were exhausted. The angelic warfare now entered its second phase, sword to sword combat.

Lenar realized that this was a risky proposition. They were badly outnumbered. Still, he saw no other option. His blood was pumping. He was doing the thing he was created for. It was almost instinctual. Then again, they weren't alone in this, were they? From the chaos that he could discern among the demonic ranks, he already deduced that the ACs were busy.

Yet before his meager forces could clash with the demons, three more particle beam blasts erupted from the ground—from a different location. One found its mark. It was an action that further confused the advancing demonic force. Members within it began to scatter. And with the confusion came opportunity.

The dark angels engaged their sworn enemies 500 feet above the jungle. The fires below illuminated their struggle.

Below, Tom was constantly on the move. Taking a few shots when he could, then moving to a new location to keep the demons from zeroing in on his position. Yet he was trying to work his way back toward the ring, which was being guarded by a lone dark angel.

From the ground, Satan watched the battle in amazement. His arm was wrapped in gauze bandages, and he appeared to still be in considerable pain. "So, there are angels here as well," he said.

"Yes," confirmed Molock, "dark angels."

"Dark angels! Then where have these warriors come from?" asked Satan.

"Presumably from your old kingdom, my lord," said Molock.

"I shall get to the bottom of this," swore Satan. "In my absence, things have gotten out of hand. I swear this shall not continue." There was a pause. "And it was one of your followers that allowed all of this to happen, one named Cordon. You appointed him as interim governor of your region when we left for the war. Then he rose in power to become the lord of all Hell. I've heard about the mess he made. He made peace with the dark angels and with the humans. He had the audacity to change the order of things, an order that I myself established. He might even have intentionally cut off our escape route during the war in Heaven. Even now, he plots against me."

Molock was stunned. He didn't know what to say.

"Now he is trying to take Serena from me, too," said Satan, in a rambling and slightly slurred voice. "Here is what you shall do, Molock, and hear me well. You will destroy these abominations. Make sure that none escape me. And when it is all done, bring me the head of Serena Davis."

"Her head?" asked Molock, "Why?"

"So I can look at it," said Satan. "So I can spit in it and know that I have won. I must have this thing!"

Molock reached to stabilize his monarch, who seemed on the threshold of collapse. "Come, my lord, your servants shall take you through the ring and back to your quarters in Paris. You are not well; you need to rest. I shall see to it all."

Satan nodded and went with his escorts toward the ring. A moment later, they vanished into its foggy depths.

Molock just shook his head. "What a mess."

Overhead, the battle continued. It was nearly an hour before both sides mutually disengaged. This battle would not enter the classical third stage of sword to sword combat on the ground.

Lenar returned to the ground to find the building within which the ring was housed severely damaged. Across the island, fires still burned, though there was insufficient dry fuel to support the fires for very long. Within the building, he found Tom with his flashlight, examining some instrumentation that was currently partially buried under a pile of rubble against the near wall. He rose to his feet and shook his head.

"None of the fireballs did any real damage other than this one," said Tom. "They seemed to have concentrated their fire on the fusion power plant. Our power supply, the one that will provide the juice to get us home, is buried under there. We'll need to clear the rubble. Maybe, if we're lucky, it's only a snapped cable. If so, I could reattach the power supply further up the trunk cables."

"How long would that take?" asked Lenar.

"A few hours," was the reply. "But if the power supply itself is damaged, we're sunk. We only have the one, and I don't have any spare parts."

Lenar stepped forward, picking up a 100 pound block of rubble and tossed it to the side. "Let's get to it then. The sooner we get this rubble moved, the sooner we'll know."

Two other dark angels joined in the task, tossing blocks that a normal human would find difficult to handle. One way or another, they would soon know the fate of their rescue mission.

Krissie and the others stumbled through the narrow, dark tunnels. Sometimes they waded through shallow water and at other times squeezed through narrow spaces. Twice now they had to double back 100 feet or so after coming to a dead end. She'd begun to realize that seeing these tunnels through the ethereal vision of a demonic spirit was not quite the same as dealing with the physical reality.

All the while, Bedillia and Leland Senior were growing weaker. Were it not for their power suits, they might not have been able to walk at all, and Bedillia's power suit was only partially functional.

Serena faded in and out of consciousness, occasionally coughing up a foul mixture of blood and other fluids. She seemed to be getting worse.

Leland and Leland Senior walked together, exchanging stories, reaching across the generations. If only they had more time.

Once more, they had reached a fork in the tunnel. Krissie stopped. Right now she didn't know which way to turn. She couldn't make another mistake. It was her confidence and determination that had brought them down here. Might she have been too confident? She prayed for guidance.

It was only then that a flash of light caught her eye, a flash of light from the right branch of the tunnel. She focused upon it. There it was again. "We have company," she whispered.

Bedillia drew her weapon, though she hardly had the strength to lift it. The light was growing brighter. Then she saw the beam itself. It reflected off of a pool of water before them, illuminating the whole group.

"Krissie?" said a voice, coming from the light.

"Abaddon?" she said.

The figure quickly approached. It was Abaddon, accompanied by another dark angel.

"Are we glad to see you!" said Bedillia, practically falling into his arms.

Abaddon looked at her with concern. "You don't look so good. We need to get you back to Refuge." Then he saw the young woman in Chris's arms. He slowly approached.

Serena opened her eyes to see a familiar face. "Abaddon, you're really here," she murmured. "You've come to take me home."

"I'm here," said Abaddon, caressing her cheek. His attention turned to Goliath, who sat curled up upon her chest. "It looks like you've found an old friend."

Serena nodded, but said nothing.

Abaddon looked to Chris. "Here, I'll carry her for a while. It will be my pleasure."

Chris nodded and gingerly handed his wife off to Abaddon.

"Like old times," whispered Serena, "being in your arms."

Abaddon nodded. He turned to Krissie. "You've done very well. You almost have them to the exit. Another 10 or 15 minutes and this journey will be over." Abaddon took the lead. They walked through ankle-deep water for about 50 feet; then they began to climb once more. The atmosphere was growing fresher, less claustrophobic. One could smell the salt air. Then they emerged from an almost hidden sea cave about 20 feet above the waves.

The sky was bright. Sunrise couldn't be more than 20 minutes away. Turning, they saw building one just a couple hundred yards away. Their hearts sank when they observed its condition. It had been battered severely by some sort of weapons fire.

They struggled up the hill through a tangle of foliage. At the front door of the facility they encountered Tom. Bedillia practically collapsed into his arms. She was very pale, and her hair was actually starting to fall out.

"We've got to get you home," said Tom, helping her into the main building. "We've had some problems, but it's not as bad as it looks. I think I can fix it. I just need some more time. We'll get you home."

"How are you feeling, Tom?" asked Abaddon.

"Actually, a lot better," said Tom. "Last night, for a time, I was feeling a bit ill, but it passed. Right now I'm just tired and a bit hungry." He hesitated. "I'm thinking about staying."

"Staying?" asked Bedillia.

"Yeah," confirmed Tom. "Here is where the real battle for the future of humanity is going to be fought. I have a lot of skills and knowledge to share. Maybe I can make a difference."

"But you don't know if the sickness will creep up on you," objected Bedillia. "Sure, you feel fine today, but what about tomorrow?"

"Tomorrow will take care of its self," replied Tom. "Don't you see? I have to do this."

Bedillia nodded, but said no more.

"I better get back to work or none of us is going anywhere," said Tom. "Try to get some sleep, OK?"

Abaddon took Bedillia, Serena, and Leland Senior to the control room. They would be more comfortable there.

Tom turned his attention to the banged-up power supply and the makeshift circuit junction he was fashioning. This was going to be iffy. He might be able to open the wormhole, but he couldn't keep it open long.

A winged demonic lieutenant dropped down in front of Molock. He made his report. "My lord, I have seen the extent of the damage to building one and the ring with my own eyes. We did extensive damage. I truly believe that these invaders are now trapped here."

"But you are not certain," deduced Molock.

"Well, no, not certain," was the reply.

"If it were my decision, we would withdraw," said Molock. "There is nothing more to be gained here. In all likelihood, the ring is inoperable and Serena is dead. But it is not my decision." He paused. "We now have about 150 troops on the ground, do we not?"

"One hundred and seventy four, including me," said the lieutenant.

And how many reserves do we have standing by in Paris?"

"An additional 110," replied the lieutenant.

"And how many dark angels are there?" continued Molock.

"We are not sure," admitted the lieutenant, "surely fewer than 15."

"Then this is what we shall do," said Molock. "Bring all of them through the ring and assemble them here in 15 minutes. We are going to stage an all-out attack on the defenders of that building. I want it leveled to the ground. Then we will go through and search this entire island inch by inch, even the caves. Only then will I consider this operation complete."

"My lord," objected the lieutenant, "we only have eight hours to escape the devastation that the comets shall surely bring."

"All the more reason to begin now, wouldn't you think?"

The lieutenant bowed before his master and departed. Molock looked toward the building in question. Even from here he could just make out a dark angel pirouetting on the trade winds above it. It was time to end this thing and get out of here while they still could.

Fifteen minutes found the assault underway. The winged demons, over a hundred in number, took to the sky to resume their fireball barrage. Those who possessed a human by union or by the more conventional method began their advance upon this makeshift fortress on foot. Their orders were simple—to secure that hill within three hours and bring back the bodies they recovered.

"It's no good," lamented Tom, turning from the power supply. "I'm sorry, Abaddon. I can't make it work. There must be more damage to the system than I'd originally thought."

"So what do we do now?" asked Abaddon.

Tom seemed deep in thought. There had to be a solution. Then he happened upon it. "No, no, wait a minute. There was another ring set up on a barren atoll some 20 or so miles to the south of here. Aaron told me about it in a briefing several days ago. I'm sure I could find it. It is almost certainly unguarded at this point. They removed its power supply, but this power supply I brought with me still works. We could hot wire it. It would probably be good for one transport, maybe two, assuming they didn't take any of the other guts out of the unit. It could work."

"We have a massive force approaching, by air and ground," came the warning over Abaddon's radio.

Abaddon turned from his radio and looked toward Tom. "How long would it take you to be ready to leave?"

"Three minutes," replied Tom.

"Very well, keep working," said Abaddon, running toward the control room.

What he saw pierced him to the heart. Serena lay beside her mother, weeping. Both Bedillia and Leland Senior were dead.

"She gave her life to save me," wept Serena. "I wish we'd have had more time."

"They're coming; we've got to go," said Abaddon.

He gently picked up Serena and headed for the door. Leland and Chris followed. Both wore pairs of lab overalls and steel toed shoes they had managed to pick up from a nearby storeroom.

Returning to the main room, they found Tom still busy. He'd opened an access port at the rear of the platform upon which the ring stood.

"We've got to go," warned Abaddon.

"I need a few more minutes," said Tom, working furiously. He looked up but momentarily. "Where's Bedillia; where's Leland?" The silence led him to only one conclusion. "Oh God," he murmured. Tears came to his eyes. "Now I know I need to do this."

"Do what?" asked Abaddon.

"I'm going to leave those demons a little gift to remember us by," said Tom, working all the faster, "though I suspect that memory will be measured in the microseconds."

"A bomb?" asked Chris.

"Oh no," said Tom, anger in his voice, "not just a bomb. I'm going to break some eggs on this one, eggs of the atomic variety."

"A nuclear bomb?" deduced Chris.

"Something like that," said Tom. "I've wrapped eight power cells around the still live field coil of the ring. If they knock out the reserve power to the ring with one of their fireballs, the coil will discharge and this little gem will blow this whole island to Hell, where it belongs. Otherwise, I'll set it to detonate in two hours."

Tom was already zippering up the access plate. Abaddon would give him the time he needed.

set," said Tom. He glanced back at the ring. "This one is for
a."

The group met with their small force of dark angels and ACs at the front door to the facility. "I have asked much of you during this mission. I will need to ask still more," said Abaddon. "I'll carry Serena. Four of you will accompany me, carrying the humans, to an atoll some 20 miles south of here. The rest of you and all but 20 ACs will engage the enemy. Don't take unnecessary risks. You'll need to engage the demon forces for about ten minutes while we get the humans to safety. Then split up. Just get away from the island any way you can. Once you are sure that you are not being followed, turn due south. Meet us at the atoll; we'll wait for you. From there we'll gate back to Refuge."

It took but two minutes for them to get organized. Seven dark angels vaulted straight into the sky, while the others, with their human cargo, flew off to the north. They flew barely above the spray of the ocean at the highest speed they could muster. Then they slowly turned to the west, then the south. They were not detected.

Three miles off to the left, Abaddon witnesses the distant glow of an angelic battle. They placed the battle ever further behind them. He prayed that his fellows and his children would have time to escape before the device that Tom had set out detonated.

It was the better part of an hour before Abaddon and the others set foot on the deserted atoll. The ring was still here, but was it functional?

Tom immediately went to work on it. It was several minutes before the verdict was in.

"It's all here," he announced. "I'll have it powered up inside of an hour. You folks are going home."

It was about 45 minutes later that the first of the other group of dark angels began to arrive along with the ACs. The last two were in sight, coming in from the northeast when a flash of light erupted along the northern horizon. The classical luminous mushroom cloud quickly followed.

"Now that's a pretty sight," said Tom, gazing upon the work of his own hand. "That one is for you, Bedillia."

It was a comment that gave Abaddon some measure of concern. He was certain that vengeance was a part of Tom's motives in orchestrating this display of power. He decided not to say anything about it.

It was over a minute later that the low rumble reached them. By then the ring was powered up. The blue starry mists appeared within it, obscuring what lie beyond.

"Are you sure you won't come with us?" asked Abaddon, turning to Tom.

"No," said Tom. "My work is here. Anyway, I have to see that the others are teleported to safety."

Abaddon turned to Serena, who lay in her husband's arms. She looked back at him with her eyes about half open. "It was good to see you again," he said. He kissed her hand. "Until we meet again."

Serena managed a slight smile. "Until we meet again."

"I owe you more than I can ever say," said Chris, shaking the hand of the dark angel.

"Just take good care of her," said Abaddon. "That will be thanks enough."

Chris nodded, "I will."

"We have a solid lock on the ring in Refuge," announced Tom, "stable wormhole established, but I don't know for how long. Come on folks, let's move it."

The dark angels and ACs rushed into the wormhole. They weren't particularly fond of remaining here. It was then that Serena noticed that Goliath wasn't moving.

"Go, you've got to go," she whispered. "I'll be just fine, but there are others who need you. Please, go."

Goliath nodded, rubbed his fur against her chin, and flew into the mists. Serena was positive she heard a voice in her head, a goodbye. Was it from Goliath? Yes, she was sure of it.

The mists dissipated. Tom was making some quick entries into the small keyboard within the housing to the one side.

"This thing sure is primitive," he grumbled. "We have 34 percent power left, more than enough. OK, I've been thinking. You said that you entered the wormhole through a barn in Illinois. Well that link is still available according to this. I can't think of a safer destination on Earth. We might need to take care of some bad guys on the other side, then again, maybe not. At least we'll be in the good old U.S.A."

Krissie smiled, "That sounds good to me."

"Go for it," said Leland.

"Here we go," said Tom, punching in the coordinates. Yet when he hit the enter key the whole display went dark. "What now?" he grumbled. He rebooted the system, it came up all right, but it wouldn't accept the coordinates when he reentered them. Tom stood there for a moment then entered a new set of coordinates. "OK, we'll go to New Zealand first, then form the wormhole to the U.S. from there." Yet, when he hit the enter key, the screen went blank again.

"I take it that we have a problem," said Leland, walking over to Tom.

"Yeah," confirmed Tom. "I'll figure it out. It has to be a small problem. I'll solve it. Everyone just relax."

And so they did. During the next three hours, Tom had just about every access panel on the instrument off and on, but success eluded him. It was just past one in the afternoon when he found the problem. He gingerly wiggled then pulled the circuit board from its slot in the instrument. He scanned it carefully, confirmed what he'd seen from the access port. "This is at least part of it," he announced. "It's a burned power trace. This is why the relays aren't firing." He shook his head. "This thing is just so primitive." He looked still further. "No, it's worse than that we've got some component damage. Forming a wormhole to Hell was just a bit much for this ring."

"Can you fix it?" asked Chris.

Tom sat down, leaning against the ring. "I don't know. Let me think."

"Don't think too long," said Leland. "We've got about, what, three hours?"

"Not that long," said Tom, looking at the board. "Just give me some time."

And they did. Leland and Krissie sat together under the sheet metal pavilion arm in arm. If they were going to meet their end out here, at least they would be together.

Chris sat there, leaning against one of the concrete pillars, with Serena in his arms. How she had survived this long he couldn't even begin to guess. She seemed so peaceful right now.

The others had barely noticed that Tom was on the move again, literally rewiring the circuit board. The two couples had managed to fade away into a light sleep even as Tom worked furiously. He had an idea. He only hoped that he had time to make it work.

CHAPTER 30

The USS *Maryland* surfaced at 2:34 P.M. local time in sight of both the Russian guided missile sub *Arkhangel* and the British guided missile sub HMS *Vanguard*. The three vessels would be involved in a coordinated launch against the comet fragment Florence C3.

Even though it was broad daylight, the skies overhead were ablaze with meteors that seemed to radiate out from a central point in the sky. Occasionally, the passage of a particularly bright meteor was accompanied by an almost blinding flash, followed a minute or so later by a low, ominous rumble. Somehow, they had to slip their missiles between those meteors.

And it was their missile that would be most likely to survive the passage through the debris field and impact the comet itself, not the land-based ones. Their crews would also be in the greatest danger if they failed, being less than a hundred miles to the northeast of the predicted impact point.

With the network of communications satellites now completely destroyed from horizon to horizon, they were on their own, totally out of contact with their individual governments. They would execute the last instructions that were sent to them, now over four hours ago. The three subs were linked by their computers, acting as a single powerful engine of destruction.

At 2:49, the first of the *Maryland's* missiles was lofted skyward, atop a roaring column of fire and smoke. In concert with the *Maryland's* missiles, the missiles of the *Arkhangel* and the *Vanguard* also thundered into the heavens. Every 12 seconds the sequence was repeated.

After about four minutes of launches, they said their goodbyes and submerged, descending to a depth of 500 feet. Then they proceeded to the northeast at flank speed in an attempt to place additional miles between them and ground zero.

On the Arizona State University campus, Sam Florence looked on in dismay as their satellite links to the rest of the world went silent, one by one. Yes, they were well outside of the danger zone. By the time the Earth's rotation carried them around and into the shooting gallery, the comet's fury would be spent. Still, they would experience the poisonous ammonia and methane rich clouds of dust as they swept eastward, which would dim the light of the sun for what might be over a year.

Then there was the comet's impact with the moon. No one here was quite sure as to what the ecological implications of that event would be. Perhaps, if they were lucky, it would be minimal.

There was nothing more to do, nothing more to calculate or measure. Sam headed for his office. Here he prayed for the planet and its people. He prayed for the Christians who were already suffering in the midst of the last-days tribulation. He even prayed for the blind followers of a false god. "Forgive them, Father," he said, "for they know not what they do."

A few minutes later he headed for home. He gazed up into the sky to see his comet. It dominated the southern heavens. Even the combined light of the moon and that of the city did little to dim its glory. He would have a still better view from home. Somewhere between here and there, the first of the large comet fragments would either strike the Earth or be vaporized in space.

He thought of the Book of Revelation, of John's descriptions of things to come. He'd never imagined seeing them all for himself. Now here they were.

Almost two hundred miles up, the first of the *Maryland's* missiles was destroyed by debris. The missiles launched by the *Arkhangel* and the *Vanguard*

met similar fates, destroyed by marble-sized rocks moving at 20 miles per second. The second round of missiles fared little better, as did the third. It was with the fourth round that they got lucky. Two of the three missiles slipped through the gauntlet and hit the comet fragment head on. The sky literally exploded with brilliance. Yet this impact generated even more debris. Of the 60 missiles launched toward the comet fragment, only eight found their mark. A cosmic bullet had been turned into a cosmic round of buckshot with a central object that still measured over half a mile in diameter. A minute later it hit the atmosphere.

Many of the fragments detonated upon hitting the stratosphere. Those detonating 15 or more miles up blazed with a brightness that rivaled the sun for several seconds then faded into an expanding gray cloud. But others, dozens of others, penetrated deeper before exploding with the power of a hydrogen bomb, creating a wave of searing heat and a blast that pushed the ocean's surface downward dozens of feet and sent a tsunami wave out in all directions.

Then there came the largest fragments, those that actually hit the deep ocean. So great was their impact velocity, nearly two dozen miles per second, that they were almost instantly vaporized.

The blast carried some material completely out of the atmosphere, where it followed a parabolic trajectory before coming down a thousand miles away. In this way the devastation spread.

In the Central Pacific, a second group of submarine launched weapons experienced equally poor performance. Now a tsunami wave 300 feet high was bearing down on the Hawaiian Islands, where nearly 40 percent of the population still remained.

In eastern China, a quarter-mile diameter fragment came down near the City of Hangzhou with catastrophic results. Nearly two cubic miles of earth were sent skyward by the impact even as a wall of hot pyroclastic material spread out in all directions, incinerating homes and fields.

The list of devastated cities and towns grew, spreading across the eastern hemisphere, as scores of smaller fragments detonated but a few miles above the Earth with the power of half a dozen Hiroshima-type bombs. Hell had come to Earth.

On the atoll, the sky was filled with bright mid-afternoon meteors. Then a bright flash appeared along the horizon, far to the northeast. You could actually feel the heat, even from this distance. The glow persisted for three minutes, then faded. Now billowing red clouds erupted from that quarter of the sky, clouds that seemed to be moving rapidly in their direction.

The flash had attracted everyone's attention. Leland and Krissie rose to their feet to see the horror that was moving in their direction. All the while Tom labored on the ring. He reinserted the board into the instrument, only to pull another.

"How much time do we have?" asked Krissie.

"A bit over half an hour," replied Tom. "I'm sorry I can't be any more precise than that."

"I guess it doesn't matter," said Krissie, sitting back down.

"It might," said Tom. "I'm almost finished."

"You've figured it out?" asked Leland.

"Yes," confirmed Tom. "I've bypassed a bunch of safety protocols to make this work, and the wormhole won't last long once I've formed it. When I say jump, we'll have only five or six seconds to make the passage, but yes, it will work."

"How close are you to finishing?" asked Chris.

"About 20 or so minutes," said Tom, setting two jumpers on the circuit board and reseating it in its slot. "Yes, I know I'm cutting it close."

A few seconds later, the atoll shook as in an earthquake. The shaking lasted about 15 seconds and then subsided.

All the while Tom worked at fever pitch. No one dared to disturb him. Then he was screwing the cover plates back on the unit. He returned to the monitor and rebooted the system. It gave him a total of five error messages, but he told the system to ignore each one.

To the northwest, Chris watched the horizon bulge. It was the tsunami wave.

"The seas are a bit shallow around us," noted Tom. "It will slow the wave down a bit."

Chris looked into Serena's eyes. "We're getting out of here in just a couple minutes, my love, just hold on."

Serena smiled at him. "Yes, we are."

The wave grew ever larger as the seas around them seemed to flow toward the north. Within a minute those seas seemed more like a thundering river than an ocean; they withdrew from the atoll on all sides.

The computer seemed to be going through some sort of self-diagnostic. Within a few seconds it was requesting coordinates. This was it, the moment of truth. Tom entered the coordinates and prepared to hit the enter key. This would have to work the first time. It was only then that he noticed the growing glow all around him. He turned to see that all of his companions had become luminous beings, becoming ever brighter.

Serena sat up and embraced her husband. Together they rose to their feet. At the other side of the pavilion, Leland and Krissie stood hand in hand. Streams of living light wrapped around them and swept toward the sky. A second later, their feet left the ground. They flew hand in hand into the air and away from the encroaching wave.

Tom turned to Chris and Serena, whose feet had also left the ground. They looked like angels. They moved toward Tom.

"Push the button, Tom," said Serena. "You've got to get out of here."

Tom turned to see the wave, which now towered above him. He grabbed his rifle and his gear and hit the enter key. The ring began to fill with mists, only to clear once again.

"Oh no," he gasped.

A second later, Serena's hand touched the ring. The mists reappeared, filled with sparkling stars. "Go, quickly," said Serena, who, with her husband, hurtled skyward in a globe of luminous vapor.

Tom didn't have to be told twice. He rushed into the vapors and vanished. Eight seconds later, a 200-foot wave swept over the atoll removing everything that man or demon had endowed it with.

Chris and Serena climbed ever higher within that globe of light. From their lofty vantage point, they witnessed the full extent of the destruction.

Chris looked in wonder upon his wife. She had been completely restored and more. She looked so young, like she had looked on the day they had met. She was dressed in flowing white robes. She was so beautiful. Then he looked at himself. He too was dressed in dazzling white.

Around them, the world seemed to fade into a realm of billowing, white clouds contrasted against a deep, blue sky. Then he saw the others, people like himself, all dressed in white. They were coming from every quarter, converging upon an area of brightness up ahead. The love that emanated from that light was indescribable. Yet he had experienced it before during his time in Heaven.

In the midst of that light, he beheld a figure, His arms outstretched. He knew him immediately. It was his Savior, Jesus, the Nazarene.

"It's all so beautiful," gasped Serena. "I'd never imagined that it would be so beautiful."

The brightness grew steadily until they were surrounded in nothing but white light. A minute later, the brightness faded. They stood in a vast open-air arena bordered on all sides by a ten-foot wall. And beyond the wall were spectators dressed in white. They sat in ever ascending rows around the great arena. Their numbers must surely have been in the tens of thousands.

Beyond the people were tall, marble columns that stood hundreds of feet high, reaching toward great, billowing clouds set against a clear sky. Before them stood a great and luminous being sitting upon a golden throne. His eyes followed the two humans as they approached.

Both Chris and Serena knew this place. It was the Great Hall of Judgment. Years ago, they had both stood in this place. For Serena it brought back painful memories. This meeting, so long ago, had been the prelude to Hell. She looked to the right. Yes, there was the angel and the book. She tried to remain calm.

It was then that a man in the stands stood up and began to clap. Another man and two women quickly joined him. Chris recognized them. It was Johann Kepler, David Bonner, Sister Elizabeth, and his own mother. Then more joined in and still more. Within a minute the great hall was filled with the sound. It was over a minute before it at last died down.

The great luminous figure on the throne smiled. "It would seem that the two of you have found favor with the saints of Heaven. Let us dispense with any further formalities." He turned to the angel who stood behind the book. "Does the name of Chris Davis still appear in the Lamb's Book of Life?"

It took no more than two seconds for the angel to reply. "Yes, Lord, his name is still here."

"And what of Serena Davis?" continued the luminous being. "Does her name appear in the Lamb's Book of Life?"

This time, a good five seconds passed. Serena clung to her husband.

The angel looked up. "Yes, Lord, the name of Serena Davis appears in the Lamb's book of Life."

In that moment, Serena was smiling through her tears. The luminous being, the Father of the Universe, looked upon Serena smiling. "Well done, my daughter, well done indeed. Few could have endured all that you have. You have snatched many souls from the great Deceiver. You have confronted him face to face and remained true to Me. I could not have asked for more." There was a pause. "There is but one more issue to be dealt with here." The Father stretched out his hand and the spectators turned their attention toward the far side of the arena.

From a rear entrance two people emerged, a man and a woman. They too were dressed all in white. Serena's eyes grew wide as she watched them approach. "Mommy?" she gasped.

Again the sound of applause arose from the stands. It grew until the majority of those present had risen to their feet and made both their presence and their will known. Serena rushed to her mother and embraced her even as Chris shook the hand and then embraced one of those who had rescued him and his wife from the darkest being in the universe.

"We have here an unusual situation," began the Father. "Both of these people have stood here before. Both were condemned to Outer Darkness long ago. Yet they stand before us today." The Father turned to the angel. "Does the name of Leland Brown appear in the Lamb's Book of Life?"

The angel looked down into the text. "Yes, Lord, his name appears here."

"And the name of Bedillia Farnsworth," continued the Father. "Does her name also appear in the Lamb's Book of Life?"

"Yes, Lord," said the angel, "her name appears in the book."

The stands erupted with a cheer as the saints rose to their feet. Indeed, some were jumping up and down. Serena looked to the Father. There was a look that might best be described as one of amusement upon his face.

The Father rose to his feet. The cheering ceased.

"Bedillia Farnsworth, Leland Brown, I don't need to tell you that second chances are rare. Today you have been given just that. Your love and your sacrifice under a most dire situation speaks of the condition of your heart. Today you shall enter into My Kingdom."

In their midst, a figure appeared. He was a handsome man with a short beard and the trace of a nearly healed puncture wound in his wrists. "Come, My friends, it is time for you to enter into the Father's Kingdom. We have much to do in the next 42 months. Your friends Leland and Krissie James are waiting for you." He placed his arms about them and led them away. They vanished into a cloud of sparkling stars.

Even before the comets hit, Abaddon's children had poured like flood waters from teleportation rings around the world. They even erupted from certain oil wells in the Middle East. They immediately attacked the allies of Satan, those who had become one with the new religion. Yet they followed their instructions well; they killed no one.

They spread out in all directions, bringing the judgment of God with them. Those who had not followed Lusan, those who had not embraced his new faith, were left in peace. They judged the heart, and their judgment was severe.

Several hours after their arrival, the true children of God, those called by his name, vanished amidst glowing tendrils of light. The suffering Christians in Europe, Africa, and Asia had been liberated.

Politicians, philosophers, religious leaders, and scientists scrambled for an explanation for what they had just seen. For some the conclusion was inescapable; they had just missed the last flight from God's judgment. Even as the clouds of dust darkened the sun and made the moon appear as red as blood, they begged for forgiveness.

The great tsunamis had destroyed a third of the world's ships, and unimaginable catastrophe had been visited upon the Pacific Rim. Radioactive fallout swept around the globe even as materials brought to Earth by the comet, mainly ammonia and methane, poisoned the waters.

Following the impact of the main body of the comet upon the moon, a shower of contaminated lunar material rained down upon Earth for days. The green Earth was becoming Hell on Earth, and its people would have to live with that reality.

EPILOGUE

Within the mysterious ring setting in the old barn, a blue mist formed. The hundreds of tiny creatures that had become its new residents took notice. A few seconds later, a man in a black suit stumbled from the fog, following which it dissipated. They eyed him closely in the dim glow provided by the one light bulb hanging from the rafters.

The man gazed about at the many eyes watching him. "Welcome to Earth, my friends," he said. "I hope you had a pleasant trip."

One of the creatures flew from its lofty perch and alighted upon the man's shoulder. Tom Carson looked over to see the curious little face gazing upon him. He knew right away that it was a female.

"Hello, ma'am," he said in a pleasant voice.

She gazed into his eyes and smiled back. Within the depths of his mind, Tom heard a tiny greeting. He knew immediately that he had just been judged and found acceptable in their sight.

Walking toward the partially open barn door, he noticed a trail of blood leading away into the darkness. He turned toward the small creature on his shoulder. "My, you have been busy, haven't you?"

The creature nodded. Tom knew that he wouldn't need to fear Satan's agents; they were long gone.

"Let me tell you," said Tom, gazing out into the cool night air, then back toward the AC on his shoulder. "I don't know that I've met you and your particular group of Abaddon's children before, but that doesn't matter. You make a lonely traveler feel right at home; thank you very much."

The AC smiled broadly. There was no doubt about it, Tom did have friends here.

Tom walked away from the barn to see the farmhouse 50 or so yards away. There were lights on. Again he turned to the creature. "Is there anyone home?"

She shook her head. "They are all gone. They were bad."

Tom was surprised. He'd heard her thoughts almost as clearly as a human voice. He had been fortunate to encounter an AC whose mind was so closely attuned to his own. "God is good," he said. "I thank Him for His kindness. I wonder what He has in store for me."

The tiny creature on his shoulder shrugged. It made Tom laugh.

"No, my friend, I didn't expect you to have that answer," said Tom, stroking her soft fur. "It was what we humans call a rhetorical question. I suppose that I'll have the answer in time."

Tom turned his attention to the clear autumn sky, toward the bright moon about two days before last quarter. The moon wasn't alone. The comet held it in its deadly embrace. Its tail seemed to encompass the whole lunar disk. Here and there, Tom saw flashes of light on the moon's darkened hemisphere as fragments of the comet impacted the lunar surface. He stood there mesmerized.

"Now that's something you don't see everyday," he said to his small friend. "Too bad we don't have a telescope."

Then there was a bright flash right where day met night on the lunar surface. It was so bright as to briefly illuminate the field around them in its stark, white light. Then after about half a minute, the light faded to a bright orange glow on the lunar surface, surrounded by a growing gray cloud expanding in all directions from the impact site. Within that gray cloud were a myriad of crimson flicks of light, expanding with the cloud. Within a minute, the cloud had completely obscured the features of the moon. All that remained was a gray, featureless disk.

"Can you imagine what might have happened if that comet had hit the Earth?" said Tom. "We're in enough trouble as it is with the tiny piece that did hit us."

Tom stood there for the better part of ten minutes. The dust slowly cleared, and the familiar features of the moon reappeared. Still they seemed muted, somehow less distinct.

Tom realized that he had just been a witness to one of the most awesome celestial events humanity had ever experienced. He wondered what the ramifications of this impact might be. Still, he was tired. His new body didn't seem quite as resilient as the one he had possessed these past six and a half years. He needed to get some sleep. He turned toward the farmhouse. Perhaps he would find a comfortable bed there, one not made of rock. He walked toward it.

The farmhouse seemed rather modest on the outside, but the inside was another matter. It appeared to have been recently remodeled and was well furnished. The renovations had, no doubt, been funded by Satan's many earthly enterprises.

Exploring further, Tom found food in the kitchen, and clothing in a bedroom closet that fit him quite well. Heading on into town wearing a black power suit might raise unwanted questions. He would have to try and blend in if he could.

He also found quite a stash of money in a suitcase in one of the bedrooms, all in 10s, 20s, and 50s. There had to be tens of thousands of dollars there, at least.

Well, what next? What could a legally dead physicist do on Earth during the last half of the Tribulation? What could he do to become a thorn in Satan's side? He really wasn't sure. Then again, he was really very tired. This farmhouse offered comfortable accommodations for him and loads of security. He would sleep in a soft bed tonight and figure out the other stuff in the morning.

ABOUT KENNETH ZEIGLER

Kenneth Zeigler was born in Harrisburg, Pennsylvania. He is a high school chemistry teacher, currently teaching at University High School in Tolleson, Arizona. He earned a master's degree in chemistry and his graduate work was in quantum mechanics. He is a research scientist who has taught secondary and college-level science and mathematics for 30 years. He and his wife, Mary, have two grown children, Rob and Beth, and two grandchildren, Kindra and Kristen.

You may learn more about Kenneth Zeigler by going to his website:

www.thetearsofheaven.com
Author also has FaceBook page.

In the right hands This Book will Change Lives!

Most of the people that need this message will not be looking for this book. To change their life you need to put a copy of this book in their hands.

> *But others (seeds) fell into good ground, and brought forth fruit, some a hundred-fold, some sixty-fold, some thirty-fold* (Matthew 13:3-8).

Our ministry is constantly seeking methods to find the good ground, the people that need this anointed message to change their life. Will you help us reach these people?

> *Remember this—a farmer who plants only a few seeds will get a small crop. But the one who plants generously will get a generous crop* (2 Corinthians 9:6).

EXTEND THIS MINISTRY BY SOWING
3-BOOKS, 5-BOOKS, 10-BOOKS, OR MORE TODAY,
AND BECOME A LIFE CHANGER!

Thank you,

Don Nori Sr., Publisher
Destiny Image
Since 1982

DESTINY IMAGE PUBLISHERS, INC.

*"Speaking to the Purposes of God for This Generation
and for the Generations to Come."*

VISIT OUR NEW SITE HOME AT
WWW.DESTINYIMAGE.COM

FREE SUBSCRIPTION TO DI NEWSLETTER

Receive free unpublished articles by top DI authors, exclusive

discounts, and free downloads from our best and newest books.

Visit www.destinyimage.com to subscribe.

Write to: Destiny Image
              P.O. Box 310
              Shippensburg, PA 17257-0310

Call: 1-800-722-6774

Email: orders@destinyimage.com

For a complete list of our titles or to place an order
online, visit www.destinyimage.com.